Wise Woman's Telling

Book One
in the sequence
Daughter of Tintagel

Fay Sampson

HEADLINE

ISBN 0 7472 3263 6

Typeset in 10/11 pt Mallard
by Colset Private Limited, Singapore

Printed and bound in Great Britain by
Collins, Glasgow

HEADLINE BOOK PUBLISHING PLC
Headline House
79 Great Titchfield Street
London W1P 7FN

To Jack

Author's Note

In physics, Dark Matter forms an unseen world
that is the inverse of the matter we observe. The
two were created to exist in equal proportions.
Together they hold the universe in balance. But
when they come into contact, the result is mutual
destruction. Morgan's story is the Dark Matter of
Britain.

The name Tintagel, formerly believed to be
Norman, may be much older and Cornish. If so, it
should be pronounced with a hard g. One possible
meaning is 'the strong place where the two currents
meet'.

The Tintagel of legend is a fortress, the birth-
place of Arthur and the seat of King Mark of
Cornwall. The archaeologists who excavated it
believed that in Arthurian times it was in fact a
Celtic monastery. Others have challenged this.
The headland was certainly occupied in the fifth
century, but as yet there is no conclusive evidence
of its function.

The Western Sea

The Sisters

The Convent of the White Nuns

Tintagel Haven

Barras Nose

Tintagel Island

The Mother's Hole

The grave of Gorlois

To Padstow

To Dimil

Bossiney Haven

The Oak Forest

Le Great Oak

Pasture

Bossiney

Pasture

Waterfall

Nectan's Hut

Peter McClure 1989

Chapter One

It was the worst thing we ever did when we forgot Morgan, that night above all nights. Many's the time I've wept for it since. And that's nothing to the harm that will come of it yet.

And such a night it was. The gale screeching like the Black Hunt across the sky, and the sea howling up at us out of the caves around Bossiney Haven. And the rain! I can feel the cold of it stabbing into my joints to this very day. You'd have thought the Mothers' own waters had broken in the heavens above and they were all three of them screaming in labour.

But I couldn't close the door and get to bed. Not that night. Every door and window had to stand open, never mind the rain, and every knot let loose. There mustn't be anything closed or tied 'til the baby was safely born.

So I sat in that cruel draught, with my thighs wide open to the night, and holding the lips of my own blood-hole apart, though it had been dry these many years. Easy, easy, I was grunting. I was casting the spells of opening, and at the same time heaving and groaning, just as if I was bringing the child I'd never had into the world.

Morgan wasn't the only one they'd forgotten, my Lady Ygerne and her fine Uther Pendragon, that liked to call himself King of all the Britons. In Gorlois's time she'd have wanted me beside her, where I'd been when her three daughters were born. It was my craft she'd have trusted to bring her and the baby home through it then, never mind the midwife. But Gorlois was dead, and I was out of favour. Maybe King Uther thought I was only good for getting girls.

That's all Morgan was to him, that strutting fool of a man. A little girl. The youngest of Lord Gorlois's brood of daughters. But he should have known better, after what he'd seen. Only nine she might be, but he could hardly pretend she was too young to understand what had happened to them all. Though in fairness none of us guessed what was in her mind even then, though we found out soon, to all our cost.

Nine months they had been forgetting Morgan, King Uther Pendragon and his new queen, Ygerne. Queen before her husband's body was cold in the grave and the worms had hardly begun to nibble his parts. Nine months those two had petted and pawed each other for everyone to see, though not so much lately as they had done at first. Well, not on her side, anyway. But that didn't stop Uther Pendragon from having his pleasure wherever he could find it. And now her time had come, her hour of reckoning for that first night that broke Morgan's heart, and the lamps were burning late in our queen's bower. They were busy now. We could see shadows passing before the light. The baby was pushing to be born.

And all this time that little maid Morgan stood in the doorway with her wet face turned to the storm, and there was nothing I could do to shift her.

'Come away in, my lover,' I begged. 'You'll catch your death of cold, and it will be my back that pays for it with a beating, not yours. Tomorrow will be bad enough as it is, me crippled up with the rheumatism already, and sitting with my feet in a puddle like a leaky boat, without having you ill as well. Come to bed now, there's a good maid, and snuggle under the blankets.'

She never even heard me. I could only see her back. Still, she was. You would have thought she was lifeless, like a storm-struck tree. Hour after hour she'd stood, with her face to the rain and the lights and the bustle. And never a word she spoke or a muscle stirred. But she was living, all right. I could feel a spirit buried inside her that made the rest of the world seem half dead. It made me afraid, I can tell you.

I am an old woman now and I wasn't so young even then, for I had been nurse to Morgan's two sisters that were grown girls, and to their mother before that. Those two were lying there in the darkness under the furs. I could tell Elaine was sleeping because she was snoring like a pig, though before another year had turned she might be sweating and straining with a baby of her own. Pretty and plump and pink she was, and no trouble to any of us. Though not so innocent as she looked, either. She could see further than most. She was always her mother's favourite, and the queen had whispered her what she knew. Mother to daughter. Woman to her own blood. But I had no daughter of my womb. Or son, either.

So it made me cross, hearing her snoring. Young though she was, she could have helped me a little if she'd wanted to, and Margawse too, though that one was newer in the knowledge than Elaine. It was their own mother in pain, wasn't it? But there, they were neither of them wives yet, and it was no work for maids. And they'd no more call than Morgan to help the Pendragon's child into the world.

It was Margawse now who lifted her head. She

3

cried, 'What's the matter? Is something wrong? Has she dropped the baby yet?'

I could smell the excitement strong on her, like a soaked breech-cloth, and I thought, not for the first time either, that it was time she was married and away from that place. The eldest, Elaine, was betrothed already to King Nentres. Uther had seen to that. A handsome queen she'd make. And a wise one too, if you take my meaning. Margawse had come to her womanhood only lately, with no father of her own. And that was a dangerous thing for all of us. I had seen her up against a wall with Uther Pendragon, that day in the treasury. He wasn't the man – for all he called himself a Christian king – to care that he was married to her mother now. He took what he wanted, as we had cause to know. And Margawse was not the maiden to say no – if maiden indeed she was, which I very much doubted.

But what was I to do? Those girls were too head-strong for me. And their mother's head was so turned she couldn't see anyone but the king. Yet they called her a wise woman, Ygerne. And I should know, for it was not her own mother that had the whispering of that one. It's not every peasant woman can claim a queen for her daughter, by the Mothers' blood. They say it was Merlyn brewed the spell that tricked her, and I don't doubt he did, but in a man's world it's the man's story the bards tell. I've often wondered if there was more to it than that. Of course, I wasn't there when she went to the king's fine court, my little Cornish lady. But when she and my Lord Gorlois came galloping home with the king hard on their heels, there was more than a little look of Margawse in her face. She wasn't ill-pleased with herself. And why the king should be so hot after her, when he could

have had any lady in Britain for the asking, it's not for
me to tell. She never went high in our mysteries. Not
as high as me, if I do boast. Still, she did know enough
for that. And she wanted to be loved. She wanted a
son. Best of all, she wanted a son that might be king.

But she and her daughters had slept in Tintagel on
a terrible night, when the spirits were abroad. And in
those days Tintagel was a women's place. Merlyn
wove his own magic, oh, yes! But it's my belief that
under the rock the Mothers were laughing at the lot of
us. And true it is that none of us have been the same
since that time.

So the night went on, cold-footed as a toad, and
Margawse fell back to grumbling.

'I'm freezing. Give me another cover, Gwennol. I'll
die soon.'

'You've had every one there is. There's only this old
blanket I've got about my shoulders, and I'm not giving
you that. I'm as damp as a ditch in February, as it is,
and lucky to live 'til then, sitting here shivering with
the door open and the bed-chamber like a bog.'

'Make Morgan come to bed then. Or shut the door
and leave her outside.'

She knew I couldn't shut any opening 'til the baby
was born. But she didn't care.

I was past arguing with either of them. I was too
damp and cold and tired even to move my jaws. My
head was so heavy, I'd have given a month of my life
to lay it down and sleep. But I had power to use for a
birthing, even for those that didn't want it now. I
could still show them. And then, I daren't leave
Morgan to watch alone. Only nine years old she was,
and there wasn't one of us could bend her to our will.
Not even if we had beaten her. Least of all then. Her
father was gone and he was the only one that she'd

ever let touch her. There was nothing any of us could
do for her but wake and watch. And there was no one
left to do it but me. Her father was dead, and her
mother had forgotten her.

But I'll swear to this. I had never whispered
Morgan, not so much as a word. Not then. That was
her mother's place. A year before she'd bespoken
Elaine, and then Margawse, when Uther Pendragon
was coming. But never Morgan. To tell you the truth,
my lady was more than a little frightened of
Margawse and Morgan, her own daughters. But for
all I believed her, I knew there was power in that
child already. And when I think how it must have
come to her, through no human being, it makes my
hair creep sometimes.

A gust of wind slammed the door back against the
wall. It blew a stink of wet wool and leather across my
face. I shuffled back, trying to get out of the draught.
But Morgan never moved, though the gale was dashing
rain into her eyes and there was black water swilling
about her feet.

An ugly, drenched scrap of a thing she was. As thin
and draggled as a black kitten that's just been born.
To see her like that you would never have thought she
would have grown into a beautiful queen. Margawse
now, you couldn't miss her, with her red hair and her
skin like buttermilk. Or Elaine, that everyone said
was the prettiest of the three, though I never saw
much in her myself. But Morgan had always been a
strange maid. 'Like a crow in a thunderstorm,' Uther
Pendragon said when he first set eyes on her. Yet she
had a way with men when she wanted to. The way she
used to smile at her father.

And then I caught sight of something fluttering,
pale as moths in the darkness, down Morgan's skirt. I

peered closer and then I let out a scream. Her little hands were twisting her girdle, tying it tight, knot after knot, over and over. No wonder that baby was slow in coming.

'You little black witch!'

The words were out of my mouth before I knew what I was saying. I tore her crooked fingers from the cord and tugged out those cruel knots 'til the whole thing fell free. I felt those tight cramps in my belly moving loose and I could breathe deep and strong again. She didn't try to stop me. Just laughed at me with her little white teeth, though never a sound she made.

Well, I daren't take my eyes off her after that, though it made them swim, peering through that murk. I was nearly crying from the fire in my joints and the icy cold in my feet. Then Morgan let out a gasp that was almost a shriek. In spite of my rheumatism I was in that doorway as fast as I could move, never mind the mud squelching under my feet. She clutched at my dress with the bones of her skinny white hands.

'Is it born, Gwennol? Is it here?'

We heard Queen Ygerne cry out louder than the scream of the wind, and there was a thin high wail through the rain and the darkness. He had come. The baby was born alive.

For a moment I forgot Morgan. I am an old woman that never bore a child. Any woman's baby starts a hunger in me, and a queen's baby is more precious than most. And if what I guessed about Ygerne was true, then in a way that child came partly from my doing. Almost my own blood it felt. Then I remembered Morgan. I looked down to see how she was bearing it – and she was gone. I'll swear it was only a

7

moment I forgot her. But I had lost her, like a black cat in the darkness.

Then someone lifted the curtain. I saw the queen's bed, gold in the candlelight. A woman ran out, shouting to us all, 'It's a boy!' And there was Morgan, running towards the light, with her skirt sticking to her knees.

A shadow came between her and the doorway. I can see it now. A man's shadow. You couldn't mistake the shape of big Uther Pendragon, striding into my lady's bedchamber. We saw his shadow huge across the curtain. He was like a giant bending over the bed. Over his wife and son, that should have been the wife and son of Gorlois, Morgan's father. We saw him lift that golden child in his arms before the door slammed shut.

A boy. And Gorlois's little maid was left outside in the dark and the storm. He never even noticed her.

'Morgan!' I cried, though I could hardly hear myself for the wind. I knew it would be no use. She had gone. What hope had I got of catching her, old and stiff as I was, and the rain fit to wash us all out to sea? I knew what she was going to do, poor little scrap, for child she was still, and could still be hurt. She would make her body suffer 'til it was as bitter as her soul. She'd gone beyond my help now. The darkness had taken her. And we may all suffer for that.

Chapter Two

She was happy once, in her own way. Though it seems so long ago now that I sometimes wonder if I didn't dream it.

It was only her father she loved. He had the power to swing her off to the Blessed Isles with one hug of his big strong arms about her. And the same power to hurt her. Like a puppy that hasn't got the sense to get out from under its master's feet. She could be sharp with her teeth like a puppy too, but she'd come crawling back as if she was wagging her little tail and begging him to love her again. That was a bitter lesson she had to learn: to make herself be loved and not to love back. There isn't a woman in Britain has learned it better.

It was hunting that her father loved best. So nothing would satisfy Morgan but she must go with him. She was riding into the forest with the hunt almost as soon as she could sit. When other little maids were crawling about the floor playing with dolls, Morgan would be out with the men. I remember the day she came back, her face smeared with blood and her eyes shining like the dew on May-Morning. That was her first kill. I warned her father then.

In those days one of the huntsmen would carry her on his saddle in front of him. Not Gorlois, of course. If she had been a son he might have done. But my lord

9

was too proud a spearman to slow his horse or spoil his aim for the sake of a scrap of a girl-child. It was enough for her that he let her follow him. She would twist her fingers in the horse's mane and crouch down low, as if she was whispering in his ears and urging him on faster.

My lady and Morgan's two sisters, now, they'd ride in the greenwood if the sun was shining. Sidesaddle, like the fine ladies they were – or wanted to be. And the ponies tricked out with bells and baubles that you'd have thought would have frightened every hare and deer for miles around, so loud they jingled. And their gowns and their skirts spread over the horses' rumps so that the light would catch the silken embroidery and the gold. And you can't go dashing under branches and through briars like that without tearing your gay gowns to shreds and messing your pretty hair.

But Morgan, now, she would hunt in any weather. Though if I'd been her mother I wouldn't have let her. But who would listen to old Gwennol? I was just their old nurse, too slow in the joints and too quick with her tongue. By daylight, anyhow. True, I had a name for a powerful skill with charms, but that was no more than women's medicine, or so the men thought. I didn't want Gorlois to know any different. But my lady did, for all her fine airs. She ought to have listened to me then. She'd heeded me once, when she was younger, or she wouldn't be called wise now.

Morgan was eight summers when her father let her hunt on her own pony. I saw them set off that day. She was gripping it between her knees that were as white as two peeled hazel wands, and not much thicker. Riding astride, she was, like a boy, with the skirt of her dress tucked up so high on her thighs it was hardly decent, even for a child so small, with all those men around. But that summer there was never a thought of such a thing in her little mind. Why should there be? It came to her too soon as it was, and from those that should have watched over her to keep her from harm. She'd have worn breeches like a boy then, if I'd have let her. She knew she was all the son her father would ever have. But she was never anything like a boy. She was too fey for that.

I watched them go, with the hounds and the horns and the spears tossing in the sunlight. And my heart was heavy with fear for her. I was twisting my apron between my hands like fishermen's mothers when they stand on the beach, watching the boats fighting their way back to harbour against a gale. But she was laughing, and her father with her. That great, black-bearded spearman and his little black-braided daughter. A giant with a dwarf. Well, they always say giants are stupid. It would be enough for me if he brought her safely back to us.

The hunt turned their backs on the sea and the sunlight, and rode in under those great branches of the oak forest. All their brave colours and bright harness were swallowed up in that old twilight. Hours, they could be lost before anyone caught a sight of them again, except for what lived there. That made me shudder. Gorlois didn't know the half of it. There's places there, old pools and bogs and circles of standing oaks, I wouldn't go near even in daylight without strong spells to guard me. There's times and seasons for places like those, and a right way of coming to them if you want to get away again with your life and your wits. And often as I have been, I'd never have had the courage 'til I'd drunk that cup that makes me more than old Nurse Gwennol when the moon is up.

11

So I wondered how long it might be before I'd catch a
glimpse of them again, up on the clear ridge where
the road runs past to Padstow. And it wouldn't be the
first time if they came out of that forest fewer than
they went in.

We women were left in Bossiney. It was a pleasant
enough place – a clutter of houses, a hall big enough
for a hundred warriors, and a wall round them.
That's all it was then, before the king moved in. Bright
sea and sky in front of us, black woods behind. It
wasn't that Gorlois didn't have stronger forts in
higher places, but what would have been the point in
living up there and making ourselves more uncomfortable than we had to? They'd made him Duke of
Cornwall, hadn't they? Leader of all their war-hosts.
Who had he to fear this side of the Tamar?

But I had plenty to worry about, even if he hadn't.
And worse to me than any Saxons.

All day I feared and fretted. Margawse screamed
at me for a clumsy idiot when I tugged a tangle of the
red hair clean out of her scalp with the comb. I dropped
a jug of milk, and trailed my skirt through the fire so
we almost had the hall in flames about our ears. And
all the time my ears were listening for the horn and
my eyes watching for the first horses breaking out of
the trees.

Like the little luck-cat she was then, she came back
from it alive, and laughing as if she had been in paradise. And her knife still covered in blood.

Her father was mightily pleased with her too. I
could see that, and for once I was glad for her. He
rode up beside her, his big horse towering over her
little pony, and he clapped his hand on her shoulder
so hard that she almost fell under the blow.

'Well, Gwennol, what do you think of that? She's

galloped all the way across the Alan and up to Caer Delinuth, hunting the biggest boar I've seen in a twelvemonth. And she came in at the last in time to have her knife in his side with all the others, before he'd done squealing. Look, she's got his ear to show you. A boy couldn't have done much better on his first ride.'

He grinned and hugged her to him, and she smiled at him, so happily, it made my heart turn over to watch it. I've never had a child smile at me like that, for all I've nursed so many and broken my heart over one of them. But it's not the same as your own.

I suppose that made me a little sharp.

'Poor lamb! Just look at her. She's almost dead with weariness. We'll have her in bed for a month before she's fit to ride again.'

And I wasn't far from the truth, for she must have driven herself as hard as a grown man. When he took his great hand away from her shoulder, she fairly fell into my arms off her pony, and it was all I could do to hold her upright and set her safely on her feet.

The gown she'd kilted up fell back to her feet, all ripped and splattered with mud as it was. And when she put up her hand she couldn't stop it from shaking now. She picked off the ribbon I'd braided her hair close against her neck with, so she shouldn't hang herself in the forest. She always hated to be bound, and she shook her black hair free.

He saw her then for what she was. A drooping little girl, filthy, tired out, and never as strong in health as any of us would have wished. He knew she could never be the son he wanted. He swore by names I'd never heard him use and didn't think he knew, and he turned his back on her. He flung himself from his horse and strode off to his wife, all splashed with

13

blood as he was. And it wasn't love he'd be pushing himself into her for.

Poor, foolish man. I knew what drove him, while I picked my baby up in my arms. He was praying that Morgan wouldn't be the last child he spawned. And I saw by the look in her eyes as they followed him that she knew what he was thinking too.

Chapter Three

Summers end in killing-time, when the scythe's in the corn and the hare hides herself in the last stand 'til the reaper throws his sickle at it and there's blood in the stubble.

We drank the harvest home, and those that hadn't got their bellies big at May-time had another go. But we were hardly sober before those whetstones were shrieking again, and it wasn't sickles they were brightening this time. The men were off to war again.

I've never seen a Saxon. Summers come and summers go, like the tides in a cove. You don't expect the world to change. The sea's not going to come pounding in and then refuse to stop. It's not going to come flooding up the coombes and washing into our duns to sweep us all away, is it? There's spring tides and neap tides, full moon and dark. What has been will come again. There's a pattern to everything. Cornwall was like a high ground we'd built on. I couldn't think that those Saxons might just keep marching west and never stop until they crossed the Tamar. Every flood comes to its top and flows back.

Summer after summer it had been going on, the gentry riding out on their brave little horses, all jingling with gold and silver and bronze, and our young lads marching behind them in their breeches and plaids with the pack-horses. They made a gay

15

sight. We never thought they wouldn't come back – most of them, anyway. Mind you, I've seen sights that might have made you wish they hadn't. A face split open by an axe. An arm hacked half off at the elbow and turning green. I couldn't save them all. The Raven must have her share of blood. So the young girls would cling and cry when their sweethearts went. But the older women just twisted their aprons a bit, and sighed, and maybe hung a little something round their man's neck for luck. There's hard work to do without them, but, on the other hand, you can get a sound night's sleep, though it begins to get cold on your own when autumn's putting a frost on the grass.

Of course, it's different if it's a son.

So Gorlois was off again, and laughing as if he was glad to be away from his womenfolk and out of Cornwall. First off it had been Aurelius. He was the one that got his own back on that traitor, Vortigern. But Aurelius was dead, poisoned they say, and now it was his brother Uther that all the Britons were following. To tell you the truth, wise woman I may be, but I never bothered much about where our men were going to fight, or what it might mean for us down here if they won or got beaten. As far as I could see, it was all another kind of hunting and bloody sport to them. They said my own man fell in Kent, when his master was fighting him they called Hengist. I used to tie strong magic round his neck and a hard leather jerkin over his heart. But when his time came round it seems it wasn't enough. I wailed for him when they told me, and cried for him too, in private, in the straw. He was a good man, as husbands go. I've never married since. I didn't need to. I was well provided for, with my lady's babies to bring up, and as for the other, I know those that can bring the thunder in the blood better than any mortal man.

The night's my time. And by day my life was those three girls, and most of all Morgan.

I suppose that's the difference between us and Merlyn. Men off and doing, as if they could change the world by running about. Women staying at home, to hold things as they are. They move in straight lines, while we weave circles. What has been must come again, or so I thought. So I never spoke a spell against the Saxons. It wasn't them I feared.

All the same, I wasn't wise enough to stop our world from changing, though it wasn't a Saxon army that came marching over the Tamar in the end. Of course, I'd heard of Merlyn, even then. Who hadn't? That clever brat that was got by a devil on a nun. The weasel Vortigern, that sold our land for Saxon swords, he meant to make the boy a blood-offering for his stronghold that kept tumbling down. But Merlyn was too sharp for that. 'Dig under the walls and you'll find a pool.' So they did. 'Drain the pool and you'll find two stones.' So they did. 'Break open the stones and you'll find two dragons.' So they did. And the dragons fought, backwards and forwards, 'til the white one killed the red.

That's power that could make your hair turn white if you think about it too long. It's one thing for the wise, who have the far-sight, to see what's coming. But to make a king and a court and an army, plain men with not a morsel of magic between them, see it too, that's something few druids on earth could do. It drains the strength out of your heart even to imagine holding such a spell. But he was alive to prove he did it, and right-hand counsellor to Uther now. For all that, it was the red dragon he was fighting for.

Morgan darted away from me and ran up to her father's horse.

'Take me with you!' she begged him, as if this was just another hunt they were going on.

'Women don't go to war these days,' he laughed at her.

'Boudicca did! And Mab. And it was Scathach taught Cu Chulainn to be a warrior.'

'Times change. We're Romans now. We're not living in those old stories any more. Would you like to see your pretty mother slashed with battle scars?'

She made a face to show it wasn't her mother she cared for.

'When I'm grown, I'll fight for you. And if you die, I'll hunt the man who kills you, through the length of Britain. They'll make a new story about us that will be sung for a thousand years and more. How Morgan, daughter of Gorlois, avenged his honour.'

Oh, Morgan, Morgan. How could the little mite know how close to her the man that killed him would be?

The men were all laughing at her by now. Well, she was just a skinny, black-haired scrap of a child to shout so bold. Only her father wasn't laughing this time. It never did to speak to Gorlois of dying. He was the bravest man that ever I knew, and I don't doubt he was as foolhardy in battle as the rest of them. But if he fell, he had no son to follow him yet. And not for want of trying. So he glared at her with a face as black as his hair and swore at her to be quiet.

But she'll make good every word she said.

My lady rode a little way beside him to the high road, with the rest of us following along behind as if it was a May-time picnic. Dressed in a clover-coloured gown, she was, with a cloak of gold and black flowing out behind her. As brave and beautiful as the furze and heather that were blazing on the hills. She'd taken mighty good care of the way she looked that day, to make sure he'd hold that sight of her in his mind 'til he came back again. But Morgan had spoilt it for her, talking of death.

So Ygerne bit her lip and glanced sideways many a time to see from Gorlois's face what kind of mood he might be in now. It was a narrow, tricky road she had to tread, being wife to him. He'd married her for the great beauty that she had, and still had after fifteen years, if you'll believe me. It's the soft Cornish air that kept her pretty cheeks as delicate as the wild roses and curled her hair when there was damp in the wind.

But she'd disappointed him three times now. Two girls she'd given him, and in pretty quick time too. So he'd still had hope the next one would be a boy. Then, nothing. Years they'd waited. Many's the time she'd come to me in tears and begged me to help her. As if I hadn't taught her everything a wife should know, and done a few things in private on my own account that should have quickened any barren cow this side of Bodmin. It worked at last, and mighty proud she was when her belly swelled for the third time. But she wasn't laughing when it came to the birthing. I've never heard a woman scream so. And Ygerne was no coward. I truly thought the child was killing her, and itself as well. But we got it out at last. And it was a girl. Morgan. You wouldn't think a thing so small could have done so much harm. Black as a raven she was, even then, with her hair already grown down to her waist while she was still in the womb.

I laid her beside her mother, who was as white as death. Ygerne asked one question, and I answered her. Then she turned away, and it must have cost her a mighty effort to move her bloody buttocks even that

19

far, after what she'd been through. She wouldn't look
at Morgan. She wouldn't touch her. The wet-nurse
had her from that moment. And then she was mine.

I didn't believe she'd ever have another child, and
nor did she. But the two of us went to lengths I hadn't
even dared up to then. I took her to places, women,
yes, even men, that Gorlois might have killed her for if
he'd known. The old faith is still alive, or you wouldn't
be listening to me now. It's more than a bit of harm-
less medicine, a few charms in a bag, or a poke up the
bum under the horse's skirt on May Day. She must
have blood.

Ygerne had other ideas too. She went to the saint.
To Nectan. As if that white-gowned hermit knew anything about woman's work. Lily-livered folk that call
wine blood and bread flesh. Strong voices and soft
hearts those Christians have. But it seems he knew a
bit more than I gave him credit for, and she came
away from his cell with a flea in her ear, duchess or
no. She still went beside Gorlois on Sundays after
that. She had to. She couldn't very well tell her husband what the saint had said, could she? But she'd a
hard job keeping the anger out of her face every time
she looked at Nectan. And there'd be times he'd keep
his keen blue eyes on her when he preached about
witchcraft. He tried looking at me, but I'd pull the
hood round my face and stare at the ground or the sky
'til he'd finished ranting.

Oh, yes. I took their Eucharist with them. We all
did. The gentry expected it. They say it was a Roman
emperor first had the idea that a crucified man could
win the world for them in battle. Well, the Romans
have gone from Britain now. It seems their fighting
Christ couldn't keep the North-gods out of Rome after
all. And what have they left behind but monks and

nuns without a sword between them? A shepherd's
crook, and a bell, and a pen. That's all their weapons
now. And maybe they're more dangerous like that.
But the men can't see it. Gorlois still rode out to battle
against the Saxons under the cross. But who his wife
prayed to for his safety was another matter.

So she had to tread carefully. She was his treasure.
The most beautiful thing he owned, as long she could
keep her looks. The envy of every lord in Cornwall,
and further than that, if they came west to see her.
But every time he ploughed her now the seed never
sprouted. She knew she'd failed him.

They'd reached the crossroads before she'd
plucked up the courage to smile and put her white
hand on his bridle, and lean across to kiss him.

'God-speed to your banners, my lord. Let Uther
Pendragon know there is high blood beats in
Cornwall. Come back to us swiftly with victory and
with honour.'

And she hung a charm round his neck, like any
good-wife.

She was a brave woman, and a beautiful one. She
smiled at him and turned her head so that the cloak
blew back from her shoulders and the sun shone
behind her through her hair. She wanted to be sure
he'd remember her so, and bring him hurrying back to
her bed.

He grinned at her then. The wind was blowing over
the hills and the white pebbles shone along the road,
going east out of Cornwall. There was hard riding and
brave adventure and maybe glory at the end of it.
There was a light in his eyes that told me his heart
was across the Tamar already. He gave her a great
bear-hug that swung her clean out of the saddle.

'Never you fear, woman! By Beli and by the Bride of

Heaven, those Saxons shall never set foot in Cornwall to steal Gorlois's treasure!'

And he galloped away from her at full speed with never a thought for the lads that were striding out after him on foot.

He never noticed Morgan, holding up her arms to him for a last kiss.

Chapter Four

We were coming to the height of our own killing when they rode back. Samain, I still call it. Fat sheep and sleek cattle for the butcher. They drove them down from the moors with the wool curling on the lambs' backs and the shine of summer on the cows' red rumps. We couldn't keep them all. Not with the grass turning to sour mud in the winter and salt blowing in over us from the sea or snow down on us from the hills. Winter, we were all shut in, folk and beasts. There wasn't room enough for them all in a narrow place. Or food, either. So some must die and others live. Those we kept were the ones that were the best for breeding.

It was a noisy, smelly old time, what with pigs' blood running into barrels and cattle roaring at the knife. And pilchards and mackerel hanging up to dry, all split and skewered, with the seagulls screaming over the buckets of guts.

We kept the feast the old way. We doused every fire to show the summer was dead and gone. Then we scared ourselves silly in the dark. To some like Margawse it was just a game. But Elaine knew better. We still had one of the Old Ones to kindle the new fire on the top of the hill that would light every hearth for another year. It was a good old blaze we made, and then we broke the oatcake, and him that got the burnt bit ran for his life. I daresay we were a bit freer that year, with so many of the gentry away. We didn't mind my lady, somehow. For all her fine clothes, she was not so very different from us.

I can see Morgan's eyes as she crouched beside me, watching it all. Wide and black as two pools in a bog. She didn't need to be told what it was all about.

I could take my girls that night, and not be worried they might come back sprouting. Samain's not like May-time. We huddled close, but I don't need to tell you it wasn't for want of that. We daren't look over our shoulders into the dark for fear of what we might see. It was the night of the dead.

May-time and Samain.

Sometimes I wonder if that's all life is. Breeding and killing. The men to kill. The women to breed.

There's just a handful of us set apart, between the right hand and the left. It's left to us to watch over the heart of things, to keep the world from tearing itself in two.

That lanky saint, Nectan, spent Samain a different way from us. A lamp burning in his chapel all through the night, and him flat on his face, praying for the souls of the dead. And if you'd passed close enough by Tintagel, you'd have heard the white nuns singing psalms.

Gorlois had done his share of killing too. He and his men came back slower, and looking well satisfied with themselves. Like a cat that's eaten a hare and come home to sleep it off.

When all the yelling and the kissing and the boasting had died down, they slept all right. Sprawled out and snoring, as though some fairy-woman had cast a glamour over them to stop their eyes and ears for a year. Like a woman after childbirth, they were. All the struggle and the pain and the fear behind them. They

24

were mighty pleased with what they'd done.

We heard that tale sung so many times I was heartily sick of it by Christmas. But Morgan could never have enough of listening. We were coming to the time of the year when we keep the fire blazing high on the hearth at supper-time and the white logs are still glowing at their ends by morning. It was good and warm to be crowded in the hall, with apples and nuts roasting on the hot stones and the ale going round more slowly as our heads began to nod. Morgan would curl up on the floor with her arms round her father's leg. And if the harper fell silent or the men ran out of bawdy stories, she'd dig her pointed chin into his knee and say, loud enough for them all to hear, 'Tell us, Father. Tell us the story of how you saved Britain at Mount Damen.'

And he'd give a great roar of laughter and toss the wine-cup back. But he never said no to the telling of that.

Blaen the harper would touch his fingers over the strings 'til they began to dance.

Jordan and Britael would leap to their feet on either side of Gorlois's chair. Like two tall schoolboys, they were, hardly more sensible than the day the three of them rode up to Ygerne's father's gate, for Gorlois to court his daughter. And it wasn't long before Jordan tumbled me in the orchard too, though nothing came of that. Well, they were fine warriors, both of them, that could make a man's blood beat faster and a woman blush and a boy's eyes burn bright with talk of battles. It was a fine tale they told.

'The Saxons came marching down from the north.'
'They'd sailed a great army across from the lowlands.'
'Fire flared where they passed.'

25

'They ruined towns and farms.'

'Octa, Hengist's son, and Eosa rode at their head.'

'Hateful helmets and armour spread over Britain's land.'

'They came down on York, proud city of the Romans.'

'It seemed that no one could save the people.'

'Uther summoned warriors out of all the west.'

'From Cambria and Cornwall and Rheged of the Lakes.'

'They marched across Britain, the Pendragon leading them.'

'The Cross of Christ was on their banners.'

'Gorlois rode at Uther's right hand.'

'A man cunning in battle, skilful and fearless.'

'The ranks of the Britons were few against the hosts of the Saxons.'

'Red blood flowed and brave men fell.'

'Terror came with the white dragon of the pagans.'

'By nightfall we were driven back to Mount Damen.'

'High on the hill we hid amongst rocks and hazel trees.'

'The Saxons dared not follow us in the dark.'

'Like foxes we hid in hollow holes in the earth.'

'Like owls we looked down upon the camp of our enemy.'

'Vast the hordes waiting for us on the plain.'

'They slept in their tents, certain of victory in the morning.'

'Uther summoned his chieftains in the darkness.'

'The noblest warriors of Britain met in counsel.'

'Gorlois of Cornwall spoke words of courage.'

'Gorlois, battle-hardened, gave daring counsel.'

'The chieftains sprang to their feet under the stars.'

'Hope returned to the heart of Uther Pendragon.'

Well, by this time, they were on their feet, swords out. Real swords, with real edges on their blades, mind you. Acting it out and going at it, hammer and tongs. Morgan was ducking her head to keep out of the way of them, and her eyes flashing with the glamour of it, like any boy's.

They were creeping round the hall now, with long, stealthy strides, and making sudden dashes to frighten the women screaming into a corner if they could. Some of them enjoyed that, I can tell you. And you can be sure that Margawse was always just in front of those swords, so that it brought the heart into my mouth. She was a girl that loved danger, when it came from a man.

'The brave band of Britons crept down the hillside.'
'Night and mist were friends to the Pendragon.'
'In silence they drew near to the Saxon sentries.'
'The stars shook with the shouts of men alarmed.'
'Fear ran like fire through the tents of the invader.'
'The Morrigan washed a bloody shroud for them.'
'Men fell in darkness. Brother turned against brother.'
'Octa, that mighty leader, was taken prisoner. Eosa was captured.'
'Gorlois of Cornwall taught Uther the paths of victory.'
'The Britons marched upon York with their banners flying.'
'At the gates, in the sight of all the people, Uther Pendragon spoke.'
'He gave chief honour to Gorlois, Duke of Cornwall.'

Morgan's little eyes were shining by then, and there was colour in her white cheeks for once, almost as high as her mother's.

'The night is a lucky time for Cornwall, then? A time to dare! We take our enemy in their sleep and win the game.'

I heard a little laugh behind my shoulder. It was Elaine.

'And who shall be our enemy in the night-time?'

I didn't take any notice of her, fool that I was.

I was looking at the three of them, towering over Morgan. Jordan, and Gorlois, and Britael. The firelight dancing in their faces. And them laughing and slapping each other on the back as they remembered how they'd won. I saw those three creeping up on a camp in the darkness. Their white teeth grinning in the mist before dawn. Taking their prize.

Gwennol Far-Sight, they call me. I should be ashamed.

Well, there'd been killing enough to last them 'til another summer. But as for the other . . .

I'd seen Gorlois look at his wife almost before he swung a leg down from his horse. She had a fair, round belly, after bearing three children, and she wore her gowns slender and her girdle pulled tight. But one look, one spark in his eye, and then he could see that was all it was. She hadn't kindled. I've seen that darkness in a man's face many a time, when my husband sat across the fire from me, looking at my barren belly.

Chapter Five

It was one day when the rain was sheeting down outside and we were all filling in the restless time before supper, cramped up together in the hall and everything stinking of damp.

'I suppose you're Uther Pendragon's best friend now,' laughed Morgan.

She was sitting between her father's thighs and pressing her head back against his kilt.

He jumped up pretty quick when she said that, and kicked her, though he never even noticed.

'Yes, by God and the Blessed Head of Bran! I'm the best friend he has.'

He was striding down the hall, striking his fist into his palm and shouting. But I saw Jordan looking at Britael, and the two of them lifted an eyebrow at each other. There's more to this yet, I thought to myself, for all they shout and swagger so loud about their great victory. What's come between Uther and Gorlois, then, if they were so thick as they say at the gates of York?

'But it was because of you he beat the Saxons, wasn't it?' Morgan was on her hands and knees like a black cat. 'You told Uther what to do. You took Octa and Eosa prisoner and freed the North from the hand of our enemies. It was all your doing, wasn't it? If you hadn't led them down the hillside in the dark, the

Saxons would have beaten you in the morning and Uther wouldn't be alive and wearing the crown of all the Britons now.'

She was mightily proud of her father then. And had good reason to be, if the tales the bards sang were only half true. He'd saved Uther's skin, and the rest too, and turned the tide for Britain that year. They'd gone rampaging up to the North after that, all the way to the other side of the Wall. And goodness knows what kind of chancy folk or devils they fought with there. And everywhere they went the red dragon had put the white to flight, or so they boasted.

Gorlois grinned. He couldn't help himself. Like Ygerne, he wasn't as young as he used to be. But like her, he didn't look as old as he was. Just a bit of grizzle in his black beard, like an early frost. And his step was spry and firm. For all the battles that he'd fought he hadn't a limp or a scar to spoil his looks. He was a handsome man, and a proud one too. And he liked to be praised. Well, that's what they pay the bards for, isn't it? And why he kept a hundred warriors in meat and ale. 'Gorlois of Cornwall!' they cried when they raised their drinking horns. 'Gorlois the Generous!' 'Gorlois the Gold-giver!' 'Gorlois who saved the North from the sword of Octa!'

Well, that was well enough in Cornwall. They were his liege men. But how would a shout like that sound in Dyfed and Gwynedd and Rheged beyond the Wall, and such outlandish places? How did the other chieftains like to hear Gorlois praised above the Pendragon himself? Did Uther's bards sing the same song at the king's court in London as Blaen did here? I bet they didn't. It would have set the Pendragon's teeth on edge, I reckon. No gold ring for the poet who sang a song like that. It's a dangerous thing for any nobleman to be praised above his king. It's shortened many a man's life. What Uther wanted was a man to give him good counsel, but then the sense to keep out of the way and leave the fighting and the glory to him.

But Gorlois couldn't see it. That's all his life had ever been: blood and glory. A woman's blood or a man's. He'd have victory on a bed or a battlefield. Either way, he had to win. He wouldn't care that he was riding into the jaws of death, with his breeches on or off. Maybe he was right. Maybe it was better to live and die the way he did, and not go creeping and careful. He wasn't the man to save his skin and lose his honour. Was he to change because Uther would rather have a soul-friend that had no need of a sword?

All the same, something was heavy on him. We waited for him to come out with it. I know all our heads were up and listening then. I've seen folk like that at haymaking, when you can hear the wind rising in the trees and you know the rain will be on you any moment.

He turned at the door and came striding back and thumped the table. I think he wished it was a man's head.

'I *was* the king's friend!' he said. 'After Mount Damen. He's young yet. He trusted me. I gave the Saxons into the palm of his hand when they could have split and skewered our skulls upon a stake next morning.

'I rode into the north beside him. Gorlois, Duke of Cornwall at Uther's right elbow. We crossed the Wall.

'But there was a snake in the heather. Sliding and slithering into the king's good graces. One of those that slough their skins and shift their shapes.'

I sat forward pretty quick at that, and my heart was thumping faster, for he was getting pretty near to my own business here. I daren't meet his eye. I didn't know how much he knew, but he was sometimes shrewder than I took him for. Besides, I'd half guessed the name he meant. I hadn't thought that one would have come to the surface again so far north. But that was before I knew him. Like an otter, he was, that can swim miles under water, hidden from sight. You never know where he'll rise next. Or like summer lightning, he'll strike at you out of a clear blue sky without any warning.

'I say Vortigern should have killed him when he meant to, prophecy be damned! The fatherless boy! It's plain why his mother would tell a tale like that, isn't it? Either his father was the devil or she's no nun. He talked his way out of that, and he's been talking his way to fortune ever since. Worm-tongue! I'm a plain soldier. I say what needs to be said, and that's the end of it.

'I gave the king good counsel, and it worked. I only say what can be done tomorrow, and I'm proved right or wrong. I don't deal in dreams. I don't try to paint the future.'

All this while Morgan had been staring up at her father's face, like a puppy-dog at her master. But when he started to talk of dreams I saw her eyes wander to the door. The rain had stopped, as it often does just before sunset. The sky was flaming under great purple clouds, like the edge of a creeping fire in the heather that can't be smothered. And I remember all the beads of rain on the ends of the thatch began to glitter. You'd think they were rose-crystals on the trees of fairyland.

'Who is he?' she asked. 'Who is it who can dream a king's future for him?'

'That trickster,' he said, 'that came from no good man's bed. Merlyn, they call him. Emrys Merlyn. Like a jackdaw, he is. You never know where he's going to be popping up next, stealing what doesn't belong to him. And he's no warrior or even a licensed bard. Yet he struts beside the king now as proud as a prince.'

'And will the dreams he weaves for the king really come true?'

Her eyes were wide. But I didn't heed her. It was her father I was watching closely then, and I held my breath to hear him answer. Gorlois was no fool. Not when it came to wars and land and the big affairs of men. It was only the things closest under his nose he couldn't see. Emrys Merlyn was a big enough affair, in all conscience. But I hardly knew if Gorlois counted him as a man.

A chancy, crafty, dangerous creature, he must be.

It's a funny thing. I'd never met him, and never thought I ever would, then. But I'd heard enough. Even to think that name sent a quiver down my spine and set the blood throbbing between my legs. You'd think I was a young girl staring after a man who's never looked her way, but that her body's panting for. We're not so far away in Cornwall that tales don't come our way, and Gorlois could be generous to any passing poet. And lately the songs of Merlyn had begun to grow.

There's many a brave Briton lost his life because of that traitor Vortigern. He thought the Saxons were his friends and called the council of Britain to a peace conference. Fool, that saw the flower of our leaders hacked to death before his eyes. But the fatherless boy he wanted to sacrifice to save his stronghold was

33

cleverer than them. Merlyn slipped out of his grasp,
like a tadpole through your fingers. There were some
who swore he was a child of hell and others who
whispered he was heaven-sent. But what's heaven
and hell to the wise like us? Our power is in the earth
itself. In springs and stones and under the hollow
hills.

For a while after that Merlyn vanished from the
tales. He'd hopped out of sight, like a toad in the
grass. Some said afterwards he'd fled to the forests
beyond the Wall, others that he'd sat on a mountain
from which folk come back madmen or magicians.
But suddenly here he was again. And now it seems
our fairy toadling had turned into a prince, or one
that walked pretty close with them. Closer than Duke
Gorlois, by the sound of it. Our good lord wouldn't
forgive that in a hurry. He thought he was the one
who'd earned the right to have the Pendragon's
ear.

I was Gorlois's bondwoman, since the day he married Ygerne. And I've served him loyally, living and
dead, down to this hour. For his sake I ought to have
hated Merlyn then, even before what happened. Yet,
I don't know how it was, but every time I heard the
name of Emrys Merlyn spoken it was as though someone had put a finger on that spot between your legs
that I needn't tell you of. The one that sends a thrill
right through your body. Sometimes religion's like
that. I've known those that can kindle lightning in the
soul as hot as in the flesh. And sometimes both at
once. He was one of those.

So when Morgan asked if Merlyn would dream true
I knew the answer, even if Gorlois didn't. It scared
me. There are times when I can see the future. And
more often than not I wish I hadn't. I've seen a man

34

trapped under the sea, with the fish picking his face away. I've heard an unborn child walled up alive in its dead mother's womb. Weeping comes out of the future louder than laughing. But I haven't made what I see. I'm like Gorlois. I'll pluck and brew, and cast and chant, to bring about what we need for this year. I don't interfere any further than that. I wouldn't know how. But suppose a man or a woman fasted and suffered and prayed hard enough to sweat blood, and went out into the wild places and wrestled with devils 'til they were nearly driven mad. Wouldn't they come back with powers greater than a mortal witch? A man like that might change the course of the world.

Just for a moment I saw clear. There was something Merlyn wanted from us here in Cornwall. It was only for a heartbeat, but it nearly stopped my heart. But Gorlois was a plain man, a soldier.

'I told Uther we would beat Octa's host at Mount Damen, and come off that hill with our lives and honour. Then I took my good sword in my right hand and made certain that what I'd promised him came true. Well, this trickster Merlyn is a different sort of warrior. We'll see if he can hold his weapons as firm as I hold mine. But I don't doubt he'll use all his craftiness to turn what he says he can see into certainty.'

It was Morgan who dared to ask, 'What does Merlyn see for the future?'

But Gorlois just turned his back on her and yelled to the steward to ask if supper wasn't ready yet.

All this time Ygerne had been sewing. She bent her pretty head over the sweet honeysuckle she was embroidering, as though it all meant nothing to her. Swords and sorcery. What was that to Ygerne? The Duchess of Cornwall, safe in her hearth and her hall in Bossiney. She was far away from the glamour of kings

and enchanters. I could kick myself now, looking back.
I knew better than to believe that on one score, didn't
I? She had more ambitions of sorcery than her
husband dreamed of. I was as big a fool as him not to
have guessed she might have ambitions for the other
too.

Chapter Six

So we came to primrose time. A wet, old winter since
Christmas it had been, too, with all the tracks out of
the dun running like rivers, and my Lord Gorlois sulky
because there'd hardly been one day in seven that
was fit for hunting. And all of us coughing and shivering, and the wood too wet to give a good blaze. I feared
for Morgan then. I never thought we would bring her
through the winter. There was always that feeling on
me when I looked at her, as though she was never
surely with us.

I've lost many a night's sleep over that child. Aye,
and it began right back before she was born. I held
her mother's shoulders when she was doubled up
with pain. We feared for the child even then. We
never thought we would get her to the birthing. And
when we did, it seemed as if my lady would die too,
with the child still trapped between her legs. And
when it was all over, and the blood and the mess
cleared away, what had we got to show for it but a
scrap of flesh and bone, like a half-picked chicken leg
that my lord would have thrown to his hounds?

I sometimes wonder if it would have been better if
she had died then. If all that pain and labour wasn't
for worse than nothing. But I can't think it. Even if I'd
known what was to come, I couldn't have taken the
pillow and smothered her, though there are some who

say it would have been better if I had. It's funny how it's the ones who give us the most trouble that we love deepest. Take Elaine, now. She was as easy a child as you could wish for. Hardly a tear or a frown we had from her. You could tell she would make a fine mother from the day she was old enough to play babies with her dolls. But I danced at her wedding when she married a king and went to bear him fine sons, and I never shed a tear. But Morgan. Even when they took her away from me, before she was half-grown, I never stopped thinking about her.

But now the wind had changed, and the sea settled like cat-skin, and the sky was as blue as a girl's gown. My lord was restless. He'd been cooped up too long in Bossiney. The wind was drying the tracks and news began to reach us again from outside Cornwall.

I remember that day. It was healing weather. A little mist coming up off the streams at sunrise. Then it was swallowed up in that bright blue sky, as if the heavens themselves had opened their arms and lifted all our chills and tears away from us. For the first time you could feel the sunshine sinking into your bones and doing you good. There are some of the wise have a touch like that, when they lay their hands over your heart.

Gorlois and the men were off at dawn hunting, and Morgan with them. For once I was glad of it. Her legs were growing longer, and mine were getting slower with every year. Sometimes the child would sit for hours, hardly moving. Then she'd be off, as quick as a stream over a waterfall, and how was I to keep up with her, or know what was in her head? Let her father look to her for once, I thought.

Small hope of that. I waved to her when they rode off, but she never turned her face to see. She was too busy trying to keep her pony's head as close behind her father's horse as the men would let her. And him? He couldn't wait for the hounds to give tongue to gallop away at the head of them all. He was so hot to kill whatever might cross his path that I don't think there was a thought in his head about her.

It was always peaceful at Bossiney without the men. We all found some excuse to be out of doors, and outside the walls too, if we could find the chance. The sheep were crooning in the pasture, and the lambs beginning to come. In a few weeks it would be Maytime, and summer on the hills. The whole place was like a daisy-flower opening up its petals to the sun.

I busied myself about our sleeping-hut a bit quicker than usual. Elaine's corner wasn't much trouble. Neat and warm and soft as a dormouse's nest. Margawse was the one that made me work. Clothes flung everywhere as she'd rummaged through her chest, sorting out what to flaunt herself in this morning, and the bedclothes all over the floor as if she'd been snatched from her sleep by a gang of Irish pirates. I scolded enough, bending my stiff back to pick everything up, though there was no one around to hear me.

I'd no need to scold Morgan, and I could have wished I had. Her bed-place was straight and tidy as a nun's, or a soldier's. That sometimes made me want to cry. It didn't seem natural. I was not so silly as to think she did it for my sake, to save me work. It felt more like a warning, telling me to keep off. She didn't want even my hands on her things, prying and poking. Not Gwennol's hands, that had reached inside her mother, when the midwife didn't dare, and pulled her into the world.

When that was done, I took a girdle I was plaiting,

and sat outside on a bench where I could feel the sun
on my face. I looked about for Margawse, but I
couldn't see her. Yet I didn't go looking for her. Not
then. I was pretty easy in my mind that morning. With
most of the men off hunting, and only a handful of
slaves about the place, there was little she could get
up to. There was a ruddy-faced shepherd boy I'd
noticed her sidling off towards lately. But I'd taken
care to have a word in his ear and I'd frightened him
good and proper with a picture of what evil I'd put on
him if he laid a finger on her. I left him shaking so that
the poor lad couldn't have got his tool up if Arianrhod
herself had come tempting him.

But I'd got used to looking for a whisk of her gay
gown round some corner, and I couldn't see her. Or
Ygerne and Elaine. They could be in my lady's bower
across the way, but why would they sit cooped up
indoors on such a sweet morning? I tried to put the
thought out of my head, but it wouldn't let me rest.
Every time I looked across at Ygerne's half-open door,
it had a still, empty look about it. There wasn't a
flicker of movement or a woman's voice from inside.

Presently it got so I had to find out. I unknotted the
wools from my waist and went across to look. I didn't
need to push the door wide open to know the truth of
it. There was no one in the chamber. I went across to
the hall, though what would they be doing there at
that time of the morning, among all the sweeping and
scrubbing after last night's supper? Issey, the
steward, must have seen me staring round and asked
me what was the matter. But I didn't tell him. I had my
pride. He was a decent enough man, but I wasn't
going to have a hall full of slaves knowing my lady had
taken her two daughters off, without even a word to
their nurse about where they were gone. I didn't want

them thinking I was too old for my job.

But you can't hide much, living as close as we did. I was taking myself off across the yard, and thinking I was keeping my dignity, when Ewa came past, carrying a bucket of ashes. A cow-faced slave, she was, from up Devon way. She'd never liked me. She grinned at me now, black teeth and all.

'If it's my lady you're looking for, she's long gone. She and her woman Ruan took themselves off just after sunrise. Carrying baskets, to gather the new herbs, they said. She called young Lady Elaine to go with her, and Tual to follow behind to guard them. And then I saw the Lady Margawse go running after them. Funny you not knowing that.'

I could see now why she was smiling so slyly. All the women knew well enough what I was. Not the whole of it by a long way, of course, but enough to make them look up to me more than ever they'd have done if I'd been just those three girls' nurse. They feared me more than a little. And it didn't make them love me, though there's many had reason to be grateful to me, and some for their lives, and their children's. But my lady and her daughters had gone off this morning with their baskets, on what should have been my business before anyone else's. And if I didn't know it, then maybe it was more than Gwennol Far-Sight's legs that were getting stiff and old? Maybe I wasn't the powerful wise woman I used to be, I could see her thinking, plain as if she'd said it out loud.

'There's those that can gather weeds and others that know who to use them on,' I snapped back at her. And gave her a look that sent her hurrying off to the midden with the blood running out of her cheeks.

But it hurt me sorely. Maybe I was getting too soft and slow, drowsing there on the bench when others were busy, and not seeing what was going on under my nose.

I put a shawl round my shoulders and a basket over my arm. I had a good look round to make sure that Ewa wasn't spying and I was off, out of the gates, as fast as I could go.

When I was out of sight of the dun, I stopped to catch my breath. It was a fair, fine day. There were little leverets hopping about in the grass between the hawthorn bushes and red squirrels leaping and shaking gold from the hazel catkins. But I stopped myself smiling at them and shut my eyes. I listened, deep inside. They couldn't hide from me. When I knew where they were, I went into the coombe and up the side of the brook, towards Nectan's waterfall. I didn't need to get that far. Just once I stopped to get my bearings. Then I left the water and began to climb up the steep bank through the trees.

I caught sight of Tual first, sitting on a big mossy stone, with his cudgel on his knees. Then I saw Ruan and Margawse were curled up at his feet. He was telling them some tale from the old wars with the Irish pirates that made them laugh pretty loud and shameless.

He saw me before they did and broke off quick, and they jumped up as though they'd seen a spirit-woman at Samain. Ruan turned her head very sudden, and opened her mouth as if she was going to call out to her mistress. But she thought better of it and laughed at me instead.

It seemed it was a smiling sort of day wherever I went. The sun smiling so sweet and friendly. The faces smiling so sly and secret.

Margawse said, 'Have you come all this way looking for us, Gwennol? You shouldn't have worried.

42

Look, you're all out of breath. Mother said she knew what herbs you would want us to pick. Then she took Elaine, and told us not to follow for a while. It seems there's things I'm not old enough to know yet!' And she laughed, so I could have slapped her face.

'We're all right. We've got Tual to look after us.' And that made Ruan laugh as well.

I was too full to answer her. For once it wasn't Margawse I was worried about. Tual was a slave. He wouldn't touch her, though he could foul her thoughts with his stories. I climbed right past the three of them as if they hadn't been there. Ruan called out after me, but even she daren't try and stop me, though she was pretty thick with her mistress these days.

I found Ygerne and Elaine. They were where I had seen them all this time, under a sycamore tree that was making yellow patterns of sunshine on the floor. They must have heard Ruan shout. They were crouched like two startled hares, watching me coming. I didn't say anything. I stood over them with my hands on my hips and stared down at them. I named over the leaves in their baskets and pursed my lips. I knew there was more than that to it. Then I saw it, half hidden under the skirt of Ygerne's kirtle. They hadn't been sharp enough when they heard the warning. I bent to pick it up. A chain of flowers. A dainty thing. Any village maid might have made such a garland to hang round her lover's neck. Until you looked closer and saw what was woven into it. Well, I needn't tell you. They both had blood, and more, under their fingernails. They'd used hooked flowers of course. Those that catch and claw and bind. I held it under my lady's nose, so she had to back away. But still I didn't understand what it was she wanted.

'What's this, then? A spell of summoning? Your

43

man's not at the king's court on the other side of
Britain now. Do you need such a chain to bring him
back to you from a day's hunting?'

She smiled at me, sweeter than any of the others.

'Elaine's new in our ways. There are things she
needs to be taught. And after such a cruel winter the
forest is full of fallen trees and dangers. The wolves
are hungry. There's no harm in us wishing Gorlois's
safe return, is there?'

She never thought of Morgan.

I looked her squarely in the face 'til her eyes fell.

'There are charms for a man's safety. I've filled
bags with them by the hundred. And there are spells
of binding. Do you think I'm so old and witless I can't
tell the difference?'

She always had an answer. 'Summer is coming.
Don't you feel it today, Gwennol? Soon Uther
Pendragon will be at the wars again, and Gorlois with
him. Should I not try to bind him to me, while there is
time?'

I saw her put her hand over Elaine's to keep her
quiet. The daughter's face was as sweet and smiling
as her mother's. But her eyes looked scared. I made
up my mind I'd have it out of that girl before the day
was over.

It was noon before we got back to the dun, and by
then I didn't need to be told who that pair had been
summoning. There was a horseman in the yard
already.

Chapter Seven

By nightfall the whole dun was in an uproar. That messenger wouldn't tell his news 'til Gorlois came home. It seems this message was too important for women's ears, even Ygerne's. But we found out pretty quick he came from Uther Pendragon's court up in London. Well, you can imagine the wild stories that went flying round.

'Are they going back to war already? They must be, mustn't they?' says Margawse, gripping me by the wrist as though she'd like to break it.

'Tual says the Saxons have brought a huge army over from the Lowlands to rescue Octa and Eosa.' Elaine's eyes were so big, I didn't know if she was more frightened of the Saxons or of what she'd done.

'They've captured Glastonbury.'

'The Picts have crossed the Wall and they're pouring south.'

I hardly knew where to turn or who to believe. It was too far even for my seeing, and it sounded like fighting men's business, none of mine. Except when Ruan said that about the Isle of Glass. The womb of Britain. That shook me for a while. I've never been so far, though I could take you to other tors, true daughters to that one. But we all know of it, of course, through the Old Ones. And I could feel it then, like a cord that's not yet cut, as if I was a baby feeding on its mother's blood. I'd have known if they'd touched that.

I was watching Ygerne as close as I could through all that flying about and foolishness. She'd got Uther's messenger in the hall and had the fire built up, and she was giving him the best wine in a jewelled horn, just as if he'd been the king himself. And all the time her little white fingers were tap, tap, tapping on the table-top. It didn't do her any good. He knew his job better than to unbutton his lips at the first drink he downed. She had to wait, like the rest of us.

It was still early in the year, and the light was turning purple over the forest before the hunt came home. And then, of course, I had Morgan to wash and get to bed. The poor little mite was so weary she could scarcely hold her eyes open. Still, she half knew there was something going on. She stirred and struggled a bit as I picked her up. Then her head dropped on my shoulder and she let me carry her to our hut. I stripped the muddy clothes off her back and bathed her and salved her scratches. She was so limp and spiritless you'd think she'd been drugged for the Offering, and I don't mean any Christians' Eucharist, either. I chased that idea away pretty quick. I laid her down on her bed, and lifted the black hair away from her little face. She was asleep before I kissed her. A little baby thing she looked on her pillow. And the only still creature in the dun, or so it seemed that night.

I couldn't wait to be off and running across to the hall as fast as I could go. It irked me to be called a wise woman and now to be the last to know the news. I'd have to keep my mouth shut and my ears open, and make believe I knew more than I did. But I needn't have worried. Margawse came flying across the hall as soon as she saw me.

'Gwennol! You'll never guess the news! It's not the

Saxons. Just the opposite. King Uther Pendragon is going to wear his crown at a great feast in London. All the lords in every part of Britain who helped him to victory are summoned to his court on Easter Day. And their ladies with them. Think of it, Gwennol! Mother's going to London to meet the king!'

I looked across at Ygerne and nodded. So that was the way of it. She'd been a better pupil than I thought, this daughter who was not of my own blood. She'd got what she wanted, and hadn't even asked my help. Only Elaine's. I watched her now, still smiling over the Pendragon's messenger, like any good housewife with a guest. Well, good luck to her, I thought. It's dull enough for her here in Bossiney, out of the way of all the great happenings. We don't see many kings down here in Cornwall, except him who calls himself King of Dumnonia. Of course, I'd been up Exeter way once. His court was a bit grander than our Cornish rounds. They'd built it up with stone the old Romans had left. It must have been a fine city once, before the pillars started tumbling down and the trees grew up through the pavements. But his house wasn't much richer inside than we were used to. That was long before, when Ygerne was newly-married, a slip of a girl as bright and golden as a Lent lily. She turned men's heads wherever she went. Since then, I'd had her children at my knee and stayed at home when they rode off to their kin across the Tamar.

Gorlois was like a dog that's seen a hare. He was mad to go. Anything to be off and doing, meeting with other lords and ladies and playing the great man. I could see him now, his arm round Ygerne's shoulders and fondling her more than I'd seen him do for many a year, except at night when he was drunk and couldn't wait to have her in bed. I knew what he was thinking.

Uther could wear his golden crown, to show to all the
Britons. But Gorlois had his golden Ygerne, and the
king might hunt a long way to find a wife more beautiful than his. She'd be his jewel.

As for his men, there were hands on daggers before
they'd hardly started drinking. Gorlois couldn't take
a hundred warriors to the feast with him, but he'd
want an escort. The Duke of Cornwall's got to look
like a noble lord. He fancied himself as a great chieftain now, since that battle. Uther's general. A bigger
man, they said, than our king up in Devon. So some
could go and some must stay. And who would he
choose for the honour, and why? They might have
beaten the Saxons for the moment, but there'd be
more blood shed in our hall over that victory, long
after it was won.

If we thought we'd had excitement enough that evening, it was nothing to what the place was like next
morning. All of us were sent flying about, and
screaming at each other like birds at mating-time.
There were the finest clothes to be looked out and
made good, and the jewels and the armour, and the
horses to be seen to. And all the food for the journey.

And in the middle of it all, while I was stooping over
the well, I heard Elaine's voice behind me. Clear and
calm, she sounded, just as if she'd been expecting it.

'Gwennol, you must get out my finest garments as
well, and make them ready. I am to go to London with
Father and Mother to feast with the king.'

I turned round sudden, and she was smiling down
at me, with that same smile on her face she'd had in
the woods, only not so scared now. Like a cat that's
had the cream and knows you're too late to stop it.
That look gave me a queer kind of jolt. It's one thing
to whisper a maid and watch her grow into a wise

woman, as I had with Ygerne, in place of the daughter
I never had. But when your spirit-daughter whispers
her own, and the two of them go spell-speaking in
secret with never a word to you, you feel as though
the world has turned a bit too far. Your star's already
gone down into the dark under the earth.

Well, I could see what was in her mother's mind
straight away. It was plain to all of us. Elaine was a
woman now, with a bloom in her cheeks like the wild
rose. And what better chance could there be to marry
her off to one of the highest in the land? Though I did
think that feast might be a bit like the midsummer
horse-fair, with the men sizing up the fillies for breeding and beauty, and their wives knowing it wouldn't
be just their sons' pleasure those lords were thinking
of. There'd be some sharp bidding and bargaining. A
duke's daughter may be bought and sold, the same as
a slave. And Elaine was a beauty, or so they told me. I
guessed that when that feast was over she wouldn't
stay a maiden much longer, and a good price paid, for
those that reckon in farms and forts. But when she did
come home, and sooner than any of us had looked for,
she had a tale to tell that was stranger than any I
dreamed of then.

There are some that get what they want through
the old knowledge. But there's other ways too, for
those that haven't been spoken. We had reckoned
without Margawse. Well, I can't be keeping my eyes
on them every moment of the day. I had enough to do
with helping to get all my lord and lady's gowns
washed and mended and trimmed, and Elaine's too.
You'd have thought they were going to London for a
year, they wanted so much, and we'd be lucky if we
could find wagons enough to carry it all.

I heard screaming in the great hall. I put my head

inside, and there were Margawse and Elaine, fighting
on the floor like two cats. That was a fine to-do, with
all the house-slaves standing round and gaping. Some
of them were laughing their heads off and the rest
were scared out of their skins. But there wasn't one of
them that dared lay a hand on those young ladies.
Ladies? There was hair and spit and straw flying
about in the air and I could see pretty soon there'd be
blood too if I wasn't quick.

'Stop them!' I screamed.

Well, those slaves looked at me once, but they
wouldn't move. And I hadn't the strength to separate
them. Elaine's strong. She may look plump, but
there's muscle there under the fat. She'd got
Margawse's wrists in a grip and was forcing them
away from her face, and kneeing her at the same time
for all she was worth. Margawse's eyes were blazing
like a smith's forge. She knew well enough she had
weapons at her fingertips. But she was so wild she
hardly knew where she was hitting, or Elaine's pretty
face might have been in rags before then.

I doubled out of that door and yelled for help at the
top of my voice. Well, that brought the warriors that
were in earshot running. They must have thought the
Saxons had found their way to Cornwall at last. The
swords were out before they reached me. They soon
saw what was what, and that it wasn't fitting for
slaves to see what they had seen, in daytime, and not
even strong drink to blame it on. Though goodness
knows I've seen worse than that at a feast when a fine
lady's husband has been given a portion meaner than
she thinks he deserves. Anyway, it was Endoder, our
horsemaster, and Hedrek, Gorlois's huntsman, that
had the separating of them, as if they'd been a pair
of their own bitches. They'd put up their swords and

dropped the shields they'd grabbed when they saw it wasn't men they had to deal with. But they'd have been glad of them. They took a wound or two, before they had those two under control. If they'd been boys, I think the men would have ducked them in the horse-pond, for all they were Gorlois's children. But they daren't do that to his daughters, even then.

I was gasping as if I'd been in a fight myself.

'You wicked girl! What if you'd scratched your sister now and spoiled her looks, just as she's going to the king's court to find a husband?'

Margawse laughed in my face. I'd handed her the weapon she wanted.

Well, she went straight to her parents, as though she was the one who'd been wronged. I fancy my Lady Ygerne must have heard what was passing. Her bower was not so far from the hall, when all's said and done, and she'd sharper ears than I had. But she wasn't going to interfere, or daren't. But when Gorlois understood how they'd shamed each other, with their skirts up round their bums for half the world to see, he was for whipping the pair of them, never mind who had the right or wrong of it. But Margawse put her hands on her hips and said, 'I want to go to the crown-wearing. And if you don't take me, I'll put such scratches on Elaine's face that no one will marry her, now or ever.'

Well, they threw me out pretty quick, and the rest of us besides. But half the dun heard them shouting at each other. He was furious, for she made him look as if he couldn't manage his own womenfolk. But he knew she meant it. She'd got the upper hand of them all. They could have threatened to banish her or whip her, but she only needed a moment. They couldn't act quick enough to be certain she wouldn't reach her sister before they could stop her.

And besides . . . she might not be fully woman yet, as I knew. But I'd seen her stroking her breasts when I bathed her. It wouldn't be long now. And there were few that saw her that would have guessed she wasn't. She could make every head turn when she walked through a group of men, and she knew it. And it wasn't only heads she stirred, either. There'd be more than a few wet breeches. She couldn't be wed yet, but there'd be plenty would be willing to offer. So she got her way, and I'd more work than ever to do making ready for her, and less time to do it in too.

The moment they told me Margawse was going with them, I knew what would follow. *She* didn't fight her sisters or run to her mother. There was only ever one person who counted with Morgan.

She stood in front of her father, pale as ever I'd seen her, and deadly serious.

'Take me! You must take me with you. You have to,' she said, very low and clear, and looking hard into his eyes.

It twisted my guts to hear her. She was trying to make it sound like an order. But I could tell she was desperate. It was just as if she knew he was going to say no, but was driving herself on to do it just the same. She'd damn herself first in her own heart, but she wouldn't stop 'til she'd heard him do it to her with his own lips.

Well, of course, he did. How could they have taken her? A little runt like her, who didn't even look the eight years she was. They'd have laughed her out of court, and him with her, parading herself like her lady mother and her sisters. Margawse would get away with it, and brighten plenty of eyes into the bargain, but never Morgan. That was always the way of it. Her father tried to laugh his way out it, of course.

That great laugh, that men think will set the world to
rights and make women love them again. He put his
arms round her to swing and hug her the way she
always wanted. But she slapped his face and wriggled out of his clutches. That didn't please his
lordship. He was as quick to anger as she was. So they
were not good friends when he left for London. But
what could she have done if she'd gone with him? He
was no more cruel to her than she was to herself.

She ran out of the door. It never crossed her mind to
threaten Margawse's trick. She wasn't like that. If
she'd wanted to strike her sisters, she'd have done it
there and then, without any warning. No matter that
it wouldn't have got her what she wanted. It would
have been quick and sudden, while the fire was eating her heart. She wouldn't think to wait in the dark,
plotting to get her own way. She had a boy's temper,
not a woman's wiles. Not then.

Chapter Eight

I remember the day they left for London, with Morgan
still torn between loving her father and hating him.
We were all up before dawn and in such a commo-
tion, you'd think the king was coming to us, and not
the other way round. Elaine was the calmest. She was
ordering the packing of her mother's things, and her
own as well, and making a better job of it too, for my
lady was as excited as any girl. Margawse was
nowhere to be seen, and goodness knows what she
might be up to behind the armoury, but she was too
big for me and I was too old to go chasing after her,
and so I'd told her mother many a time.

Down in the stables they were grooming the horses
'til you could see your face in their backsides, as if
they wouldn't be spattered with mud and sweat by
the time they crossed the first ford. I found Morgan
down there talking to her father's horse. She was
twisting her fingers in his mane as though she wished
she could turn into a fly and hide herself away there
when he rode off. We must have been the only two in
the dun standing still, and not dashing about with our
faces all red and bothered. And then Issey, the
steward, came running, like a man demented, and
calling out that my lady had ordered sweet-meats to
be baked for the journey and the honey was all gone,
and there wasn't another spare pair of legs to go to

the bee-woman and get more, and would I fetch some for the cooks? I burst out laughing in his face. The sun was over the trees already. This was no time to start baking cakes. They should have been on the road and over the hill long before this, and so I told him. But he was as crazed as the rest of them.

'Use your eyes, woman! It will be hours yet before they're ready. Hurry now, before they think of something else to trouble us with.'

Then Gorlois's horse reared up at the shouting and swung Morgan off her feet. She screamed, and dropped down to the ground almost under his hooves. And as bad luck would have it, up came Lord Gorlois behind me, yelling, 'Get that child away from here, you old fool, before she gets trampled to death.'

Well, I can tell when I'm not wanted. I grabbed Morgan with one hand and the empty crock Issey was holding out in the other and took them both off.

I had trouble with Morgan. She tried to snatch her hand away from mine and run back, though her father had marched off out of sight again.

'No, Gwennol! I'm not going! You can't make me. They're going to leave without me and I won't even have said good-bye to him.'

'You great fool,' I told her, sounding like Issey himself. 'Look at them all, running about like a troupe of mummers at Christmas-time. It'll be noon before they're on their way, and they won't leave without your mother's sweet-cakes by the sound of it.'

'They will! They will! You know what she's like. She'll forget she even ordered them. I *won't* go.'

She had the stronger will, but I had more weight. I was fairly dragging her towards the gate, and she had marks on her wrist afterwards to show for it. But I'd lost patience with them all. If I was to be ordered

about like a house-slave, I'd do my share of ordering
too. Still, I had to calm her, or she'd be darting back
like a swift the moment I let go of her.

'Now then, you can see they haven't harnessed the
horses yet. And it isn't so far to walk to the bee-
woman's. You'll have them in sight when we're on the
downs. If they look like leaving, you'll see it soon
enough to run and catch them.'

'Are you sure, Gwennol? Are you really, really
sure?'

'And your father wouldn't leave without a kiss from
you, would he, now?'

She looked at me then, with eyes so dark it was like
peering into the night. They told me nothing. But I
think it was me saying that that decided her. She was
putting him to the test. She must have known he'd fail
her.

She darted off ahead of me out of the gate. I picked
up my skirts and hurried after her. But I soon slowed
down. I couldn't walk very fast, even then. It was
quiet up on the cliffs. Just a bit of a breeze in the grass
and the gulls flashing overhead, and the little spring
flowers beginning to come out. It would have done me
good to have sat down and rested in the sunshine.
Across the bay we could see the white huts of the
nunnery on Tintagel Head. Very still and quiet they
looked, like birds nesting on a cliff, hatching their
young.

It was a queer feeling. You'd have thought we
should have been bitter enemies, me and those Christians. That hoarse-voiced beanpole, Nectan, up the
coombe, ranting at us for our sins on Sunday. Those
clear-faced nuns, busy as bees, growing queens to
stock new hives all over Cornwall. And so we were,
when we were each about our own business. I can

still feel it like a blow to the stomach – the day they overturned the Stone Man of Trigg. I looked for the heavens to open and shiver their cross to splinters, and the unholy hands that raised it. But the gods must have hid their faces from us that day. Next year we watched those white-robed women marching over the bridge to Tintagel Island, with their cross held up in front of them, singing psalms. Yes, and we did more than watch, some of us. I was a young woman then, drawn up with the rest of the wise on the cliffs opposite, hurling slates and screaming curses on them.

The stones didn't reach them, and the wind took our curses away and turned them back on us, it seemed. Gorlois saw to that. He thought himself a proper Roman then, giving those Christian women the land. Never mind that it had been sacred to us long before their time. He wouldn't let us near enough to harm the nuns. Not with our hands, anyway. There's other means. The Romans have gone, and we'll see who lasts longest now, the Latin psalm-singers or us.

Well, they could drive us from the high places under the sky. But most of them didn't know what went on still, in the dark places you all know of. Though there were some even among the nuns that kept the old faith in secret. That made me laugh. And Gorlois never guessed where his own wife went by night when the month came round again. Most of our gods are like any war-lords. They can be beaten. But the Mothers will go on giving birth. You can't stop them.

Gorlois's people followed him to Nectan's chapel, willing or not. And there were some of the gentry who sent their daughters to the nuns to school, to learn to read and write and weave a pretty embroidery. But we weren't idle, either, though we had to be careful and secret the way we went about it.

So you'd think I'd have hated those nuns, looking across at the place that was once ours. But I couldn't somehow. We were like a pair of wrestlers, sizing each other up. The men who ruled us couldn't see what was going on under their noses. But those women did. Not the whole of it, of course, but enough to respect us. We understood each other's ways. And sometimes I envied them, never mind their cold, narrow beds and their meek rules. They were on the winning side now. You could see by the light in their faces.

But the wise women know how to wait.

That morning I could have sat and looked at Tintagel for a long time, and those little white-robed figures going peacefully to and fro. It was so different from the folly we'd left behind us. But Morgan couldn't wait. She was as restless as a butterfly, flitting from one side of the path to the other. She kept getting further ahead and calling back to me to hurry. All the same, I could see she was glad to be out of doors again and feel the wind fresh on her face. I know I was. I couldn't even mind that it was blowing Morgan's hair all any old how, and I'd be half the day combing out the tangles, if I could keep her still long enough. It was enough for me to see her happy for a moment and safely through another winter, though there wasn't a drop of colour in her cheeks, just the tip of her nose red with the wind.

She'd found flowers now, hiding in the moss under the stones, and she was picking a bunch of them for her father. Primroses, mostly, and a few violets. But she couldn't make them into a dainty nosegay as Elaine would have done. She snatched at them too quickly, so that some of them broke off short and others she pulled up by their poor bruised roots. It was all pretty spring above her fist, but underneath you could see the torn stems hanging down.

She was chattering away, as busy as a starling.

'When we get the honey, I'm going to make cakes for Father too. Some he can have for the journey. But I'll make special ones, Easter cakes, that he can give to the king. He'd like that, wouldn't he? The king would be pleased with Father if he gave him Easter cakes, wouldn't he, Gwennol?'

'That's as may be. As like as not you'd run off and forget about them, 'til they were burnt. The king wouldn't thank your father for offering him a plate of charcoal, would he?'

'I wouldn't! I wouldn't! They'll be the best cakes in the world. And the king will send for the maiden who baked them and offer her his hand in marriage. And I shall be the greatest queen in the land. And when Uther Pendragon is killed in battle, they will bring his body back to me and I shall raise his sword and lead his warriors to victory over the Saxons. And all the people will shout, "Long live Queen Morgan, leader of the Britons!" '

'Get along with you! You couldn't lift King Uther's scabbard, let alone his sword. And if you dance too near the edge of that cliff, you'll end up the seal-king's bride, and a kingdom under the sea.'

Little we guessed then who Uther Pendragon's bride would be within the year.

I was all for staying and chatting at the bee-woman's cottage on Barras Nose. If I was to be treated like a kitchen servant and shouted out of the way, I'd get my own back on them by having a morning's gossip where no one could see me. And the steward could whistle for his honey. But before long Morgan began to tug at my skirt. She was in a hurry to go, and full of the

presents she'd planned for her father, the little
flowers and the Easter cakes. My heart softened, for I
couldn't ever say no to her, though I made sure to
scold her for the fidget that she was.

All the same, I couldn't hurry back as fast as she'd
have liked me to, with the great crock on my shoulder
full of good thick honey now. We came over the cliffs,
and the flashing and movement from Bossiney was
like a fairground in front of us. Then we dropped into
the track that led up beside the stream away from the
sea and lost sight of the dun for a while.

It was a hollow way, and soft underfoot. Above our
heads the twigs of the hawthorn were bare yet. But
the Lent lilies stood as brave as golden war-trumpets.
It was very still and quiet, just as if we had stepped
into another time and another world. Down there
between the hedgebanks we lost the noise of the dun.
Morgan looked at me, and I saw the fear in her face.
She started to run.

We came out of the hollow road into the sunshine
before the gate. And it was a different sight now. The
horses were saddled and drawn up in lines, and the
slaves holding the pack mules' heads. Even before
they saw us, my lord was lifting Lady Ygerne into her
chariot. Margawse and Elaine were already sitting
up in theirs and smiling. Morgan stopped short with a
shudder, like a boat that's struck a rock. She dropped
her poor little flowers in the mud. Then she dashed
forward through the warriors and flung herself on
her father as he settled himself in the saddle. I was
left too far behind to hear what she cried at him. Not
that I needed to. She hadn't learned then how to trick
and act and smile falsely at men. I didn't need to come
within sling-shot of her to know what she would be
saying. Every line of her body and every twist of her

hands was shouting to high heaven. She had her
fingers knotted in her father's cloak and her black
hair was trailing down his horse's flanks like dried
blood. But he flung his arms open and laughed at her,
with his teeth white in his beard. Then he tossed her
in the air and set her over his horse's neck. By the
time I caught up with her, she was hugging and kissing
him, though I could tell that underneath she was still
angry to think that he might have ridden away without her, while she was still on the downs picking
primroses for him.

You couldn't have told her, but it was her own
faults in him that made her angry. She always did
what she wanted. And when did she ever stop to think
of the hurt she was doing to other people? Afterwards
she'd give you a laugh and a kiss to make it all right.
And where did she get that from but her own father,
laughing at the world through his black beard?

Lord Gorlois handed her back to me.

'Bring me a present,' she cried. 'Something splendid
from the king's court.'

'What shall it be? A golden goblet, studded with
jewels? A cloak trimmed with fur? A wolfhound's
puppy?'

'A sword! A magic sword that will kill every enemy!'

He laughed at that, and trotted away from us
through the gateway. A fine, proud sight, with his
warriors and ladies behind him.

Morgan looked up at me when they had gone past
seeing her waving.

'I didn't give him the flowers. He didn't deserve
them. He was going away without saying good-bye to
me.'

She gathered up the flowers then, what was left of
them, for they'd been trampled into the mud 'til they

were pulped and broken. She should have left them there. But she could never let a wound alone. She always had to be testing it to see how much it could hurt. She laid those poor, battered stems across her hand and tried to straighten what petals there were left. I watched her little fingers, stroking and smoothing, as if even then she thought she could heal them. And I wondered, not for the first time either, if perhaps she shouldn't be whispered too, young though she was. No one that knew such things could doubt there was power in the child that she didn't know herself yet. It scared me sometimes. And if she knew the charms of mending she might be a great healer one day, as great as any I'd known.

But all of a sudden I shivered. I cut off the thought short, like the sun going behind a cloud. You can't build walls round a power like that. It goes where the wise woman wills. Left or right. To heal or to harm. I loved the little maid dearly, but I wouldn't trust her with knowledge like that.

So I fell to scolding anyone who was left to listen.

'Yes, and there's me with my arms nearly dropping off, carrying this great crock of honey. And what for, I'd like to know? A slave might just as well have fetched it tomorrow, for all the use it's been. It's not my place to go fetching and carrying like a mule. But your father's like a little boy. He's that excited to be going to see the king, he can't wait. And my lady's not much better, though I don't blame her for that. We see little enough of fine courts and palaces here, and she's beautiful enough to be a queen.'

Young Keby, the stable boy, was coming back from the gate. His cheeks turned red when he saw me and it crossed my mind that it might have had more than a little to do with Margawse disappearing that morning.

And maybe that was why he was in such a hurry to turn my thoughts another way.

He burst out laughing. 'Our lord's a lucky man, and he wants the king to know it. But if I had a wife with my lady's breasts, I'd be leaving her at home when I went to the Pendragon's court. I bet she's still good for a tumble in the straw, even if she has got two tall daughters and the little one. And from the tales our lads brought back last year about King Uther, he's not the man to keep his weapon under his cloak when there are pretty women about.'

'Shame on you, Keby Eval's son! We're not all as free with our hands as some I could tell of. That's no way to be speaking of the High King of Britain. My lady's a good woman, and true to her lord, and has been these fifteen years.'

'Don't shout at me. I didn't make the tales. And it's not my hands we're talking about, is it? I'm not the keeper of the High King's weapon. It wasn't me Gorlois swore his oath to, to give the Pendragon whatever service he asked for. You think of that, Gwennol Far-Sight.'

'My lord's a proud man who can take care of his own. And if you want to keep a whole tongue in your head, you'll keep your dirty thoughts to yourself.'

He looked round that empty yard with his insolent grin. There was only me and Morgan.

'Who's left to hear us now but you and me, Gwennol? And don't tell me you hadn't heard the Pendragon's put more than Saxons on their backs all over Britain. I'm only saying what half of Cornwall knows already.'

'Then Cornish folk can know from me that my lady's a pure wife, and always has been. And she's too wise to be having her head turned by a gold crown at her age.'

I don't know why, but I was trembling with anger so that I could hardly hold that stupid crock of honey in my arms. Time I got rid of it, and gave Issey a piece of my mind for putting me to all that trouble for nothing. It wasn't my place to fetch and carry. I looked round for Morgan. She shouldn't have been listening to such talk. But the wind had blown the tangles over her face and I didn't think she'd heard us. I should have known better.

Chapter Nine

It was a sweet spring, that year – with clouds like young lambs chasing across the sky, and the sea so quiet you could hardly believe how it had been tearing at the cliffs like a pack of wolves all winter. I've often wondered what it must be like to live inland and not to hear the come and go of the waves like blood in the ear.

Our coast looks north, and there's many a tumble of black rock that never sees the sun. But below Bossiney there's one sweet stretch of golden sand when the tide is down. You can sit there in the sun in the middle of the day and watch the green water washing in past the Sisters and a boat or two bobbing out at sea. There's tall old cliffs on either side. From there I couldn't see that stone cross on Tintagel Head, let alone what lay beneath it. When I look back, those are the days it doesn't hurt me to remember, when there was no one to trouble me but Morgan, and I didn't need to be looking up every moment at a warning of what was going to take my baby away.

It was an easy time for us, with our chieftain and his lady away at the court of King Uther Pendragon. And if I was resting my old bones in a bit of sunshine on the beach, mending an old gown for Elaine, who was to worry if Morgan was sometimes out of sight? I was feeling my rheumatism even then, and what would a stiff old body like me be doing scrambling over the rocks of the sea-shore after an eight-year-old that was as nimble as a goat? If it had been Elaine, now, I'd have been worried sick that she'd slip and drown herself in the sea. But not Morgan. She was as sure-footed as a cat. Her sort don't fall. I scolded her often, mind you, but I knew she'd come to no harm. The sea was her playmate.

'Gwennol!' she said, and I nearly fell off the rock with fright, for I hadn't seen her in the shadow of the cliff behind me. She trumpeted with laughter and set me straight again and picked up my sewing from the sand. Then she squatted down in front of me and tipped up her sharp little face.

'Will they come here?' she said. 'My father and the king? If they're out hunting and it starts to get dark, would they ride this way and stay in our dun?'

'Goodness me, my lover! The gods forbid!' I said, and I crossed my fingers for good measure. 'They're miles and miles away. Across the Tamar and a lot further than that. A week's hard riding, or so I've heard tell. And a good thing too, the state we're in. The larder's almost empty and there's hardly a thing growing in the gardens yet but kale. How would we be feasting a king at the back end of winter, with not even a day's notice to brew and bake?'

'But they'd bring meat for the feast with them, wouldn't they? A great stag over the horse's back. Or a boar with savage tusks, and their spears red with its blood.'

'And what about your dear mother? Would you have her galloping half across Britain at her age?'

'I wasn't thinking about Mother.'

'I don't need telling that. You're too fond of hankering to run after the men, my handsome. But it's a woman's world you'll have to live in, so you'd better make up your mind to it. I've enough trouble with your sister Margawse that hasn't eyes for anything that doesn't walk in breeches. We'd all sleep a lot sounder in our beds if that one was at school in the nunnery on Tintagel.'

'I'm not like her. Margawse doesn't want to *be* a man.'

She spoke true enough there. To tell you the truth, it wasn't just idleness that kept me in the dun most of the year. Elaine was as happy as a bird to borrow her mother's power over the hall and the kitchen, and see things were well-set and proper. It was Margawse I worried about. I could never see her disappear round some corner or into a dark doorway but I wondered who might be waiting for her there. She'd no pride. Only a red hunger that wouldn't be satisfied. As soon as she was a woman she ought to be married. I thought of May-Eve that was coming. If I could take her with me then . . . That was what she needed. There is a right season for everything. And those that open their bloodhole to the Mother's Son can sleep more easily in their beds on other nights. It wasn't as if she would be the first of her folk to travel that road, for all Ygerne's family were nobles and called themselves Christians now.

Elaine was still a maid. I'd taken good care of that, even after she was spoken. But her mother was a different story. Many's the time she's been into the Mother's Hole with me. She put on a mask and hood, and I blacked her face below so that no one would guess who she was. There's loose tongues among the wise, let me warn you, the same as other women. But there were some that had to know. Well, we have our own lords and ladies by night, as they have theirs by day.

Gorlois never knew the half of it. I told him there were women's times when he must keep out of her chamber. And what I threatened would happen to his parts if he didn't was enough to make any man sweat. He'd curse and shout if his blood was up that night, but he feared me too much to cross her threshold.

So we wrapped a mist round his eyes, the two of us. He may have known there were times and places I had to go where it would have been death for a man to follow me. But I swear he never guessed his own wife went with me. The gatekeeper knew better than to peer under the hoods that went past him. And she wasn't going to tell him. What we do in the Mothers' name we don't call adultery.

There was only one thing that chilled me – if that stringy Nectan should ever make a proper Christian out of Gorlois and tell him our threats were nothing but moonshine compared to his power. Oh, don't mistake me. My power is real enough. I can feel it sometimes, coming up through the soles of my feet out of the good earth. It runs out through my hands into things I touch, like blood from an open cut. But there's one thing can dry it up. A Christian unbeliever. Lucky for me, he never knew that 'til the day he died. And luckier for his sweet lady's life.

But Morgan was not like her sisters, or her mother. There was a proud spirit in every inch of her. You'd be cutting off pride with every snippet of her finger-nails that curled on the fire. You could see it even in the way she slept, so still and stiff under the furs, while Elaine snored so peaceful and Margawse tossed about. There was always that pride. She would risk anything to get what she wanted, that child. But it wasn't what Margawse wanted. What Morgan dreamed of was to be a queen – or better still, a king.

She sat quiet, looking out to sea. There was a mist starting to rise from the woods in the coombe behind us and the sun was going down over the clifftop for another day. She could sit very still indeed, when she wanted to. I looked down to see what she had been making in the sand. I gave a great start and then hoped she hadn't noticed.

It frightened me. I'd never taught her. But it was there in front of me, or almost. She hadn't the pretty flowers her mother had used. She'd taken living things of the sea, or things that had been living. Empty shells, limpets mostly, and strands of cold wet seaweed, with holdfasts like fingers. But the pattern was the same. It only wanted blood.

'What's that you're doing there?' I asked.

'*You* know! Making a spell,' she said, jumping up with that wicked laugh and hugging me. 'To bring him home to me.'

I kicked that circle into little pieces. I didn't know why it was I had to keep that knowledge from Morgan. I'd never worried when Elaine was whispered. But there was a warning shouting inside me as if the tide was rising. And so it was. The sun had gone from our cove and there was a damp chill in the air. I grabbed her hand and hurried her home.

At dusk they shut the gate of the dun, and though we had nothing but cheese and beer on the table we were sitting late taking our ease when the dogs set up an almighty racket in the yard. Keby went running to the doorway and shouted out. 'Bran's balls, it's my lord and lady! And just look at the horses! You can hardly see them for dust and sweat. They've been ridden fit to break their hearts!'

Well, we were hard on his heels. And what a sight met us. The wild eyes of the horses rolling in the

lantern light like night-mares. There were riders
leaping down off their horses and shadows of cloaks
swooping about like great bats. There were those that
shrieked as though they thought the Black Hunt had
come to take us. But they were human, all right, and I
don't know which of us was more frightened. Gorlois's
bodyguards had their swords half-drawn, as if they
expected to be attacked at any moment.

We women flew about like hens when a fox gets in
among them. And squawking just as loud. The beds
weren't aired, and there wasn't a loaf of fresh bread
in the place, or a mouthful of stew in the cauldron.
And some were dashing to change the rushes on the
floor of my lady's chamber, where the puppies had
got in and fouled it, and it hadn't seemed worth the
trouble of changing them 'til we knew she was coming
home. And now, when I look back at it, I can see we
had fouler things than that to worry about.

I was running to and fro like a madwoman, not
knowing what to do first. The chariot was empty
when I got to it, and the furs all tumbled in the mud. I
couldn't find my lady and the girls in the dark and for
a terrible time I thought they had been killed or taken
by the Saxons. And then I caught up with my lady
stumbling towards the hall doorway fit to drop, with
Elaine and Margawse holding her by the arms on
either side of her.

As soon as I saw their faces, I knew that ours were
nothing but children's troubles, slaves' troubles,
beside what had happened to them. My Lady Ygerne
was weeping and trembling something terrible. Yet
for all that, her eyes were bright and you could see she
was excited. It struck me suddenly that she was not as
much like our little Elaine as I'd been thinking lately.
There was something of Margawse in her still, even if

72

she was twice her age. And it's not to be wondered at, for Morgan and Margawse were her blood too.

I didn't like the look of Lord Gorlois. He was angry but he was afraid, too. And that's not a thing I'd ever thought I'd see in him. He was as brave a warrior as you'd find anywhere, our Duke of Cornwall. He couldn't keep still and he had to be shouting and giving orders, though I don't suppose he knew what he was doing half the time. He just had to be on the move. He ordered the gates to be barred again and all the weapons in the dun sharpened and a strong guard to watch through the night. So we all looked at each other, but nobody dared to ask what was the matter.

I caught a glimpse of Morgan's white face as she ran from her bed towards her father. I called out to her, but she wouldn't listen. I could see he had no time for her, but she followed along behind him like a puppy-dog, waiting for him to notice her. I let her go. I had my hands full enough as it was. We took my lady round the waist and helped her to her own bower. She fell to weeping on my shoulder and she was all fluttering and trembling, like a woman when a man strokes her flesh and takes his time about going further. Elaine and Margawse came crowding after us into the bed-chamber. Elaine looked fairly shocked, but Margawse was dying to tell us all about it.

We set her on the bed and shook the cloak from her shoulders. All spattered with mud, it was. I set to brushing her hair, thinking that would calm her. But when we asked her what was the matter, she threw back her head and laughed, and then frightened us more by laughing and weeping at the same time. So Elaine ran to the kitchen for a beaker of hot wine and herbs. When we had quietened her down they told us everything.

Chapter Ten

Well, you must know by now what happened as well as I do. The bards have sung that lay the length and breadth of Britain. But what was strange was the different ways those three told it.

Margawse was gabbling away as if she couldn't get the words out fast enough. Her red hair was all tumbled over her shoulders and her eyes sparkling like a cat's. I'd seen her wild before, but never as excited as that. You'd think her gown would have split, her breasts were heaving up and down that fast.

'We've been in Fairyland, Gwennol! Such a city! I thought it couldn't be real. White statues on pillars, as if living people had been turned to marble. And such floors in his palace. They'd think shame to put rushes over them. They had pictures in little coloured stones. Can you imagine that, Gwennol? Pictures even on the *floor*! And as warm as summer. You could dance in your bare feet and it was as though the sun had been beating on the tiles, although it was night, in April, inside stone walls.'

Well, there was more of such nonsense. Baths steaming like boiling lakes. Couches of marble. Halls big as our grove in the forest, all under a great tiled roof. Whole streets of such palaces, she said, and the streets themselves paved with giant stones. Temples and churches to foreign gods and goddesses. Market squares. No wooden walls and thatch, you understand, but all made of great blocks of stone, if I was to believe her. Well, I saw Exeter years ago, and that was grand enough for me. But that was a hovel compared to London, if I was to believe her. You couldn't imagine such a thing, could you? I thought her head was turned and her wits were wandering.

Elaine was the one I could get most sense out of, though she was more scared than any of them, poor soul.

'Such crowds of people there were, Gwennol! And I don't just mean common folk, though the streets were thick with them staring at us. But fine lords and ladies from every part of Britain. I didn't think the world could have held so many. And the clothes and the jewels! We were like brown hedgehogs, all covered in dust and mud. But they took us into fine rooms and oh, Gwennol, they had hot baths as big as horseponds, and they washed our hair and oiled our bodies with scent, and we put on our second finest clothes, for we must leave the best ones 'til the grand feast of the crown-wearing. And then they led us to the great hall for supper and I thought that everyone would titter at us for country bumpkins.'

'The very idea!' I scolded. 'You two young ladies are pretty enough for princesses, and so I've heard say many a time, and you've gowns good enough for any duchess.'

'But they *didn't* laugh, Gwennol. All the heads were turning when we came in. I'm sure I was blushing like a gorse-fire. You know how it is when you feel everyone's looking at you. And they all seemed to have Roman names, like Lucius and Eusebia. And some of them called me Helena!'

Margawse couldn't hold herself in any longer. 'The king, Elaine! Tell her about the king.'

My heart seemed to jump a beat, and then took to hammering like a galloping horse. For what could she mean but that the king himself had looked at them, and which of my two young ladies would it be he'd set his fancy on? And then I remembered what young Keby had said and I turned cold again. It was true it wasn't the first time I'd heard that said about Uther Pendragon. I thought how a king can do pretty much as he pleases, and it's a bold father would say no to him, though it is his own daughters the king would have the maidenhead of. But when all was said and done, he surely wouldn't be ungrateful. A king's a king, and there would be few noblemen who could refuse to wed her for a cause like that, maiden or no maiden, and he'd know there'd likely be jewels and favours to follow for her and hers.

And it crossed my mind just then to hope it might have been Margawse he'd set his fancy on, child though she was, though you'd never have guessed it. For it would be common knowledge if the king took her, and none could shame her after that or know what she might or might not have got up to behind the armoury already. And I'd a shrewd idea the king wouldn't tell, whatever he found out about her, for he'd shame himself to let it be known he was not the first.

But which of those two was it, in truth's name?

'Be quiet, Margawse,' says Elaine. 'I'm getting to that. All in good time.'

'Tell her about the goblet. How the king sent it from the high table.'

Margawse's eyes were shining like two jewels in a goblet themselves, so I made sure now it must be her.

'*Well*,' says Elaine, getting cross because she wouldn't be hurried, 'we were all led to our places at the supper tables. And I could see Father was angry because he thought we should have been on the king's table.'

'And he was saying how he'd fought last year for Uther Pendragon against the Saxons in Elmet, and how he saved York for the Britons. And he was shouting it out loud enough for the king to hear, and people were beginning to look at us for more than our fair faces.'

'I started to be afraid then,' Elaine confessed. 'And I'd been so enjoying it 'til then. It was like a fairy-tale. Everyone treating us as though we'd always been princesses but never known it. And then I got frightened because of Father shouting, and I thought perhaps we couldn't have been princesses or we would have been up higher, as Father said. And maybe those lords and ladies always treated each other like royalty and there was nothing special in the way they looked at us.'

'But there *was*! The king! Go on!'

'Then the feast began, and the pipers started to play, and such food they brought in! Oh, Gwennol, it was all decked out like a May-Day procession with flowers and frills. You'd think it couldn't be real food. But every plate of it was for eating. Then the king signed and the pipers stopped and the chief bard began to sing a love-lay. Oh, it was so sweet! And King Uther Pendragon stood up, with everyone watching him.'

Her cheeks were flushed like roses now, and I began to think I'd been wrong about it being Margawse, and I was all of a flutter. Even Margawse couldn't stop her telling her story now.

'He took his own knife, with the gold handle, from his belt and he kissed the blade. They'd set a swan before him, that seemed to be swimming in a lake of violets. He cut the first slice from the breast. And he laid that portion of honour on a golden platter and whispered to his steward. And everyone watched to see where the plate would be taken. It went past all the under-kings and queens on the high table. Past the benches just below them, with the fine dukes and duchesses, down our side of the hall.'

'And all the heads were turning, and only the king still smiling after the plate had passed people by. You never saw such long faces!'

'But I never thought. I swear I never thought it was coming to us.'

'Oh, Elaine. You ninny! The king's portion? You must have wanted it to be for you!'

'I didn't think of that, I was so busy watching. It came to our table and the steward stopped. It was like a dream. I was so silly. I thought he was going to give it to Father, to make up for not inviting him to sit on the high table.'

'Oh, *Elaine!*'

'And then . . . Gwennol! He put it down in front of . . . Mother!'

I was as stunned as she had been. They were both looking at me, those girls, laughing and frightened at the same time. But I couldn't take it in. I mean, I knew she was still a beautiful woman. But the High King himself!

'The noise, Gwennol! The stamping and the shouting.'

'The men were laughing, and the women were angry. It was wonderful.'

'And Mother went white, and then red, and white

79

again. And then I looked at Father, and I was frightened. He was furious.'

My eyes went to Ygerne then. She was staring across the room as if she was in a trance. There was just this little smile on her lips. When I saw that I could have slapped her face.

'Three times Uther sent her gifts. We'd never guessed. He must have fallen in love with her. The king, Gwennol!'

'The second time he gave her a golden goblet of wine, with a jewel in it. A little dragon brooch of red enamel and silver.'

'He smiled and lifted his drinking horn to her.'

'Then he sent sweetmeats in a casket of silver wire, all decked with lilies.'

'If I had been Father I would have killed him, then and there.'

A small, thin voice like the mew of a cat that's tasted blood. We'd all forgotten Morgan. She was crouched at the foot of the bed, her little white face peering up at us over the furs.

Her voice seemed to wake my lady out of a dream. All this time she'd sat there and never uttered a word. You'd have thought the Sisters had put a spell on her tongue. But when she spoke it hardly made sense.

'I thought it was all a dream. Lost with the Legions. But I have heard the tramp of the emperor's army on the streets. And the lays of the emperor's battles at the feast. And the hymns of the emperor's priest in the church.'

I don't know why, but that put me in a terrible temper. I was shaking with anger.

'And what's wrong with the British tongue, my girl? And the old straight track on the backs of the hills?

And a sky-roofed temple to worship our own gods as we've always done?'

But she didn't hear me. And I began to fear she'd tried to spell-speak Uther Pendragon and it had turned back on her. She wouldn't be the first that had happened to. Her eyes were miles away. And was it the past she was looking into or the future?

'I never knew that Britain was so wide or so fair. Day after day we rode. Past forests that seemed to have no beginning or end. Lakes like silver cobwebs in the morning sun. Corn springing green. And still when we lay down at night we were among our own. But the white dragon is cruel. They murdered Aurelius in his bed. And Uther has no wife to bear him sons. If he should fall . . .'

And then that little sharp voice, like claws scratching.

'What did Father do to Uther Pendragon?'

Chapter Eleven

Elaine seemed to be staring into the dark beyond the windows.

'Father sprang to his feet at the third gift, and his hand went towards his knife. Though he couldn't have struck the king in his own hall, could he?'

'I would have done,' cries Morgan.

'And then . . .'

'What? What did he do?'

'Nothing.'

'Tell her about the other man! The man in the archway.'

But Elaine wouldn't say a word more. I looked from one to the other of them. There was a queer look in Elaine's eyes. I've seen it in others. The look of those who can see more than they want to.

It was Margawse who rushed on. There was no stopping her now.

'There was a tall, thin man in one of the archways, on our side of the hall. No one seemed to have noticed him but Father, and then us, when we followed his eyes. He was about the same age as Uther Pendragon. Not too old. Not exactly handsome, because he had a crooked sort of face, but laughing. He was different from every nobleman in the hall. You could see it first in the way he was dressed. A plain white gown. But with a deerskin thrown over it, and the head left on

and hanging down over his shoulder. But he wouldn't
have been ordinary, even if he'd been wearing a toga
or tunic and breeches like everyone else. He even
made the king look a bit like a shadow, he was so . . .
alive. He was the one who was holding Father from
moving or shouting, I'm sure of it. And all he was
doing was just crooking his hand a little and pointing
a finger at him. And smiling that lop-sided smile. It
looked as if Father was in a fit or a trance. I was sure
he was going to fall down stiff on the floor at any
moment. All we could see doing it was that one finger
and his smile. But you felt as if there was a spider's
thread between them, and Father was a struggling fly
caught fast in it. Then I looked round at King Uther.
And he was smiling back at the man. They had the
same smile. As if they were brothers.'

'Who . . . was he?' I asked, and my tongue felt dry
in my throat.

It was my Lady Ygerne who answered.

'Merlyn! Who else could it be? You guessed that,
didn't you, Gwennol? Who here should recognise the
Old Ones better than you and I?'

I'm not sure but that didn't give me the biggest
shock of the evening, her coming out with it like that,
in front of everybody. And I'm not just thinking of
Margawse and Morgan, who were too young yet to be
hearing about such things. I had the name through
Cornwall of a powerful wise woman, and that suited
me. And everyone knew I'd shown my lady some little
skills of healing. But I'd taken good care they said no
more than that about us. There are some names we
have that are better not spoken. It's true there were
not so many women in that room, but some of them
were none of our side, and never would be. And she
had spoken out loud a thing which we'd always kept

secret, and which should have stayed so.

Emrys Merlyn. I'd known it must have been him, of course. And she'd seen I knew. I was just an old nurse on the cliffs of Cornwall and Merlyn was the king's soul-friend that was known for a great enchanter at the court. And what the two of us might have in common it wasn't for others to know. My mind was in a turmoil now. If I was right, and she had tried a charm to catch the king, she'd have met her match a thousand times over in Merlyn. Even the mighty Pendragons would dance to his tune. And where that dance might lead us now, if Merlyn was pointing his finger at us, I shuddered to think.

All the same . . . Not so old. Not exactly handsome. But laughing. It was not King Uther I hankered to see when they told me all the marvels of his court. I wasn't so old but I wouldn't dearly have loved to come face to face with Emrys Merlyn, just once in my life, though I doubted I'd have the courage to lift my eyes to his, and let him see there what I knew well he would. Well, the world's a stranger place than we have any notion of, and sometimes Fairyland may be closer than we think.

But I was still cross with my lady. If I'd have had my way I'd have sent the others all packing out of the room, and asked her straight out what she meant by it. She's not so old nor so grand that she can't remember me smacking her. But in that dun she was the Lady Ygerne and I was her children's nurse, and what could I say to her with all her waiting-ladies and serving-maids fussing round her?

So I said a bit shortly. 'Well, then. If the king's taken such a fancy to you, what are you doing galloping back here in such a lather before the feast of Easter's over, and acting as though the giants of St Michael's

Mount are on your heels with their cudgels?'

The two girls looked at each other then, as if neither of them dared to tell me what came next. So I looked at Ygerne, and her face was red as a horseshoe from a smith's furnace. But she wouldn't bare her shame to me.

'Is the thing so evil, then, that none of you are going to tell me?'

I might have known it would be Margawse that couldn't keep silent. It was the sort of folly that would put a sparkle in her eyes. What was modesty to her?

'The next day the king did Mother even more honour. We all went to church. And then ... Oh, Gwennol, he was forever praising her beauty and calling for his bard to make lays for her. He made her walk beside him in the garden and cast petals on the paths in front of her. And when the evening came, he led her with him to the high table, while Father was left with us, halfway down the hall. Afterwards, when there was dancing and singing, we heard ... Elaine and I heard ... they were saying on our table ...'

She broke off into giggles. Shameless, she was. As if I hadn't lived long enough in a man's world to guess what was coming next.

'They said ... everyone was whispering it ... the king was having a bower prepared, next to his own bed-chamber. And he'd had it filled with flowers, and silks, and perfumes, and silver mirrors. And guess who it was for? Mother!'

Poor silly woman. Couldn't she have seen the way the wind was blowing, long before it got to that? She'd lived long here in Bossiney, with only a handful of Cornish lords and a white-robed priest for company. But she'd feasted in kings' courts too. She wasn't as green as all that.

I looked her straight in the eye.

'And what did you do?' I asked. 'When you found that out?'

'What any loyal wife would do. I told my lord,' she said, with her eyes cast down. Very demure, she looked. 'He was in a terrible rage. He called our people together. He had to keep his voice low, but he was so angry it was as if he was yelling to heaven. He ordered the men to saddle our horses in the dark and bring out our chariot. Of course, Uther's grooms went rushing to tell the king we were going, so Gorlois had them killed, every one, and the guards at the gate too. Even the yard-hounds he killed. So we rode out into the night, like thieves. But Gorlois went back towards the palace with his sword drawn, and Jordan and Britael with him. When we looked round there was a bright light in one of the doorways. Merlyn was standing there. He didn't say anything, Gwennol. He didn't do anything. He just stood and smiled. He has a terrible smile. And Gorlois turned like a man sleepwalking, and came back to us and mounted his horse. When morning broke, we were galloping as hard as we could for the west and Cornwall. And who knows if Uther Pendragon is coming after us now, with half the troops of Britain at his back?' There was a catch in her voice somewhere between sobbing and laughing, so that I couldn't be sure if she was sorry about it.

'Let him cross the Tamar if he dare. He won't rouse Cornishmen to do you wrong. They'll fight for my lord, never you fear,' I told her stoutly.

'Ah, you say that now, Gwennol. But you don't know Uther Pendragon. And he has Merlyn behind him. Uther's not like other men. There is something about him that makes even kings follow him. And love him too. I've seen it in their eyes at court. You don't

87

understand, Gwennol. Even a Cornishman would find
it hard to say no to him.'

And a Cornish woman too, I thought to myself. So
that's how the land lies. And little you care that
good men will have to die for this. And so I told
her.

'Lucky for me,' I said, 'that my man is dead, and
never gave me sons. There'll be many a woman weeping before this is over.'

But I judged her too hardly. She was right. I hadn't
set eyes on Uther Pendragon – or on his soul-friend,
either. It would have taken a stronger woman than
her to have refused the glamour of that pair. But for
all that, I'll swear she was never unwilling. And what
I'll never know is who began that magic. Was it just
the little spell she made that called him all the way to
Cornwall? Or were there bigger powers than that at
work already, to get her to make that boy the bards
sing of? Either way, I should have known better than
to meddle with them.

That little voice came again.

'Is Merlyn our enemy then?'

I didn't care to answer that. I left the child sitting
on the floor, watching us.

We got Ygerne to bed, and her waiting-woman,
Ruan, made ready to sleep with her, and by the time I
looked round, Margawse had gone. The times I've
wished my Lady Ygerne had given me a brood of boys
to nurse! I should have been shot of them to their
foster-fathers long before this. I went puffing out into
the dark to look for her. And sure enough, there she
was with some of my lord's young warriors, in the
torchlight by the stables, laughing and as excited as
her mother. And I don't doubt she was giving them a
version of the story a sight more colourful than the

one she had told me. I scolded her to bed and left her frightening Elaine with talk of battles coming.

And then there was Morgan to look for. She wasn't in her mother's chamber. I didn't need to go far. I knew I should find her with her father. He, poor man, had drunk himself stupid over the great table in the hall, with the pick of his warriors and house-servants watching by him. And there was Morgan, under the table, curled up asleep beside his feet like a puppy. I got old Sulian, that had seen more battles than any of them, to help me lift her, and she stirred in her sleep and cried out. She seemed heavy for such a skinny little thing, 'til we swung her clear of the table and a great sword fell out of her hand. It was no magic present from the king's palace. Only Gorlois's own sword that she had been clutching while she slept.

'No, no,' I scolded her gently. 'It will take more than you to save his life now.'

Chapter Twelve

I don't think any of us got much sleep that night, except my lord, though he never went to bed at all. It was a grey, misty sort of dawn, and chilly, too, for the year was still early. And so quiet. Even the birds seemed as if they were listening. There wasn't a sound from outside, and nobody dared to unbar the gate until my lord gave the order. He slept on, with his head on the table and his beard all wet in the spilled wine.

I huddled close in my shawl as I went to get water for my girls to wash. At least they would die proud and clean. Elaine was shivering and complaining, but then she always did. She wrapped herself in her fur robe and ran away to her mother to find some comfort. I had a fight with Margawse to strip her of her shift.

'Come on, my lass. You'll never make a fine queen with a dirty neck.'

By the time I had towelled her dry, her eyes were sparkling.

'Will there really be a war between the king and Father? Will Uther bring his whole army here to fight us? And all because of Mother?'

'You can wipe that smile off your face. Fighting means dying. And how do you expect your father to stand against King Uther Pendragon and all his fine

91

warriors? If it ends the way I think it will, you'll be laughing on the other side of your face.'

Morgan stripped down to her skinny white body without needing to be told. She didn't smile, and she didn't shiver. You'd have thought the cold had no power over her if you hadn't seen the goose-pimples on her. She washed more carefully than usual, then dressed herself and fastened her girdle tightly. I looked down at her proudly. Even then, she was more of a queen than Margawse. I wondered what would become of her if her father died.

The night had cooled my lady down, and she was frightened now. There are few that can feel romantic in the cold grey of the morning. Now that she was more sensible, I felt kinder towards her. Poor lady, who had thought herself almost ready to be a grand-mother. And then to be courted by a king as though she was a handsome young princess. It was enough to turn any woman's head.

And so we all waited for my lord to wake up. Young Keby came by and saw me standing in the door of my lady's bower.

'What did I tell you?' he grinned. 'I said there'd be trouble if he took Lady Ygerne with him to court. I wouldn't mind having it off that one myself, even if she is old enough to be my mother. You can see she knows a trick or two. And Uther Pendragon can spot a good lay when he sees it, by all accounts. I reckon the king'll be standing in that doorway where you are before the week's out, or he's not the man they say he is. How's that for far-sight, Gwennol?'

'You cheeky devil,' I said. 'You want to watch that tongue of yours, or you won't have one much longer. My lady will hear you.'

But it was not her I was worrying about. All the

92

time I was casting my eyes about to see where
Morgan might be hiding herself.

'*She'll* be all right. It isn't her throat he'll be cutting,
is it? It's the likes of you and me that will catch it in
the neck if we stand in his way.'

But he was always a brave lad, Keby, for all he was
cheeky. And he was true to his lord and lady to the
end.

It was mid-morning when Gorlois walked out of the
hall. The men stopped whatever they were doing and
looked at each other, wondering who dared speak to
him first. But they hadn't made my lord Duke of their
war-hosts for nothing, and the morning had made a
man of him again. He sent riders to the east to find if
there was any news of King Uther coming. And others
he sent south and west, to his kinsfolk and his friends,
to call them to fight with him for his wife's honour
against the king, if need be. And when the messengers
had ridden away, the gate was barred again, though
it was broad daylight. We couldn't see out unless we
climbed on the ramparts, and all we could hear was
the honing of swords and the clang of hammer on iron
from the smithy-end.

My lady talked a long time to Lord Gòrlois. She was
no fool, once she'd gathered her wits about her again,
now she was away from the glamour of the king's
palace. It made me feel better, for it should have
taken more than vanity to turn the head of a wise
woman, though she was of the lesser sort. But whatever she'd done, she'd have met more than her match
in magic there, as my lord was likely to meet his
match if it came to a battle.

By and by the sun came out, and we all began to feel
a bit safer, with so many men busying themselves for
war around us. It was foolish, really. What could they

do? But I've seen a sick child stop crying just to hear its mother sing a lullaby, though she can't save its life.

Morgan followed at her father's heels. She was quieter than usual, seemingly listening and thinking. Once she came running back to me, full of questions.

'Is this all because of Mother? Is she as beautiful as that? More beautiful than any woman in Britain? I never wanted to look like her.'

Which was just as well, seeing her hair was as black as a luck-cat's.

'She's beautiful, yes. And I don't mean just what you're supposed to say about any noble's wife. She scarcely looks older than the day she married your father. They say she's the handsomest woman in all Dumnonia, that I do know. Though I dare say they're only counting the gentry.'

'And is it so very important to be beautiful? Kings would really go to war because of it? Against their own friends? Father was Uther's friend, wasn't he, last year?'

'King Uther Pendragon would, by all accounts. And he's the only High King we have between us and the Saxons.'

'I used to want to be a king,' she said thoughtfully. 'But perhaps it's more powerful to be a beautiful woman. What do you think, Gwennol? If I was beautiful, would kings go to war because of me?'

I couldn't help laughing, for, much as I loved her, she was a sharp-faced, ugly child. If she had power, it would come from somewhere else.

'Handsome is as handsome does, my fine young lady. And if you want to grow up beautiful, like your sister Elaine, you'd better start drinking up your milk and put some flesh on those sparrow-bones of yours.'

She didn't heed me.

'So my father has the most beautiful woman in all Britain for his wife. Even King Uther Pendragon envies him. You can buy horses and jewels, but you can't buy somebody else's wife. You can only steal her. So Father must fight to guard her. She belongs to us. We won't let the Pendragon take her away from Cornwall.'

That surprised me. It had never struck me that she cared much about her mother 'til then. All the shine in her eyes was for her father. But she was proud like him. And when she saw her mother was a lady that a king might covet, she began to look at her in a new light.

Ygerne was with my lord, walking the ramparts and arguing about what they should do if the king sent for her. Morgan went back to them. And she stood looking at her mother as though she had never seen her properly before. As a man may look at a mare that he's thinking of buying. And presently I saw her walking behind them. She wasn't dancing about, but copying my lady's steps. And she was twisting her hair in her fingers as though she was thinking of braiding it with pearls as my lady did. Her father looked round then and saw her. He thought she was playing. He grinned through his beard and tossed her up in the air. But Morgan didn't shriek with laughter at him as she used to. She let him put her down. Then she smiled at him like a grown woman, and studied her mother closer than ever.

We hadn't long to wait.

Chapter Thirteen

I don't know what I expected. The fairy troops of Gwyn, with their silver helmets, galloping out of the mists to snatch us all away. Or the Black Hunt screaming down on us in the darkness on their night-hags, while we lay shivering with our faces turned to the walls. Or those old Romans my granny used to tell of, that stood in squares like human walls, fighting and falling without ever moving a foot.

Not normal human beings anyway. Not like our fighting Cornishmen, grinning through their beards and brandishing their long swords, bragging and showing off like men anywhere. I couldn't square that with what I'd heard of Merlyn.

Well, I did what I could while we waited. Gorlois wouldn't let me leave the dun, and that angered me. I could have helped him more than most, and the gods knew he needed it. It would take more than a strong sword-arm and high courage to save him from this. With Merlyn against us it needed nine times even my strength to build the sort of rampart that had any hope of keeping us safe. And even then I wouldn't have trusted it to hold for long. But he wouldn't budge, and I daren't tell him all I'd planned. I did go so far as to threaten him, but he hardly seemed to notice what I said. I wondered then if it was the beginning of what I'd always feared. That one day he'd slip the

bonds I put on him before he married Ygerne. He'd
stop believing I had power. I could have shown him
then, before it was too late. I could have struck him
down. But I held my hand. He had troubles enough
coming to him as it was.

So I grumbled away and summoned Ygerne and
Elaine and two others that were wise among her
women. And do you know, my lady put her fine nose
in the air and told me she had more important things
to see to. Well, I'd spared Gorlois, but I was
sorely tempted to call a curse down on her, there and
then.

That left the four of us, and Elaine had been spoken
less than a year, though she was a sensible maid and
quick to learn. And nowhere for us to go but a grubby
lane behind the kitchen, where anyone might chance
upon us. The Mothers forgive me, I set Morgan on the
corner to give us warning. I built a fire, and we did
what we could. A little patterning. A handful of herbs
on the flames. A cock killed. But it was poor, thin
stuff, and we knew it. All the time I had this sick
feeling in my stomach that if this was all the strength
we could manage, it might do us more harm than
good. But I was like Gorlois. I had to try.

After that, there was nothing but waiting. I don't
mind admitting I was almost glad Gorlois hadn't let
me go where I meant. It's not much of a wall around
Bossiney. It wasn't built for war. But it felt a good
deal safer than walking out there on the cliff, with the
gulls slipping on the wind over the rocks and nothing
but thin air between you and the sea. A cold, lonely
place to be caught by what I feared was coming.

And yet. It's a funny thing, but I found my blood was
beating faster, like all the rest. And I can't swear it
was an unpleasant feeling entirely. I'd lived too much

in the old songs and stories. When the world was all battles and magic and high deeds, and things turned upside down for pride or love, and kingdoms lost and won. All of a sudden we found we were living in such a story, and I don't think there was one of us that was wholly sorry, for all the evil that we guessed would come of it. We'd all rather that something happened to us than nothing. So we watched the skyline with our hearts in our mouths. And whether we hoped or dreaded what we might see, it's not for me to say.

But it wasn't much when it came. Three riders, or so it looked. A little after noon next day. They rode lighter than my lord and lady, without chariots. It's a wonder they hadn't overtaken our people on the road. But then, they didn't know the ways into Cornwall. They weren't winging straight homeward, like swans at evening. Or maybe they had reasons for not hurrying. Maybe it suited them to let the birds flock back to Bossiney. It gave them a chance to ride right up to our walls, and look around, see how the land lay and where a strong king's army might do most damage if my lord proved stubborn. Was it the vixen they wanted, or her earth as well? There was one at least that looked long and shrewdly round him before he left us.

They'd ridden hard, but not so fast the horses had foundered. They stood for a while where we had all been looking for them. That little nick where the road comes over the hill from the north-east. We never doubted who they were or why they had come.

They stood so still those first few moments, you might have thought three new pines had sprouted over there on the ridge. They looked hardly human. With the bright air behind them it seemed almost as if you could see through them. Then they moved, and we saw the glint of their armour, and knew then what we had to deal with.

Morgan caught her father's hand.

'Fight them, Father! We will never give in to them as long as we live.'

He just gripped her fingers. I heard her gasp. I don't think he even knew he'd done it.

They started to trot down the hill, and it was so still I could almost swear I heard their harness chiming like bells, though I couldn't have done. You'd think we'd never seen horsemen before. We were all of us on the walls and staring at them as if we couldn't move. Every soul in the dun was there – my lord and his wife and daughters, right down to the smallest slave baby in its mother's arms. Yet there wasn't one voice raised, not even Gorlois's. Just a sort of low murmur, like the sea on shingle under a fog. We were all holding our breath, to see if Uther and all his army were coming over the skyline behind them.

Looking back on it, I don't know why we didn't let her go there and then. We were beaten before we started. But they were high-blooded folk, and I suppose it had to be done the way it was.

We watched them come, and there was just enough dust on the road to hide the horses' legs so that they seemed to be swimming towards us on a brown tide. All this time the cows in the meadow outside the walls went on tearing at the sweet grass. They weren't thinking what might redden it before long. Though our own horses, that we'd picketed inside the dun, began to lift their heads and prick their ears.

Then I gave a great start. There was another rider had come over the hill. It wasn't the whole host of Uther Pendragon, but I don't think it could have shaken me more if it had been. Just one man. There wasn't even a flash of armour on him. As soon as I realised that I knew who it must be. And I couldn't take my eyes off him. He rode alone and slowly on a white horse. And as he drew near, I saw that he was dressed fantastically. A great cloak that seemed to be made of rags, every colour of the rainbow. And his hair white with lime. That made me shiver. I'm not lying when I tell you this: I felt his power, even from where I stood. And something worse than that. I felt sure that power had picked me out, even where I stood packed in amongst all the others. Old Gwennol, the children's nurse. And yet I swear he knew me. My knees were trembling like weak brawn, but I was as drawn to him as a magpie to a silver knife.

I had good reason to fear him, and he let me know it. Halfway to the dun he stopped his horse, at the far edge of our pasture, where the Great Oak grows. He got down and he was a younger man than I'd expected, even after Margawse had told me. He strolled under those huge branches, and he laid his hand on the bark of the trunk as familiarly as you please and tilted his head back to look up at the crown. He lifted his hand in a sort of salute. Even from here I could swear his crooked face was smiling. Well, I'd never in my life dared touch any oak-tree like that, as if we were friends. Never mind that one.

Suddenly I heard noise all around me. I'd only had eyes for one man, but the rest of them had been watching those three in front. Poor, silly fools, as if the danger that threatened us was steel and iron. Men can't see further than a sword and a shield, and most women aren't much better. And all at once the newcomers weren't ghosts or noontime shadows. They were flesh and blood, with men's faces we could see clearly and sweating horses under them. One of them carried a herald's staff.

They were still a good bowshot from the gate when Gorlois leaped down off the wall into the yard, with everybody tumbling down after him. I must have been the last, except for the sentries and a few boys that couldn't take their eyes off a coat of mail. I was always slow. But I was slower that day than I need have been. To tell you the truth, I didn't want to turn away. And it wasn't soldiers I was watching. I'm past bothering with them. Dangerous he may have been, but turning away from him was like being dragged out of a dream into a rough, cold world. And at the same time I was mortally afraid that the gate would open and he'd ride in, and I should have to meet him, eye to eye.

Well, such a to-do there was everywhere, I almost laughed at them when I saw it. Gorlois packed Ygerne and the three girls off into the bower out of sight, and barred the door after them, as if they were mares on heat, which in a way they were. Well, three of them, anyway. Morgan made a fuss, but he wouldn't listen to her. He set warriors with spears everywhere, lined up by the gates and all the way to the hall, and he was shouting for his best mantle and the clasps of silver and garnets, and polishing up his scabbard on the skirt of his own tunic. Pride. The sheer foolish pride of the man, flaunting his jewels and weapons at them, as he'd flaunted his wife at Uther Pendragon. I must have stood gaping like a fool. Next thing I knew I was bundled into the sleeping-hut. They almost threw me on the floor and the door slammed shut behind me. This was to be men's work, seemingly. There wasn't a woman left in sight.

I got to my feet as quick as I could and hobbled back

to the window. I couldn't see them open the gates, but they seemed to swing back as if a giant's hand had pushed them. It was so bright over the sea it made me blink my eyes. All the same, even while my sight was dazzled I knew Merlyn hadn't come. I should have felt it in my blood.

Uther's three messengers dropped from their horses. Their legs had that wearisome roll of men who have ridden hard and long. But they were proud and haughty under their dirt, even so. Their leader was a proper lord this time. They told me afterwards his name was Ulfin, he that stood as close friend to Uther as Jordan was to Gorlois. I should have studied that face while I had the chance. I'd be seeing it closer than I wanted to . . . if you could call it seeing. But then, I just watched the fine flash of their cloaks go by me as they walked through our spear-guard into the hall. Then we all had to wait.

After a while I couldn't help myself. I found a stool and clambered up higher on it. I couldn't see much over the stockade even then. But there was a place where the headland reared up above the rest of the cliff. A green mound, caught between the top of the wall and the sky, that I knew was sweet with wild flowers if you could see it closer.

He was there, with a deep blue sky behind him, and the sunlight glistening on his white hair and his coloured ribbons. Sitting on a white horse among the walls of the old people you can still see in the grass. He could have come straight out of Fairyland. But I didn't doubt for one moment he was real, and here in Bossiney now. I think it was the rest of the world I'd have doubted first.

They were carrying wine into the hall now. The best jars too, that they said had come all the way from

Palestine. Gorlois would make a fine show of politeness, though there was a dusty answer at the bottom of the cup. We knew what Uther's men had come for, of course. Our Gorlois had insulted him, good and proper, leaving his court without permission and killing his people. He'd ordered him back to London with his lady, on pain of death. We knew what message they'd take back with them, too. Still, a guest's a guest. Gorlois wouldn't have the king say that he hadn't shown them hospitality first.

Our men on guard shuffled their feet and growled as they waited, but the birds in the trees were singing away now as though they hadn't a care in the world.

The king's party came out at last, and walking quicker than before. They looked angry, though I can't think what they had expected. But perhaps it was just a show they had to put on for honour's sake. I often think that so much that happened that year was play-acting. It's always like that with the nobility. Common people like us say what we think, or show it in our faces. Like children.

And that made me gasp all of a sudden and turn my thoughts for the first time that day to Morgan. She was still young enough to wear her heart naked in her face. Even without being told I knew she'd be watching from the window of her mother's bower. I wondered what she'd seen. I scrambled back on my stool and let Uther's warriors ride out with their backs to Bossiney and our fate in Gorlois's answer. I hadn't time to look after them. My eyes went straight to the downs.

There was no horseman any more up on that mound of turf above the sea. The place looked as empty then as ever I've seen it. Merlyn had gone.

And you young ones may laugh at this. You think the blood runs cold when you're past fifty. But I tell you this. I never felt such a loss when my own man was gone and I lay alone month after month. It was so bad that moment I had to pull up my skirts and thrust my own finger into my blood-hole to satisfy myself, and never mind who heard me crying. Afterwards, I was ashamed. It had been too small a thing for what I felt.

I couldn't tell you if Morgan saw him or not.

Chapter Fourteen

I don't know why she did it. It's a thing I can't forgive.
She went to Nectan, and not to me. Ygerne, that I'd
sung lullabies to in the old tongue before she could
speak her mother's name. Ygerne, that I'd taken into
the woods showing her leaves and roots even before
she knew the power of them. Ygerne, that coaxed me
to use a deep charm of mirrors and apples to bring
young Gorlois to her door. Ygerne, that I'd whispered
into the old way, having no little maid of my own. Did
she think I'd failed her, bringing her nothing but
daughters?

I chided her to help me build a wall. She just stared
at me, with her blue eyes very round.

'They say his parents wore the Roman purple.'

'Rome's gone. Uther Pendragon's flesh and blood.
He's king over us only as long as the Britons want him.
He can be killed, whatever his father wore.'

'But it wasn't just his father, Gwennol. His *mother*
wore purple too.'

And what did she mean by that? I should have seen
the way her hopes were turning.

Well, as soon as the gate was opened again she was
off. Just her and Ruan, in plain cloaks and hoods.
Gorlois was in a fury when he found out. It would be
days yet before Uther got his message, like a slap in
the face. But he wasn't going to have his prize running

FAY SAMPSON

loose over the countryside like any milkmaid. He sent
Jordan and Britael galloping after her. But they were
too late.

It wasn't far from us to the coombe where the saint
lived. A sweet, rocky valley, it is, with the river
rushing over the stones, cool and green, and the trees
and ferns hanging over the water. And then you come
on it suddenly. A great hole in the rock, as if a giant
had punched his fist through it. And a white spout of
water flinging itself down through it into a pool. They
knew how to pick their spots, those Christians. He'd
made his hut there, and grew his little garden of
herbs and kept a few fowls. Just for the eggs. They say
he wasn't man enough to kill one.

I'd been there once, when curiosity got the better of
me. Just to see what we were up against. I didn't get
close. I was still coming through the hazel trees when
he heard me. He'd been sitting on a mossy stone out in
the water with his long shanks dangling in the stream,
and singing to himself or his god. But I hadn't set foot
in his clearing before he'd whipped round and was on
that bank and snatched up his staff where it was lying
in the grass. I thought for a moment he was going to
beat me with it. But he just held it at both ends,
stretched out like a bar between us. His blue eyes
burned and words came out of his mouth. Hard-
edged, like steel. Latin, I suppose it was. I couldn't
understand it. But I knew what he meant, all right. I
don't think he cursed me. I didn't take any pain from
it. But I couldn't stir one step forward from where I
stood, do what I would. I never tried again.

But it wasn't his staff that stopped Jordan and
Britael, so I've heard. It was the sight of my lady,
standing among the primroses beside the water, with
her hands lifted, praying. Think of that: the wise

Ygerne of Cornwall and a bloodless Christian hermit. It made me spit like a cat. What was she, that he'd let her into his holy ground when he'd barred me? I'll tell you what she was. False. For all the power I'd given her, she'd swing from one side to the other where she thought it would do her most good. Though what help she thought she'd get from a childless man like that is more than I can say. And I dare say he thought she was a lamb come back to the fold. She was a wise woman, all right. There was none of us truly knew what was in her mind.

When they'd done their prayers, he put his hands on her head, and she crossed hers over her breast and cast her eyes down very modestly, or so Ruan said. Then she walked over to her husband's men, very meekly. And Britael set her on his horse and led her home. Gorlois raved at her, but she never answered him. Just stood before him with her head bowed down and a little smile on her lips. When he'd blown himself out she said just one thing.

'I have prayed, my lord, for the safety of Britain.'

I could have wished I'd had Gorlois for a son, instead of that one for a daughter.

But she was as false to Nectan as she was to me. Elaine was missing a long time that night, and when she came back she wouldn't meet my eye. It didn't take me long to know what the two of them had been up to behind my back.

I was sick of the lot of them. If they didn't want my help they could seethe in their own cauldron. Why should I burn my fingers plucking them out of the stew? So I stayed where I was. I never called the wise even then. I had messengers as swift as any of Gorlois's. I could have summoned a host that was stronger than his. Our weapons are different but they can shield and kill as surely as metal and wood. I let them lie. Many a time I've grieved over that. I was so angry with Gorlois and Ygerne, I never thought what might happen to Morgan.

Before evening the first of Gorlois's messengers came galloping back, and the news was as cold as the sea-wind that was beginning to rattle the thatch. All next day it was the same tale. It seemed all the chieftains of Cornwall had gone off to that Easter crown-wearing and there was no one left who dared to raise a sword against the Pendragon.

'They'll come back to the west now the feast is done with. My kin will fight for my honour. Blood of my blood. Sword-brothers and father's friends.'

Oh, yes, I thought to myself. Who are you fooling? For which of our chieftains of Cornwall can't count more enemies than friends? Fat cattle stolen. A daughter dishonoured. A son killed in his cups. The gentry know no other way of passing their time but fighting and boasting and raiding. Gorlois had as ready a sword as any of them. And they've long memories in these parts. Our duke couldn't rally heart and hand across the country now. They'd fight for him against the Saxons, but not against Uther. He hadn't Merlyn's glamour round him.

Yet I don't think it even occurred to him to let Ygerne go. Not though this Uther Pendragon claimed to be High King over us all to the Land's End, and Gorlois was only war-lord of Cornwall. I think he knew she fancied Uther. It was that that stuck in his pride. It made him angrier than I'd ever seen him before. He didn't shout and bluster. It was a deep, dark anger, that turned him in on himself. Oh, he'd had fights a-plenty. Cattle-raids, pirates, Saxon wars. But he was always laughing in his beard beforehand as if it were some great sport. And when enough blood was spilt and enough armour dented and enough booty snatched from whoever wasn't quick enough to hide it, both sides would break and ride away. And they'd fill their heads with ale and raise a lament over their dead and in the same breath be planning the next raid.

He wasn't laughing now. He'd fight this battle to the bitter end. He'd see every last one of us dead before he let her go.

But he still had one dagger up his sleeve.

There was a shout from the sentry at the gate, and we all jumped like hares. But Gorlois grinned.

'Let her in,' he cried, and strode across the yard with us crowding after him.

It was no horseman this time, sweating back through bogs and forests to bring us bad news. It was a woman we saw marching in through the gate. Well, three women, to tell the truth, for she'd brought two of her nuns with her. Bryvyth, who'd built her nunnery on Tintagel Head. She had a tall staff in her hand, curled at the top like a shepherd's crook, a white wool gown over a linen smock, and bare feet. She'd cut her hair, and you might think from all I've said that she was a slave. But you'd never have thought that if you'd seen her. Her way's not mine but I can tell those that have power from those that haven't, and she had it. She wouldn't look a man in the face if she could help it, and she kept her head covered for modesty. But she had a way of folding her arms that was as bold as if she'd looked him straight in the eye. She was a big woman, too.

'You sent for me. Is the business so urgent that your man must come yelling at my gate while we're singing in chapel?'

'I've reason enough to rouse the whole of Cornwall.'

'So I hear. And what has Gorlois's quarrel to do with the nuns of Tintagel?'

'It has everything. Uther wants my wife, and he shall not have her. When he hears my answer, there will be an army in Cornwall. I must have a fortress to fight from.'

'The Duke of Cornwall has many strongholds. Did you call me here to tell you which one to pick?'

He moved quickly then, and we thought he was going to strike her. But he caught his hand back.

'Bryvyth Crook-Staff, you may be a woman but you are a learned one, and no fool. There is one place, and one place only, that could hold out against such a war-host: Tintagel.'

We must have all drawn our breath sharply then, like a nest of adders. It was no more than everyone must have thought in their minds many a time. That rocky island, with the sea coming at it on all sides. And just one neck of rock, so high above the waves it made you dizzy, joining it to the land. What chieftain mustn't have envied it for a fortress, these hundreds of years? But if we thought it, it was never spoken. For everyone knew Tintagel was a woman's place. First ours, now theirs. It had a name: the strong place where the two waters meet. There were few standing there that understood the meaning of that, or guessed how it was used. But the men kept away. Why else had those nuns chosen to set their cross there?

'You are thinking that Uther Pendragon would respect sanctuary? A king that would violate a Christian wife?'

'I'm not asking you for sanctuary, woman. I want a fort! A hundred warriors. Three lines of ramparts.

Ten men alone might hold that bridge for me against half of Britain.'

She had a temper like his. She raised her staff to him then, like a bar across a door.

'On your knees, godless man! Shame, that you should even think of it. There's one way only Gorlois will come to Tintagel – when he brings his lady wife to me for sanctuary. No warrior passes our wall bearing weapons, nor ever shall. If Uther Pendragon comes, it will be Bryvyth Crook-Staff will meet him on the bridge. But Gorlois, war-lord of Cornwall, will have to fight his bloody battles somewhere else.'

She didn't wait for him to argue. She turned her back and strode out of the gate with her nuns after her. She never once looked back.

Gorlois had a face like thunder. We feared he'd send the guards and have her struck down before she'd reached the downs. But he let her go. There were only a dozen nuns on Tintagel, and a handful of schoolchildren. But whether it was her he was most afraid of, or the place, Gorlois never tried to take it from them by force.

Chapter Fifteen

Still we sweated. And I soon feared it wasn't only Ygerne that had been spell-struck, up there in London. Gorlois was like a fly trussed in a cobweb. He'd had this one idea, and Bryvyth had thwarted him. Now he didn't seem to know what to do.

That frightened me. It wasn't like him, that was always so quick to leap on his horse and draw a sword. Bossiney's no place for war, but Gorlois had forts enough on the hilltops, above the forests. Chilly, windswept old crags. They weren't the sort of places you'd want to live in, when you could have sweet grazing on the downs and good fishing in the sea. But that's where we should have fled by now. That's what they were built for, in the old times, when it was clan against clan and we hadn't a king over all Dumnonia or a Saxon army to turn our thoughts elsewhere. Gorlois was known for a canny war-lord, but there wasn't the youngest kitchen-maid couldn't see that we should be somewhere else but where we were. And my courage seemed to fall into my boots, for I guessed who'd done this to him, and there'd be worse to come.

His warriors didn't like it one bit either. They buzzed loud enough. I saw Jordan and Britael arguing with him, and old Sulian trying to steady the younger bloods.

'Why doesn't Uther come?' says Margawse. 'What is he doing?'

You'd think she wanted us murdered. She was always impatient, that one, whether it was good or ill coming.

'Let's hope he's changed his mind. Maybe he's put up a doe that will make sweeter hunting than your dear mother,' I told her.

I glanced round at Ygerne as I said it. She tossed a braid over her shoulder and looked away as though she hadn't heard me, so that I couldn't tell if she liked the thought or not.

'He could be in Cornwall by now,' said Tudy. 'Wouldn't he take the high road over the moors to make for the forts? The Pendragon's a man of war. He'd never think we'd be such fools as to stay in Bossiney, like cattle at Samain, waiting to be butchered.'

That struck home. There was a loud growl ran round from near a hundred men. Gorlois had been sitting hunched over the fire, staring into the flames. But when he heard that he straightened up and gazed at Tudy, round-eyed as an owl. But even then we never guessed what was in his mind.

'Maybe he's come to his senses and gone off to fight Picts or Saxons instead of good Cornishmen,' Keby said.

'It's a long march from London,' Sulian tried to warn us. He was the oldest warrior Gorlois had, and he'd fought in many a battle against the Saxons. 'And the Pendragon will have an army to muster if he wants to besiege us. Likely enough it will be Pentecost before he crosses the Tamar.'

'Not he,' said Jordan. 'There were warriors enough came with their lords to the feasting to make a fair old war-host. He hadn't got halls big enough to hold us all. There were camp-fires burning in every market-place and tumbledown temple the Romans had left. My lady may have turned his head but Uther's a soldier. He's not so mad with love he wouldn't have the sense to keep those spears about him 'til he got my lord's answer.'

We came to Sunday. And still we hadn't moved from that round in the meadows, where an army could march right up to our gate, and nothing to stop them. I'd tried what I could to rouse Gorlois with nails and thorns and more besides. But he'd gone beyond my reach by then.

It struck me folk were a sight keener to go to chapel that morning than ever they'd been before. There hadn't been such a crowd gathered round it since the day Nectan came striding up from the beach with his psalm-book on his back and his bell in his hand.

My lady was there inside, of course, fresh as a girl at her first communion. I'd love to know what was hatched between those two, and what they'd prayed for.

The nuns came trooping along from Tintagel Island too, singing as though their God was still in his heaven. They were the only ones that didn't look afraid. What had they to fear from Uther Pendragon? A religion for slaves, my mother used to call it. Nectan feeding us with bread, though he'd hardly a scrap of flesh on his own bones. Big Bryvyth in her housemaid's gown, serving us rich wine from a chalice set with jewels. But they'd caught more than slaves now. I glowered at them from where I stood. Morgan was standing beside me, singing away in her clear voice. I don't think she cared what the words meant, then. Her eyes were fixed on her father. He glared back at those two, and mostly at Bryvyth.

But it was Nectan he collared afterwards, speaking hoarse as though the words choked him.

'When Uther comes, I shall expect you to do your duty as my priest. You cannot wield a sword, but you can call down curses on our enemy.'

I've seen a bull's nostrils widen like Nectan's did then. If I'd been Gorlois I'd have jumped well clear.

'Aye! The prayers of the Lord are more powerful than pagan battle-axes. But do you think I would aim them against a Christian prince?'

'Uther, Christian? A king that turns to a druid for his soul-friend?'

'Emrys Merlyn is the son of a holy virgin. Who are you to slander them both? You who keep a great witch to teach your daughters!'

Gorlois swung round on me then and his eyes went wide. I stood my ground and gave him back look for look. Let him think what he would now. Then he gave a great laugh.

'Old Gwennol! You'd compare her with Merlyn? You haven't met him, man!'

But nothing he could do would shift the saint. There wasn't one of them would give him what he wanted. And when I turned round, there was Morgan, staring at me like a little owl.

The time had seemed long, watching those empty hills. Now, looking back on it, I could have wished it had gone on for ever.

But Uther Pendragon was in more of a hurry than we bargained for. And whether it was just my lady's sweet face, or hot anger because Gorlois of Cornwall had refused to hand over what he wanted, or whether he'd noticed the first grey hairs frosting his beard, it's not for me to say. He was a bold war-lord before, and now he had Merlyn at his elbow. When his heralds came back with Gorlois's dusty answer, I wouldn't mind betting he had his saddlebags packed for war already. Lord Gorlois was known to be a proud man and Uther Pendragon was not a king to sit about waiting for an insult.

We watched Gorlois pace the ramparts, 'til the stars started to prick through that April sky. He was a dark man in daylight, and he looked darker then. I should have been getting my girls to bed, but none of us wanted to move. It was pretty near like waiting for a sentence of death. I stood outside my lady's bower, with my arms round Morgan. And she was stiller than I was. Stiller than any child her age had a right to be. Watching her father.

He turned his head suddenly and the watchman gave a great cry, so we knew they were coming. Two messengers came galloping in as hard as they could ride. We didn't need to hear them shout.

'Uther has crossed the Exe. He'll be in Cornwall tomorrow!'

That brought Gorlois back to life at last. He came striding down the steps into the dun. The yard was full of our shadows, crowding round him, like a town of ghosts. We held our breath to hear what he would do. We thought we knew the choice. To fight Uther Pendragon and die, or give Ygerne over to him and be shamed. We never guessed the madness that was going through his brain.

He smiled at us, and played with his sword, so that it clinked in his scabbard. It was the only sound in the evening air, except for the sea far off that was like our own breathing.

'I will not stay here!' he said harshly, like a man condemned to die. 'I cannot fight him in the open plain, and he knows it. Nor can I hold this house

against him. We shall march to Caer Dimiliock and
make a stand there, 'til enough Cornishmen come to
my aid to make a fair battle.'

And not before time, I thought, though it won't save
you. Poor fool. Who but your own kin will fight for you
now? There's a richer king than you coming, with
glamour in his train and the promise of glory after for
those who follow him against the Saxons. And what
has Gorlois got to offer them now that he's out of
favour?

Well, the men burst out cheering, of course. My
lady was the only calm one among us. Win or lose, she
didn't count on being harmed. She put her hand on his
arm and smiled up at him.

'But Uther is on the road already. He may be close
behind your scouts. What if he catches us before we
reach Caer Dimiliock? Why can we not stay here and
defend our own Bossiney?'

Oh yes. I could see the way her mind was shaping.
Bossiney's a homely round. It's not one of your high
rock forts that will stand months of siege. That wasn't
what she wanted. A bitter, wasting war. Growing
thin and scrawny like some hermit woman, to fall into
Uther's hands when all her looks were gone. She
wanted Gorlois to ride out to battle on our cattle
pastures. She saw herself standing on the ramparts,
watching two lords fight it out to the death over her,
and she waiting to give herself to whichever of them
won, like a prize at a fair. Ygerne the Beautiful. She'd
been a virtuous wife, as I account it, but she was too
much like Gorlois herself. She'd the same taste as he
had for fame and fortune, but it took her a different
way. So she turned white like the rest of us when she
heard what he was planning.

'You will not ride the same road as me,' he said,

barking it out in the voice of a man who knows he is speaking folly but is not to be argued with. 'Dimiliock's strong. It can stand out for many weeks. Maybe Uther Pendragon will grow tired of dashing his head against Cornish granite for what he cannot have. But if I fall, he will find himself cheated of what he came to steal.'

Morgan caught her breath, sudden-like. There wasn't one of us understood him, even then. My lady said, in a strangled kind of voice, 'Then . . . where shall I be?'

We heard the waves far off beating at the foot of the cliffs and I think I was not the only one who saw the height of that drop in my mind and wondered how far Gorlois might go to cheat Uther Pendragon.

'Here!' he cried, and he laughed at last, like the old days, splitting his beard and grinning with his white teeth.

Morgan's was the only laugh that followed his, just as if this was some new game he'd thought of.

'Here? You'd leave me here for Uther Pendragon?'

'Three soldiers and a handful of servants. You won't need more. Tudy was right. Here's the one place he'll never dream of finding you. He'll think the place is deserted when he hears I've gone. He's High King of Britain. He'll go where there's a strong fort and a great war-host. You know that man's pride.'

She was terrified now.

'You're mad to leave us to his army!'

'No madder than he is, that thinks he can steal my wife.'

'But he ordered us back to the feast at London. You told him no. You defied him. His troops will burn every village, every dun, every farm, before they reach Caer Dimiliock. What if some of them come here without the king?'

Couldn't he see what she was trying to tell him? It wasn't falling into the Pendragon's hands that she was afraid of. There were those under him who wouldn't stop to ask her name.

He nodded to the warriors behind him. 'I'll leave you a faithful guard. Sulian, Tudy, Coan. They'll know what to do if you're found.'

If they hadn't been grey before those three would have changed colour then. Years now, they'd been too stiff in the elbow to ride to war with the rest. But there was only one stroke he wanted from them this time. I saw the men's hands drop away from their sword-hilts as if they'd been burned.

My lady gasped at that. She could see that he meant it. The words came rushing out of her.

'And what of your daughters? Would you have them killed too?'

That stopped him. I felt the muscles of Morgan's shoulders tighten under my fingers as we waited. Gorlois went white for a moment. He had no answer to that. He would have died himself and taken her with him if he had to, but not his daughters.

Ygerne seized her moment.

'At least send us somewhere safer than this,' she begged him. 'Let us go to the nuns on Tintagel Island as Bryvyth said. They'd give us sanctuary.'

That touched him on the raw. He swore at her then.

'There's only way I'll have you go to Tintagel now. If you hear Gorlois is dead, then shear your hair and take off your gown, and go to Tintagel with my daughters and take your vows as nuns.'

Well, we all looked at each other. We didn't know what to do. I stood clutching my little Morgan's body in front of me for dear life. I'll tell you, I was terrified. If I'd thought him spell-struck before, it was nothing to the madness that had bewitched him now.

But we were only women, and the men had been cooped up long enough. It was Jordan moved first. And then it was like a spark in the straw, and everyone shouting their heads off. It was coming on twilight, but in a moment the slaves were dashing about, emptying the storehouses, though dear knows we had little enough left that was fit to eat after that wet old winter. They were packing it all into panniers and carts. And the war-horses were whinnying as they threw the saddles on.

Ygerne just stood there dumbstruck, with Elaine and Margawse, and watched them bring two chariots out. Three of her women wrapped themselves in cloaks and climbed into them. And Britael lifted a little kitchen-maid into the second one, bundled up so she might have been Morgan.

All Gorlois's warriors mounted and lined up, before and behind, with a train of pack-horses loaded with all the gear they could carry.

I thought Gorlois was gone mad. But at the last he surprised me. He looked me straight in the eye and said, 'If they come near, Gwennol, try all you know. There's more things than morning mist that can deceive the eye, though I fear you've left it too late to gather your brood. Look after my daughters. Fight Merlyn any way you can.'

I hadn't heard his voice so gruff since his hound died. I just stood with my mouth hanging open like a fool. All those years, and maybe he'd guessed more than I thought. Morgan twisted her head back to smile at me, as though she'd always known.

I don't mind telling you, tears stood in my eyes. He was always a brave man. And it was all my doing. When he was just a young lord and whole of heart, I'd pared the apple that had brought him to Ygerne's gate. I put my hands on either side of his face and kissed his head. I felt my power going into his blood then. I couldn't save him. But he wouldn't go into the dark unblessed.

He hugged Morgan strongly to him.

'Be brave, little warrior. Look to the honour of my name.'

It was hard for him to say it. She answered him fiercely.

'Never you fear, Father. Whatever you hear shall make you proud of me.'

She buried her face against his breastplate, and I had to prise her off. But she didn't cry, though she must have known what that parting meant.

He kissed Margawse and Elaine, and whispered to them and fondled their hair. Even Margawse looked pale. And last of all he embraced Ygerne, long and hard. She didn't say a word.

Then he gave the order, and the column started to move. For a long while we heard the tramp of hooves and the creak of carts going past us. When the yard was quiet we scrambled up on the ramparts and watched them go, a host of shadows marching away in the twilight. But they scorned to hide themselves. As dusk turned into night we saw torches spring out and fire flashed red on their spears and armour. All up the hill there were rivers of lights moving. Gorlois's kin were hosting in the dark.

Then our men shut the gate, and we were left in an empty dun.

Chapter Sixteen

We didn't know if Uther would come on us in the dark, as Gorlois had taught him that night at Mount Damen. We were starting at every sound. There weren't many of us, and we must have looked like a handful of ghosts. My lady and her waiting-woman Ruan, the three girls and myself, young Keby and a couple of kitchen-women. And those grey old warriors, Sulian, Coan and Tudy.

We daren't show a light. The dun was meant to look hollow and deserted. If any nosy folk looked in next morning, then we'd make ourselves out to be a parcel of greybeards and slaves left behind to mind the place, with all the glory and high blood gone somewhere else. But it was better no one saw us at all.

We moved into the great hall, where at least we had straw and water and a little food left. I got the slaves to fetch all the blankets they could find, and we made ourselves ready for weeks of cold hiding. And who could tell what would happen to us after that?

We couldn't use my lady's bower. That was supposed to be empty. But nothing that any of us could say would persuade my lady to dress herself and Gorlois's daughters like common peasant women, still less shear themselves like slaves. She was a brave woman, Ygerne, when all's said and done. She'd meet her death if she had to, but it must be nobly, like a duke's lady, not a kitchen-maid left behind. But I didn't think that dying was as much in her mind as it was in mine just then. And when you come to think of it, she had less need to fear death than the rest of us. There was just those three old men guarding her, and I could see that under their fine mail they were more nervous of what they'd been ordered to do than I was.

No. Ygerne would live, all right. She was what this whole game was about. She was a wise woman who would make shift for herself. When Uther Pendragon came, as come he must, Ygerne would be waiting for him, as beautiful as the day she walked into his feasting-hall and won his heart.

So she changed her dress as well as she could by starlight. She chose it even more carefully than she usually did. She had the decency not to put on her best feast-day robe. The dress she settled on was two years old, and faded with washing, but for all that it was a pretty thing and made her look not more than seventeen years old, and so Lord Gorlois had often told her. Sky-blue it was, by daylight, embroidered with roses and violets, and she tied a girdle of silver about her waist. She still had pearls in her hair. And she dressed her daughters finely too, though she had a tussle with Morgan. That one would rather have gone bare-legged in a coat of mail if anyone had let her. Over it all they put homespun cloaks of dun and russet, such as farmers' wives and daughters wear, with hoods for their jewelled hair. That was for outside only. It was no proper disguise. We all knew that in a twinkling of an eye they could throw them off and show themselves for what they were. Ygerne wouldn't pretend. And it was nothing but that black jealousy of Gorlois that stopped him seeing this was the only safe way.

Yes. There's the rub. Safe. That's the sort of word you and I would think of. I know it was mightily on my mind that long night. But it's not a word that men that are highborn have any use for. They live in some dream of pride and glory, so you'd think they had no fear of death like common folk. And they'd take wives and daughters with them to the grave, like slaughtered hounds, if they had to. A Christian, he called himself, and went to Nectan's chapel, but I hadn't noticed my lord was so very different from the old chiefs that the bards still sing of. I don't think he wished to be. And my lady had always kept one foot, and more, on the old road.

The moon rose late that night. And when it came I minded my lord's last pleading as well as I might. I knew I couldn't keep Uther Pendragon away from us, with Merlyn beside him, but I might yet be able to wrap us round in a Cornish mist so that some things might stay unseen a little while longer. This time I ordered Ygerne to help me and she didn't dare refuse now.

That was the night we whispered Margawse. We needed all the help we could get. But when she was joined to us, it couldn't be done proper. I often wonder if the Mothers were angry with us over that.

But Morgan we never spoke, either of us. Not even then.

I was for lighting a fire under the stars, the way it should have been done. Who would be awake to see us now? But Sulian wouldn't let me. He was a plain-thinking soldier that was more afraid of Uther than of me. So I paid that price for a promise that the men would keep their eyes shut and their backs turned. We sat cross-legged in the yard, under the half moon. I'd put Morgan to bed long ago. But I knew she hadn't stayed there. I could feel her watching us through the dark doorway, like a cat at a mousehole.

I battled against Merlyn that night, as I hadn't dared do before. I should have saved my strength. I had left it too late.

Ygerne's heart wasn't in it. All the time I could see her eyes going over her shoulder, though you couldn't see anything above the ramparts but treetops and stars. She let her cloak fall open, showing her pretty dress, and she put up her hand in the moonlight to touch her hair and her white throat. Even as she chanted the words with me her look was far away. She never wanted to be invisible. It was a poor, weak circle we made, like trying to bind a giant with a daisy-chain.

But then, perhaps she was more sensible than us. How could those four ever hope to hide what they were from the king, with their high bearing and their soft white hands?

When it was done, it was almost daybreak. I stomped up to the ramparts in no good temper. For I knew already it had all been wasted effort, and it had left me tired. I let the sea-breeze blow on my face and I wished I was back in my childhood home in Polzeath and rid of the lot of them.

Then I felt a small, cold hand slipped into mine. Morgan was smiling up at me, as if she was trying to coax me into something.

It made my heart turn over, not for the first time by a long way. For she had a way of smiling, as though you were the only person that mattered in the whole world. And sorry I was for what I had been wishing to her and hers just then.

She squeezed my hand.

'That's not how it should be done, is it, Gwennol? Not like that. Not here.'

And her little lips were still smiling, but her eyes had gone very dark and bright, staring deep into mine.

'Where, Gwennol? Where is the power, really?'

My own eyes went sideways then, though I tried to pull them back. She followed where I looked. And I was pleased to hear her gasp. It wasn't everything she knew, at eight years old. And even then I didn't tell her all of it.

Tintagel Head. That proud stack of rock that was almost an island. Just that one narrow ridge from cliff to cliff that was more dreadful than any drawbridge. The nuns had got it now. It even looked a bit like a fort. There was a ditch and a bank dug in front of the bridge, and they'd put old Padern there in the porter's lodge. He lived alone, and he was the only man they'd let near them, and then only when there was heavy work to be done. But beyond the causeway it was as peaceful a scene as you could wish to see in an April dawn. The white walls of their little huts scattered about the grass like so many daisies, tucked into the ledges with their backs to the winter storms. The sheep grazing on the hilltop. And the stone cross above it all.

Well, they say they'd carved a cross on it. You couldn't see that from here. Just a shaft of stone pointing at the sky. I needn't tell you what it looked like to me.

So she didn't see my eye go downward. She was gazing like a child spellbound at what she thought I'd shown her. For I didn't give that nunnery more than a glance. My mind was seeing deeper than that. You'll know where I mean. On the beach below those cliffs there's a deep cleft, where a hand has reached inside the bowels of the land and plucked out a hollow way

right through the rock. Like a hole between two legs.
The sea comes washing in from either side. Even then
I thought I could hear the stallions of Manawydan
neighing.

I'd left Morgan still staring at the cross of the
nunnery with her eyes wide and startled. Well, she
wasn't wholly wrong, was she? Those white nuns
couldn't have lived where they did, and heard the
waves around them, lain in the night alone and still,
and not felt something of what went on beneath them.
And there were some who did more than that. Though
there was the devil to pay later when Bryvyth found
out.

So I let Morgan believe what she would that morning. In the end she knew the whole of it, better than
anyone.

'Couldn't we go there?' she said, very fierce. 'Can't
we go to Tintagel and make magic with them there?
Real, powerful magic.'

I shook my head.

'It's too late, my lover. I'm not stirring one foot outside these walls until this is past, and nor will you. We
must bide where we are, and use what strength we've
got, though it's little enough for what's coming
against us.'

'And Father?' she asked. She had a way of piercing
straight to the heart of things. 'Does he have those
with him who can make magic to keep him? As strong
as Merlyn's?'

What could I do but look down at her with the tears
beginning to brim in my eyes and hug her close to me.
She saw where the real danger lay.

When I lifted my head I thought I could hear a bell
on the wind and I pictured those little white figures
going to their chapel in the grey dawn light. Well,

what if they were? They'd be at their prayers now. I caught myself wondering if they were praying for us.

All the same I wasn't prepared for what I found later that morning. Morgan, with her hands lifted, praying out loud, and not to any god I'd sung to her of. She smiled when she saw my face, and then she looked frightened.

'What's the matter, Gwennol? Why are you looking so angry? Didn't you mean it? Haven't the Christians got the power to save us?'

'Them! No, my girl, they haven't,' I told her pretty short. 'So don't let me catch you looking to them to help you.'

I don't know to this day if I did right. I hadn't the power to save her myself, had I?

At sunrise we shut ourselves in the hall again. There was a ladder to the loft over our heads. Just in case. Elaine was weary and crying, but to Margawse it was all adventure. She'd enjoyed what we'd done last night. It was her first taste of our power, and it had quickened her blood. She was only sorry she couldn't be riding off to Dimiliock now to watch the battle. She hadn't the seeing, like Elaine.

Lady Ygerne sat with Elaine's head on her shoulder. She looked older by daylight. I wouldn't like to tell which way her hopes were turning. Morgan was quiet, too. She was more frightened, now that her father had left her.

Chapter Seventeen

We hadn't much longer to wait. When they came it was sudden, like a flood in February. Keby shouted out to us and we went running to the walls. I could hear our small old guard drawing their swords, grasping at spear and shield. But there was no hope of fighting.

I'd never seen such an army. I thought the hills themselves were moving. It was like the shadow of a great cloud in the east.

'They've taken his bait,' said Coan, very hoarse. 'They're bound for Dimiliock. They're going to pass us by.'

'Don't tempt the gods!' I screamed at him. But it was too late.

We watched the Pendragon's men pouring off the ridge towards us, like a river that has burst its banks, and spreading out over the countryside, in little rivulets. For a while the forest hid them. We could see smoke beginning to go up here and there. Then they were on us. Green and blue, their cloaks were, sweeping in to drown us where we stood. And the light on their weapons and harness flashing like water in the sun.

We weren't waiting out there in the open to see any more and be seen ourselves. We didn't need telling that the only safe place for us was up the ladder into the rafters over the great hall. Lady Ygerne and the three girls went first, with Gorlois's men after them. Their faces were grim and their swords were drawn, and not only for Uther Pendragon's soldiers, I knew.

Now Ruan and the slaves were scuttling up that ladder as fast as they could move. I told them all to go in front of me, for I knew I'd be the slowest. And all the time I was gabbling spells aloud that I'd forgotten I knew.

But when it came my turn to climb that ladder, my stiff old joints clipped at my sinews like the black-smith's red-hot pincers. Morgan leaned over the hole, and her little white hand was clawing down for mine.

'Come on, Gwennol! Quickly!' she screamed.

There were many things happened that day that I wish I could forget, and can't. But I shall remember that one thing 'til the day I die. Morgan cried out for me as though she loved me.

But nothing I could do, not even the wet, shaking terror of the Pendragon's men, would get my limbs up those rungs. When they knew it was no good, old Sulian drew the ladder up into the shadows, and their faces disappeared.

That hall seemed bigger than I'd ever remembered it. Too big for me. But I daren't go outside again. So I crept into a corner behind the beer-pots. And then I thought that was the worst place I could have chosen to hide from soldiers, so I crawled away like a rat into another corner and hid myself in the straw. And only then I remembered Keby, that I'd last seen standing on the wall with nothing but an axe in his hand.

We couldn't know 'til the very last if they would pass us by or not. The coast road runs close by Bossiney. Surely they couldn't have helped but see our dun? I lay with my head pressed to the ground. I

134

could feel my whole body shaking with the tramp of their feet and hear the neigh of their horses. They were coming fast, like hounds that have sighted their quarry. The sound was getting louder, like the tide coming in.

Then it seemed to go quiet and I thought we were saved. Maybe my spell-weaving had been stronger than I'd dared to hope. I lifted my face from that scratching straw. Too quick. There was a shout from outside. Then loud yelling. I dived back under that straw like an old trout under a stone. And there I lay, shivering with fright.

It didn't take them long. They burst through the door. I'd have given anything to be able to see with my ears then. I could hear shouting and banging, but I couldn't make sense of it. There didn't seem so many of them as I would have thought, and more of them inside the hall than out of it, by the sound of it. I could tell when they found the beer, and I thanked my lucky stars I wasn't behind it. Let them drink themselves stupid, I prayed. And I curled myself small like a newborn baby in a cold world.

But they found me. When they pulled the straw off me and rolled me over, they looked like a ring of giants with their backs to the light. Laughing down at me at the thought of what was coming as if I'd been thirty years younger. And they weren't drunk enough for my liking. It only made them rough. I tried to let them take me as easily as I could, for I was an old, used woman and long past the age of bearing, and what did it matter so long as it was over quickly? But I must have been stiff and difficult for all that. It was a long time since I'd had a man between my legs – except in the Mothers' service, and that is something different. Then there's that pulse in the blood that makes us all

135

young maids again, wet inside and out and too eager
for stopping, and the one who comes to us then takes
us like a king. So they hurt me, and I cried out with the
pain. But it was a cruel long time before they had all
finished with me.

Someone else came then. A young warrior lord by
the look of him, but he wasn't Uther. He was half-
drunk as well. He shouted at the men, and they went
grumbling out of the hall like whipped curs. But he
stopped behind. It wasn't me he wanted. He looked all
round and cursed. If he was hoping to find a treasure
of weapons still hung on the walls, he could have
saved himself the trouble. He might have known that
Gorlois wouldn't leave so much as a horseshoe-nail
behind for Uther Pendragon to find. So he had me like
the rest before he left, since there wasn't anything
better.

There wasn't one of them saw the treasure hidden
over their heads. I never had Merlyn's power, and
what I'd had felt to be slipping away from me fast, but
I couldn't help having a grim sort of smile to myself,
even then. That's one spell I'd made stronger than I'd
thought.

He strode out of the door, and I heard him call for
fire, and I thanked the gods that all our hearths were
cold. But one of them must have had a flint. I heard it
strike, and then a crackle in the thatch. I thought of
my own skin first, even before Morgan's, crouching
there as I was in that stale straw with the fire beginning to sparkle in the roof. And anyway, what had any
of them done to help me? I'd done my best for them.
Those that went up that ladder could get down it fast
enough without help from me.

The noise died away. I limped out to the doorway
and breathed clean air again. There was a dark cloud

of dust up on the ridge going away to the south. It seemed King Uther had taken Gorlois's bait. But his men had left Bossiney burning.

Well, let it burn. There wasn't water enough to put it out. All I wanted was enough to wash myself clean. I'd find some in the well behind the kitchen. I could only go slowly and painfully. There was no one yet to help me.

I pulled myself round the corner of the wall. And it was there I found Keby, hanging over the well with his throat cut like a pig.

A little voice spoke behind me. I might have known Morgan would be quickest down that ladder.

'Is Keby dead? He is, isn't he? And those things they did to you. Was that because of Mother, too?'

I was too sorry for myself to tell her anything but the truth.

Chapter Eighteen

Bossiney burned. I hadn't the heart to weep for it.
Sulian's three and the slaves did what they could to
pull off the burning straw from the roofs with rakes
and beat out whatever flames they could reach. But
for all that, the great hall was a blackened shell, the
stables had gone, and the slaves' quarters were nothing but smoke and ruin. They'd managed to save my
lady's bower, though there was a great black hole in
the roof. They'd all of them worked themselves to
death there to salvage what they could. Even my lady
and the girls had fought the flames and run through
the smoke with whatever armfuls of stuff Uther's men
might have missed. All except me, and I could hardly
put one foot in front of another. They were all of them
black and weary by the time they'd done.

Lady Ygerne pushed back her hair with her sooty
hand and said, 'If Uther Pendragon could see me now,
I doubt if he'd think I was worth the trouble of finding.'

And her voice trembled, so that I could tell she was
near to tears. Poor lady. She hadn't had a mouthful of
hot food for a night and a day, and she'd been frightened half out of her wits. But she was as proud as
Gorlois, and that's where it hurt her most. She could
bear it if her lord died in battle and King Uther took
her by force. But what she couldn't bear was for him
to come and find her like this, old and tired and dirty.

'There now,' I soothed her. 'We'll wash your pretty face and see if we can find you a clean gown, and there's still a corner to sleep in.'

'I won't stay here.'

'There's nowhere else for us, my handsome. We'll make shift somehow.'

'We can't spend another night waiting for common soldiers to come and burn us in our own thatch like rats,' said my lady.

'They won't come back. Not now they think the place is burned, and only a dead boy and an old used baggage like me inside.'

'And what are we to eat and drink?'

That made me pause a bit. I'd been bleating away at her like a foolish ewe, but I saw she had the better of me now. Sulian and Coan and Tudy had beaten back the flames from the storehouses, but they might as well have saved themselves the trouble. Bossiney was stripped bare: every last grain of corn and joint of salted pork gone. It was little enough Gorlois had left us to eat as it was, marching off with his own men at the thin end of winter with all the provisions they could carry for a siege. They'd even herded our cattle down the road to Dimiliock.

Siege? I couldn't see it, no matter how I tried. A proud man like Gorlois of Cornwall, waiting to die in his hole like a starved shrew, with Uther outside his gates, taunting him for the honour of his wife. A man like that would never stay cooped up for long.

But gone he was, and all our good corn with him, and what little he had left us, Uther's men had stolen.

And there was something worse. There wasn't one of us wanted to lift a bucket from that well, seeing what had fouled it. The men were old soldiers. They'd seen blood before. But even they didn't have the stomach for that.

I didn't care then if I died, so long as I didn't have to move from where I was. All I wanted was somewhere to lay down my head and rest.

'We're to stay here. That was my lord's orders.'

'And how much longer will Duke Gorlois be alive to give anyone orders?'

'Ssh!' I scolded her, for Morgan was listening, with a face like white chalk under the soot. 'We'll face that news if it comes.'

'I won't stay here, like a pig shut in a slaughter-pen. It is not fitting.'

'But where would you go, my lover? You can't reach him now.'

She lifted her chin with that proud look that warned me I was not her nurse any more.

'Where we should always have gone. To the nuns at Tintagel.'

I looked to the warriors for help. They were Gorlois's men, after all, and under his orders. But I could see how it tempted them. They didn't like what they'd been told to do. And whatever Bryvyth said, even three old warriors might make a valiant stand there, defending my lady's honour on Tintagel causeway 'til the very last. You could watch the thought shaping in their minds.

'But my lord said . . .'

Ygerne looked me straight in the eye.

'Gorlois will not come back, Gwennol.'

I was too weary to argue with her.

I made the slaves get the better of themselves and dip the bucket in the well 'til they got one that was no worse than pink. You wouldn't have thought a young boy would have so much blood in him. But the Mothers have more. They'll swallow all we give them 'til we're bled white. But the water will still be bubbling up out of the earth after we're gone.

Ruan chose a dark cloth and washed the soot from their faces. There wasn't one of them dared to ask where the water came from. And after they'd finished, I cleaned my own legs with it. You can wish to die, and yet you go on living.

But none of us cared to drink from that well, though our throats were rasping from the smoke.

The men buried Keby in the meadow. Poor souls. Their old arms were so weary they could hardly lift a spade. But the pigs had been rooting for acorns under the oaks all that wet winter, so the ground was soft. If we lived, my lady would come back and ask Nectan to give him a proper burial. The Church always had them when they were dead.

Then those four wrapped themselves in their cloaks, and put up their hoods to hide their faces. But what was the good? You could no more have hidden who they were than a white mare can hide in a herd of bay and brown horses. Even the way they carried their heads told they were nobly-born. The king would find them out sooner or later. But Ygerne made sure she would choose for herself the place where Uther would see her again.

His men had gone long since. All the same, it was queer and silent on the track. We all felt as naked as babies as we stepped outside that gate. The pasture was empty. There wasn't a body moving on the road. Margawse was quieter than usual. She was looking round her nervously instead of with that bold stare of hers.

The cottages we passed had a dead sort of look. Some of them had their doors wrenched off their hinges and their gardens trampled and every bit of food gone. If they hadn't, the doors were shut, and the smoke-holes were still, as though the hearths below them were cold. They had an unfriendly feel. And with good reason. The bards sing fine songs of the warriors who fall in battle. But there are others the lays don't tell you of. There were common men as well as lords walled up in Dimiliock now who'd never come home again, and women and children who had cause to weep already. If they were inside, peeping at us through the cracks in the door as we passed by, they wouldn't have any reason to love Gorlois's family.

Elaine looked pale and scared, and kept close behind her mother and Sulian. Morgan was the bravest of the three, with her little head held high.

By the time we reached the cliffs, I was so worn out I couldn't look at more than the next step in front of me in the grass. Every time I moved a foot it hurt me. But when I had dragged myself out to the headland I drew a big breath and made myself lift my face to look south.

It was what I'd feared. The sky was filled with a great dust-fog, and I heard men screaming and the clash of weapons. But when I looked round at Sulian and his men I could tell by their faces they hadn't heard anything but the cry of herring-gulls and the splash of the breakers on the rocks beneath us. And they were soldiers that had known more battles than ever I would.

I'd have liked to believe they had the truth of it, and I was just a foolish old woman who'd seen too many horrors for one day. Then I looked at Elaine, and I knew she'd heard it too. It's a bitter burden we carry.

Morgan caught at my hand.

'How far is Dimiliock? Will we be able to see it from Tintagel?'

'No,' I said, to comfort her and myself. 'It's too far for the likes of you to see the fighting. Dimiliock's an hour's hard galloping from here.'

Still so close as that? They seemed to have been gone a lifetime.

'He should have taken me with him. I'm not afraid of the Pendragon. I'd have fought him. Like I fought the fire.'

'No, no,' I told her. 'You weren't made to be a warrior. You're forgetting. I thought you'd made up your mind to be a beautiful queen, like your mother.'

She pulled her hand away, sharpish-like. 'Don't dare say that! What made you do it, Gwennol? She's not a queen. Not while Father's alive. And anyway, I don't want to get married now. Not to a king or anyone else.'

And I didn't need to ask what she'd seen that day to make her change her mind.

There's a valley runs down below Tintagel. We came to the head of it, and there was the nunnery, standing against the sky like a fairy fortress. There was the cross on top, and little houses for the nuns all dotted around the sides. Peaceful, that's what it looked, like a farm in the evening when the cattle are coming home. Uther's men hadn't touched it.

They all of them started to hurry when they saw it. But I couldn't have gone any faster if I'd tried. Every step I took was agony, with the raw flesh chafing me as I moved my legs.

Morgan waited for me where the path crossed the stream and began to climb again. She smiled as she held out her hand and pulled me up. But then she was away again up to the next bend, darting backwards and forwards like a squirrel. She was always impatient.

I was far and away the last to reach the top. I couldn't help it. They were all standing there on the edge of the cliff, and I don't flatter myself it was me they were waiting for. An odd, quiet place, it was. Not a soul to be seen. There was a bank in front of us, with a narrow opening, to show that it was holy ground beyond. God's rampart, they called it.

And below it a deep ditch that must have taken days to dig. It made me feel queer looking down into it. But that was nothing to what I knew was waiting for us on the other side.

There was no one about. But for all that, I had a feeling we were being watched.

Chapter Nineteen

There was no one about, so we started to walk through. But we hadn't taken more than a few steps towards it before old Padern came out from behind his hut. From the way he was yawning I should say he'd been taking a nap in the sunshine, just as if Uther Pendragon's army wasn't raiding and burning the whole countryside. Well, they'd steered clear of Tintagel. There wasn't a wisp of burning thatch here.

His mouth fell open in a different way when he saw who'd come. Sulian gave him his marching orders.

'Bring your mistress here, fellow. And look sharp about it.'

He didn't need telling twice. He went hobbling away over the bridge as fast as he could go. Poor old man. I don't know what they kept him for. They were a tough lot, those nuns. Half of them were stronger than he was. But then, he was hardly likely to turn any woman's head.

While we waited we couldn't help looking at that neck of stone between us and the island. It wasn't very wide. I could hear the waves pounding on the rocks below, and it seemed to me as if each one that broke was biting a little bit deeper into the sides. I could almost fancy I felt the land shaking beneath me.

Padern was coming back. A little brown figure he

looked on that causeway, like a shrivelled old leaf
that the wind might blow away. He was fairly out of
breath by the time he got to us.

'You're to go across, my lady. She's waiting for
you.'

So Ygerne wasn't the only one who would have her
visitors meet her where she chose. I thought our
duchess might argue, but to tell you the truth, we'd had
enough of standing out there on the open downs. We'd
all feel a lot safer on the other side of that bridge.

So we kept our dignity and went on through the
gate. Ygerne first, then her daughters, with Ruan and
me following. But when it came to Sulian's turn
Padern stuck out his hand.

'I'm sorry, sir,' he said. 'Just the womenfolk unless
you give me your weapons. There's no armed men
allowed on Tintagel Island.'

Sulian had the sword half out of his scabbard. He
had his job to do. But Ygerne turned to him with a
sweet smile.

'Put up your sword, Sulian. I shan't need you to
defend me here.'

I felt sorry for those grey old warriors. They'd
rather have been at Dimiliock, any day. It was a hard
task my lord had left them. But they knew their duty.
They'd wait by the rampart if she ordered them. They
wouldn't budge from it, whoever came. And they
were not so old but they wouldn't sell their lives
dearly to anyone who tried to pass them.

My lady was walking out on to that high path, so we
had to follow her. It made me turn dizzy crossing that,
and I wouldn't be the first one, by a long way. You
could look down into the sea on both sides, ten times
deeper than the deepest well. Green water breaking
on black stone. And you could see where lumps of

rock had tumbled off and lay smashed on the beach, like bits of broken pot. Up here in the sunshine it might be all peaceful and holy to Christ. But underneath there was something else. A different holiness, where the two streams meet. The Mother's Hole. The nuns should have known they'd never be rid of it entirely.

I wondered then if my lady had more than I guessed in mind when she chose this place. There was power beneath us. I could feel it with every step. What troubled me was what she meant to use it for.

I looked down at Morgan. But for once her little face was hidden under her hood.

There was a nun waiting to meet us on the other side. But she was too small to be Bryvyth. She wore white wool that had never been dyed, the same as they all did, and walked bare-footed. But she greeted us like a lady in her own hall.

'The peace of Christ welcomes you,' she called out to us, 'and the rest of the Spirit upon weary travellers.'

'May your peace return to you,' we answered, as they had taught us.

Peace? Small hope of that, I thought to myself, what with the pain in my guts and the thought of Keby with his blood running away into the well, and Uther Pendragon laying Cornwall waste, all for the sake of my lady's face.

Well, as for her, she held her head so high she might have been visiting another lady in her castle for a feast. 'Lady Ygerne and the three daughters of Gorlois claim sanctuary here from Uther Pendragon.'

That made the little nun gasp.

'Follow me!' she said.

She was off up the path with her skirt flapping, like a startled hare. All over the island we could see white figures turning round or peering out of doorways to get a good look at us.

'That's made a stick to stir the hive,' I muttered to Ruan.

The little nun showed us into the guest-house.

'Wait here,' she said, 'Bryvyth is coming herself.' And she bobbed away backwards out of the door.

I'd never been inside a convent before. Seeing those plain, white nuns, I'd always thought they must live in a poor, bare place. But whatever their own cells were like, when I looked around their guest-house they had tables and benches as finely made as anything we'd had in Bossiney before it was burned. And the curtain that hung by the door was made of wool good enough for a chieftain's cloak.

But I hadn't much time to be nosy. Next thing we knew, there was Bryvyth in the doorway. A big, broad-shouldered woman she was, and she stood on her own threshold like a barn-door. I thought for a moment her knee began to bend when she saw us, as if she was going to bow to Lady Ygerne. But if she had old habits pulling her that way, she got the better of them.

'Peace be to all in this house, and the blessed rest of angels this night,' she said.

'And to you also,' we answered.

'And which of you would be the Lady Ygerne?'

They still had their hoods on. But she knew, of course. Hadn't her own hands given the wine to my lady that very Sunday? You couldn't have hidden a fine duchess like Ygerne among a hundred women. And anyway, Bryvyth was looking straight at her when she said it. But she was mistress in her own house, bare feet or not, and she was enjoying it.

My lady drew herself up tall. For all she had come

through, she looked as fine and handsome in her homespun cloak as if it had been cloth of gold.

'I am the duchess,' she said. 'My lord Gorlois is fighting with Uther Pendragon at Dimiliock, and I and my daughters have had our hall burnt down about our ears by his soldiers. We claim sanctuary here, with you, for our lives and honour.'

I thought that nun looked at her shrewdly.

'And you're thinking Uther Pendragon would respect my convent, now? What's to stop him going through here like a blacksmith's poker through butter?'

'Uther is a Christian king.'

'A fine sort of Christian, isn't it, that makes war on the husband to steal his wife?'

'He is High King of all the Britons. He is used to having what he wants.'

'For a king so recently made, it's not taken him long to get into the habit. And if you've come from his feast in London, you'll know it's no Christian confessor he keeps company with for his soul-friend.'

There was not much she hadn't heard, that Bryvyth. And she was sharper than Nectan.

'Is it Merlyn you speak of?' my lady asked, and I thought she spoke the name soft and carefully.

'Emrys Merlyn it is. And no friend of the Church.'

I waited for my lady to answer that. When she did she startled me.

'Uther Pendragon carries the cross into battle. Whoever helps him fights for you, Bryvyth Crook-Staff.'

'And if he wins, who will be master on Tintagel tomorrow? My Lord, or Merlyn's?'

'If the Saxons win, there will be no tomorrow for either of you.'

The nun snorted and straightened her shoulders then, like a farmer's wife getting ready to draw a pig.

'Well, they'll not be coming tonight, by the look of it. We'll see what the morning brings. There are clean beds here for the women, if that will suit you. Padern will look to your men in the gatehouse. So I'll see you at supper. We don't get many guests at Tintagel. It's a long time since I had a crack with layfolk that could talk about more than the price of beans.'

She looked across the bridge at the porter's lodge.

'And send word to those men of yours that they can put their swords away and sleep sound tonight. This is a holy place. If Uther Pendragon should come to Tintagel, it's me he will have to reckon with.'

She left us then with a grim smile. The guest-mistress brought warm water and washed our feet, even mine. It was sweet to the touch, that pure spring water. It cleaned more than our skin. And when we drank it cold it tasted better than wine.

The sun was getting low, though we couldn't see it now. A mist was creeping in and the tide was hushed. Presently a bell rang and we could hear the nuns singing in the chapel higher above us. Away in Dimiliock, the first day's fighting would be nearly over. It was a heavy thought that there'd be men dead now that I'd known all their lives. And nothing any of us could do but wait.

They served us a fine supper in their refectory. It opened my eyes, I can tell you. Red wine in glass goblets, just for the gentry, of course. And roast lamb, newly-killed, on fine, glazed dishes. Bryvyth laughed at our faces.

'Yes. We lead a simple life most of the year. But it's our rule to see our pilgrims well-served. Guests are doubly welcome!'

And when I looked at the nuns I could see what she meant. They were sat at tables down the sides, and they were enjoying their feast, I can tell you. Across the bottom of the room there were the schoolgirls. Princesses as well as farmers' daughters, so I'd heard. They weren't allowed to talk, but they were staring at us for all they were worth.

The wine loosed Bryvyth's tongue, and she was all evening telling Ygerne about her schooling in Dyfed. Of how she'd travelled in Ireland, following him she called Patrick. And of the work of her nuns that were fine potters and weavers and bee-keepers and scribes, and were supposed to busy themselves with everything that was wholesome and beautiful.

Pilgrimage, that's what she called her life. A journey of the soul. Always travelling on to something new.

More than once her eyes went to my face. But she never challenged me. And I was too weary to think it strange for me to be sitting at her table. It was like a dream to us at the end of such a day to be full and warm and at ease, and to feel the arms of the sea guarding us on every side but one. It ended with Elaine asleep with her head on the table, and Morgan creeping into my arms to close her eyes.

We got them to bed at last. The guest-house had three small rooms, opening off a passageway. My lady slept in the far one, with Ruan stretched at her feet. Elaine and Margawse next to them, and I was left with Morgan. We were too tired out and full of food and wine to fear that anyone might come on us in the dark. We didn't trouble ourselves how Coan and Tudy and Sulian might be passing the night on the other side of the bridge.

I shuffled in to put the older girls to bed, and I'd

hardly the strength to brush their hair or fold their gowns. We should none of us want rocking that night, after all we'd been through. I'd be gladder than most to close my eyes and put the pain away.

When I got back to Morgan she was standing in her shift at the open window, watching the mist come creeping up over the cliffs and curling in wisps in front of her eyes. She had her back turned to me, and her voice sounded hollow in the fog.

'Where are we? What place is this?'

'Why, maid, you know very well where we've come. To the nunnery at Tintagel, as your mother said.'

After a bit she swung round to me, her eyes black and staring.

'Who are you? Who am I?'

That made me shiver, I can tell you, thinking of some of those charms I had put about us. How did I know what she could see or couldn't see when she looked at me? It made me cross and frightened.

'Hold your tongue now, child, and come to bed. Do you want to ill-wish us all? I'm old Gwennol, and you're little Morgan, that's Lord Gorlois's daughter.'

'Am I? Am I, old woman?'

I couldn't bear to listen to such nonsense any longer, nor meet the look in her eyes. I rolled over, hunched up tight under my blankets, and tried to wish that long day away. Beneath us I could hear the slow beat of the sea. Like the breath of a living beast, it was, closer than I had ever slept to it before. I knew the tide was rising in the Mother's Hole. And even there in the darkness, with my eyes tight shut, I had a picture of Morgan still, kneeling on her bed in her white shift, staring at me as though she didn't know me.

Chapter Twenty

I woke suddenly in the night, with that feeling you have when you know there's something wrong. I sat up in bed, and that made me draw my breath sharp. My scars had stiffened while I slept and the crust was splitting. I listened. I couldn't hear a sound now. And somehow that was worse than if I had. I waited, with the skin crawling on my neck, and then I heard it. A scratching on a door, and then a bumping in the passage, and the sound of men's voices, very low.

I'd no thought but that Uther's men were coming to attack us in our beds. Then I heard women whispering. And I thought perhaps they might still be outside the gate and old Padern had come across the bridge in the dark to warn Lady Ygerne. And what could we do if he had? We'd nowhere left to run.

I clambered out of bed, and I don't mind telling you it made me moan to move. I went to the chamber-door and I must have gasped out loud, for there was a white-clad figure whisking out of the house-door into the night. I made the sign against evil. Then I blinked and came to my senses a bit, for as she vanished over the step I saw the heel of her bare foot and knew it must have been one of Bryvyth's nuns. The little guest-mistress probably. She'd left the outer door open, but I couldn't see far. The moon was up, but so was the mist. The air was white, yet I could hardly see two paces beyond the step. It was a night to trick the eyes. Far below I could just about hear the hiss of the sea. Even that had gone quiet now, as if it was listening.

I put a bar of my own kind on that door, just to be sure, mumbling a bit, as you do when you're not really thinking. And I cursed myself for an old fool that had broken a good night's rest for nothing, and got the cold dew on me. Then I turned back, and I had such a shock! It sent the blood out of my face all at once when I saw what I'd done. If my bar had worked, it had shut the good outside and trapped the evil in with us.

Two men were standing on either side of my lady's chamber-door, like sentries. Tall men, cloaked and hooded. They were none of our three old veterans, that we'd left at the gate, for they carried themselves straight and easy, like warriors in the prime of life. I couldn't move for fear, and my tongue stuck in my throat.

I knew they were watching me, though they had shadows for eyes. Then they turned their heads to look at each other and I heard them laugh low.

Well, if I'd been afraid to venture outside my room, first off, it was worse now. I was trembling like a dog in a thunderstorm. I'd have given a year of my life to be back in bed with the covers over my head. But I daren't step past those two men and turn my back on them, even if they'd let me by. Then another shape separated itself from the shadows between those soldiers. A woman's, it was.

'Ruan?' I gasped, with my heart in my mouth. It's not often I've been glad to see her, but I couldn't think who else it could be.

It was her, all right, and she giggled to me, with a bright, wicked look in her eyes, that put me in mind of Margawse.

'Ssh!' she whispered. 'What's the matter? Don't you recognise these two? It's Jordan and Britael.'

My lord's two bodyguards, that hardly left his side? I couldn't make sense of it. Or only one way.

'Is he dead, then?'

'No! You ninny, Gwennol! Lord Gorlois is here. He's in my lady's room now.'

'He never is!'

'It's true. He'll be having her in her bed by now.'

'But he's in Caer Dimiliock, with the Pendragon's army round him. How could he get out?'

There was a movement from the middle room behind us, where Elaine and Margawse slept. I heard Elaine cry out.

'No! No!'

And then Margawse hushing her.

'Ssh. Don't disturb the children.' Ruan put her finger to her lips. 'What does it matter how he did it? Let's leave my lord and lady in peace. They'll sleep sweet tonight. If they sleep at all!'

I looked past her. Those two tall guards had never moved, nor lifted the hoods back from their faces. But I could see their white teeth grinning in the shadows.

One of them murmured, 'Goodnight, Gwennol.' It was Jordan's voice, all right.

I breathed a little easier. To tell you the truth, I wanted to believe her. I'd had enough terror to last me a lifetime. I'd known those two since my Ygerne had married Gorlois. A wild-spirited pair they'd been then, like Gorlois himself. That was the sort of harebrained trick those three would have played, to steal out of a fort under siege, past the very nose of the king himself. Like schoolboys scrumping. And our Cornish orchards grow a rosy apple.

And then the smile slipped from my face. He was

FAY SAMPSON

Duke of Cornwall, wasn't he? And Ygerne was his
own wife. He shouldn't need to steal in to her like a
thief in the night.

I shook my head and closed the chamber-door
behind me. I couldn't understand a word of it. I'd been
so sure we'd never see Lord Gorlois alive again. One
Cornish lord against all the hosts of Britain? Besides,
I knew his temper. If Gorlois couldn't win, he'd never
run away. He'd chosen to take his stand at Caer
Dimiliock, and he'd die fighting there. And who could
have told him he'd find us in Tintagel?

Tintagel! Gorlois, to beg his way in past Bryvyth?

It wasn't exactly a sound I heard behind me. More
like a chill stir in the air, as though someone had
unbarred the window. But I knew, even in the darkness, what it was. Morgan was awake and listening.

'What is it? What did she say?'

'Hush, my lover. It's nothing. Go back to sleep.'

'No. Tell me. She said something about Father,
didn't she? Is he dead?' She screeched it out at me.
'He is, isn't he? Is that what they've come to say?'

I went to her, and felt for her shoulders in the darkness. She clung to me like a wild thing, and I stroked
her hair.

'No, my pretty. It's not that.' And then it came out in
a rush, to comfort her. 'Your father's alive. He's here.
He's come to your mother.'

I should have known better. She was out of my
arms, and what chance had I got of holding her?

Then she screamed, outside in the passage. And
hurt or not, I was out of that door faster than you'd
have thought possible.

I couldn't see her at first. But I saw someone else. In
a patch of moonlight, from the door. Not Ruan, this
time. Oh, no, not Ruan. The other of those men had

moved. Taller than any warrior I'd ever seen, or so he
looked then. Standing in a shaft of gossamer light,
brighter than mist and thicker than moonshine. With
a hood drawn over his face, shadowing it. Then I
made out that he had Morgan by the wrists and she
was fighting him like a wildcat.

'Let me go! Let me go! I want to see my father!'

Then the hood fell back as he struggled to hold
Morgan. I breathed a sigh of relief. I'd been having
nightmares with my eyes open for nothing. His face
was half-lit in the witchlight, but it was the one I
knew: Britael's, that had been my lord's bodyguard
these fifteen years, and his friend before that.

'Take your claws out of me, you little screech-owl,
or by the hounds of Annwn, I'll put that on you that
will bind you stiller than stone from now till morning.'

He had a deep, strong voice, like wind through the
standing stones, but this time my knees fairly shook
when I heard it. I wasn't a fool. I knew every man in
Gorlois's dun. The voice was Britael's, I didn't doubt
that. But Britael would never in his life have spoken
words like those. I could only think of one man who
would.

But Morgan didn't care who he was. She ducked
her face to his hand and he let out a yell. And from the
bedroom behind him there came another shriek. A
woman's cry, that stopped us all in our tracks. To this
day I couldn't tell you if it was joy or pain, or both at
once. But as long as I live I shall still hear that cry. It
was as if the land itself had been entered.

That voice that was Britael's laughed long and
loud.

I snatched Morgan to me and covered her ears with
my arms. None of us should have heard what we had.
Inside my head I could hear my own voice crying out,

'Where are our guards? Sulian! Oh, Mother, where are the guards?' When I listened again there was only the splash of the waves below us, and I knew I hadn't spoken a word. All I saw was what seemed to be Britael's face, smiling at me from the shadows, and the shape like Jordan's grinning at me too. There wasn't a sword in the world could have saved us from those smiles then.

Morgan was flying at him again, but that tall man threw her across the passage, as a wolf might toss a whippet over a stream.

'The little weasel! She bit me. Get her to bed, woman, 'til tomorrow. And look to it well that she doesn't trouble her mother again.'

I could hear Elaine weeping behind the wall, and Margawse whispering. But I hadn't a thought for either of them.

Morgan was sobbing now.

'Father! Where is Father?'

'Hush, my pretty,' I told her, dragging her back into our chamber. 'Your father is sleeping now. Sound and long. We shall all of us go to join him soon enough.'

Chapter Twenty-one

Somehow I slept again, and as heavily as if I'd been drugged. When I woke it was full morning. Morgan was sitting at the open window, with the sea-wind slapping the hair across her face like a whiplash. The mist had gone and the breeze was skimming up the crests off the waves like flags.

I looked at the door, and though I knew it was foolishness, I was afraid to step out into that passage. I knew he wasn't there but the terror of it was still on me. You'll think me a silly old fool, crying my eyes out one day because I hadn't met him, and shaking with fear the next because I had. But you haven't known him. I'm not talking about an ordinary man.

Morgan turned her head slowly to look at me, with a strange, cold stare.

'You needn't be afraid. I heard them go.'

And there was a queer thing for her to say, when she'd been so hot to see her father last night. Hadn't she so much as opened the door to see if I was telling her the truth? My mouth fell open, but I didn't know what to say to her. There was a bleak, shut look in her face that I had never seen before. I didn't like it. She'd always worn her heart naked in her eyes.

'See for yourself,' she said, very cool and scornful, not like her tempers or her wheedling smile.

I went to the door, stiff and slowly. But I knew she

was right. The passage was empty. There was no sign of any men.

The bell was ringing the nuns to their chapel.

I don't know what I was afraid of finding out, but I didn't go to my lady's room straight off. I stopped at the older girls' door and poked my head in. Elaine was fast asleep, curled up like a plump, round dormouse for comfort. There were tear-marks on her face, and she was sighing in her sleep. But Margawse was sitting up with the covers thrown back and her shift open to her breasts. There was a funny, wild look about her.

'Is he come yet. Gwennol? Has Uther Pendragon found us? We thought we heard voices in the night, but we daren't look. Listen! Isn't that the gallop of horsemen coming?'

'Never you fear, now. It's only the sea on the rocks. You're safe here,' I said, helping her to dress.

It wasn't like Margawse to be frightened. She wasn't the only one. I had a cold feeling that something had happened here that was too late to mend.

I went back to dress myself, and Morgan too. Then I straightened my shoulders and tried to act braver than I felt. Even then I daren't have told you what I feared. I tiptoed to the end of the passage, to my lady's room, and scratched at the door. When I opened it, Ruan was lying at the foot of the bed. Her eyes were open, watching me. She put her fingers to her lips.

Ygerne was asleep, in that narrow convent bed, with her face turned towards me. She hardly looked any older than Elaine. But there were no tears on her cheeks. She was smiling in her sleep. And far be it from me to speak ill of my betters, but when I saw her lying there like that I could have slapped her face.

What right had she to look so pink and pretty, when the rest of us were as white as whey?

Whole, she looked, when the rest of us were wounded. Full and satisfied, when her daughters had been robbed. I knew what that look meant well enough.

I went outside to cool my temper in the good sea-wind. It seemed quiet enough in the sunshine, though the waves were roaring on the beach. I could believe Margawse's fancy, that it was like a great troop of horsemen galloping nearer. All over the island I could see the nuns busy at their work. And it seemed to me that their movements were brisker than the day before. I've seen birds darting here and there like that when their nest is threatened. Two were herding the cows out from milking, and some were sitting out of doors, seemingly writing. It was strange to me to see those women with pens in their hands. Their houses were not like the buildings of a dun, all tight together inside a wall. They were scattered about the grass, with their doors open to the sea and the wind, as though those nuns didn't mind being alone with their thoughts. But they were lifting their heads pretty often to look at the bridge.

As I watched, there was a bit of a flurry among them, like wind passing over a field of corn before a storm. I turned just in time to see Bryvyth striding up the path towards the guest-house.

'Bring the Lady Ygerne outside to speak to me!'

A fine, commanding voice she had, that nun.

From inside, I heard Ruan's voice call out.

'My lady is sleeping. Tell her to wait.'

But Bryvyth was not a woman to be kept waiting.

'Lady Ygerne! Come out!' She thundered.

There was a silence. And then Ygerne stood in the

doorway, with a white and gold gown we'd rescued from the fire slipped hastily on and her pretty hair unbraided. Her chin was up, but she looked younger than ever.

'Come here!' the nun bellows.

The rest were all creeping up to watch. Bryvyth stood on the path with her nuns gathered behind her, like a stag guarding its does.

'Kneel!'

Ygerne's mouth opened then, and I thought she would say no to that. There was a mighty long moment of awful silence. Then she smiled, and down she went, Gorlois's lady on the muddy grass in her fine gown. And it was so quiet you could hear the sea sliding down between the stones, like horses whinnying. I've often wondered how much she was laughing at all of us.

The nun wasn't laughing.

'The holy gate of Tintagel was opened last night, after dark. They told me Lord Gorlois had come with two companions, in danger of their lives, to see his wife. For Christian pity I broke our rule. I had the gate unbarred and let them in. Armed men entered this holy island, the Blessed Virgin forgive me! As you value your soul, answer me. Was it your lord who came to you? Did you take him to your bed, here?'

'Yes.' No more than a meek whisper, it was.

'Yet now it is morning and what was done in the darkness is made plain. Uther Pendragon's herald is at our gates. Lord Gorlois is dead. Woman, your husband fell last night at sunset, fighting against the king at Dimiliock. He died of his wounds. And Uther Pendragon has come to claim his wife.'

Well, I'd been watching Ygerne pretty close but it was only a moment I saw it – that flash of lightning in her eyes.

Then I spun round fast enough like all the rest. And
what a sight met our eyes! Beyond the causeway was
a great troop of horsemen drawn up on the hill facing
us. The sun was bright on their weapons and shields
and armour and the brave colours of their cloaks.
They sat still on their horses with their heads high,
waiting as bold as brass, and every so often a horse
threw up its neck and whinnied. It wasn't a raiding-
party this time. There wasn't a sword drawn. He'd
won. You could tell even from here there was a grin
on all their faces. Oh, no, the Pendragon hadn't come
here to fight for Ygerne. He had come to claim what
was his own already.

Then Ygerne flashed out at Bryvyth, with her sweet
little chin in the air.

'Fool! Look! Can you not see it is Uther Pendragon's
spears that keep you Christians safe? Where do you
suppose the Church will be if the white dragon comes
west?'

'Where it began! Under a tyrant. Did you think the
Lamb was a stranger to the knife? The road runs
straight from Gethsemane to here.'

Big Bryvyth folded her arms. You'd have thought
she wasn't afraid of a Saxon army, or a British one
either.

'Go! To your king, and his banners, and his spear-
men. Adulteress! Did you imagine we needed your sin
to shield *this*?'

Ygerne changed colour then. She went a deep fox-
glove red. Not just her face, but down her neck and
her breast. If she'd been a slug across the path, I think
Bryvyth would have looked at her more kindly.

The nun wiped her hands then, as if she'd been
gutting mackerel. I've a notion she was enjoying herself now.

'Go!' she thundered. 'Go to that godless man! And never set foot on this holy ground again unless you come with your hair shorn and your clothes rent to do penance for your blasphemy.'

We were dismissed from Tintagel. Tipped off their land. The land that had once been ours. I could feel the earth beginning to burn under the soles of my feet.

There was nothing else Ygerne could do, except keep her dignity. She got to her feet without a word and started down the path. The nuns stepped away into the grass to let her pass, and pulled their skirts aside. That family would never be right with the Church again.

But there was one they forgot. I don't know if the nuns could have healed her even then, but Bryvyth never thought of it. It cost her dearly afterwards. She lost the place that was dearest to her heart, not to the Saxons but through a slip of a girl barely come to womanhood.

I was as bad as the rest.

We'd none of us noticed there was something else between Ygerne and the Pendragon. A tiny black figure out on the bridge of stone. Morgan. Alone on that causeway. Facing a whole army. With the wind tearing her hair backwards like a raven's wing.

Chapter Twenty-Two

Ygerne stopped. It wasn't the drop to the sea she was afraid of, but her own daughter, staring at the Pendragon's army as though she could kill them with her fierce green eyes.

It was a fearsome place, that causeway. No walls on either side, not even a handrail. And the breakers so far below it made you giddy to look, smashing themselves on those rocks, one after the other, 'til the end of time.

We all seemed to stand there bewitched, nuns, warriors, king, lady, as if she'd put a spell on us. Then I straightened my shoulders. After all, she was my little maid. I'd carried her in my heart these eight years. And likely enough she was the last child that would ever be put in my lap to nurse. If her own mother couldn't go to her across that gulf that separated them – and it was more than sea-wind and gusty air – then I would, who had lived closer to her than her own blood.

There wasn't one of them tried to stop me. I walked past my lady, who was stopped as still as a standing stone, and down to that road of rock. The king was riding slowly down the slope on the other side. I knew it must be him, with his two tall warriors on either side. I wouldn't let myself look at them.

I'd seen Morgan tense. She was as still as a

thin-backed stoat, rearing up in the grass when it sees its prey. And near nine years though I'd known her, I'd no notion what she might do next.

I was afeared of them all. That drop to the waves, the king and his soul-friend smiling beside him, that had tricked us, the hundreds of swords in front, and that big nun behind. And most of all, if you'll believe me, that fatherless child no higher than my own chest.

I thought I'd call to her as I stepped out on the bridge. But my tongue was dry, and the wind snatched the breath out of my mouth. The pounding of those waves seemed to crash through my head and drove all the sense away. And yet it felt so quiet where we were. Just the two of us in a world of our own, high up there in the blue air. My old feet shuffling without a sound over the soft turf towards her. Her back was turned to me. All this time she never stirred a muscle. I could only guess what she was going to do. The only bit of her that moved was her black hair streaming out past her shoulders in the wind.

At last I found my voice, when I was hardly an arm's length from her. And very gruff and sudden it must have sounded, fool that I was.

'Come here, my lover. Come to Gwennol. There's nothing you can do will bring your father back to us now.'

I saw her start, just as the stoat jumps in the air. And she was whirling round and flying at me, teeth bared and nails clawing. I stumbled backwards and lost my balance. I heard men's voices shouting and women's screaming, and I don't doubt my own scream was somewhere there amongst all the rest. I saw the blue sky wheeling past me, and then the flash

of the sea on the horizon. There was silver, then
emerald green, spinning closer underneath me, purple
weed, white surf, black rock, and I was falling towards
it. Something caught me at the last. I felt the jolt
through all my bones as I went pitching over the edge.
I heard the sound of cloth tearing and I knew I was
going again.

Then her hands gripped me hard. She hauled me
back from the brink and staggered on to the path with
me. I was sobbing and panting like a woman in labour.
But Morgan flung her little bony arms around me and
buried her head in my breast, weeping fit to break her
heart.

We clung to each other, so close you couldn't have
separated us. She sobbed, 'I'm sorry, Gwennol! I'm
sorry!' And I just stroked her tangled hair and gasped
her name, over and over, as though I had lost my wits.
And for all the terror of it, I have wished often and
often that I could have that morning again. That was
the last time Morgan, Lord Gorlois's daughter,
hugged me and cried in my arms.

Then she twisted apart from me and turned away.
When she faced me again she was a different person.
It was as though she had gone from me further than I
could ever reach. Her face was hard and cold as
stone. I knew then I had lost her for sure.

My fall had broken her spell. On the far side of the
bridge the king's voice called, 'Ygerne!' I looked up at
Uther Pendragon then for the first time. Tall, he was,
and he sat proudly on his horse, for all a little maid
had just stopped him in his path. The warrior on his
right hand wore his cloak tossed over his shoulder
now, and his armour twinkled in the sun. He watched
us all with a crooked smile. I didn't swoon over Emrys
Merlyn this time. I stood my ground between Tintagel

and all the men and faced him back. Even in the morning sunlight, with his hood thrown back, he had still a little of the look of Britael about him. But not enough for me to forgive him what he'd done.

When Ygerne heard Uther Pendragon calling to her, she seemed to come to her senses and remember who she was. She turned her back on those Christian nuns she'd knelt in front of, and lifted her head and smiled at him. Then she walked across that bridge of stone, straight past her daughter Morgan, as though she couldn't see her.

Widowed that very day she may have been. But in her white gown, with her hair loose on her shoulders, she only needed a wreath of flowers round her head, and she would have looked for all the world like a May Queen.

Chapter Twenty-Three

You may think by now that I hated Uther Pendragon. But that was before I knew him.

When my lady went out of Tintagel to go to him, there was nothing the rest of us could do but follow her, though Morgan hung back at the last. We passed the porter's lodge and went through the gate in the rampart, and suddenly Ygerne seemed to move as if she felt she was free. She almost ran to Uther.

And he sat on his horse, like the high king that he was, watching Gorlois's wife come to him, with a great, satisfied smile on his face. And a tall friend on either side of him.

As she passed Merlyn, she turned her face to him for a moment and their eyes met. They smiled at each other. Short and polite, it was, like two swordsmen meeting, searching out each other's strengths and weak points. I stopped short when I saw that and it made me shiver. For wasn't she Ygerne, that I'd nursed on my knee when she was still soiling her napkins? And hadn't I taught her all the wisdom that she knew? But there was a good deal more that I could have told her I'd kept to myself. So, duchess or no, who was she, that she could smile so boldly back at Emrys Merlyn, when I daren't? What had she got more then me, wise as I was, save a pretty face and a womb that could still bleed?

Then Uther sprang down from his horse to greet her as though she was already his queen. But now that she'd got him, she wasn't going to have him seem less than he was, in front of all those people. She sank down on the grass in front of him, with a great billowing curtsy, and bowed her head. She had beautiful hair, had Ygerne, thick and golden, and with her face hidden you couldn't have seen those first wrinkles in the corners of her eyes.

He raised her up, of course. Not daintily, either. It was like a great bear-hug, and they kissed each other as warmly as if they'd been man and wife. I daren't look at Morgan's face.

He had chariots waiting. Very sure of himself was Uther Pendragon. He never doubted that he could take what he wanted, even from the holy house of a nunnery. He lifted Ygerne into one, as if she had been an armful of swansdown. Then he turned to the two older girls and took Elaine by the waist.

She was crying now for her father, and for fear of the soldiers, I don't doubt, and all the sudden terror and strangeness we'd had these two days. He put his arms round her and held her close to him, and he whispered in her ear for a little while. When she lifted her head from his shoulder she smiled up at him and started to dry her eyes.

As for Margawse, I needn't tell you the look that passed between them when his arms reached out to take her. It's not for me to say if that one wept for her father. But she knew very well how tears could put a sparkle in her eyes. He wouldn't be the first she'd flashed her dewdrops at, by a long way. And never a red eyelid or a puffy cheek on her. Not like Elaine, that seemed to be the only soft-hearted one of them, though I've sometimes wondered if she was all she seemed. When he swung Margawse up into the chariot after her sister, they were a mighty long time separating his cloak-pin from the breast of her gown, and there were roses in her cheeks by the time he'd finished.

Then he turned to Morgan, but she twisted her face away from him. And his eyes met mine across her head. Bright brown eyes, he had, and laughing for joy because he'd got what he wanted. And, may the Mothers give me peace, I almost forgave him. I was an old woman, older by far than my lady, and I'd had many men. But that was all it took. One smile from Uther Pendragon. And if he could make me feel like that after all he'd done to me and those I loved, it was time I started thinking less hardly of Ygerne.

But Morgan wouldn't let his hands touch her. She sprang up into the chariot all by herself, and if she could have made those horses rear up and strike their hooves in Uther's face, you could tell by the look in her eyes that she'd have done it.

I'd dearly loved to have ridden pillion behind one of the men, the way I was feeling. But you don't expect the gentry to notice things like that. They'd all forgotten me. So they moved off, all those fine riders with their spears held high and their gay cloaks blowing in the wind and the horns sounding, and Ygerne in her chariot at the front. I was left to walk behind. And my parts were still sore.

I looked round for some sign of Sulian and the other two. But I never saw them again after that. Or Jordan and Britael. There'd be more than a few women weeping around Bossiney after that night's work, and many a week before Nectan and his like had finished singing litanies for the dead.

I trudged along the track choked with their dust.

173

Then I heard horse's hooves coming up beside me. A pure white mare. That startled me, as you can guess. What Cornishman would have dared put a leg over her? No ordinary one, anyway. We've been the people of Rhiannon's horse as long as anyone knows. So I didn't need to look further.

Well, it's one thing to be warned, but another thing to build a wall in the time you've got. That tall, lean man was close above me in his skirt of mail and his green mantle with the hood thrown back on his shoulders. A proper warrior he looked this morning. Nothing druid about him now, except for the mare. But for all he was smiling, I could see close up that his face was lined deep, as if he'd seen more blood and heard more screams than a man so young could bear lightly. So I knew he had the seeing too. And I pitied him, whatever he'd done.

He was looking down at me with green-grey eyes that went clean through my head and out the other side. It was not like the way King Uther smiled at a woman. But it set my blood beating like the drums on May-morning, I can tell you.

'Gwennol,' he said, very low and courteous. 'Gwennol Far-Sight, is it? Do you know who I am, this morning?'

That brought me back. I don't know how I dared, but I looked him straight in the face.

'Merlyn, I should call you, sir. This morning.'

'Merlyn, it is. So it seems there is more than one wise woman in Cornwall.'

And what did he mean by that, I wonder? There were many of us in Cornwall, but few higher than me.

'There are some that say so.'

'Then we should be allies, you and I. I serve the king and you the queen.'

'She's not queen yet.' It came out so sharp it might have been Morgan's voice speaking through my lips.

'But will be soon, when Gorlois is buried. And she is still your mistress. By daylight at least.'

'It was Lord Gorlois gave me my meat these fifteen years.'

I saw his hands tighten on the bridle, and I had a hard job not to flinch.

'Then listen, Gwennol Far-Sight. Listen to me well, if you have any love for Gorlois's youngest daughter. That's a wild young hawk you have in your nest. See to it that she keeps her talons away from the king's flock. He's a man that likes to have nothing stand in his way.'

I was too full to speak. I couldn't answer him. Couldn't any of those grinning red dragons understand what they'd done to my little maid? But for all that, when he spoke so grave, I was all of a tremble, and I couldn't look him in the eye any more. He saw too much.

Then all of a sudden he laughed. And before I could let out a gasp, he'd got me by the waist and swung me up on the horse behind him. And I had to cling on tight as we galloped back to the army. Me, Gwennol Far-Sight, on the white mare that should have run free without a bridle, with my arms round the greatest druid in all Britain. The Mothers forgive me, I think I was laughing.

I soon saw that it hadn't taken some others long to forget to cry, either. There was the king on his horse beside Margawse and Elaine's chariot, and teasing and laughing with them both. It was that plump little hen, Elaine, that surprised me. Giving him back jest for jest she was, as if she'd forgotten she'd ever been shy. Forgotten too that he'd just killed her father, and then done worse than that.

I'd never seen Elaine quicken to a man before. It was like seeing her come awake from a long sleep. All her life she'd been one for mothering things, kittens and dolls and such. And here was Uther Pendragon teaching her that if she wanted to be a mother she'd have to learn to be a woman first. And he was a man that taught that very well.

But Morgan was only a child with a flat chest, scowling at him. He hardly looked at her twice. He'd forgotten already how she'd made him check at the bridge. Only Merlyn would remember that. You couldn't fool those eyes. I knew that he'd seen that last change in her face as well as I had. He knew what it meant. There was one at least that would never forget her father . . . or her mother either. And if she lifted the first little finger against the Pendragons for revenge, it would be more than all my wisdom could do to keep her safe.

Well, it seems a great druid can be more of a fool where women are concerned than I thought.

We came in sight of the poor burnt roofs of Bossiney round. They sounded their war-horns again and the horses broke into a trot and Uther's men burst out with a victory-song. Then Merlyn gave a great whoop, and he kicked his heels into the mare and away we went, galloping in great circles around the dun. There was me clinging on to his waist for dear life, and Uther and Ulfin and Merlyn laughing their heads off and all their army with them. Shameless, they were, coming back to Gorlois's home singing like that, as though his women were cows herded in after a cattle-raid.

Chapter Twenty-Four

When Uther saw the state the place was in, he was all for taking Ygerne away at once. To be fair to him, he turned mighty pale when he learned how close his men had come to roasting her alive. Sometimes, afterwards, I'd pass him looking up at that hall-roof with a sick, scared look on his face. And if my guts were twisting worse than usual, I could find myself wishing he'd got what he deserved.

She wouldn't come with him. Not yet. I knew she had her reasons.

First, we had to bury Gorlois. Uther pitched a tent for Ygerne in the Great Meadow, and a snug little bower it made, with couches of lambskin and striped hangings at the door. There were shelters for the rest of us too, and the weather fell warm and blue, so we took no harm of it, in our bodies. I had a feeling that we were cattle put out to grass, in place of the herd we'd lost.

A sore time I had keeping Morgan off her father's body when they brought him home. A child shouldn't have seen it, hacked into bloody rags, with the splinters of bone showing through.

Uther gave Ygerne men, with orders to do whatever she wanted. Then he left us alone with our dead. Nectan came stalking out of the woods when he'd gone. A bit pale and hollow-eyed, but he hadn't been harmed. So many good, red-blooded Cornishmen lay dead, but Uther had left those white Christians alive to bury them.

I'll give Ygerne her due, she did Gorlois proud. Well, the way you put your man in the earth says what he was and that tells who you are. There's a deal of boasting even after death. The number of gentry that come, the size of the feast, the height of the stone.

If she'd had her way, she'd have done it in the old style, in a golden chariot, and full armour, with his sword and his shield and his hound, and much more besides. She knew what was fitting. But Nectan stopped all that.

'We brought nothing into the world, we take nothing from it. He has gone to one who offers riches beyond our dreaming.'

What's this world for? Are we supposed to throw it away like a worn-out clout? Nectan spent long enough sitting in his glade beside the pool, playing his harp to the birds. He seemed to like that. What's his heaven if it's more than the best of the best things on earth? Wine and feasting and song . . . and the women beautiful. Couldn't he feel the life that was in the earth he trod on? Life to death and death to life again. That's how it's always been. The dead are here, among the living. We do well to keep them sweet.

But the Christians buried my lord up on the headland beyond Tintagel. Bryvyth came striding up, with all her nuns, singing their litany for the dead. She stood across the grave from Ygerne and scowled at her many a time. My lady had made some sort of peace with Nectan, though I don't know how she did it. But never with Bryvyth. That nun had scolded Gorlois often for his wild ways. But I think she'd loved our black-bearded duke in a queer kind of way, or what passes among those white-blooded women for love. But I couldn't forgive her. She'd denied him what he asked her. She'd cost him his life, and what for? Did she think her prayers were stronger than a man's sharp sword? She hadn't even saved his honour. So I wasn't sorry when she got her comeuppance in the end.

It was a fine day for the funeral, and you could see all the way out to sea as far as Lundy. I heard them shovelling earth on to Gorlois's corpse and I stared across the waves at Tintagel. He might have been there now, wielding his sword on the bridge and laughing through his beard at the whole of Uther's army. Then I looked round for Morgan and I could tell she was seeing him too. Bryvyth was her enemy now along with all the rest.

Afterwards that priest buried Keby and the rest with the same words. As if there was no difference between them.

And then Uther came riding back and married Ygerne. And none too soon. I didn't need to wait for her belly to swell to know why she was looking so pleased with herself.

Uther Pendragon was still for taking her away to one of his palaces up east. But she wouldn't go 'til the child was born. I could have told him why, well enough. She was a beautiful woman, but she wasn't as young and light as she used to be. She wasn't going to appear before all those fine, slender ladies with her waist thickening like a tree-trunk, and too heavy to dance in front of them all. No, she'd wait 'til she had something better than beauty to show off to them. The king's first son. Gorlois had never given her a boy. Three times she'd waited to bear him a child, and each time it had been a girl. And the last time had been bitterest of all. So she'd use every bit of power I'd taught her now.

Well, he built Bossiney up for her again. He had walls made of fine, planked timber, instead of clay and wattle, and hung doors of carved oak, and put on a new thatch as gold as a buttercup. So in the end it was a handsomer place than it had been before. Then he had the walls painted inside with flowers in all the colours you'd see in a summer meadow. He even had the cheek to ask the nuns of Tintagel to embroider hangings for them, for they were known far and wide for pretty needlewomen. He should have known better. Bryvyth was no more afraid of him than she was of Gorlois. She told him no, and I'll bet she gave him the wrong side of her tongue, too. His cheeks turned purple when he got her answer, and the woman who brought it nearly lost an ear. So my lady and her daughters got out their own needles and set to work themselves, meek as you please. I didn't offer to help. There's things I can see far off, and things I can't see under my own nose, and it was fine work. So I stuck to plain stitching and mending.

Still, for all that, he built a chapel on the end of the hall, which was a thing Gorlois had never done. Nectan came and blessed it when it was finished. But there was another that had got in first.

It was the night after they'd dug the trench for the foundation. Something drew me outside to go and look. I caught him at it. He'd put up a circle, but he wasn't troubling to hold it. I stepped right through it, and hardly felt any hurt.

He was just dropping stones in to cover up what he'd done. But not so many that I couldn't see. He smiled at me like a little boy that you've caught with his fingers in the honey-pot.

'Well, Gwennol. We were here first, weren't we? We'll see which of us will have it at the last.'

There was someone else saw what he'd put there. Morgan had followed me. She never asked me what he was doing, or why. She didn't need to.

As soon as the roof of the hall was up, we all moved in and had a great feast. We were pretty merry that night, I can tell you. I looked up at that clean new thatch that hadn't a trace of smoke. And Ygerne's clean new husband, with the blood washed off his hands. But it was Merlyn I mostly had my eye on. He watched them both. I'd seen what he had put under the walls. He meant that hall to stand and he meant that marriage to stand, too. And he understood what had to be given to pay the price. Yet I had a shrewd idea Bossiney wasn't the place he really wanted, nor Uther neither. Time and again I saw them standing out on the headland, looking across at Tintagel Island. Like a baby hanging from its mother by the cord. Well, let them take it from the nuns if they could. I didn't know which would grieve me most. For men to have it that knew the old way, or women who followed the new. Either way, I'd follow what I knew, if I did have to wait till night fell.

Still, it seemed this marriage was going the way Merlyn wanted. I caught him once, running his hands down Ygerne's body just as if she was a figure he had carved himself. She was enjoying it, 'til she looked at his face. Then she pulled away from him saying, 'You may be a great magician, Emrys Merlyn. But there are some things only a woman can do.'

It wasn't his hands on her parts that displeased her. I could see that. It was his looking at her as if she was something he had tooled. Oh, she was very sure of her power just then.

So she sat smiling to herself and embroidering, while our sweet Cornish spring turned into a hard, hot summer. Then Uther Pendragon rode away to fight the Saxons.

That frightened her. She would have stopped him if she could. Many a time she'd feared that Gorlois might come back and find her old and barren. But as the years went by she hadn't seemed so worried about him getting killed. Now she'd got her new king, it was a different story. She kissed him bravely enough as she buckled his sword about him. But when he was gone, her pretty face crumpled up and she cried in my arms as she hadn't done since long before Gorlois died.

When I looked up, Merlyn was standing in the shadows, laughing at her without making a sound.

'Little fool,' he said. 'Did you think you could keep him? Do you suppose I gave him into your arms for a plaything? We gamble for higher stakes, the Pendragon and I. The survival of Britain.'

'And so do I!' she rounded on him. 'Do you think I want him dead before his son is born?'

'Born to *what*?' he roared. 'A few stones and bogs? The last black lakes and the sea-lochs of the west? The hollow mountains of the dead? All that will be left of Britain if the red dragon fails!'

She turned white, and put her hands on her belly. She knew the danger she was in now. Her face grew thinner as her body thickened. If Uther should fall, there were few of those fine folk outside Cornwall that knew their new queen or cared about her, and none of Gorlois's kin in Cornwall left to love her.

Merlyn left us too before Midsummer. He was one of those that lean more towards the sun than the moon. He'd have his holy place in those stone circles they call the Giants' Dance.

She turned to me then. She begged me to help her weave a strong spell of safety for Uther's return.

I snapped at her, 'If your spells fail, take yourself to your priest and his prayers! It wasn't me you looked to, to bring a king to you. Why should I help you get him back?'

Well, believe it or not, she went. When she was desperate she'd try anything. I never understood what hold that bloodless saint had over her. What power could he use that wasn't forbidden him? Or was it her that used him? But she'd come back from his cell with some of the lines smoothed out of her face, though there were traces of tears on her cheeks too.

And, may the shade of Gorlois give me peace, I softened a little and put what strength I had left to hers. It wasn't just for the sake of Uther's bright, brown eyes, either. The Pendragon was our king now, and her wedded lord. He was all we had.

He came back, in the heat of summer's end, and mightily pleased with himself. The red dragon was driving the white back. Then the drought broke, and from then on it was teeming rain. We were all shut up in Bossiney, waiting for the child to be born. All except Merlyn. Storm or shine, you could no more hold him in one place than you could trap the wind. He'd be in and out, like the sun on a March day. And where he went to, none of them dared to question.

The days grew short and cold, and the wheel-ruts were full of water, and every dog in the place had mud up to its shoulders. You could leave your shoes by the hearth at night, and in the morning they'd still be cold and sodden.

Our world got very small. We couldn't go out, and the mist was so thick you couldn't see the woods

beyond the gate. It even drove Morgan home from the
cliffs. All summer she'd run wild at the edge of the
sea, with her legs growing longer now, so that it was
more than I could do to keep pace with her. I'd had to
let her go. I'd hoped the sun would heal her wound
and the wind wash her mind clean. But too often I'd
come up with her and find her kneeling on the very
edge of the cliff, staring down at the surf on the rocks
as if she wished herself dead. Now winter had come
and she was like a cat in a cage. The rain made
prisoners of us all. We began to feel as if we were the
only people left in the world.

Seeing King Uther pacing up and down the hall I
used to wonder how long it might be before he got
tired of his new lady. I remembered what they'd told
me about his great cities of stone, like London and
Winchester, and the houses the Romans had built,
with pools of hot water to bathe in. What had we got
to offer but a wooden bucket in a poor wooden dun,
for all it might be a bit grander now than we'd been
used to.

Hours I spent worrying about those fine ladies of
Britain, and how Uther might go rutting after them.
And I thanked my stars the seas were closed as well
as the roads, or I could see he'd have been off. Yet I
never saw the danger under my own nose. A blind old
fool I must have been, too, and never ought to have
been called wise.

My lady – it came hardly to me to say 'the queen' at
first – had sent me to the store-house to fetch more
wool for spinning. I was coming back past the treasury
when I heard the sound of voices inside. A man and a
woman. That pulled me up short. There were none,
only Uther's trusted guard, that had the right to go in
there. Then I shrugged my shoulders and started to

move on. What was it to me now what the queen's women did with the king's soldiers? I'd seen many women this year made widow first and mother after, and maybe by the same man. I wasn't standing out in the cold to bother with them.

It was her laugh that warned me. She hardly bothered to smother it. I'd known that laugh for thirteen years. Well, that moved me sharp enough then. Another step, and I'd have flung that door open and caught them both with their breech-clouts down, and praying I'd be in time to stop the worst.

But as I reached for the latch I heard the man's voice, low but clear enough. The blood left my face. Margawse and Uther Pendragon? I'd known she was shameless, but I never thought it had gone that far. Wouldn't she even stop at the man who was now her father?

I was shaking all over, for to tell you the truth, I was more than a little frightened of the Pendragon, for all his flattering ways. I thought of what Merlyn had warned me, how he was a man that liked to have what he wanted. And I tell you, I felt older and more tired then than I'd ever felt before.

Still I couldn't leave it without knowing the worst. I moved very softly to find a knothole to peep through. He'd got her up against the wall, facing me. I got a glimpse of her white thigh, and her skirt up round her waist. I was squinting round to see how far he'd got himself.

Just then, like a small black cat creeping over the mud, Morgan comes sidling up to me. She must have been watching it all from the shadows of the door across the path. She slipped her hand into mine and looked up at me with a small, sweet smile I hadn't seen much lately.

'You can't stop them, Gwennol. I don't want you to. Don't worry. She doesn't love him, you know. And she doesn't love Mother, either. None of us do. Margawse will avenge Father in her own way.'

And that was a chilly thing for a child of nine to say.

Well, I couldn't stop it. But a few more months and I'd have to give that young woman something to stop what might come from it. I still had power enough for that.

I was back in my lady's bower before Uther was. The fire shone red on Ygerne's face, and when he came in his was red too. He smiled down at her and kissed her long and softly, and put his hand on her belly and down between her thighs. A smile from Uther Pendragon is worth rubies from another man.

Then the door swept open with the wind. But it wasn't Margawse this time. Merlyn was with us again in the firelight. Weeks, he'd been gone from us, and nobody ever asked where he went. But he came dancing in now, dressed all in leather, sewn with little bells that rang when he moved, even to the pointed cap on his head. He looked a proper fool. He rubbed his hands and called for hot wine, and he and Uther Pendragon hugged each other, like a couple of schoolboys wrestling. When they parted, Merlyn looked pretty keenly at Ygerne's belly and smiled to himself when he saw how it had swelled. He always had that cunning look on his face as though it had been his own doing, and not Uther's.

Merlyn stayed close by us then. We were coming to the darkest time of the year. My lady was often tired and resting in bed, but Uther Pendragon always had Margawse and Elaine to laugh and flirt with and keep him company. When the rain fell, they used to get out the chequer-board and play the game of the hunt. I sat in the corner, stitching in the firelight and listening to the harper, 'til my head nodded. What they did when I slept, I shouldn't like to say.

Merlyn sat by the fire with me, watching all of us, or maybe jumping up to show off some trick of his own. I never saw him sleep. I never got used to that. Emrys Merlyn sitting across the hearth from me, as it might have been man and wife. He witched my thoughts, like the rest of them. It wasn't him I should have been thinking of. But what I was worried about was nothing to him. Even he wasn't wise enough to see the harm that was coming of it.

Only Morgan never laughed or played with Uther. She'd rather go to bed early, without light or fire. But often I found her lying awake in the dark.

Chapter Twenty-Five

Midwinter's Eve. In Gorlois's time we used to keep it the proper way. The bonfire should have been stacked on the cliffs and the torch ready to kill the dark and bring the sun to life again, and all of us dancing and drinking around the fire.

But the storm blew and the gale kept us pinned down, like sheep under a hedge. That year I left the kindling of the light to hardier souls than myself. Besides, we had another birth to wait for. Her pains had started. She'd given orders not to let me into her chamber, and that made me angry. But I couldn't help myself. This was my business, before anyone else's. I got my things ready for what had to be done.

We had a bit of cheer in our own hall, but it wasn't like the roof-raising. Our new queen was missing and Uther had a face grey as a snow-cloud. He was striding up and down, up and down all evening, with the drinking-horn in his hand empty as soon as filled. He only stopped to stare at the fine shields and swords he'd hung on our new-painted walls. I dare say he was dreaming of a young hand that might one day hold them. I doubt very much if he was looking at the fine embroideries that Gorlois's daughters had sewed and thinking of their fair hands. He wasn't dreaming of another little maid.

The waiting put him in a sour mood for the dances

and bawdy games that we'd always used to chase
away the shadows of winter and put fresh heart into
the sun. And to tell you the truth, we were a little shy
when it came to dancing the hobby-horse in front of
him. The Cornish have always been Horse-people, and
he was a Dragon-man, and he still felt like a stranger
among us. So it wasn't like it should have been.

Then, like a clap of thunder, he rounded on us and
sent us all packing off to bed. Margawse started complaining. She ran to him and threw her arms round his
neck, kissing him and trying to wheedle another hour
of fun. There are few enough feasts for her liking, and
she was the only one, bar the hall-servants, that was
truly enjoying herself. But he threw her off as if she
was nothing to him now. Elaine had the sense to see
there was no arguing with him in this mood, and
between us we hushed Margawse and led her off to the
sleeping-hut. Morgan had got there before us, but she
wasn't undressed, and nothing I could do would make
her go to bed before that baby was born . So I worked
what I could and waited, 'til I could hardly keep my
eyes open, in spite of the draught. And little help I got
from Elaine and Margawse.

The child was slow in coming, as though he was her
firstborn. But for all it was long, they tell me she had no
great pain. And that was a wonder when you think how
Morgan nearly killed her, struggling to be born into the
light. The Pendragon's child just waited his time.

He came at midnight, as near as I could tell, when the
fires were low and the night at its darkest. Hours she
had been waiting, Morgan, that was his half-sister,
standing there in the wind and the rain, 'til her hair
was plastered to her head like seaweed on the rocks.

And then the curtain flew open and the woman's cry
went up that it was a boy, and it was all light. Light in

the queen's bedchamber. A great cheer from the hall and logs thrown on the hearth to make a great blaze, so that you'd think they were trying to set fire to the thatch again. And everywhere people running out of doors into the light to hear the news. Boys as young as Keby would have been, and women older than me. Uther went striding off into the queen's bower to claim his own.

Well, there was more cheering when he came back to us, looking like the sun itself, and called for more wine and mead to toast the baby's health. And all the lot of them went crowding into the hall out of the rain, even Ruan that had never left my lady's side since the pains began. She was so proud that night, to see her you'd think she had dropped the baby herself.

All except one.

When Morgan heard that cry, and knew that the Pendragon's child was born, and that it was a boy, she dashed off into the night like a wild thing. I knew then that I had lost her a second time, and the dark she'd gone to now was worse than before. I dragged a cloak over me and stumbled off after her, scolding and shouting her name. It was wasted breath, what with the wind tearing my words away and the water coming over my shoes. She wouldn't have listened, even if she could have heard me calling. But she was my little maid, my last baby. I couldn't cut the cord that bound us together, for all it hurt me.

So there was I, standing out in the storm between the dark where we'd been and the light where the new child was, and, believe you me, my cheeks were wet with more than rain for Gorlois's daughters. Then Margawse went dashing past towards the hall. She'd barely the decency to cover her shift. She wasn't going to be cheated of her wine and merry-making this time. Well, it took them different ways. Morgan wept, that night and many besides. But I dare say Margawse will laugh when she has her revenge. Elaine keeps her own council.

I felt sorely tempted then to go after Margawse. I like a drop of hot mead as well as anyone, and I was so chilled with wet and cold I was aching in every joint and bone. And traitor you may think me, but I'd worked hard enough with Ygerne to bring that boy into the world. I had something to celebrate now, after all my trouble.

But there was another thirst on me too. Some of you will understand what I mean. It was a long time since I last held a baby in my arms. And none that were given to me to look after had been boys. I was a lively young woman when I took Ygerne from her wet-nurse. I could race on the beach with any lad, and wrestle too. But she'd never had brothers. Or sons, either. And now at last she had done for King Uther what she never did for Gorlois of Cornwall. She had given him a son, a prince of Britain. And the little babe was there, just behind that curtain, lying on the pillow of her bed.

I scratched softly at the door, but I knew no one could hear me for the wind. So I slipped inside. My lady was lying with her eyes closed and her body under the covers as slim as a girl's again. There was only the midwife left, sitting on a stool beside her. And she was nearly asleep after all her work, with a great jug of mead steaming on the floor by her side.

And there on the bed between them, wrapped in white bands, was that precious baby that we had waited for so long. Fair, he was. Handsome. I never saw a child come out of the womb so perfect. Not a wrinkle on him, nor a red mark anywhere. He lay so peaceful, in a pool of lamplight, with not a thought of what his coming had cost his sisters. His eyes were open, looking up at me.

And for all that I might be bitter towards the king and queen, I lost my heart to their child. He was only a baby, and it wasn't his fault. When I looked down into his little face, there wasn't a thought in my head about Morgan.

Chapter Twenty-Six

Ygerne was looking as pleased with herself as a cat
that's found a fat salmon. You could almost hear her
purring as she smiled at me. Her hair was brushed
out around her on the pillow, like an unbound sheaf of
corn. She'd had Ruan bathe and tidy her pretty
quickly before the king came, and the lamplight was
kind to her. She was beautiful before, it's true, but
there was something else glowing through her now. I
hadn't seen her as happy as that, not even when she
got her pretty Elaine.

Yet I noticed her eyes were a bit anxious, as though
she thought it might all be a dream. My hand was
reaching out almost by itself, and wanting to stroke
that baby's soft cheek, when she caught at my wrist.

'Is he pleased? Gwennol, is the king pleased now?'

I could feel by the tightness of her fingers how
much she must have been afraid these nine months.
She had taken a high risk. It was like walking over
that causeway again. One false step to left or right
. . . It might have been a stillbirth, or another girl. But
she'd passed the danger, and now her king was waiting on the other side, laughing, with his arms open.

'He's as happy as a boy with his first sword. That is,
if he's still sober enough to remember what he's
celebrating.'

My eyes strayed to that big jug of mead on the floor.

But it was three parts empty already. The midwife saw my look and pulled it closer to her skirts. She wasn't going to share what she'd earned so dearly, though I could see the glint of gold under her other hand too. Uther would have given her something more lasting to remember him by. He'd be a generous lord to anyone who so much as smiled at him that night, now that he'd got what he wanted. He'd even have slapped the shade of Gorlois on the back if my lord had come back to haunt him.

Ygerne had let go of my wrist. She had the baby in the crook of her arm and she drew him close to her side. The two of them stared up at me. Two pairs of round blue eyes, they were. Smiling. Both half-asleep. I could see there was nothing for me here.

I suppose I could have softened towards her a bit. Stroked her forehead, or kissed her cheek, as if she was still my little maid, and asked her to let me hold the baby. But somehow my pride wouldn't let me. I was dying to touch him. But I wouldn't beg him from her. I don't know how to explain it properly, but I felt as if that boy was ours by rights, and she and Uther had stolen him from us.

So I turned on my heel without telling her about Morgan, and went off over to the hall to soothe my hurt and drink the rest of the night away. It was as hot and noisy as a smith's forge. By the time I'd had two cups of ale inside me, the world looked a rosier place. Elaine was there now, still soft-eyed and pink with sleep. As pretty as her mother. But she'd taken the trouble to put on a proper gown, and braid her hair. Uther had his arm round her. His face was red and his drinking-horn was not as steady as it should be, for all he was a strong man who could hold his liquor well. He'd need helping to bed when morning came. I

looked round for a flash of red hair and there was
Margawse, with her shift unlaced at the neck under
her scarlet cloak, flirting with half a dozen of Uther's
young warriors.

There was someone else too. Crouched on the stones
in the corner of the hearth, as if the cold had got right
into his bones. Merlyn. It's a funny thing, but he
seemed a different person each time you saw him. He
was a man that came and went. You never knew
when or how you would see him next.

He was here now, all right. But not looking at all like
what I'd expected him to do on such a night. He had
an old goatskin pulled round his shoulders, that stank
to high heaven, and the rest of his clothes were in
rags. A proper beggar, he looked. But what gave me a
start was how old he seemed. Older than I'd thought
he could have looked, for a man that usually carried
himself so tall and moved as if he was going to break
out into dancing at any moment. He wasn't dancing
now. And it wasn't lime that made his hair look white
this time. It was as if that little boy that had just come
into the world had drained all the life out of him and
left him an old man.

He saw me coming and raised his beaker to me. I
wondered then if he had Margawse's fever, for his
eyes were red and watery. He hardly had the strength
to lift his arm.

That cheered me up and put a bit of pride back into
me. I felt a bit like Ygerne then, and there must have
been a pretty broad grin on my face when I walked up
to him.

'Well,' I said. 'You may have brought the stallion to
our mare. But there are some things even Emrys
Merlyn can't do. It needed woman's wisdom to bring
this foal into the world.'

Me, pulling Merlyn's leg, like a milkmaid with a farmhand. I must have been drunk already. He sounded so weary as if it cost him an effort to talk.

'There are many things that Emrys Merlyn cannot do, or the world would not be as it is. And where were you, Gwennol Far-Sight, when this foal was dropped?'

That made me wince. He meant it to.

'I was working my weft, never your fear. I still have power, though I get little thanks for it these days.'

'I told you, Gwennol. We should be allies. Our time is passing. A little space of sunshine before the storm comes. I need your help.'

'Me? Help the Pendragon?'

'Not him. All *this*.'

He stared out then with a wild, flashing sort of look in his eyes, as if the walls weren't there and it wasn't pitch-black night. There was no telling how far he could see across the land.

I couldn't understand what he meant. I was looking round for something else. And what I was hoping to see was a draggled black thing, like a half-starved cat, that might have crept in out of the storm at last for a bit of shelter and comfort. But I hadn't much faith I'd find her here, and I was right. No matter where I looked, there wasn't a sign of Morgan. Still, I worked my way round the crowd thinking she might have slipped into one of the side stalls where Uther's warriors slept, and curled up in the straw. I found more than a few merry couples enjoying themselves but I couldn't find her. Fuddled I might be, but I started to worry where she might have got to on such a night as this. I could curse my way past a closed gate after dark even now, if I had to, though Uther's warriors were not so feared of me as Gorlois's Cornish boys had been. A little maid like Morgan

couldn't. But she didn't need to. She was as nimble as
a cat. I knew she could be over that rampart in two
shakes of a duck's tail. And who was going to stop her
in the dark? She could be on the cliffs by now. I
pushed that thought away. It was like watching a rat
poke its head out of the wall, and then turning your
back and trying to pretend to yourself that you
haven't seen it.

I needed another beaker of ale. As I pushed my way
back round the hall I saw two figures, like giants they
were, on the dais. The fire was throwing their
shadows high on the wall behind them. Uther was
leaning his fist on the high table to hold himself
upright, and Merlyn was standing over him now. He
was drawn up to his full height again. It struck me
then that Merlyn was the taller of the two, though
Uther Pendragon was a big man. Merlyn didn't look
old now, though his hair was white, and he was the
only sober man in the room. He had a clear, singing
voice. He kept it low, but I could hear it through all the
shouting.

'You made a promise, Uther. On the honour of your
father's grave you vowed the boy to me before ever he
was conceived. It was a fair bargain. I have fulfilled
my part. Now keep yours.'

Uther's fist thumped down on the table. But he
wasn't sober enough to keep it steady.

'But he's my son! My only child.' The drink was
slurring his speech. He'd be crying soon.

'And therefore most precious and most vulnerable.
Our time is shorter than you think. These days are
dangerous. I must have the boy. Soon.'

'When?'

But Merlyn looked up and saw me watching. And ill
though he'd looked, in three strides he was across the

hall like a hawk swooping. He towered over me, and I was mortally afraid. His eyes glittered, and not with firelight either. He gripped my arm like a noose round a hare's neck.

'Gwennol Far-Sight! So it seems your ears pierce the distance as well as your eyes.'

We weren't allies now. We were no milkmaid and farmhand.

'I was only watching out for my young ladies, sir.'

His eyes swung round the hall, and he muttered under his breath, 'Elaine. Margawse.' Then his fingers tightened on my arm, 'til I fairly yelped. 'And where is Morgan?'

I couldn't meet his eyes.

'It all happened so quick. When the baby was born she went dashing off into the storm like a mad thing. That great fool of a man . . .'

'The baby! The queen's bower? Are you sure she's not there?'

A blacksmith's pincers couldn't have gripped me harder.

'No, sir. It was the first place I looked. There was only the midwife with them. And the little babe was dropping asleep, bless him.'

I didn't tell him it wasn't any thought of Morgan that had taken me there. His hand let go of my arm and he seemed to draw his breath a bit easier. But he wasn't satisfied yet.

'I have business to finish with Uther. Find her, Gwennol. And watch her well these next few days. I warn you, do not forget Morgan. Even for a moment.'

He didn't exactly push me out of the hall. But he looked at me so stern that, I don't know why, I turned and went out into that storm without another word. Merlyn wasn't a man you said no to.

All the same, when I came to, I wasn't best pleased at finding myself the wrong side of that door again. I'd never had that last beaker of ale and it was sheeting down with rain. I looked in our sleeping-hut, but she wasn't there. So I crossed the path to the queen's chamber again, just to make sure.

My heart was beating fast as I opened the door.

They were all three asleep. Ygerne with her face half-buried under her hair. The midwife rolled on the floor, snoring. And that sweet baby tucked up in a wicker cradle all threaded prettily with ribbons of gold.

There was no one to see me now, so I bent my old stiff back and reached out my hands to take him up.

I never heard her coming, but her shadow fell over the basket and made the baby blink. I felt who it was, like a chill in the room when the wind has changed. She was standing close behind me. The water was running out of her hair in rivers, and her dress was black with rain. But she smiled at me sweetly. Oh, very sweetly she smiled!

'Poor Gwennol,' she said. 'Did you think he would be your baby? Did you think they would give him to you when the wet-nurse has finished with him? Were you dreaming of dressing him, and playing with him, and singing him to sleep, as you did with Gorlois's daughters? Don't you know who he is? He's the eldest son of the King of all the Britons. He'll be the greatest prince in the land soon. Fine ladies will feed him gruel. Court bards will sing him lullabies. And the wisest scribes in Christendom will teach him. Did you think they would leave him here in Bossiney with you?'

Oh, she was clever for nine years. Like a hot poker to the eyes it was. Yes, I'd been a foolish old body, dreaming what I had dreamed. And it didn't hurt any the less for knowing she was right. It was the way the child did it. She knew she was all I had left now, but she'd enjoyed bringing tears to my eyes. They'd killed the light of her life, so she'd put out the light for the rest of us.

Her voice woke Ygerne up. She opened her eyes and saw her daughter.

'What is it?' she said, and you could see her move quick to gather the baby close to her. But the pillow was empty. Well, her eyes went wide with fear.

But Morgan laughed and swooped for the cradle. She had the baby in her arms before any of us could stop her. Then she looked up at us with her green eyes, as wide and innocent as you please.

'What's the matter with you all? What are you staring at? He's my little brother, isn't he?'

She bent her black hair over his face and we thought she was kissing him. Then the baby let out a yell. And when that maid lifted her head, there on his tiny white neck were the red marks of her teeth.

Chapter Twenty-Seven

Those few short days before Christmas I never had an easy moment. I'd been used to letting Morgan run free. She was a child that needed to be left on her own. In summer, as long as she didn't wander into the forest, I'd let her play where she wanted amongst the bramble brakes or paddle her way through the pools on the beach. Just so long as she didn't get quite out of my sight. She might seem to be reckless, but she never came to harm that way. It was Margawse I'd worried about. Tossing her red hair and flashing her green eyes at every man in the dun.

But now I had worse than that to fear. I had lost my little Morgan that I had wept over so many nights when we never thought she would live to see nine summers. When I looked at her white face now since the year had turned, it was just as if there was a stranger in the room. And no child either. Hours she would sit silent, brushing her black hair 'til it shone like a chough's wing and cleaning her nails. And where was my little maid that used to run home to me with her hair tangled in the wind and her hands full of sea-shells?

And then suddenly I'd look up and she would be gone, like a soul out of the body. Only her empty stool beside the door. My blood turned cold each time and the first place I'd run would be my lady's rooms. Her women would be there, or the wet-nurse, and that sweet boy that still had no name, and all looking as peaceful as a field of lambs in spring. And there I'd stand panting in the doorway like a silly old fool, staring at them. And as like as not, when I got back to our own hut Morgan would be there, sewing in the light from the doorway. She'd lift her green eyes and smile at me. But there wasn't any warmth in her smile now, and no kindness either.

Still, she hadn't learned to be deceitful then, though there were others who'd deceived her cruelly. Sometimes she would sit scowling over her work, then jump up suddenly and laugh in my face. She'd be off like a greyhound, straight to her mother's room for everyone to see. And all the women would start to their feet and pull their skirts away from her. They all feared her. The one that was nearest would snatch up the baby, and Morgan would burst into laughter at their looks. She enjoyed frightening us. But I wonder now if she hadn't been crying out to us to stop her.

Hours, I lay awake worrying over her. For who was there to keep her now from harm? Merlyn had the strength, I didn't doubt that, but he'd sooner have cursed her than taught her what he knew. I even thought about the white nuns on Tintagel. Yes, you may stare at me. But they hadn't saved her father, or her mother either. There was only me.

I was sorely tempted then. I knew where there was healing for her hurt. I had led her mother and sisters down that way. But when it came to Morgan, still I drew my hand back. There was this strong feeling on me, as if there was a barrier across the path that I daren't cross. I knew that once I took the first step down that road with her, that way would lead deeper than I wanted to go. Deeper than I'd been myself. And

who knows what would come of it? It frightened me.
So I held my peace. I don't know if I did right.

Still, I couldn't be watching her all the time.
Morgan had hurt me deep, saying what she had about
the baby. But it was no more than the truth. He
wouldn't be with us long. Who's to blame me if my feet
were sometimes straying to that bower when Ygerne's
back was turned?

On Christmas Eve, Merlyn, that had been with us
since the boy was born, packed his bags to go. It was a
strange time to be taking to the road, but that was the
way he was. He never said where he was going and we
didn't ask. We crowded round him in the yard as they
saddled his white mare, and the two of them were
dancing about as if they were in a hurry to be gone. The
wind had changed. It was blowing from the north now,
chasing the rain away and freezing the puddles.

And just as we thought he was ready to ride off,
there was a flurry of white in the gateway, like a
shower of hail.

Nectan, with his cloak blowing round him. Come to
shrive us all before the feast of Christmas. Well, what
those Christians call a feast. To tell you the truth, I'd
forgotten about their holy day. I had so much else on
my mind, good and bad, just then.

We were coming into their time now. It was too raw
weather for his bell to gather everyone in the open
air. There'd be candles in the chapel and the hall.
He'd spread his table with a fair cloth, a book, a
chalice and a dish. And he'd make our rafters ring
with his hymns. A very different sort of singing from
Midwinter's Eve, that would be, though he did it gladly
enough. It always surprises me, that folk that live so
thinly can sing so heartily as that. Uther's warriors
would make a brave sound singing with him.

Then I turned my head, and I saw something that startled me. Merlyn had forgotten the Christians too, or I could tell he'd have gone sooner. It had struck me often that when the chapel bell called us for Sunday or a Christian feast-day, Merlyn always contrived to be somewhere else.

There was a cloud passed over his face when he saw that lean saint coming, and it made me feel queer for a moment. He looked so old. I don't just mean tired and white, like he had after the boy was born. No, worse than that. You'll think me daft but you might have seen such a look if you'd invited the Old Ones to join you at Samain, and the Older Ones had come in their place. The ones our own gods drove under the hollow hills when they took the land.

I thought Nectan checked too at the sight of Merlyn. He crossed himself. I don't think he was afraid. More like a man buckling on his armour. Though I wouldn't have blamed him if he had to screw up his courage. Then he gathered his muscles together and came on. They didn't say anything. Just looked at each other, eye to eye, like two warriors before a battle.

Yes, I thought. That fool of a hermit should have listened when Gorlois warned him.

It didn't last long. I don't think anybody saw it but me. Next moment a smile broke out on Nectan's face, and he turned to Uther.

'Well, your honour? Is your new son keeping healthy this cold weather? I must talk with you about his christening.'

Uther clapped him on the back and laughed.

'All's well with the queen and her son, thank the Lord. Go in and warm yourself by the fire. They're ready for you in the chapel. Give us a moment to bid farewell to Emrys Merlyn.'

The saint thanked him and strode indoors out of the frost.

I had known Merlyn for a man that was very sure of himself. He was like a piper that could make all of us dance to his tune. And he was always quick with a jest or a clever word. But I saw for a moment he didn't know what to do when the saint spoke of the christening. He almost looked as if he was thinking of unpacking his saddle-bags. Then he grinned at us sudden, with that queer one-sided smile of his.

'I don't wait to give my gifts 'til Christmas Day,' he said.

And I knew then I was right. I don't doubt he had his plans to make for the boy, but we shouldn't see him again until the psalms and the prayers were over.

But he wouldn't let the Pendragons forget him. He reached down into his saddle-bags and drew out something for all of them. Fine, feast-time gifts they were. He gave Margawse a bronze mirror. Beautifully patterned on the back, it was, with leaves and song-birds' heads. I knew she'd be hours admiring her pretty face in it. And for Elaine he had a little case with fine bone needles, and a pair of scissors shaped like a swan's beak, and skeins of coloured silks, that made her turn pink with pleasure. Uther got a set of dice in a silver cup, and Ygerne a golden comb. I didn't see what he handed her for the baby.

I must have been as daft as the rest of them, pressing round him, hoping for a smile before he said goodbye. His eyes met mine. Grey eyes, he had, like the blade of a fine sword. He looked at me keenly. And when he did smile, I felt the thrust of it deep inside my belly.

'Come here, Gwennol,' he said, and reached into his leather satchel again. 'This is for you.'

Well, I gasped. I'd never expected him to give me anything. A red shawl, it was, that he told me was made of goat's hair. I stood with it over my arm, stroking it, for I'd never had anything of my own so fine and soft, and I could feel the warmth of it already in the cold wind. I know he laughed at my face. Years, I kept that shawl.

When it came to Morgan's turn I was sure she wouldn't be there to see him off. But she was standing a little way off, leaning against the doorpost of our hut, watching us from the shadows that were blue with frost. Merlyn took out a little hunting-knife, with the bone handle carved like a boar, all bristles and tusks. It was a rare piece of craft. He held it out to her.

'For Morgan to stab us all in the heart with,' he said. And the smile never got past his mouth.

Last Christmas Morgan would have loved a present like that more than any pretty thing her sisters had. Wasn't Gorlois the finest huntsman in all Cornwall? And didn't she ride at his heels whenever he would take her? She'd have run straight off with that knife and played that she was the son her father always wanted.

But Gorlois was dead. And this Morgan was a stranger to us. She'd never hunted with Uther.

She said angrily, 'That's a boy's present. I'm a woman now.'

Though she wasn't yet. Not as I understand it, anyhow. Merlyn knew that too. He smiled down at her slowly, and even, I thought, a bit sadly.

'When Morgan, daughter of Gorlois, becomes a woman, then the whole of Britain will have something to fear.'

She looked at him and there was doubt in her face,

as if she feared he was laughing at her. She let the knife fall to the ground between them. Then she turned her back and went inside our hut.

'Watch her,' he said to me sharply.

He took my arm then, over that red shawl, and his eyes held mine.

'A little time we must keep him safe, Gwennol. A few more days. And then you may leave the future to me. Watch Morgan.'

I knew what he meant, though I was too choked to answer him.

Then he kicked his heels into the mare's sides and cantered out of the gate with everyone waving and calling after him.

When he was past the oak I turned my eyes away. I was quicker to be rid of him then than I had been that first time. I remembered I had to pick up the knife. It was too fine a thing to be left lying in the mud. But someone else had got there first.

Nectan had come out into the yard again. He was holding the knife out to Morgan. It seems they were the only two in the whole dun who hadn't been caught up in Merlyn's glamour.

'This is yours, I think,' he said. He smiled at her pretty kindly for a childless man. 'It's a good blade. You could whittle a piece of boxwood with it to make an angel for the Christ-child's crib.'

She turned away from him without a word, as she had from Merlyn.

He must have felt me watching. He faced slowly round.

'Well,' I said, with a grim sort of smile. 'The son of a holy virgin, is it?'

He had the grace to laugh, though there wasn't much humour in it.

'Yes, Gwennol Far-Sight. You have the better of me there. I was a fool. Too trusting. But we grow wiser. He has run away and I am here. Uther will trust his child to me. And whose side are you on, Gwennol? Will you help me care for the child?'

I smiled at him, as innocent as you please.

'I have always cared for the child, sir. Since the day she was born.'

Fool of a man. He never even noticed.

He held out the knife to me.

'Will you give it to Morgan?'

He had bigger things to think about than that. So he never saw, as I did, that she had turned her head and was staring after him with a sort of hunger in her face.

I'll never forgive him for that. She'd seen he wasn't afraid of Merlyn. She might have turned to him then.

Yes! Don't hiss at me. I'd rather he had taken her for his Church, if it had made her happy.

But it was only the boy that mattered to any of them.

Merlyn had gone. Those that cared to told Nectan their sins. Then we sang their hymns, and made ready for another child's coming.

When it was done I went back to the sleeping-hut. Morgan was there. She was holding Margawse's mirror and smiling at her own reflection as she touched her hair. That gave me a start. Just for a moment she looked like a small, dark copy of her mother. Then she heard me coming and put the mirror down. She picked up Elaine's sewing-case and began to play with the scissors. I heard her draw her breath sharp. When I looked down, one of those dainty blades had pierced her finger, drawing blood.

But the hunting-knife lay on the chest beside her bed where I had left it. She never touched it.

Chapter Twenty-Eight

We kept that Christmas as we never had before. And it was the first of many days' feasting. Uther was as pleased with himself as a dog with two tails, and both of them wagging fit to bust. He carried the baby round the hall for everyone to say how handsome he was and how like his father. Tiny though that mite was, he dandled him on his knee through the mummers' play and the horse's dance and all the sword-swinging in the hall. He couldn't be done with showing him off to the world. I never saw a man tempt the gods so, not even Gorlois, and he was proud enough. In the end I couldn't stand it. I snatched the child off him and took him back to his mother. Let Uther show off his daughters now.

Well, as soon as he'd finished toasting his son he gave it out that he meant to marry Margawse off like Elaine to a king up north, beyond the Wall. They'd be betrothed just as soon as spring came and ships could sail north again to seal the bargain. I think he knew as well as I did we'd need to be quick about it. Margawse had come to her womanhood these last few days.

I didn't grieve over her when I heard the news. There never was a girl I'd be gladder to see wed. I'd had enough of her light-headed ways. Though it was no liege-man of Uther's she'd be marrying, by the sound of it, but a king that he had need to be better friends with. He'd sell Gorlois's filly off at a fair price, to keep the north at peace. At least I needn't fear her shaming us much longer.

And still the Pendragon's boy had no name. There were some that held that he was safer so. What has no name can't be named, and no one can get power over it. But some of the Christians had a different view of it. They said it was a dangerous time. If a child should die unchristened, their Heaven would have none of it, and it would become a pixie spirit, wandering the moors and leading baptised folk astray. But Nectan wouldn't have it was so. And I could have told them there were worse things than babies loose on the moor at night.

But we had no fears that this child would die before its time. You never saw a healthier baby. Day after day we watched him grow. His little cheeks were pink and full and his eyes bright and clear, and the winter sunlight seemed to catch in his hair. He was a child of the light, that one. Every day he grew stronger, like the sun. Many a time I'd make some excuse for passing the door so I could put my head round the curtain and have a look at him lying in his cradle. And if no one was looking, I'd pick him up and cuddle him, and croon in his ear the songs I used to sing his mother. We had no snow that winter, though it froze hard. But for once I was casting charms to make it long and bitter, with snowdrifts up to the roof. When the spring came, I knew what would happen. They would mount their horses and chariots, and Ygerne would take her son up in her arms, as proud as you please, and they would be gone, out of Cornwall.

Still, no good crying about it 'til it happened. We would make a great feast for him while he was still ours. So we kept that midwinter season as never before. I must say that Uther Pendragon was a merrier man than ever Gorlois had been, and a richer one too. It was a gay time we had, and Elaine and Margawse looked as merry as their mother, whatever they felt inside.

The boy was to be named on what they call the feast of Epiphany. Nectan had planned it. A double celebration, that would be, for the baptism of the King of Heaven and for King Uther's firstborn son. Uther had sent word to all the lords and ladies in Dumnonia to come to the christening, if the roads would let them. Bossiney had never seen anything like it in all my days. The kitchens were busy baking and brewing and roasting 'til the steam came out of the thatch so thick and wholesome you could almost taste it. Both hall and chapel were decked with armfuls of holly and ivy. And so many lamps everywhere, you'd think they'd never have found oil and fat enough for them all.

Uther thought he had Nectan dancing to his tune, though I wasn't so sure myself. The saint might seem pretty thick with the king and queen these days, but it was his own battle he was fighting with Merlyn over the boy. They were all the same. They only thought about him. But there was one thing made Uther frown. There was someone he could never wrap round his little finger, for all his bright eyes and golden gifts. Bryvyth had been bidden to the christening, with all the other high lords and ladies round about. She might live plainly, but she was a mighty learned woman, and they treated her just the same as if she'd been a bishop. And now she had sent back word from Tintagel she wouldn't come. Things had been done there that couldn't be mended. And that boy was at the heart of it. Uther and Ygerne made

more show of treading the Christian way than ever
Gorlois had done. They might fool Nectan, but it did
them no good with Bryvyth. The Church was never
best friends with the Pendragons.

So we came to Twelfth Night, and the boy was to be
named in the morning. And as if I wasn't busy enough
already, Margawse went down with the fever. It was
nothing more than a winter chill, and she was as
strong as a horse. But there was no one but me to
nurse her, and she was as cross as a dog that's lost its
bone because she was missing the last days of the
feast. She couldn't bear to be dull. And how I was
supposed to see to her and keep my eyes on Morgan is
more than I can tell. I took Elaine aside and told her to
watch her little sister closely and see she never left
the hall. But you'd need to be as watchful as an owl
and as fast as a hawk to keep up with that one. Elaine
was no match for her. She put me in mind of a plump
house-cat that keeps to the warmth of the fire and
doesn't like to get her fur dirty in the mud.

I wished Merlyn had stayed. Bryvyth spoke true
enough when she said he was a strange soul-friend
for a Christian king. He was as slippery as a trout. I
knew the times and the reasons, and I could guess
better than most some of the places he went. And
Merlyn knew that I knew. Many's the time he got up
from the bench and looked at me before he went out of
the hall with that quick half-smile in his eyes. And I
always felt that if I'd been only a little bit younger he
might have pulled me by the hand and whipped me off
with him. It's a strange thing to say, but I was never
sure whether he and I were friend or foe.

But surely he'd be back for the christening? He'd
had a way of talking to Uther almost as if the baby
belonged to him.

It fell dark early on the eve of Epiphany. The wind was rising 'til you could almost feel the earth shaking beneath you where the great waves were flinging themselves against the land. There was no rain with it this time. It would be bright moonlight a bit later on, if only the wind could tear a hole in the clouds. They were pressed thick across the sky now, like a black herd of galloping cattle.

The feasting-hall looked a brave sight across the yard, with all the lamps burning and the fire leaping up the logs. But there'd be no games for me that night. I was left sitting by Margawse's bedside. They sent us food, goose-meat and mead, and a bowl of good broth for Margawse. But it wasn't the same. There's no fun in getting drunk by yourself. I missed the company. It's a hard life we lead at Bossiney, though it was a sight gayer since King Uther was our lord, and midwinter had always been a time for laughter and a bit of horseplay and plenty to eat and drink. And what's the harm in that, even at my age, if it helps to see us through the dark of winter?

And besides, I couldn't have eyes everywhere. I'd sent Morgan off to the hall with her sister Elaine, both of them with their skin washed and the grease sponged off their best gowns and their hair plaited with silk braids. As quiet and demure as a little queen Morgan looked that night. But by now there wasn't one of us that knew what was going on behind those green eyes. So I wasn't easy.

Supper never seems to take so long when you eat it by yourself. I licked the grease off my fingers and picked my teeth and listened for the harp and the singing and the dancers' pipes. The music seemed to come and go between gusts of wind, like the sea. The mead was making me drowsy, but I could tell well enough when the food was finished and the horseplay began, by the noise. A great roar of singing and stamping. And no court bard's ditty, either, I can tell you. And they shouted louder than ever when it was finished. They'd be lucky if there weren't daggers out before the night was over, with all the wine and mead and beer I'd seen them taking into the hall. And in the morning, they'd all of them be nursing sore heads and walking to chapel like sober gentlefolk to see the baby prince baptised with his new Christian name. And he? He'd be fast asleep now, bless him, and not caring a bit for the noise they were making over his coming.

It didn't surprise me when Elaine came back early. She was never one for rough play and bawdy jokes, and there'd be plenty of that tonight. It would have been enough of a treat for her to serve the wine to Uther's guests at the high table in her mother's place. She was fourteen now. Her breasts were filling out and her cheeks thinning. She'd make a proper queen before long. But I was angry when I saw she hadn't brought Morgan.

'Where's your sister?' I said sharply. 'You haven't left her, have you, when I told you never to take your eyes off her?'

She tossed her head a bit more proudly than she used to. She had more than a little of her mother in her.

'You forget, I had more important things to look to, with so many guests.' Then she laughed and hugged me, like the old times. 'Don't worry, Gwennol. She wanted to stay and watch the sword-dancing. It's all right. Mother's still there with her.'

'And much good that will do,' I muttered.

It wasn't Morgan our queen would have her eyes on. In Gorlois's time she was more delicate. She'd have gone to bed earlier, with the baby so newly-born. But she was bolder now that she was Uther's wife. And who was I to blame her? I'm old enough to be her mother, and I'd sooner have been in the hall with the rest of them than stuck in the bed-chamber. Ygerne had come late to her crown, and she meant to have her fill of it.

Elaine must have known what I was thinking, for she said, 'Go on, Gwennol. Why don't you go and enjoy yourself? Margawse is asleep, and I'll be here if she wakes. And you can watch Morgan for yourself.'

I didn't need telling twice. I've never missed Twelfth Night. I'll sit down to a feast, any time. Old Religion or Christian, it's all the same to me, so long as there's plenty of food and drink and dancing.

As soon as I got to the hall I looked for Morgan. And she had gone from the table. I could feel the panic starting inside me. There was her mother laughing, and the king beside her. I looked everywhere. And then I saw her. Like a little black shadow in the corner by the hearth, behind the harper. Well, let her stay there. If the play got rough, she'd be out of the way of it there.

Oh, it was good to be squashed up on the bench among friends, and the warmth of their bodies better than any fire. There was still drink going round, and some scraps of food left, and I went on stuffing 'til I lost a tooth cracking nuts. They plunged hot iron in the mead, and passed it round fizzing hot. We were all more than a little merry.

Then the dogs began barking outside. All the men leaped up and reached for their swords, because who would be on the road in the dark, when the gates were shut and the yard-dogs loosed and food on the table? But we recognised that voice calling to the dogs through the wind. King Uther laughed.

'All's well,' he said. 'It's only Merlyn, come late to join our feast.'

Merlyn. On the eve of the holy-day of Epiphany? So he'd come back to battle with Nectan for the boy, had he?

The door crashed open, and the wind almost took the platters off the table. Merlyn stood there. He was dressed like a druid, in a white gown with bands of gold across his breast. He had a wreath of holly woven round his cap. But there was no smile on his face now. We just sat there gaping at him like fools. You could see his eyes going round the hall, and I shivered as they went over me. But they came to rest on Ygerne.

'Where is your child?' he roared at her.

And never mind that she had four.

Her hand flew to her mouth. She was as drunk and foolish as the rest of us. She didn't understand what he meant. But I did. Maybe I hadn't had time to drink as much as the rest, or maybe I'd seen more than was good for me. But my eyes went straight to the corner by the fire, and it was empty. Merlyn saw my face.

'And where is Morgan!' Like a river bursting into a house, his voice was.

He was running out of that door before I could get to my feet. He was in the queen's chamber by the time I came panting in. When I pushed past him I was mortally afraid of what I was going to see.

At first I thought the room was empty. Then I saw the wet-nurse, lying in her cot, dead-drunk. And that was all. The cradle was bare. No Morgan. No sign of blood.

Chapter Twenty-Nine

Ygerne let out such a scream, you could have heard it all the way to Land's End. But I'd feared worse than what I saw.

'Thanks be! At least she hasn't killed him.'

I don't think that boy's mother even knew what I meant. Wise woman or no, she'd been so besotted with her fine king she hadn't the wit to see what she was doing to her own daughters.

She was standing there, with her hand to her mouth and her blue eyes staring, crying, 'My baby! Where has my baby gone!'

Merlyn turned on her. I'd never seen him so angry, and it made me quail, I can tell you.

'This is at your door! Vain, foolish woman! I thought we were agreed. I gave you two kings. Was that too much for one woman to hold?'

'Guard your tongue!' King Uther shouted at him 'It is your queen you speak to.' But there were few of us that had much time for Ygerne that night. 'You, Gwennol! Is this Morgan's work?'

'Who else?' said Merlyn.

'By God! I should have sent the bitch to join her father!'

'Gwennol Far-Sight,' said Merlyn, gripping my wrists and looking into my eyes. 'Where would she take him?'

'Down to the sea,' I said, like a woman in a dream. I never stopped to think how I knew it.

Uther Pendragon was out of the door like a shot. Merlyn snatched up a fur from the bed and threw it round me. Then he gripped me by the elbow and bundled me out into the storm. My lady was left behind in a flood of tears. But there were plenty of folk crowding round to fuss over her.

'Which way?' shouted Merlyn. He had his mouth close to my ear, but I could hardly hear him for the gale.

I couldn't tell him. I had this picture in my mind, like the one thing you remember from a dream after you wake up. But where it was, I'd no notion. One wet rock looks much the same as any other on a stormy night.

So I set off as if I was going down to Bossiney Haven, because that's the nearest way to the beach. I could hardly walk for the wind. I had Uther Pendragon on one side of me and Merlyn on the other, and they were fairly carrying me along. When I looked back there were soldiers with drawn swords behind us. And all for a little girl not ten years old. Some of them had lanterns, though they hardly needed them. There was a queer sort of cloudy moonlight, between dark and light.

We hadn't gone far before I stopped. I couldn't say why, but I knew something was wrong. She hadn't come this way. I felt a power drawing me, and I knew she must have felt it too. I could tell now where she'd gone, all right.

There was a good deal of swearing and grumbling when we turned round. We went stumbling back over stones and potholes. But I made them follow me. I was like a hound that's picked up a fresh scent. Then the moon broke loose and we were up on the downs on the edge of the cliff, making for Tintagel.

Merlyn struck his thigh a great blow. And I could tell he was cursing himself this time for a slow-witted fool.

I'd have been plucked right over the cliff if I hadn't had those two tall men on either side of me, holding on. There was a sort of silver mist all round us, though the moon and stars were bright over our heads. The waves were crashing so hard against the cliffs they were sending the spray right up into our faces.

We were almost running now. Sometimes the wind seemed to push us back like a great flat hand. Other times it would come swirling round so I thought it would pick us up and carry us flying. All the time we were drawing nearer to that holy island.

But she wouldn't be there. It wasn't those white nuns she was running to tonight. She wouldn't cross that causeway a second time. I knew what drew her, though I'd never told her a word about it. She didn't need my teaching.

There was a way down to the beach before you reach that terrible bridge. It was a gully, running with water, and rough walking. The lower we got the wetter it was, with the spray coming down on us like rain. The roar of the waves was so loud it mazed your thoughts. I turned colder inside than out. For how could my Morgan and that precious mite be safe on the rocks in such a storm?

Then we got to the bottom and the cliffs sheltered us a bit from the wind. But we could still hardly hear ourselves speak, for the brook was hurling itself off the ledge in a great waterfall.

We could see the waves breaking on the point, shooting high walls of water up into the air, and the

flung spray turning to silver in the moonlight. But the
bay was quieter. A great black swell was running in.
Like hump-backed serpents coming at us, it looked. It
dashed itself against the rocks with a hiss a bit softer
than the crashes out on the point. The tide was full in.
There wasn't a foot of beach you could put a dry foot
on. I knew where Morgan had tried to take him, all
right. But the Mother's Hole would be full to the roof
with the sea now, and the stone in the middle drowned
deep by two currents of water. She couldn't have got
further than this.

I'd lost her heart long ago. But when I looked at
those black shining walls of water rearing up towards
us, I thought I'd lost her poor little body too.

Then we saw her. She was standing on a high pin-
nacle of rock with the waves pounding all around her.
How she got there, dear only knows. We wouldn't
have seen her, for the water was as black as the
mouth of hell, and Tintagel behind her was dark, as if
it had turned its back on us. If there was a glimmer of
light anywhere on it, we couldn't have seen it through
the spray. Likely those nuns were safe in bed, like the
good Christians most of them were. Still, for the first
time in my life I found myself wishing that Bryvyth
Crook-Staff might be awake and praying for us, up
there in the dark. We needed all the power we had
between us that night.

Even then we couldn't have seen Morgan with her
black hair and her gown dark with wetting. But she
had a little white bundle clutched to her chest, and
just then the wind blew back her sleeves and showed
her two white arms.

I must have drawn my breath sharpish. I heard
Merlyn hiss between his teeth, so I knew he'd seen
her too. But neither of us dared to utter a word.

Merlyn waved his hand at the men behind us to be still, though to tell you the truth, you couldn't have heard an army marching over the stones above those breakers. It was Uther broke the spell. He was always a man that couldn't bear to wait, never mind what it cost afterwards.

He swore a great oath and let go of my arm. And he drew his sword so fast it's a wonder it didn't take the head off my shoulders.

'Morgan!' he roared. 'Give him back to me this instant, or I'll skewer you like a sucking pig.'

My heart was in my mouth when he yelled at her like that. I knew her better than he did. A curse like that might have been all she was waiting for. I truly thought we'd seen the last of those two children then.

But she didn't even seem to have heard him at first. Still and black she was, like a woman carved out of bog-wood. And the ends of the baby's white bands fluttering in the wind like prayer-rags.

'Morgan!' he thundered at her.

The wind dropped just then, so that his voice came echoing back off the cliffs.

She turned her head, and looked over her shoulder towards us.

'If you come one step closer, I'll drop him into the sea.'

My heart fairly broke for her when she said that. I knew what it meant. If she'd really wanted to kill her brother, it would have only taken her a moment. She needn't have carried him all the way through the storm to here. One stab with that hunting-knife Merlyn had given her, and it would have been all over and done with. His little life-blood running away on the bedchamber floor, and the Pendragons punished.

But she hadn't killed him yet. I think she couldn't do

223

it unless they drove her now. How long had she been standing up there on that rock in this wild storm, holding her baby brother in her arms? I knew where she had been trying to take him, all right. But why had she held on to him for so long? Then it came to me that she was like a frightened black kitten trapped on a roof, and mewing for someone to come and help her down. I think there were two souls in her. One of them was wanting to kill the boy for the hurt he had done her in his coming. And the other one was crying out to us to save her from that.

I tried to take a step forward but the wind got up again and pushed me back, like a blow on the chest. I lost sight of the children in the spray. Merlyn held on to my arm and murmured in my ear.

'Speak to her, Gwennol. You are the only one here she loves.'

Yes, Emrys Merlyn asking me for help.

It's gone long past that, I thought, thanks to you. Precious little sign of love she's shown to me or anyone else these last nine months. But I had to try. I loved both those poor children, may Lord Gorlois forgive me for it.

'Come along with me to your bed, my lover. He's only a baby. He hasn't done you any harm.'

But even before the words were out of my mouth, I knew that wasn't true. Even sleeping in her mother's belly, he'd done her and her sisters wrong.

'Uther Pendragon killed my father. And he deceived my mother. And neither of them is sorry for it. But I will make them weep.'

King Uther took a great stride into the water 'til the waves filled his boots.

'The stinking little crow!' he shouted. 'Give me my son back!'

A king's no better than the rest of the gentry that can't keep their temper. All pride and no sense. King he might be, but any shepherd-boy could have told him it was daft to come at her like that, like a wolf on a ewe-lamb. When she saw him with the water up to his waist she moved so quickly that I thought she was going to throw herself off the rock with the baby still clutched in her arms. I know I screamed.

Then Merlyn flung out his arm with the fingers of his hand spread stiff, and called down from the sky the words of power to bind her.

I'd been a fool to think his strength was going.

I hid my eyes in my hands, but I should have covered my ears. I've said a few spells myself in my time, but I've never heard words like those before, and I hope I never shall as long as I live. None of us there should have heard them spoken aloud. It froze me where I stood like a pillar of granite.

But that power held Morgan before she reached the edge of the rock. Stiff and still she grew, like his own hand pointing at her. Just the moonlight flashing in her eyes like frost.

Then our baby prince started to slip out of her arms. It seemed he was the only one the spell couldn't hold. Very slowly he dropped, like a feather falling in a dream. There wasn't one of us could move a hand to stop him. He fell straight into a pool in the hollow of the rocks. Then we saw a great wave come rolling in from the sea and carry him towards the shore.

Quick as a heron, Merlyn went diving through the swell and gathered him up in his arms, all dripping white in the moonlight. He looked down at the child for a long, still time, as if he'd waited years to hold a baby boy like that. Then he gave a great laugh that they must have heard up in Tintagel convent and tossed the boy into the sky. He caught him again, and as the next wave washed over them both he cried out, 'By the power of the old earth and the older moon and the three dark Mothers.

'By the power of the bright face of Ludd and Gwydion and Llew.'

The wind came again, and when it had passed Merlyn laughed long and merry.

'By the power of the Father and his Christ and the Spirit of Wisdom!

'I name you . . . Arthur!'

And that moment the precious mite started crying, so that we knew for sure he was alive.

I don't know why he did it, or if you could call that a Christian baptism. Did he think that Bryvyth was listening, on Tintagel Island? Or did he fear, like me, that our time might be over? I couldn't tell you if the boy was ever brought to a priest.

Then Merlyn looked hard at Uther Pendragon and said, 'You promised. He is mine for the fostering now. Britain shall not hear of this boy again until his day comes, and the land cries out to him for help.'

He came splashing back to the shore, and in three more strides he was gone into the darkness. We had none of us stirred.

I've never set eyes on the boy up to this day.

Chapter Thirty

I couldn't tell you how long we stood there without moving a muscle. Even the sea had fallen still. All of a sudden it seemed as though the charm had let us go. The waves were slapping on the pebbles again, but lower now. All the men were running about at the water's edge, clattering and shouting, as if the pair of them weren't gone beyond finding. We'd lost them both, and more besides.

And it was only then I thought to look for Morgan. Dear forgive me, if I hadn't forgotten her like those others, for the sake of her little baby brother with a face on him like the sun. I was mortally afraid she'd be gone too, drowned deep under the water at last. But she was still there, standing on that high rock with her arms empty. She hadn't moved. I never saw a creature look so lonely, old or young, as that little maid of nine years old.

Next moment Uther came to his senses and went splashing through the waves out to the rock. She didn't fight him now, not even when he grabbed her round the waist. He carried her back and threw her on the shingle at my feet. She caught at my skirt, but she wasn't clinging to me for love, the way she had that morning on the causeway when her heart broke. She was cold and shivering, but when the moonlight fell on her I saw she wasn't crying. Her little white face was as tight and stern as any warrior's.

She hauled herself up to her feet, and it struck me then that she was getting as tall as I was. She looked into that blowing darkness where Merlyn had gone, and she spoke more coldly than any child you ever heard.

'He thinks now he has power over me. But he is not as wise as he believes. A woman could take his power away from him. And then the turn of Gorlois's daughters will come.'

I tried to put my arms round her, but she was stiff as ice. And I looked the way she had, to where I'd last seen Merlyn's back. You fool of a man, I cursed him. And worse than that. I took you for the wisest man in Britain. You had the power to charm her hurt away, though it was you that began it. But in the end you've no more sense than the king here. All you've done is turn her hate from him to you. And there'll be many will pay dearly for that before it's ended.

She lifted her face to me.

'Gwennol,' she said. And there was a little sob in her voice. 'Where is he? Where has Merlyn taken him?'

'I don't know, my pretty,' I told her. 'Somewhere where we'll never find him 'til he's a grown man.'

Uther Pendragon was marching back up the gully, without a thought for us. Then he stopped and turned, and he bellowed at us for all the world to hear, even the nuns if they were awake at their prayers.

'Get rid of that little hell-cat, once and for all! Take her to Tintagel tomorrow and shut her in the nunnery! And let me not set eyes on her again 'til those women have schooled the wickedness out of her black heart, or I swear I'll take off her head with my own sword!'

And so I lost my baby.

They sent Morgan to school with the nuns at

Tintagel. Though I could have told Uther Pendragon what else she might learn there, if only he'd taken the trouble to ask me. The air was sweet with the singing of psalms in the daytime. But there was that done in the dark place beneath that you wouldn't find in any Christian gospel. Not that Morgan needed anyone to teach her.

There was a scandal when it was found out. It broke Bryvyth's heart. The white nuns have been swept away from Tintagel now. The men have got it for themselves, as they always wanted. Though in the end it wasn't Gorlois who built his stronghold where the two currents meet.

That was years ago. Gorlois's daughters are grown into three tall queens now. Three handsome, wise women, each married to her king. You know the rest as well as I do. Uther Pendragon is dead, poisoned by his enemies, and Ygerne has taken holy vows.

Those white women weren't the only ones swept away. They're still in Cornwall somewhere, clinging to their rocks like gulls. We're not rid of them yet. But in the east the news is worse. That white dragon Merlyn dreamed of is growing fatter every day. There's many a priest and nun won't see another Easter. And many a brave British boy that's food for the Raven. The whole land's in danger now.

And so they say our little Arthur has come again and found his sword.

Well, there you have it. I've done my story, and now I'll tell you why. Morgan herself is here tonight, waiting outside that door. And she's come calling us to help her right her wrongs. So, my sisters, I'll put it to you. What shall we wise women do about the Pendragon's son?

Headline books are available at your bookshop or newsagent, or can be ordered from the following address:

Headline Book Publishing PLC
Cash Sales Department
PO Box 11
Falmouth
Cornwall
TR10 9EN
England

UK customers please send cheque or postal order (no currency), allowing 60p for postage and packing for the first book, plus 25p for the second book and 15p for each additional book ordered up to a maximum charge of £1.90 in UK.

BFPO customers please allow 60p for postage and packing for the first book, plus 25p for the second book and 15p per copy for the next seven books, thereafter 9p per book.

Overseas and Eire customers please allow £1.25 for postage and packing for the first book, plus 75p for the second book and 28p for each subsequent book.

It was seven years since Holly's husband
Nick had walked out on her and she had
never expected to see him again—
certainly not to run into him on the remote Greek island where she had been
sent on an editorial assignment. It had
to be coincidence that Nick was there—
but if it wasn't, what did he hope to
gain? Surely his love was as dead as hers
was?

SAY HELLO TO YESTERDAY

BY

SALLY WENTWORTH

MILLS & BOON LIMITED

15–16 BROOK'S MEWS
LONDON W1A 1DR

First published 1981
Australian copyright 1981
Philippine copyright 1981
This edition 1981

© Sally Wentworth 1981

ISBN 0 263 73466 8

Set in 11 on 11½ pt Times

Made and printed in Great Britain by
Richard Clay (The Chaucer Press) Ltd, Bungay, Suffolk

CHAPTER ONE

THE twice-weekly ferry boat, which was the only means of reaching the Greek island of Kinos, chugged its way noisily across the still blueness of the Mediterranean, creating a wake that gradually diminished until only minute ripples were left to lap against the rocks that formed jagged promontories guarding the wide bay and the entrance to the harbour of Melmia. The deck of the boat was crowded with goods: drums of fuel, crates of livestock, sacks of fruit and vegetables; leaving little room over for the passengers, mostly native Greeks from their dark hair and olive complexions, but here and there the lighter colouring of travellers from more northern climates could be seen as they stood together in small groups, guarding their luggage.

One girl, though, her shoulder-length fair hair blown into disarray by the breeze created by the boat's passage, stood alone by the rail, gazing intently at the approaching harbour, as if searching for something. But it was well into the afternoon now, the sun still high in the summer sky, and there was little or no movement on the jetty or on the few fishing caiques or holidaymakers' yachts tied up against the wall. Disappointed, Holly Weston drew back from the rail and went back to her extremely uncomfortable seat on top of a couple of stacked crates of beer. Hooking her equipment case off her shoulder, she placed it carefully on the deck between her sandalled feet, safe from any chance knocks or kicks, and leant back against some baulks of timber, relaxing and soaking up the sun.

She supposed it had been too much to hope for that Felix Riddell's yacht would be in harbour. A few good photographs of that would at least have been a start to her assignment. Now she would just have to wait around until the millionaire recluse made up his mind whether or not he would finally grant her the interview which her paper had been trying so desperately hard to obtain for the last two months.

The odour of pine filled Holly's nostrils as the sun brought the fragrance out of the wood she was leaning against. Around her she could hear the voluble chatter of the other passengers, pitched high to cover the noise of the old engines as they chugged protestingly along. The crew began to shout to one another as they entered the bay and one of them came over to her and said something she didn't understand, motioning her to get off the crates of beer, which were obviously of far more importance than the passengers. With a sigh, Holly humped her bag again and dragged her suit-case out of the way.

As the boat edged its way slowly to the jetty, one or two men appeared and in a desultory way caught the ropes thrown to them and made them fast round a couple of metal bollards. The engines groaned to a stop and the rusty anchor cable shrieked protestingly down, setting one's teeth on edge until it hit bottom and stopped at last. The crew exchanged greetings and news with the men on the jetty for several minutes before they unhurriedly decided to put the gangplank in place and let the passengers off. Holly waited with resigned patience, used to the procedure by now; it had been like this all day, ever since they had set off from Piraeus at five in the morning. No one hurried, it was as if they had all the time in the world. Which they probably had, she admitted to herself, but the boat had stopped at so many islands that Holly had lost count, and it had been a long, tiring day in a temperature that seemed at least twenty degrees hotter than in England yesterday morning. She longed to shower and to rest in a cool, shaded room, preferably with a soft, comfortable bed on which she could catch up on her lost sleep.

At last the gangplank was secured and the small crowd of Greeks who had been pressing against the rail surged off, laden with bags and parcels. Holly followed more slowly, the only tourist to get off the boat at this stop. Her case wasn't excessively heavy; dozens of earlier foreign assignments had taught her to travel as lightly as possible, but it was awkward with the heavy shoulder-bag, and by the time she reached the end of the jetty she had to stop for a breather. The town of Melmia spread in an untidy jumble of white, square-shaped houses all round the edge of the bay like giant cubes of sugar, nearly all of them single-storied with only an occasional brightly-painted shutter or door to break up the harsh whiteness. Behind the houses rose rather barren-looking hills with only a few small groves of olive trees on the

slopes below the brown outcrop of rock that stretched out towards the sea where it formed the promontories on either side of the bay.

For a moment Holly hesitated, wondering which
way to turn to find a decent hotel. In any other
country she would have tried to ask in either
French, German or Spanish, all of which she
spoke fairly fluently, but she knew hardly a word
of Greek and shrank from entering one of the little
shops that bordered the harbour and getting involved in lengthy directions. Then she caught sight
of a two-storeyed building a few hundred yards to
her left, nearer where the pleasure boats were
moored, and picked up her cases to head in that
direction. By the time she reached it she could feel
the perspiration soaking into her thin tee-shirt, but
at least her instinct had led her right, for the building had a terrace outside set with tables and chairs
and shaded by a trellis which supported an ancient
vine with dark green leaves and bunches of fat
purple grapes. The name 'TAVERNA HELIOS'
was painted above the door in what had once been
bright red lettering that had faded to a soft rose in
the sun.

There were several men sitting at tables at the
back of the terrace where the shade was deeper,
and they looked up to watch her curiously as
Holly mounted the steps and threaded her way
through the tables into the cool, dark interior of
the building. It took several seconds for her eyes to
adjust and then she saw that there were more
tables spread with gay, red and white checked
cloths, and a long bar counter that stretched the
width of the room and had several glass-fronted

cabinets on it containing weird and wonderful-looking foods that reminded Holly sharply that she hadn't eaten for quite some time.

At the moment the room was empty, but when she rang a bell set on the counter a bead curtain covering a doorway behind it was pushed aside and a stout middle-aged man with a balding head and a walrus moustache came to attend to her. He took one look at her and spoke to her in English.

'Yes, madame. What would you like?'

Holly smiled to herself, wondering whether he had really been able to sum up her nationality so easily or whether he automatically addressed all foreigners in English.

'I'm looking for somewhere to stay,' she told him. 'Do you have any rooms here?'

'Oh, yes, we have many nice rooms. How long you want room for?'

She gave a slight shrug. 'I'm not sure yet. Definitely for a week, but it could be longer.'

'Is no matter. Come, I show you the room.'

He lifted up a flap in the counter and Holly left her case in the bar while he led the way through a big kitchen where a young boy was standing on a box to do a stack of washing up in a deep sink, and which still smelt enticingly of all the meals that had been cooked there at lunchtime. Holly determinedly ignored the noises her stomach was making and followed him through a door which gave out to the open air again at the side of the taverna just below a flight of concrete stairs that had pots of brightly coloured flowers on either side of every step. They led up the outside of the building to a blue door that was standing open, giving on to a corridor with rooms opening off it on either side.

The Greek opened one of the doors on the left-hand side and stood back for her to enter. The room was very plain, with just a wooden double bed with a white coverlet, a small wardrobe and ancient chest of drawers, a table and chair, with over in the corner a hand-basin and a mirror with a crack across the corner. But the place was spotlessly clean and the shutters across the windows made it deliciously cool. During the course of her work Holly had stayed in far worse places; this was a palace compared to the lodging house in India three years ago, and which she still recalled with a shudder of distaste even now, but long experience had taught her always to double check, so she turned to the hotel-keeper and said firmly, 'I'd like to see the bathroom, please.'

But this, too, proved to be clean if primitive, and soon Holly had unpacked and was standing in the longed-for shower, feeling the tepid water rinse away her tiredness along with the grime of travel. Refreshed, she put on a pale blue cotton sundress and went along the corridor to stand for a while on the little landing at the top of the steps. Looking out to sea, she could just make out a smudge of darker colour on the horizon and wondered if it could be the small island of Fallipos where Felix Riddell lived the life of a recluse, the privately-owned island as securely barred to intruders and casual sightseers as any ancient fortress. But Holly had come to Greece with the express intention of bearding the lion in his den and had no intention of leaving until she had done so!

She still felt physically tired, but the shower had helped, so Holly decided not to rest now but to wait until after dinner and then have an early night. The tavern-keeper, who had introduced himself as Alexis Lambis, had told her that they would start to serve the evening meals in an hour, so she automatically took one of her smaller cameras from the big shoulderbag and set off to explore the town for a while. At first she turned her steps inland, threading her way through narrow, twisting cobbled streets that seemed to have been built with no plan or purpose, often going off at a tangent to circle a house that seemed to have been built right across the way, and joining up frequently with other streets so that it was easy to become lost, most of the houses looking exactly the same and only an occasional shop standing out as a landmark. As she went further inland the road grew progressively steeper and Holly found walking in her high-heeled sandals difficult because the cobbles were so uneven and slippery, but she eventually reached the edge of the town and sat down on a low wall to rest. Just behind her there was an olive grove and the rich oily smell of the wood came strongly to her nostrils from a nearby stack of logs that someone must have cut recently. She could see two white nanny-goats cropping the grass in a nearby field and distantly the sound of sheep bells echoed in the hills. The sun was much lower now, the shadows longer, and it was very still and peaceful, so still that you could almost hear the silence. Holly sat there for some time, her thoughts miles away, but then the clatter of hooves roused her from her reverie and she saw a man and a boy driving a herd of about ten heavily-laden donkeys coming down from the hills towards the town. She smiled; now she knew why the cobbles were so slippery, they had been worn smooth by the iron shoes of the donkeys.

The town was much busier as she made her way back, its inhabitants emerging after the long afternoon siesta, all the shop doors thrown wide open and the streets thronged with people: women with shopping bags, running children, and men who sat at low tables playing backgammon very fast. Inevitably she got lost, but kept going downhill and eventually came out quite a long way to the left of the taverna and had to walk back along the harbour past the fishing caiques and the pleasure cruisers. There were more men about now, mending nets on the harbour wall or working on the boats. Holly strolled past, keeping a trained but casual eye open for anything that might make a good photograph. She glanced across at one of the smaller boats and then came to an abrupt stop, her heart jumping in her chest, her mind frozen.

For several agonising seconds she stood and stared at a man who had briefly come on to the deck of the boat, but then he went below again and Holly began to relax, letting out her suspended breath and giving herself a tremulous mental shake. For a moment there she had thought . . . But no, it was really quite unlike him; the man had been much bigger than Nick had, his hair lighter. But the incident had shaken her; she had thought she was over that sort of thing by now.

She began to walk again, hurrying towards the

taverna. It had happened before, of course, many times, especially at the beginning when the hurt had been raw and bleeding. She would see a figure in a crowd, a man who held his head a certain way, or walked with that long, purposeful stride as if he was really going somewhere, and her heart would do that crazy jerk and then stand still until she realised with a sick feeling of bitter disappointment that it wasn't Nick. It had never been Nick. Since the day he had walked out after that last terrible row she had never seen nor heard anything of him again.

Several of the tables at the taverna were filled when she reached it, mostly by Greeks who were conducting animated discussions over their drinks, but one or two were taken by tourists who recognised her as one of themselves and nodded to her as she came in. Holly returned the greetings with a smile but chose a table by herself on the edge of the terrace, more shaken than she cared to admit and angry with herself for having let such a trivial incident affect her at all. It had been seven years—seven long years, and yet just seeing someone who reminded her of Nick could still make her go to pieces!

Her annoyance increased when she found that her hands were shaking as she held the menu, but she managed to give her order to the waiter in a steady enough voice and gradually regained her composure as she tucked into a filling dish of spiced meat which was completely unpronounceable but tasted delicious. Afterwards she ordered another coffee and went over her notes on Felix Riddell. In a nutshell, he was a second-generation

Canadian of British descent who had started off as a newspaper delivery boy from a poor family and had worked his way up to owning the newspaper group and becoming a dollar millionaire several times over by the time he was thirty. He had then set out to become one of the richest men in the world, established business empires falling like ninepins before his ruthless determination to take them over. For several years he had been one of the leaders of the jet-set scene, a playboy who had gone through three wives and an uncountable number of mistresses, until it almost became unfashionable *not* to have been one or the other. Then, quite suddenly, Felix Riddell had thrown up his life style, the yachts, casinos, women, the whole thing; left his empire in the hands of underlings and bought a remote Greek island where he had shut himself away and turned the place into an impregnable fortress where only the chosen few were allowed to visit, and those few definitely—*but definitely*—did not include journalists who wanted to interview him for a story.

Holly glanced up but could no longer see the island on the horizon. The sun was setting, turning the sky to a fierce molten crimson that blinded her to everything but its magnificence. She tried to concentrate on working out her approach to Felix Riddell, if she ever got to see him, but she felt very tired, in that soporific kind of fatigue where it is too much trouble to even move to go to bed. Gazing at the sunset, letting herself drown in the glory of colour, Holly gradually let her mind go back to the thoughts that had been hovering there since the incident earlier, no matter how much she

had tried to ignore them, to bury them in forget-
fulness. Back more than seven years to when she
had been sixteen and still a schoolgirl, and had
met a student called Nicholas Falconer and had
fallen instantly, madly in love with him.

It had been a disaster from the start, of course.
Nick had been only twenty-two and in his last year
at university where he was taking a degree in civil
engineering. They had met at a disco and at first
Nick had looked on her feelings for him as a
phase, expecting her to grow out of it and treating
her with a kind of elder-brother kindness and
affection which she neither wanted nor knew how
to overcome. But she had persevered and one
night, when he had gone to give her his usual light
kiss goodnight on the cheek, she had turned in his
arms and kissed him properly, and his surprised
response had left her in no doubt that he had at
last started to think of her as a woman.

But even then it hadn't been easy; he had insisted that they were too young, that he had still to
find a job and it would be years before he would
be making enough money to support a wife. To
Holly his arguments and reservations were nonsense. They loved each other, didn't they? So what
was the point of waiting? Gradually she had worn
him down and at last, against his better judg-
ment, he gave in; perhaps because he was an
orphan and longed for a home life of his own, perhaps because he realised just how desperately
Holly loved and wanted him, and that if they
didn't marry soon they might not be able to control their emotions for much longer.

Holly's parents could, she supposed, be regarded as upper middle class; they had sent her to good schools and had great ambitions for her, their only daughter. When Holly introduced them to Nick and told them they wanted to get married, they were incredibly shocked, looking on Nick as a sponger and forbidding him the house. At first she had been stunned by their attitude; to her Nick was perfect and she was so besotted by him that it had never even occurred to her that her parents might object. The stubborn streak that had been part of her nature since childhood, and which often stood her in good stead in her job now, had helped her to gradually wear them down, until at last they capitulated and said that if she would agree not to see Nick for several months, until he had taken his exams, and if they afterwards still felt the same, they would allow them to become engaged. This, of course, in the firm conviction that by then Holly would have got over her infatuation for him.

Holly acceded to this readily enough, knowing that Nick wanted time to concentrate on his studies anyway, even though being apart from him was a bittersweet kind of pain as the months dragged by and she marked each day off on the calendar, longing for the time to pass. On the day after his last exam she took the train to Oxford and he was waiting at the station to meet her. He looked so very dear; tall and youthfully slim—too thin for his height, really—his thick brown hair falling forward over his forehead, and his blue eyes lighting up as he caught sight of her and ran to meet her.

They grabbed each other and hugged and kissed

exuberantly, regardless of the other passengers who walked past them, grinning broadly.

Nick picked her up and swung her round excitedly. 'Guess what? I've been offered a job!'

'A job! Oh, Nick, how marvellous! Now Daddy won't be able to have the least objection to our getting married.' She kissed him fervently, hugging him tight. 'What sort of job? When do you start?'

He laughed and set her down, then flushed as he realised that people were looking at them in amusement. Grabbing her hand, he began to hurry her along. 'Come on, let's find somewhere we can eat and I'll tell you all about it.'

They found a nearby café, and over coffee and sticky buns, he told her, 'It's with a big international construction company. They've offered me a post at the very lowest of their junior management levels, but at least it's a start and it's heading in the direction I want to go,' he added enthusiastically. 'I went for an interview last month and I heard that I'd been accepted only this week. They have construction sites all over the world.' His eyes lit up eagerly. 'Just think, I could be sent to South America one year, Africa the next!'

Holly's eyes widened in alarm. 'You will be able to take me with you, won't you?'

He began to frown and said slowly, 'Well, I'm afraid . . .'

She reached out and clutched at his hand in alarm, almost knocking over her cup of coffee in her haste. 'Oh, Nick, you can't go without me. Please, please, say you won't go without me!'

His face softened and he gave her the special smile he had for no one else. He lifted his other hand to cover hers. 'Idiot, I was only teasing. Of course I can take you with me; it was one of the first things I asked.'

Holly gave a shudder of relief, then said earnestly, 'Don't tease me like that again, Nick. Promise me you won't? I can't bear it.'

He lifted a long finger to wipe away a tear that had appeared on her cheek and said softly, using his pet name for her, 'Silly young Prickles. Don't you know I won't ever leave you?'

That memory brought a wry, twisted smile to Holly's face. So much for promises. For he had left her, such a short time later.

Hindsight had shown her that it had been entirely her parents' fault. When they had heard about Nick's job they had refused point blank to let her marry at once and go slumming round the world with him, as they expressed it. They hadn't brought up their daughter to live among a lot of foreign workmen on a primitive building site without decent sanitation or medical care. And when Holly had stubbornly said that she was going anyway, they had pointed out that she was still under eighteen and unable to marry without their consent. There had been tears, recriminations and angry scenes, and in the end a compromise was reached only when Holly threatened to leave home and go to live with Nick if they wouldn't let her get married at once. They agreed to let them marry only if Nick gave up the job with the construction company and agreed to take a post in her father's business, working in the office.

The condition was completely opposite to what they wanted, but Holly's father had taken Nick to

his club and told him that Holly was a delicately
brought up girl who would not be able to stand
the rigours of living in a foreign climate, and that
if Nick loved her he would not ask her to make
such a sacrifice. Her father was eloquent and persuasive and Nick young and unsure, so that he
eventually agreed to give up his ambitions and to
take the job with her father. Pressing home his
advantage, Mr Weston had no compunction in
pointing out to Nick that he was in no position to
provide a decent home for Holly, who couldn't
possibly be expected to live in some tiny flat or
squalid bedsitter where she would be ashamed to
entertain her family and friends, and that it would
be only sensible for them to live with her parents
in the family home until such time as Nick could
afford a house.

Nick, made to feel inferior and ashamed of his
lack of background and money, and his apparent
disregard for Holly's comfort, reluctantly agreed.
Holly, when she was told of it, felt only a pang of
disappointment; it would have been fun to have
lived abroad and to have had their own place to
live in, but all that really mattered to her was that
she was going to marry Nick right away. She was
so in love that she was incapable of seeing beyond
that glorious moment. Once they were married
everything would work out and be wonderful because they would be together, nothing could
change that.

They had had a large, white wedding, insisted
on and paid for by her parents, and went on
honeymoon to a villa in Spain lent by her aunt, an
ecstatic time which had left everlasting memories

of love, happiness and discovery, when there seemed to be just the two of them in a beautiful world that was all their own.

Her parents' campaign to break them up had started from the moment they returned. Oh, it had been very subtle, of course, and conducted in an extremely polite manner, so that Holly hadn't even realised it was happening until it was too late. Her mother especially had been overtly pleasant enough to Nick, but had insinuatingly let him know that he was not one of themselves, that his social manners left much to be desired. She did it in sentences that began: 'I'm sure you won't mind me advising you, Nicholas, but . . .' or 'That isn't *quite* the way we do things, Nicholas.' While at work he was relegated to being just an office boy without being given any opportunity to use his brain or to train for management, and was also in the invidious position of being resented by his fellow clerks because he was the boss's son-in-law while those already at management level were jealous and wary because they thought he was after their jobs.

Nick must have been bitterly unhappy, but he said nothing to Holly, learning fast and making sure that he never made the same mistake twice, and at first Holly was so happy that she never even noticed. But then even their sex life, which before had been so wonderful, so perfect, began to be affected; this because, one morning at breakfast, her mother had complained, politely of course, at the noise they had made during a bedtime romp when Nick had chased her round the room the night before.

From that moment Nick seemed to withdraw into a shell, gradually losing the spontaneous gaiety and zest for living that she loved. He had begged her then to leave her parents' house and find a flat somewhere, his words urgent, desperate almost. But Holly was completely blind to what he was going through, unable to see why he should want to leave a comfortable home for a dingy bed-sitter, especially when she was having such a wonderful time showing off her new husband to all her friends. They were invited out often to parties, discos, barbecues, and Holly was engrossed in the enjoyment of no longer being a schoolgirl, of being a married woman and able to do more or less as she liked.

Nick had changed towards her then, treating her as he did her parents; with polite coldness, as if he were a lodger in the house and not a member of the family. And he made love to her only infrequently, when her parents were out of the house, until even this ceased altogether. The quarrels had started then. Holly, unable to understand why he had changed so much when he had been so passionate, so demanding during their honeymoon, and Nick bitter and resentful at her lack of understanding, made on all sides to feel inadequate and inferior. At first they had made up quite quickly after their fights, Holly tearful and repentant, Nick gentle and loving, but things had quickly got worse, the rows fiercer, the insults barbed and hurtful.

The last, unforgettable, row had taken place almost exactly six months after their marriage. Nick had tried to please her mother by spending a weekend carefully and painstakingly decorating a room for her, and then came home from the office the next day to find a hired man redoing it while her mother stood there with a friend and laughed at Nick's 'feeble clumsiness'. Unable to stand any more, he had told Holly to start packing, that they were leaving, but she was still too young and inexperienced to see that he had been pushed over the edge at last and told him he was being stupid.

The quarrel then had been terrible, each hurling abuse and insults at the other, Nick demanding that she choose between her parents and him, Holly refusing to do any such thing, and shouting that he was selfish and a fool.

'And an impotent one at that!' she yelled at him, all the hurt and misery of the nights when he had lain stiff and cold beside her flooding into her accusation.

Something seemed to have exploded inside Nick then. He had leapt across the room to her, grabbing her and dragging her towards the bed. Holly saw the look of murderous rage in his eyes and started to struggle, but he overpowered her with a brutality that he had never shown before and threw her down on the bed. Holly screamed, but her parents had gone out to dinner and there was no one to hear her cries as he began to tear off her clothes.

His voice shaking with anger and emotion, he muttered through clenched teeth, 'You bitch! I'll show you whether or not I'm impotent!' And then he had taken her cruelly, like an animal, with neither love nor passion, using her body as a means of useless retaliation for all the punishment he had taken.

Afterwards she had pulled the sheet over herself and lain, naked and crying, while he had packed his things and walked out of the room, out of her life, sitting up to call his name when it was too late, when he had already gone.

She had waited then, waited for nearly six long, grim weeks, her confidence that he loved her enough to phone her or come for her gradually diminishing as time passed and there had been nothing, not even a letter. It seemed to her afterwards that she had grown up in those six weeks, changed from a girl living in a beautiful dream to a woman facing the harsh realities of desertion and loneliness. At the end of that time, her eyes completely opened to what her parents had done, she had left their house for good, only staying on that long in the hope that Nick would contact her. When she left they accused her of ingratitude and heartlessness and told her they never wanted to see her again. Whether they really meant it or not, Holly didn't know, or care very much. She had broken with them completely and didn't even know where they were living, now that they had moved away from the family home. She had grimly set about building a new life for herself, reverting to her maiden name and living in a seedy bedsitter in a shabby, dilapidated old house while she tried to get a job, any job, and went to evening classes for journalism. It had been hard at first, desperately hard, and she often thought that she couldn't cope, that it would be better just to feed the gas meter with all the money she had left and leave the taps open, but the stubborn streak that had made her fight to marry Nick had made her carry on somehow, to overcome the desolation and loneliness, the continued exhaustion and frequent periods when she was weak from hunger because her dole money had run out.

But then Jamie had come into her life, and life had suddenly seemed worth living again when there were two of them to fight for.

The thought of Jamie made her remember how he had looked when she had left him the previous morning, emerging from sleep, his hair dishevelled, to hold her tightly and kiss her goodbye, his long-lashed blue eyes filled with love. Holly blinked rapidly, hating having to leave him behind when she was given an assignment abroad, and longing to be back with him.

She sighed, then gave a resigned shrug; once more becoming aware of her surroundings as a waiter came to place a glass bowl with a candle in it on her table. It was dark now, the sun having set completely while she was deep in her memories of the past. The lamps had been lit along the quay and out at sea she could see the lights of the fishing boats bobbing gently on the slight tide. Several of the boats tied up at the harbour also had light shafting from portholes and windows in the cabins, the larger ones even having gay strings of coloured lights outlining the rigging, giving them a fairylike appearance.

As Holly looked at the boats she noticed the man who had given her such a start earlier come on deck again and stand silhouetted for a moment by the riding-light fixed to the mast of his boat, then he turned to jump athletically on to the quay and stroll leisurely towards the taverna. As he came nearer, passing through the pools of light thrown by the electric lamps, she could see him more clearly. He was over six feet tall, the same height as Nick had been, but much broader, his muscles and strong chest outlined by the navy sweater he wore, the sleeves pushed up, hands thrust casually in the pockets of his jeans. And he was far more assured, carried himself with a commanding air of self-confidence that Nick had never had, as if he was used to giving orders and being obeyed. Another stretch of darkness until the next light, and now she could see his face quite well as he looked towards the taverna. The man's hair was thick and looked dark, although it was difficult to tell in the artificial light, one lock falling a little forward on to his forehead. The last patch of darkness and then he was climbing the steps to the taverna to stand at the entrance to the terrace, looking round. He was deeply tanned, as if he had been living in a sunny climate for a long time. About thirty, he had a strong face, with a square jaw and high cheekbones, a scar running across his left temple to his eyebrow giving him an almost satanical appearance. His mouth was thin, with a cynical twist to it, and there was a withdrawn look about his eyes, eyes that were a startling blue, as blue as the summer sky.

He walked forward and stopped in front of her table. The remembered picture of the youth she had married disintegrated as Nick, the man, said calmly, 'Hallo, Holly. How are you?'

CHAPTER TWO

STRANGELY Holly was able to return his greeting almost as calmly, the second shock cancelling out the first and leaving her completely emotionless, almost in a state of limbo.

'Hallo, Nick. I'm fine. And you?' But before he could answer, adding with a small smile, 'But I hardly need ask, need I? You look extremely fit.'

His left eyebrow, the one arched by the scar, rose a fraction, as if he was surprised by her lack of reaction. He gave a slight nod of acknowledgment and took his hand out of his pocket to put it on the back of the chair opposite. 'May I join you?'

'Of course.'

He sat down, blocking out the sea. For a moment he studied her intently, but then the waiter came up and he looked away. 'Would you like a drink?'

Holly didn't want to drink with him, she wanted to run to her room, to shut the door and hide, but she managed to shrug and say offhandedly, 'Why not? A vodka and tonic, please.'

Nick's brows flickered a little. 'A very sophisticated drink.'

Her tone hardening, Holly said tartly, 'I'm an adult, not a schoolgirl any more.'

The blue eyes came up to meet hers. 'So I see.' Then, abruptly, 'You've changed.'

She nodded. 'So have you. I hardly recognised you.'

The cynical twist of his mouth deepened for a moment. 'That wasn't quite what I meant.' His eyes ran over her face, feature by feature, leaving her feeling strangely naked and vulnerable. 'I would always have known you. You look just as I remember you the last time I saw you.'

Glad of the semi-darkness that hid the flush that came to her cheeks as she remembered the circumstances of their last meeting, she said in defensive sarcasm, 'Next you'll be trotting out the trite adage that seven years is a long time.'

Nick looked at her swiftly and seemed about to make a retort, but the waiter appeared with their drinks and he picked his up and leant back in his chair, crossing his legs negligently, his tone calm again.

'What brings you to Kinos?'

'Business,' she replied shortly, and then because he waited, his eyebrow raised enquiringly, added, 'I'm on an assignment here.'

'Assignment?'

'For a paper. I'm a journalist,' she told him reluctantly.

But to her surprise he showed no reaction, merely giving a brief nod.

'And you?' she asked him. 'What are you doing here?'

'Oh, mine's purely a pleasure trip.' He gestured towards the boat. 'I've hired a motor-yacht and I'm taking a leisurely sail round the Greek islands, just stopping where I feel like it.'

'How very pleasant.' Holly felt oddly detached,

as if it wasn't really her that was sitting here, making polite conversation. Picking up her glass, she took a long drink. Suddenly her hand began to shake, almost spilling the liquid. Hastily she set the glass down and put her hands under the table, clasping them together. The numbness had gone and her heart began to hammer in her chest. What was she doing here, sitting drinking and exchanging trivialities with a man who had walked out on her and hadn't even cared enough to find out how she was, whether she was alive, even, in the period since? Her voice uneven, she asked, 'Have you been here long?'

Luckily Nick didn't seem to notice anything amiss. 'No, not very long. I haven't seen you here before, and as this is almost the only place to stay, I presume you only arrived today?'

She nodded woodenly. 'Yes, on this afternoon's ferry.' Then she screwed up her courage to ask the one all-important question. 'I expect you'll be moving on quite soon, then?'

His lids came down swiftly over his eyes, like a camera shutter. His face expressionless, he said evenly, 'I've made no definite plans. I may stick around here for a while.'

'I see.'

His brows rose. 'My being here doesn't bother you, does it?'

Holly laughed harshly. 'Why should it?' Adding deliberately, 'You're nothing to me now.'

His blue eyes were suddenly cold as glacier ice as they came up to meet her grey ones. 'Was I ever?'

For a long moment Holly could only stare at him speechlessly, then, unable to stand the situation any longer, she got abruptly to her feet and said hastily, 'I'm very tired from the journey. You'll have to excuse me. Goodnight.'

Nick stood up to let her go by and her arm brushed against his as she passed. It was as if an electric shock had scorched through her body leaving every nerve end raw and tingling. He said goodnight in return, but Holly kept her face averted as she hurried down the terrace steps and along to the outside stairs leading to her room, not stopping until she was inside with the door firmly locked behind her. Then she almost collapsed on to the narrow bed, her whole body shivering uncontrollably as if she was very cold.

She hadn't bothered to turn on the light and she lay for so long in the darkness that the moon came out and shafted through the windows, lighting her as she huddled on the bed, hugging herself to try and stop the violent tremors that only gradually subsided. From below her room, on the terrace, she could hear the noise of voices talking, some raised in laughter, as the locals came along for their evening drinks, and then the taped sound of bouzouki music floated up from the bar, tinny and garishly unlike the real thing. Slowly she got up and went to stand at her window, gently pushing open the shutters so that she could look out. The lights of the fishing boats were far out to sea now, bobbing about like fairy lights in the wind. Tentatively Holly looked down towards the terrace, wondering if Nick was still there, but the thickness of the vine covered the area almost completely, leaving only one or two patches where it was possible to glimpse the metal tables and the people sitting round them. Lifting her eyes, she sought his boat among those moored at the quay, but it was difficult to tell them apart in the darkness, they were just a jumble of darker spars reaching up into the blackness of the night.

She drew back into the room and leant against the wall. Why did Nick have to be here? Why? She had imagined this moment so often, had had nightmares about it for years, knowing that eventually it must come, but she had never thought it would be like this; purely by chance in a foreign country. She had always imagined that it would be in a law court or solicitor's office when she would have had plenty of time to prepare herself, to be completely self-controlled and able to deal with the situation. But this—this had shaken her badly, more than she cared to admit, shattering the hard shell she had built round herself over the years into tiny fragments that would have to be painfully put back together before she could face him again.

She shivered and rubbed her bare arms, pacing up and down the small room. She supposed that it was inevitable that she would see him again; Kinos was such a small place, and Melmia the only town, that anyone staying there must of necessity bump into each other a dozen times a day. Holly smiled cynically to herself; the malignant fate that had brought him to Kinos at the same time as she wasn't going to let her off the hook as easily as just one short encounter; the knife was bound to be twisted deeper before it let her go.

Closing the shutters, she turned on the light and slowly began to undress and get ready for bed, although she knew that it would be a long time before she would sleep tonight. Her thoughts went back to Jamie waiting for her in England, and although she tried not to, she immediately began comparing him with Nick, their two faces chasing each other through her thoughts. A slow tear trickled down her cheek and Holly brushed it angrily away. She hadn't cried over Nick for a long time now and she certainly didn't intend to start just because he'd come back into her life. What the hell was there to cry about anyway? She should be *glad* that she had the chance to see him again and to know that she'd got him out of her hair for good. And the tears? They were pure nostalgia, for a brief period of happiness when she had been young and incredibly stupid. They certainly weren't self-pity for the woman she had become, or for regret at what might have been. She had Jamie and she had her job; she was completely independent financially and had no other emotional ties—and wanted none. Her life was complete and this unexpected meeting with Nick could be looked on as merely a rather unpleasant interlude that would soon be over and done with, she told herself forcefully. It might even turn out to be therapeutic, laying many old ghosts that had haunted her for years after he had gone. But she must be careful not to mention Jamie; *that* relationship was too precious to be made known to the man who had once lived with her as her husband.

The noise from the taverna below began to die away until all was quiet, the town sleeping peacefully while Holly still stirred restlessly on the strange, rather lumpy mattress, but gradually the years of self-discipline, when she had had to force herself to overcome so many torments and difficulties, began to extend their influence and she lay more quietly, feeling herself better able to cope with seeing Nick again. But her last waking thought before she at last drifted off to sleep was: He looked so different, had changed so much.

Sunlight shafted through the louvred shutters the next morning making golden bars of light across the bed and the floor. One reached Holly's eyes, making her blink and turn her head away, slowly coming out of sleep. For a moment she lay languidly, her mind still lost in the fog of unconsciousness, unaware of where she was, thinking that she was in the big bed in the cottage at home, waiting for Jamie to wake her with his usual morning kiss. Her eyes flickered open, taking in the whitewashed ceiling, the roughly plastered walls painted pale blue like the colour of Nick's eyes . . .

Holly came instantly wide awake, trembling, fully aware of her surroundings.

It took a great deal of courage to leave her room that morning, but she determinedly ran down the flight of stairs between the tubs of deep red geraniums and pink and white carnations, the scent of the flowers coming up to surround her as she descended. And when she reached the ground she saw that she needn't have worried; Nick's boat was gone from its mooring, leaving a space among the boats like the gap where a tooth had been pulled. Relief flooded her; he must have decided to leave after all, not to hang around and have old memories rise up from their graves and resurrect their grizzled heads. But as she mounted the terrace steps she saw his boat tacking towards the harbour, its russet sails set to catch the sea breeze. He had only been out fishing.

The proprietor himself brought her breakfast of rolls and coffee and Holly took the opportunity of booking two calls to England, expecting to have to wait some time for the connections, but was pleasantly surprised when he told her that the island had just had a new exchange installed and there would only be about an hour's delay. Holly spent the time exploring the little shops nearby, which luckily hadn't yet become the usual store of rather tawdry mass-produced souvenirs for tourists. What items of Greek traditional work they had were mostly made on the island by the inhabitants in their spare time. Holly reached up to admire beautifully embroidered blouses and dresses suspended on poles attached to the shop awnings, and was envious of the patience that had gone into making delicate lacework tablecloths and napkins. She bought a straw hat, knowing from past experience of hot climates how much damage the sun did to her fair hair, bleaching it almost silver if exposed to it for too long.

At ten, she went back to the hotel and sat on the terrace with a cool drink until Alexis Lambis called her in to take the first of her calls.

The familiar voice of the Features Editor greeted her and then got down to business straightaway.

'Still no definite word on the interview with Felix Riddell yet, Holly. As you know, we're still waiting for one of his employees to fix it for us. The last word we had was that Riddell was on the point of agreeing, so stay on hand so that you can get there fast when he does make up his mind. We don't want to give him time to change it,' he added fervently. 'It's taken enough persuasion and bribes to get this far. Have you fixed up somewhere to stay?'

'Yes, it's the Taverna Helios,' Holly told him, and gave him the phone number.

'Okay. You'd better stick within spitting distance of the phone today, but I'll give you a call at five this evening our time anyway to give you the latest gen. Can't have you sitting around in luxury doing nothing for too long or I'll have the Editor after me,' he added with mock severity.

Holly laughed. 'If you call this luxury, then just don't give me any assignments to any lesser places!'

She put down the receiver and left the cool shade of the building to sit out in the sun again and wait for her second call to come through, the really important call. To Jamie. Jamie—oh, Jamie! Her thoughts clung to him like a drowning person clings to a spar. He was her reason for being, for existing. Without him she would have gone under long ago. She needed him, the reassurance of knowing he was there, waiting for her, the centre of his world. Because it was that reassurance, and only that, that would give her the courage and steadfastness to face seeing Nick again.

The phone rang, its strident tones cutting through the still air, and Holly reached it almost before Lambis did. He spoke in Greek to the operator, then smiled at Holly. 'It is for you, *thespoinis*,' he said, holding out the receiver.

Holly took it, her hand shaking. 'Jamie?'

But it was Mrs Ferrers, the housekeeper, who answered, and she had to wait again before Jamie came on.

'Mummy!' His six-year-old voice piped shrilly across the line. 'I'm digging a hole in the garden so that rabbits will come and live there. Can I have a rabbit, please? As soon as you come home?'

'But you've already got the guineapigs and a hamster,' Holly answered in useless protest, knowing that she would give in to him.

He went chattering on, her little son, telling her of his day at school yesterday, of a broken toy; all the little things that were of supreme importance in his young life, and suddenly all Holly's anxiety disappeared; she was right when she had told Nick that he was nothing to her now; his child, that he didn't even know existed, had completely taken his place.

Happiness filled her as she talked. The ghost had indeed been laid; she was ready to face Nick now with perfect composure, as a man she had once known well but who didn't matter any more.

The sun beckoned after she had finished the call and she hurried up to her room to change into a swimsuit, humming a tune as she did so. Going to the mirror to rub sun-tan lotion on her face and freshen up her lipstick, she was annoyed to see the dark shadows round her eyes from the sleepless night. That would never do. Still—when in Greece, one wears sunglasses! Holly perched the large round-framed specs on her nose, stuffed a bag with the usual beach paraphernalia and went to find a quiet place to sun herself in.

She found it a couple of hundred yards away
from the harbour and the town after scrambling
over rocks worn smooth and slippery by the sea,
and little inlets of shingle, the washed stones bright
and sparkling in the sun. Beyond the rocks there
was a cove of fine golden sand surrounded by
quite high cliffs. The beach shelved gently to the
water except where arms of rock jutted out to the
sea, providing ideal platforms from which to dive.

It was too much to hope for to have the place to
herself, of course, she had guessed that when she
had asked the hotel proprietor for the nearest
beach and he had immediately directed her here.
There was a young couple further along that she
remembered having seen eating a meal in the
taverna last night and whom she guessed to be
Scandinavians from their appearance, and, on
loungers set under a huge sunshade, lay a group of
people, including two very tanned women, looking
extremely rich and pampered even though they
were only dressed in the merest wisps of material.
Off one of the big motor cruisers, Holly guessed.
One or two Greek children played by the water-
line, but there were no other islanders sunning
themselves—they were all so naturally brown that
they had no need to.

Holly spread her towel out on the sand and
slipped out of her sundress, rolling it up to make a
pillow. She reached up to clip her hair up at the
back, her body tall and slender in a dusty pink
bikini, her legs long and shapely. The water struck
cold at first, the sea dragging the sand back
around her feet, burying them like a miniature
quicksand, but as she went deeper and then dipped

her shoulders underwater, it wrapped around her like a warm blanket, unbelievably soft and caressing. And blue, so blue and clear; she could look down and see her own feet through the water, and the patches of darker seaweed that clung to the few sand-covered rocks on the shelving bottom. She let the swell pick her up and struck out towards the open sea in a strong, regular crawl, her arms cutting the water cleanly. After a while she stopped to tread water, out of breath but feeling fresh and invigorated. It had been quite some time since she had had an opportunity to swim, although she had done so regularly when she had been at school and had even won several medals for it, but that had been before Nick, of course. And after he had left her there had been Jamie to look after and the constant fight to keep them both, with no time for swimming, no time for anything except work and exhausted sleep at the end of the day.

Rolling over, Holly lay back and floated, wondering idly if this was what a waterbed was like, and thinking she must give Jamie swimming lessons when she got back to England: he was quite old enough now. Conceived during that last terrible quarrel, when Nick had taken her so violently, raped her almost, Jamie ought to have been an emotional, bad-tempered child. But he wasn't; he was happy as the day was long, only sad when she had to leave him with someone else. And that had happened often when he was a baby and had to be left with child-minders or in a crêche while Holly worked or went to classes in journalism and photography, but he had been so brave, blinking back his tears and seeming to understand that she couldn't help it. And running to her, clinging, clinging so tightly when she came back, as if he had been secretly afraid that she never would. But it had paid off in the end; she had managed to get a job on a magazine as a photo-journalist and after a few years her present post with a really good national newspaper where her feature stories appeared often in their Sunday colour supplement. It had enabled her to buy the cottage tucked away in a fold of the English countryside with a garden for Jamie to play in, and to pay a housekeeper she could trust to look after him when she was sent on an assignment, although she mostly tried to restrict these to as near to home as possible now. But this one, the chance of getting an interview with Felix Riddell, had been irresistible.

She turned and swam back to the shore, lazily now, taking her time and enjoying the feel of the sun on her back, the rainbow of colours in the drops of water that fell like crystal when she deliberately splashed her hand against the waves. Not bothering to dry herself, she lay face down on her towel and almost instantly fell asleep.

Some sixth sense brought her fully awake almost as soon as the shadow touched her. She had been dreaming, and when she turned over and looked up to see Nick standing over her, his hands on his hips, it came as no surprise to see him there, and she realised her dream must have been about him. Quickly she sat up and reached for her sunglasses, feeling deeply grateful for being able to hide behind them.

Nick dropped down to the sand beside her,

facing her. Dressed only in a tee-shirt and pale blue shorts, he half lay on the sand, his legs, brown and firm as tree trunks, stretched out alongside hers. Holly immediately swung her legs to one side, then remembered the straw hat and put it on, further shading her eyes.

There was a thin smile on Nick's lips as he said, 'Does the sun hurt your eyes?'

'I find the reflection of it on the sea rather dazzling,' Holly returned calmly, adding rather pointedly, 'Have you come for a swim?'

'That was the general idea.' He leant back on his elbows. 'But I've just had lunch—have to give it an hour or so first. Here, I've brought you a present.' He fished in his pocket and brought her out an apple, green and hard, with just a flush of red near the crown. He held it out to her.

Holly looked at it without moving, then raised her eyes to find him watching her quizzically.

'The serpent won't bite you if you take it,' he said softly, mockingly.

Reaching out, Holly took the apple, being careful not to let her fingers touch his. 'How did you know I was here?'

'Alexis Lambis told me.'

She looked up quickly. 'There hasn't been a phone call for me, has there?'

Nick's brows rose. 'No. Were you expecting one?'

She nodded silently, eating the apple.

'Something to do with your assignment here?'

'Something like that,' she agreed shortly.

'Isn't this rather an out-of-the-way place for a journalist to be sent for a story?'

'Some people might think so.'

'Which means that you're not going to tell me about it, I suppose?'

'That's right. In other words, mind your own business,' Holly said caustically.

'Tut, tut! Still as prickly as ever, I see,' Nick returned, a cold edge of irony in his voice.

Holly's head came up sharply and for a long moment their glances held, until she turned away and pulled her knees up to rest her chin on them.

Nick took a pack of cigarettes from his shirt pocket and lit one while Holly dug a hole and buried the apple core. They sat silently for some time, each lost in their own thoughts, but then Nick showed how closely parallel his had been to hers by saying abruptly, 'Why did you never get a divorce?'

Holly picked up a handful of sand and let it sift through her fingers, her whole attention absorbed in it. 'Why didn't you?' she countered.

To her surprise he laughed, the sound echoing in the bay and attracting the attention of the party from the cruiser. 'Just like a woman—to answer a question with a question. I've never known one yet who would give you a direct answer to a leading question.'

She stopped playing with the sand and lifted her head to look at him. 'You sound as if you've known a lot of women?'

His jaw thrust forward. 'Did you expect me to live like a monk just because I was still technically married to you?' he demanded harshly.

Holly stared at him for a moment, startled by his vehemence, then looked away. 'I really hadn't thought about it,' she said stiffly.

Just then the men from the cruiser party walked by them to the sea and began to swim around, noisily throwing a big yellow beach-ball to one another. Nick reached up to pull off his shirt, but he made no attempt to go in to swim. He looked very powerful, his chest broad and muscular, but his hips in the washed-out denim shorts looked lean and athletic, as if he got a lot of exercise. He glanced up and caught her watching him.

'You look very tanned,' Holly said hastily. 'You must have been sailing round the islands for some time.'

Shaking his head, Nick said, 'No, I've only been in Greece for quite a short time. I got this out in Australia while I was working.'

'You live in Australia?'

'No, I was there for a couple of years, building a bridge. And before that in Africa, working on a dam.'

'So you got to achieve your ambition and become a civil engineer, after all?'

'Yes, I managed to persuade the company that had offered me a job earlier to take me on after . . .' he hesitated, 'after we split up.'

Holly laughed gratingly. 'Let's get it right, shall we? You mean after you walked out.'

Nick stubbed out his cigarette viciously and leaned towards her, his eyes cold. 'No, let's *really* get it right. You were offered a choice, remember? Your parents or me. Well, you made your choice, and in my book you did the deserting bit, not me.'

'Well, really!' Holly opened her mouth to argue with him, but was interrupted by a trill of laughter coming from the women behind them.

Nick glanced towards them and then she saw his eyebrows go up, an arrested expression on his face. Holly turned round and saw what had attracted his attention; the two women were sunbathing topless and the laughter had been a deliberate lure to gain Nick's interest, because one of the women was openly smiling at him. Then she got up and came across the beach towards them, walking slowly, her hips swaying. She wore only the smallest possible triangles of material fastened with strings at the sides, but she had gold chains dangling from every conceivable place; round her waist and her ankle, as well as on her wrist and round her neck. She was in her mid-thirties, Holly guessed, although it was hard to tell through all the gold eye-shadow and orange lipstick, her hair dyed a silver-blonde and falling into a beautifully cut bell round her head. She exuded money, even before Holly got a whiff of the Jean Patou perfume.

Completely ignoring Holly as if she wasn't there, the woman came to a stop and stood over Nick, who leaned back on one elbow, looking up at her lazily through half-closed lids, then she slowly lowered herself to her knees in front of him, her jutting, naked breasts only a few inches away from his chest. 'Excuse me,' she said, her accent definitely French, 'but do you 'ave a light, m'sieur?' And she held out a cigarette towards him.

'Of course.' Nick sat up and took a lighter from his pocket, cupping the flame for her and letting his eyes meet hers over it, his left eyebrow raised a fraction.

The woman put her hands over his as she bent with the cigarette in her mouth, then she sat back gracefully on her heels and smiled at him brilliantly. 'Thank you, *m'sieur*.' Then, 'Didn't I see you on a boat in the 'arbour?'

Nick nodded. 'That's right, the *Argosy*.'

'We also are on a sailing holiday.' She looked at him seductively. 'Our boat is called *Mignette*. You must come and have a drink with us, M'sieur . . .?'

'Falconer,' Nick supplied. 'Nick Falconer.'

'And I am Chantal d'Arneau.' She shifted her weight so that she was leaning on one arm, the arm nearest Nick, of course. 'You will come for a drink?'

'I'd like to.'

'*Bien*. Tonight, at eight, then?'

'Thank you.' Nick watched her as she rose to her feet, her bare breast just happening to catch his arm as she moved. His mouth twisted into a thin smile. 'And may I bring my wife?'

For a moment the poise slipped and surprise and then anger showed in the woman's face, but then she recovered and she looked at Holly with a smile that managed to be polite and yet disparaging at the same time. 'By all means bring your wife, if you wish to,' she added after a disdainful pause. Then she turned and gave Nick the full benefit of her very curvaceous back view as she rejoined her friend.

Holly looked out to sea at the men playing ball, and said casually, 'You'd think with all those gold chains she'd be able to afford a lighter.'

Nick grinned. 'Cat!' He rolled over on to his elbows as he, too, watched the men. 'I wonder which poor sod she's married to?'

Getting quickly to her feet, Holly said, 'I think I'll have another swim,' and began to walk down towards the sea without looking at him. There had been a bitter edge of cynicism in Nick's voice when he made that last remark, as if he despised all women. She began to wade through the shallows, disturbed suddenly, wondering if it was she who had made him feel like that, had laid the first stone of disillusionment with her sex. She looked back and saw that he was stripping off his shorts to join her in the water. He had on a pair of white trunks underneath and she saw him now as the French-woman had seen him; a tall, handsome man, with a strong and beautifully proportioned body; a man with a dominant masculinity that would physically attract any woman. Turning, she plunged into the sea and began to swim, her mind filled with the way he had said, my wife. He had meant it only as a snub for the other woman, she knew, but it made her remember the way he had used to say it when they were first married; with such pride and pos-sessiveness, as if she was the most precious thing in his life.

He was alongside her suddenly, cleaving through the water with his powerful muscles, swimming much better than she remembered. Ignoring him, Holly struck out for the rocks at the side of the cove which stuck out into the sea like giant stepping-stones to nowhere. Reaching one of the farthest out, she grabbed hold of the edge and waited for the swell to lift her and help her climb on to its flat surface, but then she felt Nick's hands on her hips as he lifted her bodily out of the water and deposited her on the rock. One thrust of his arms and he had surged out of the sea to join her. Like Neptune rising from the waves, she thought inconsequentially.

But that she had even made the comparison annoyed her and she said coldly, 'I could have managed perfectly well on my own.'

Nick glanced at her as he put his hands up to push his wet hair off his face. His mouth twisted wryly but he didn't bother to answer. He seemed to tower over her, rivulets of water running down his smooth chest. His brief trunks had slipped a little and clung to him wetly. Holly got that far and hastily looked away, her heart beating faster suddenly.

'You swim very well now,' she said quickly, too quickly.

'I had plenty of practice in Australia.' His voice sounded amused as he sat down beside her. 'We used to go surfing a lot.'

'We?'

'Some of the men I worked with,' he supplied, still sounding as if he was laughing inwardly. 'We used to go down to the coast nearly every weekend. Some of the beaches there have the best surf in the world.'

'And that's all you did—surf?' she asked, letting disbelief show in her tone.

He turned to look at her. 'What do you mean?'

Her eyes met his disparagingly: she was angry at herself for being embarrassed and wanted to take it out on him. 'Well, you must have found some time in which to get all the experience with women you boasted about earlier.'

The blue eyes grew cold and he reached out to catch hold of her wrist, jerking her round to face him. 'Don't try and make me out as some sort of sex-crazy lecher. I've had women, yes, and I intend to have plenty more before I'm through.' He laughed jeeringly. 'Don't tell me that there haven't been other men in your life during the last seven years?'

Holly snatched her wrist away and stood up, glaring down at him furiously. 'You're quite right; there have been other men in my life, dozens of them. And even the least of them was a whole lot better in bed than you ever were!'

Then she dived off the rock into the water, but even as she did so she heard his laugh, full and masculine, ring out behind her.

Back on the beach, Holly hurriedly dabbed herself dry, but when she looked back at the rocks she saw that Nick was still there, stretched out in the sun, his head turned away. Slipping the sun-dress over her head, she gathered up the rest of her gear and started back for the hotel. The Frenchwoman gave her a speculative look as she passed, and when Holly reached the shingle path leading to the harbour, she saw that the woman had already covered her hair with a flower-bedecked bathing cap and was starting to swim towards Nick's rock.

Holly smiled cynically to herself: the woman must really be hard up if she could go back for more after the snub Nick had given her. But perhaps she thought she might be luckier now that he was alone. The shingle gave way to harder ground covered with wild ice-daisies, the plant English gardeners called mesembryanthemums, their pretty pink faces wide open to the midday sun. Holly kicked with her sandalled feet at a pebble, but the pain to her toe made her stop short. What the hell was she getting so worked up about? It was nothing to her if Nick made love to every woman in Kinos, was it? No—amend that—had *sex* with every woman in Kinos; there didn't seem to be much love in his make-up as far as women were concerned. They were merely there to be made use of whenever he felt the need.

And the accusation he had made to her? Holly's steps slowed as she pondered it. Okay, so she had met other men during the course of her work, and many of them had shown more than a passing interest, and a few had wanted to get serious, to establish a permanent relationship if she would let them. But she had always resisted this, giving Jamie and her work as her excuse. But in her heart she had always been afraid; afraid to give her trust and love to another man, unable to give herself completely in case they let her down. She knew she couldn't live through that hurt again, better to go through life alone, without love, than that. And this was the main reason why she had never bothered to get a divorce; the fact that she was married could be used as an excuse to break off a relationship that was becoming too serious, gave her a loophole to escape through without too many recriminations. Her mouth twisted into a wry smile. Did Nick, too, use his extinct marriage as a means of avoiding any entanglements with his women?

After a light lunch at the taverna, Holly spent the afternoon in her room, resting, and working

on the questions she would ask Felix Riddell, if
she ever got to see him. The editor of the paper
had been conducting delicate negotiations with an
employee of Riddell's, who said he could get the
millionaire to give an interview, but only if he—
the employee—received a substantial fee in advance. Normally the newspaper wouldn't have
touched such a dicey operation, there was too
much chance of the man absconding with the
money without their getting anything in return,
but this would be such a scoop if they brought it
off that the editor had decided to pursue it. Now
they seemed on the point of agreement, having
already paid a sum into a Swiss bank account as a
sign of good faith, but Holly had a cheque in her
purse for a whistle-making amount, which she was
to give to the employee only after the interview if
she could possibly manage it, but if he proved
really insistent she was to pay him in advance if
she was reasonably sure that the deal would go
through. But at the moment she didn't even know
the man's name; she only knew that he would get
in touch with the newspaper and tell them where
she could contact him, and also that he had insisted that a woman journalist be sent. Why, she
didn't know, but could only guess that it was because Felix Riddell had specified it. Why he should
specially ask for a woman Holly found rather in-
triguing; she had had to handle amorous celebrities
who wanted to swap their story for sex before and
her editor had always made it clear that in such
circumstances she was to chuck the story, but she
had no serious qualms that this might be the
reason with Felix Riddell; he had the power to

order as many beautiful women as he wanted to his island and they would come running at his call.

She went to the window and looked out pensively at the dark shape of the island away on the horizon, wondering how long she would have to wait before she made contact. A movement on the quay caught her eye and she glanced down to see Nick strolling along to his boat, the sun on his face. Immediately she went to draw back, but before she could do so he looked up and saw her. His eyes held hers for a moment and then he raised his hand in mocking salute before jumping on to his boat and going below.

Holly felt a sudden, fervent wish that this assignment would soon be over, that she could interview Felix Riddell and then go home just as fast as plane and boat could take her.

CHAPTER THREE

THE phone call Holly had been waiting for came at five o'clock that evening. The voice of the Features Editor was terse. 'It's all set up, Holly; our man got in touch with us through our Athens correspondent. We've told him where you're staying and he's going to contact you, probably tonight. So make sure you stay at the taverna and keep yourself available. And you must be alone, of course. Now,' his tone became anxious, 'you're sure you can handle this, Holly?'

'Yes, of course I am. Don't worry.' She made soothing noises down the phone and had to listen all over again to a lot of instructions she'd already heard back in London.

'And you've done your homework? Learnt all the trick questions to make sure it really is Riddell?'

Holly reassured him again and eventually he let her go, but not without misgivings, she knew; he would much rather have sent a seasoned male reporter on this job than a girl. She returned to her room seething with excitement. So it was really on at last. She glanced at her watch, wondering when she would be contacted and where the interview would take place. On Felix Riddell's island of Fallipos, she presumed, which could mean a short sea voyage. The breeze off the Mediterranean could be chilly at night, so she decided to change into

50

something warmer and put on a pair of crisp white slacks and a navy sports shirt, with a chunky knitted jacket to put on if it got really cold. Then she checked that she had a new cassette and a couple of spares for the tape recorder as well as her shorthand pad and a supply of pencils; she was going to make absolutely sure that she got every word of this interview. She packed these into her equipment bag, double-checked all her photographic gear and then, after some consideration, took a small slimline camera with a built-in flash from her equipment bag and slipped it into the pocket of her slacks, a critical look in the mirror reassuring her that its outline didn't show under her loose shirt, and if she carried her jacket on that side it would make doubly sure. Felix Riddell had allowed cameramen to take his photograph during his playboy years, but whether he would still do so now she would just have to wait and see.

Satisfied that she had made all the preparations she could, Holly picked up a paperback with which to while away the waiting time and went down to the terrace, choosing a table near the front, where she could see and be seen easily. It was early for dinner yet, so she ordered an ouzo and sipped it slowly, her nerves on edge and her eyes alert for anyone who looked at all out of place and who might be a likely contact.

For over an hour nothing happened, although in her nervous state nearly every man who walked along the harbour seemed shifty and suspicious, but most of them were just fishermen going along to their boats to prepare for the night's fishing. Several men came to the taverna, but they were

mostly in twos or threes, but once she stiffened,
her hopes rising, as a lone man seemed to look
straight at her and then stride purposefully to the
taverna and up the steps. Her hand began to tremble a little as he came towards her, but then he had
gone past and joined a group of men at a table
behind her. Holly gave a little gasp and then
laughed at herself; it was probably too early yet,
there were too many people about.

Deciding to order dinner, she summoned the
waiter and with his help ordered *souvlakia*, which,
he assured her fervently, she would find most delicious. He picked up the menu and went to move
away, and Holly's heart skipped a beat as she realised a man was standing by her table, hidden
from her sight by the waiter. Then she saw that it
was Nick and her heart skipped two beats.

'Hi. Mind if I join you?'

Before she could answer he had hooked out a
chair, throwing out an order to the waiter as he sat
down. Tonight he was wearing a lightweight blue
linen suit, the jacket cuffs turned back to reveal his
shirt sleeves, stark white against the strong brown-
ness of his hands. For a moment she was puzzled,
wondering why he was dressed so formally, then
she remembered the Frenchwoman's invitation to
drinks on her boat. So he'd succumbed to her
charms after all. A cold anger filled her; just like a
man, they could never resist even the most obvious
lures, even the most obnoxious of them thinking
themselves God's gift to women.

Then, almost as an afterthought, she came back
to reality and remembered that she must be alone

tonight. Forcefully she said, 'Yes, I do mind.'

'Sorry, what was that you said?' Nick, too, seemed to have been far away for a moment.

'I said I do mind your sitting here. There are plenty of empty tables,' she pointed out.

His eyes came up to study her face. 'That's very unsociable of you.'

'Very likely,' she agreed coldly. 'But nevertheless I'd prefer you to go and sit somewhere else.'

The blue eyes, somehow made even bluer by the linen suit, narrowed speculatively. 'Now I wonder why that is? It couldn't be because you've arranged to meet someone else, could it? And you've only been here a day—now that's what I call quick work,' he added in mock admiration.

'No quicker than you and that tart who was chasing you all over the beach this morning,' Holly retorted acidly.

A devilish look came into Nick's eyes as he raised his brows. 'Surely you can't be referring to the luscious Chantal? Somehow I don't think she'd appreciate you referring to her as a tart. Quiche Chantal.' He grinned in amusement.

'Well, you should know,' Holly said crossly.

The grin broadened. 'Do I detect a touch of jealousy in your voice?'

Holly glared at him. 'No, you most certainly do not! She's as welcome to you as you obviously are to her. You should suit each other admirably,' she added venomously.

The amused look left Nick's eyes and they turned chill. 'In some ways you haven't grown up at all, have you?'

Stifling a strong urge to tell him just how much she had grown up and why, Holly said coldly, 'Look, just because we happen to have run into each other again it doesn't mean that we have to be in one another's company all the time, does it? Personally I should have thought that we had quite enough of each other seven years ago to last a lifetime, otherwise we would never have parted.' Steadily she added, 'And I for one would have been quite happy *never* to have seen you again. So why don't you just take yourself off and leave me to get along with my own life without unwelcome interruptions? I'm not interested in you, Nick, and I don't want you around.'

'Well, you certainly made that clear enough.' His face set into a tight mask, Nick stood up and gazed down at her for a moment, then turned abruptly and strode across to another table on the other side of the terrace, but taking a chair facing into the café so that he could still see her clearly.

Holly looked down concentratedly at her book, trying to ignore him, wishing that he'd gone away instead of staying at the taverna. But inside she felt fiercely glad that she'd rebuffed him. It would have to have been said eventually anyway; there was no way they could have kept running into one another, even casually, without all the old quarrels and anguish raising their heads again. It was better this way, to cut it off cleanly before too many hurtful words had been said. But nothing could prevent the memories, they were already there, bitter and barren, gnawing away at her confidence and composure.

The *souvlakia*, when it came, turned out to be

herb-flavoured cubes of lamb threaded on a metal skewer and grilled over charcoal. Served on a bed of savoury rice, it would indeed have tasted delicious if Holly had had any appetite for it, but that had disappeared somehow, probably due to nervous tension about the coming interview, and she only managed less than half of the dish, much to the waiter's disappointment, who took it almost as a personal affront. Holly tried to reassure him, but she ended up with a sweet she didn't really want which the man brought her as a gift from the proprietor who thought she hadn't liked the *souvlakia*.

She rounded off the meal with coffee, all the while acutely aware of Nick, who made no attempt to hide the fact that he was watching her. He, too, had a meal, taking his time over it, and afterwards he didn't go away as she'd hoped, but, like her, sat on over a drink, which meant that he wasn't going to accept the Frenchwoman's invitation after all, she realised. It was well past nine already.

Lots more people came and went from the taverna as the night progressed, and Holly began to get anxious; what if something had gone wrong and her contact didn't come tonight? He might even have seen her with Nick and hurriedly taken himself off, afraid that he was being cheated. Holly sighed exasperatedly and ordered another coffee; better not to have too much alcohol if she wanted to keep a clear head for the interview. At ten the bouzouki music started up again, coming from a speaker on the wall, first a tune of melancholy sadness, then changing tempo completely to one of gay abandon. After a while two or three men got up to dance the *sirtaki*, their arms linked, their legs bending and twisting energetically as they moved ever faster to the rhythm of the music.

Holly became so engrossed in watching the dancers that she forgot why she was there and turned with a start when someone gently touched her bare arm. Her expectations rose wildly, but it was only a small Greek boy of about ten, his long-lashed, smoky-brown eyes gazing up at her meltingly and in his hands a small tray with pieces of embroidered cloth and lace, probably made by his mother or sisters during the winter months.

'Please, miss, you buy?' He thrust the tray under her nose and looked at her expectantly.

Holly started to shake her head. 'No, thanks, not right now.'

But he pushed the tray nearer and said, 'Yes, yes. You buy this one,' and picked out an embroidered table mat folded in four and pushed it into her hands.

'Now look . . .' Holly started to frown, then felt the crackle of paper inside the linen. Her heart suddenly beating very fast, she unfolded a corner of the cloth and lifted it so that she could see the piece of paper and quickly pulled it out so that she could read it. It contained only three words, 'Follow the boy'.

In rather a strangled voice she said, 'Yes, I think I will buy it,' and fished in her purse for some drachmas to put in the boy's outstretched hand. From the beautiful smile that lit his face she had evidently given him far more than the mat was worth, but she was much too excited now to worry about being a corrupting influence on him. The

boy moved away and went up to other tables
where tourists were sitting, including Nick's, who
merely waved him on, then the boy glanced back
at Holly before turning to leave the taverna. As
casually as she could, Holly finished her coffee,
then pretended to yawn for the benefit of anyone
who might be watching, particularly Nick, then
picked up her bag and jacket and threaded her
way to the steps. Nick watched her closely as she
passed, but Holly kept her head turned away; let
him think she was ignoring him if he liked, at the
moment that suited her very well.

Her eyes had to adjust for a minute after leaving
the bright lights of the taverna, but then she saw
the boy's white shirt a few yards ahead of her to
the left, heading for where the harbour ended and
the town began. Quickly Holly fell in behind him,
her rope-soled shoes making hardly any sound on
the cobbles. The boy set quite a fast pace for his
short legs and soon they were threading their way
through the narrow twisting streets, until Holly
began to feel hopelessly lost, and wondered uneasily where they were heading. Was the meeting
to take place here in Melmia and not on Felix Riddell's island after all? Impossible to catch up with
the boy and ask him; every time she quickened her
pace he, too, started to go faster until his thin legs
were almost running, and even if she did manage
to stop him he probably wouldn't understand
enough English to tell her what she wanted to
know. Once they stopped at a white-painted house
and she began to hope that they'd reached their
destination, but it must have been the boy's home,
for he went inside the lit doorway for only a

moment and then came out minus the tray and
started off again.

After another ten minutes they seemed to be
leaving the town, the houses thinning out and
giving way to stubbly fields where crickets
sounded in the coarse grass. Here and there appeared the darker outline of several windmills,
their eight triangular-shaped sails still now, sleeping and waiting for the dawn breeze. The boy left
the tarmacked road and turned to the right into a
farm track, the churned mud of winter made by the
passage of tractor and lorry hardened now into deep
ruts baked by the sun. Grimly thankful that she
had had the sense to put on flat shoes, Holly stumbled on after the boy, trying to find a flat path
between the ruts, but she wasn't used to this kind
of rough exercise and was soon out of breath and
wondering just how much further they were going.

The track ran along beside a stone wall behind
which lay fields where sheep slept under the out-
spread branches of gnarled olive trees, and went
on for over half a mile before the stone wall came
to an abrupt end and the surface of the track
changed, became less rutted, the hard earth giving
way to looser shingle underfoot.

At last the boy stopped and waited for Holly to
catch up with him. She took her heavy bag off her
shoulder and stood panting heavily, feeling her
shirt sticking to her and beads of moisture on her
forehead.

'You wait here,' the boy instructed in a hoarse
whisper, his eyes bright in the pale light of the
quarter moon, and Holly realised suddenly that
the child was thoroughly enjoying himself. She

grinned to herself, remembering that Jamie was into cowboys and Indians at the moment, and wondering what was the boy's equivalent—Greeks and Trojans, perhaps?

He went on alone and Holly stood looking around her while she recovered her breath. She could see now that they had travelled in a wide semi-circle and were back on the coast, but higher up, with quite a steep slope down to the sea that patterned first light and then dark, like molten silver, as the waves moved beneath the rays of the moon. Away to her right she could see a rocky headland jutting out into the sea and realised that it must be the left-hand arm of Melmia bay, they had crossed behind it and come out into the bay beyond, a bay where the steep slope made building impractical and where there was no river to create a valley and give good grazing land. There was an outcrop of rock nearby and Holly moved over to sit on it, wondering how long she would have to wait and what would be at the end of it.

Then she heard a slight noise, the soft crunch of gravel underfoot, but it came, not from where the boy had gone towards the sea, but from behind her up the track that had led them here. Puzzled and more than a little nervous, she realised suddenly that she had a cheque for a very large sum of money in her bag and that this was a very lonely place where a body could be easily dumped in the sea and disposed of. And no one knew she was there except the boy, and he was obviously very poor and could be paid to keep his mouth shut.

Her voice a tight, strangled sound close to terror, she said sharply, 'Who is it? Who's there?'

The dark figure of a man, big and powerful, emerged from the shadow of a spreading tree and loomed towards her.

Holly opened her mouth to scream and then stared blankly with her mouth open. 'You?' she gasped.

Nick emerged into the moonlight and said sharply, 'Who did you expect?'

For a bewildering moment she thought that he was the man she had come to find, then reason returned as she realised that he must have followed her from the taverna. 'What the hell are you doing here?' she demanded.

'I might ask you the same question. Rather an odd place to come for an evening stroll, isn't it? *And* with rather a strange companion. Why, Holly? Who have you come to meet?'

'How dare you follow me?' Her anger rising, she said furiously, 'And just what right do you think you've got to pry into my business?'

'I still happen to be your husband—just in case it slipped your mind,' he returned sarcastically.

'No,' Holly returned angrily, 'it hadn't slipped my mind. How could it when the sight of you brings it all back—all the whole rotten six months of it!'

Nick was beside her in two strides, his hand gripping her arm, his face murderous. 'Why, you little bitch! If I'd had any sense I would have given you the hiding you deserved when we were together.'

'Oh, really! That sort of line went out with the dinosaurs,' Holly retorted disgustedly.

The grip on her arm tightened for a moment, then relaxed. 'Maybe it did at that,' Nick agreed.

'And I doubt if even a hiding would have got through your total preoccupation with the social whirl you were caught up in at the time.' He let her go and moved away a few paces. 'But I still want to know who you came here to meet.'

'I've already told you it's none of your business.'

'Isn't it? You were scared to death when I came up behind you.'

'Of course I was startled! I wasn't expecting anyone to come from that direction. And you'd be enough to frighten anyone, looming up out of the dark like that,' she added nastily.

Nick laughed thinly. 'We are getting down to basics tonight.' He waited, but when she didn't speak, went on, 'It's something to do with this newspaper assignment you're on, isn't it?'

'What if it is? How many times do I have to tell you it's nothing to do with you?'

'Maybe not. But I'm still going to hang around to make sure you're okay.'

'But you can't!' Holly gazed at him in consternation. 'You'll ruin everything. They stipulated that I came alone!' Realising that last admission would have an adverse effect, she said hurriedly, in as reasonable a voice as she could manage, 'Look, Nick, I—I appreciate your concern . . .' he snorted in disbelief, but she ignored it and went on, 'but I'm quite all right, really I am. I'm just waiting for some transportation to take me to an interview with someone—someone very important. I know following the boy here like this seems a bit way out, but he insisted on complete secrecy. And if you're seen with me—well, it could ruin the whole thing.'

'Who is it?' he demanded bluntly.

'I can't tell you.'

'Then I'll just stick around and find out.'

'No!' Holly bit her lip, recognising the look of implacable determination on his face. Desperately she tried another tack. 'Look, I'm quite safe; they know who I am, but if they found you here they might turn nasty.'

Nick gave a gasping laugh of disbelief. 'Good God, do you think I'm afraid?'

Holly looked at the powerful set of his shoulders and for the first time began to wonder what had happened to him in those seven years, what had changed him into the man he had become. She turned her head away. 'No, I'm sorry.' Then, after a moment, 'This story means a lot to me, Nick. If I get it, it will be the most sensational thing I've ever pulled off. My success—or failure—could make it a real turning point in my career.'

'And is your career that important to you?'

'Of course it is,' she returned sharply. 'It's my livelihood.'

'Really?' he questioned disparagingly. 'Or is it just a way of passing the time between social engagements?'

'Oh, for God's sake don't be so damn patronising! Do you still think that women only have marshmallow between the ears? I work because I have to,' she told him, bitterness mingled with her fury.

From below them, carried on the still night, came the distinct sound of a boat grating on the shore, the sound of voices, talking low.

Holly gazed at him in despair. 'Please, Nick,'

she pleaded, she too lowering her voice to an urgent whisper.

He came closer, looking down at her intently. 'I have to know who it is.'

She capitulated suddenly, knowing that she couldn't win. 'His name is Felix Riddell. He lives on Fallipos, the island in the bay. *Now, will you please go?*'

But still he didn't move. 'How long will you be there?'

'I don't know. It could be several hours. I just don't know how long it will take.'

Behind them they could hear the rattle of small stones as someone climbed up the slope.

Holly opened her mouth to make a last desperate plea, but Nick forestalled her. 'All right, I'm going. But I'll keep under cover and watch you safely on the boat.' His hand came up to grip her elbow for a moment. 'I just hope to hell that you know what you're doing.' And then he had melted into the dark shade of the trees while Holly turned thankfully to meet her contact.

The boy came first and then a man of medium height but very thin build, his skin drawn so tightly on to his bones that when he turned to stare at Holly his face seemed almost cadaverous in the moonlight. He looked her over searchingly, then turned to let his eyes travel slowly all round, searching the darkness. Holly felt her heart thumping loudly and prayed that Nick was well hidden. The eyes in the gaunt face came back to her.

'You are alone?' the man asked in excellent English.

Holly nodded, not trusting herself to speak.

The man turned to the boy and gave him some money, at the same time issuing a curt order in Greek, so that the boy quickly took the money and ran off, back down the track towards the town.

Holly waited uneasily as the man eyed her again. 'You have the money?'

'Yes.'

'Give it to me,' he commanded sharply.

Gripping her bag tighter, she said firmly, 'Not until I'm quite sure I'm going to meet Felix Riddell. Where is he?'

The man's face tightened in anger, making his head more skull-like than ever. 'I have already gone into all this with your paper. They know that they must trust me.'

'They do—or I wouldn't be here,' Holly said placatingly. 'But surely at this stage you can tell me where he is, where the meeting is to take place?'

He paused, then shrugged. 'Very well.' He raised his arm to point out to sea. 'He is on his yacht, the *Alexis*. I have a dinghy down on the beach and will row you out to him.'

'He has agreed to this interview?' Holly asked, still suspicious.

'Yes, he has agreed,' the man answered, almost too quickly.

'Then why like this, at night and in such secrecy, and on his yacht? Why not openly in daylight and at his house on the island? And just who are you and how do you fit into all this?' she demanded.

For a moment he glared at her frowningly, then

seemed to make up his mind. 'My name does not matter, but you can call me Stavros, if you wish. It is sufficient that you know I am close to Mr Riddell. I was going to tell you everything on the way to the yacht, but if you insist I will tell you now. Some years ago Mr Riddell was seriously ill, so ill that he almost died, but it affected his brain. And now,' he shook his head as if in sorrow, 'now he hides away here so that no one can see what he has become.' Coming closer to her, he leaned forward and lowered his voice. 'Some days he is completely normal, others he behaves like a child, but always he has his deformity to remind him.'

Holly stared at him, 'Deformity?'

'His face,' the man explained. 'It, too, was affected, and now he is hideous to look upon, grotesque. That is why he allows no one to come here. Even before his servants he must wear a mask.'

Her eyes widening in appalled horror, Holly stared at him speechlessly. No wonder Felix Riddell had shut himself away from everyone and everything he had ever known! To change almost overnight from a sought-after playboy to little short of a monster—the shock must have been almost unbearable!

But the man who called himself Stavros was going on: 'He depends now to a great extent on drugs. And sometimes, when he has a bad bout of depression, he likes to talk, about his past, about his feelings now and of the little future he has left to him, but for some reason he will only talk to a woman. But there are no women on the island, he cannot bear to have one there in case they ever see

him without his mask, also because he is afraid
they will pity him. He is not, even now, a màn who
can tolerate pity.'

'So what women does he talk to, then?' Holly
asked, absolutely fascinated now by the man's
story.

'It does not happen often, you understand, but
several times now I have brought the boat here
and paid a woman to go out to his yacht.' He must
have felt Holly stiffen beside him, because he
added hastily, 'Please do not misunderstand me;
he does not touch these women, such things are
beyond him now, but he likes to look at them and
just talk to them. They do not understand him, of
course—he speaks only in English, but that does
not matter. He is content that there is a woman
there to listen to his ramblings.'

'Ramblings?'

'Yes, because no one asks him questions or
keeps him to the point.'

'And you think I could do so?'

'If you know your job, yes. But you must be
gentle with him, not push him where he doesn't
want to go. He is very ill. I do not think he will
live much longer.'

Holly thought it over quickly; it all seemed feas-
ible enough, but one thing still bothered her. 'You
still haven't told me how you come into this?' she
reminded him.

Stavros shrugged eloquently. 'I am a poor man.
When Felix Riddell dies it will be hard for me to
find work. I have read about the great sums that
newspapers pay for stories, so I thought of this. It
can do him no harm, he no longer reads the

papers, and perhaps it will do him some good. Maybe one of his ex-wives will read it and insist on visiting him. Give him some company in his last days.'

'They might at that,' Holly agreed, but wondered cynically whether it would be compassion that drew them or just to make sure that they were included in the millionaire's will. Then she chided herself for being over-cynical; that was what working on a newspaper did for you, you saw too much of man's greed and ruthlessness.

But Stavros was speaking again. 'You are satisfied now, Miss Weston?' An edge of sarcasm in his voice.

Holly nodded. 'Yes. Take me out to the yacht and I'll give you the money there.'

'Come, then.'

He turned to lead the way down to the beach, the moon bright enough now for there to be no need of a torch. Holly took a quick look towards the clump of trees where Nick had been hiding, but he didn't show himself. She wondered uneasily how much he had heard and whether he would make use of the information; phone it through to a rival paper and steal her thunder, perhaps. Then she chided herself again; Nick might be the man she most loved to hate, but that was no reason to believe he might play such a dirty trick on her. Unless, of course, he equally hated her!

The path was steep and the shingle loose underfoot, but it seemed well trodden and Holly wondered what it was used for, in such a quiet place out of sight of the harbour. A spot of smuggling, perhaps? A dinghy was drawn up half out of the

water and Stavros helped her in and then pushed
the boat out and jumped in after her and picked
up the oars, sending the boat through the water
with surprising ease for such a thin person.

'What have you got in there?' he asked, nodding
towards her bag.

'Oh, it's just my tape recorder and photographic
equipment.'

His voice was suddenly sharp. 'There must be
no photographs. They are forbidden. Do you
understand?'

'But if he's wearing his mask what difference
can it make?' Holly protested.

'The flash could frighten him, make him realise
what was happening. And then he could turn nasty
and might hurt you before I could restrain him.'

She looked at Stavros silently for a moment.
Then, 'Are you some sort of nurse?'

'Yes.' He looked over his shoulder to check on
their heading. 'Do you agree not to take any
photographs or shall I take you back to the shore?'

'Very well.'

He continued rowing until they were well out to
sea, and then Holly saw the outline of a large
motor-yacht, its only illumination an anchor-light
high on the masthead. Stavros pulled round to the
starboard side and made the dinghy fast to some
steps that had been lowered from the side. He
climbed out of the boat and bent to help her up,
then preceded her up the stairs on to the deck. As
soon as they reached it he turned to her. 'The
money,' he demanded, holding out his hand.

Silently Holly took the cheque from her purse
and handed it to him. He lifted it so that he could

see, then nodded, satisfied.

'This way.'

He led her along a wooden deck, so highly polished that it reflected the moonlight, to a sun lounge and on through double doors leading to an inner cabin. It was too dark to see much, but Holly got the impression of luxury from the thickness of the carpet under her feet and the gleam of silvered mirrors and onyx tables. The place literally smelt expensive. There was a glow of light in the inner cabin, low down, near the floor, and she realised with a shock that it came from an open fire built into the bulkhead, the almost died out coals giving an unpleasant warmth to the darkened room.

But it was the man who sat in an antique straight-backed wing chair near the fireplace who held all Holly's attention. He sat in the chair, gripping the arms, looking straight ahead at the curtained window, although there was nothing to see, and on his head he wore a black hood, like a close-fitting balaclava, with holes for his eyes and slits for his nose and mouth. Holly thought that it was the most terrible thing she had ever seen.

Stavros moved quietly over to the chair and said softly, 'Mr Riddell? Mr Riddell, are you asleep?'

The man started. 'No. No, I'm not asleep. What do you want?'

His speech was slow and slurred, almost as if he was drunk.

'I have brought someone to talk to you. A nice young lady. See, here she is.'

He beckoned Holly forward into the dim light of the fire. The man who had once been the most sought-after jet-setter in the world lifted his head in pathetic eagerness.

'You will sit with me?'

Holly nodded dumbly.

Stavros moved a chair forward for her, but even before he had done so Felix Riddell started to talk, and Holly hastily reached into her bag and took out her cassette player, setting it on to record. For good measure she took out her pad and pencils, but it was difficult to see in the flickering light and he was going very fast, but rambling as Stavros had said, describing a big party he had given in Monte Carlo one year. As soon as she had taken her things out, Stavros picked up her bag and moved it out of the way, making sure she couldn't take any photographs.

Breaking in on his outpourings, she said gently, 'Did you like giving parties, Mr Riddell?'

He seemed startled that she had spoken back at first and was slow in answering, but at length said mumblingly, 'Yes, yes. Always liked parties.'

'Even when you were a child? When you lived in Toronto?' Holly asked, putting in the first of her catch questions.

'Yes, always liked parties,' he repeated. Then, after a moment, 'But didn't live in Toronto. Lived in Quebec.'

Behind her she heard Stavros give a hiss of warning and decided she had better be less obvious next time. She led him on to give her his life story, and as he told her about some of the business methods he had used and the names of some of the women he had had affairs with, Holly began to get increasingly excited. This was really hot stuff! Her second catch question, about one of his wives, he got right immediately and even put her right on a mistake she had made in all innocence, so that she was convinced that he was indeed Felix Riddell. Still, it wouldn't hurt to throw in one more to make absolutely sure.

Using a piece of information she had culled from an obscure Canadian publication, she said, 'And you were with your second wife and your stepchildren, Jodi and Paul, when you entertained the American President on your yacht, the *Delphine*, weren't you?'

'That's right, not this yacht. The *Delphine*. Gave that to my wife.'

'And Mrs McGraw came too, didn't she? The President brought her?'

The voice wavered. 'Yes, he brought her. Very beautiful woman. Very good friend of the President's.'

Holly let him go on talking, but sat stiffly now, her ears pricked to catch every word. Mrs McGraw had been a she all right—and a bitch at that—but she was the President's dog! It was only a small thing, of course, and he might genuinely not have remembered, but it was enough to make her wary and by listening attentively she later caught him in another slip when he got the name of one of his companies wrong, a lesser one admittedly, but one that he first started with and had always owned, so you would expect him not to have to think twice about the name. And he seemed to be telling her too many things that would be of great interest to a newspaper, sensational revelations, instead of the ordinary everyday things you would expect him to dwell on when he was so ill.

The fire had soon died right down, leaving the cabin in almost complete darkness, but it was very hot in there with all the windows shut and the curtains drawn, and Stavros had twice quietly brought drinks for them. She had been there for a long time now, already she had had to change the cassette in the recorder, and Felix Riddell's voice had slowed, become hoarser, and he had often to reach for his drink. Holly listened and watched him as best she could in growing suspicion, but was careful to let none of it show in her voice, her mind busily trying to find a way of proving once and for all whether or not the man was really Felix Riddell. It was quite some time before she realised from the noise of his movements that he must be lifting his mask when he drank. Once he even took something from his pocket, a handkerchief, she supposed, to mop his face, which must have been absolutely boiling under the hood.

Slowly, still asking questions, Holly eased the mini-camera from the pocket of her slacks and with a soft click opened it ready to use. Lifting it to where she judged his face to be, she waited for Felix Riddell to take another drink. The cabin was very quiet really; there was only the drone of his voice as he talked of a bribe he had given to a high-up politician, and the low whine of the cassette recorder. The presence of Stavros, sitting silently in the background, she had almost forgotten, she was so wholly concentrating on waiting for the right moment.

It came at last. She heard him move forward and the chink of the glass, then a blur of darker movement as he lifted up his hand to raise the mask. The built-in flash exploded into light and revealed the man with the mask pulled well up off his face. He had swarthy features; a hooked nose, and a heavily jowled chin. An ugly face, admittedly, but not one that had been deformed and misshapen by disease, and bearing no resemblance to the dozens of photographs of the handsome playboy that Holly had studied before this assignment. So whoever the man was, he wasn't Felix Riddell!

After the blinding glare of the flash there was a shocked silence into which Holly said coolly, 'You might as well turn the lights on, Stavros. I've seen through your game even without them.'

The lights snapped on, revealing the opulent luxury of the cabin; the red leather chesterfields, the blue-period Picasso on the wall set between ornate wall lights.

She turned to Stavros. 'Nice try, but not quite good enough.'

The man who had pretended to be Felix Riddell pulled the mask off his head and brought out a handkerchief to wipe a face dripping with sweat. 'Where did we go wrong?' His voice now quite clear and normal.

Holly smiled thinly. 'Does it matter?' She turned to Stavros. 'I'll take back that cheque.'

He had got to his feet and stood glaring at her, his face more like a death's head than ever. 'I think not. After all, we deserve something for all the trouble we have gone to.'

His voice was low, menacing, and Holly suddenly realised the danger of the position she was in. The other man, too, had got to his feet and stood looking at her, an ugly grin on his face.

'What a silly little girl you are,' he said jeeringly. 'Did you really think we'd tamely hand back that kind of money?'

Holly shrugged, trying to keep the fear out of her voice. 'All right, but you obviously know a lot about Felix Riddell, why don't you tell me the true story?' Bending down, she picked up the cassette player off the table and pretended to rewind it.

Stavros laughed gratingly. 'If we'd had a story to sell we would have sold it long ago. A trick like this was our last resort.'

'And I suppose you hoped that I'd just hand the money over so that you wouldn't have to go through this charade?' Holly said as evenly as she could, her eyes darting round the cabin for a means of escape.

'Oh, no, we knew we'd have to go through with it when your paper insisted on paying us by cheque instead of in cash as we wanted. We knew that we needed time to cash the cheque and get away.' He laughed harshly. 'So don't think we're going to let you get off the boat and stop the cheque, as you're hoping. You're not going anywhere for quite some time, if at all.'

Holly pretended to take a few fearful paces away from him, bringing her near to the cabin wall—not that the fear was in any way a pretence! 'You can't do that. You have no right to keep me here!'

They both began to move towards her from either side of the big cabin.

'Can't we?' said Stavros, a foul grin splitting his

skeleton-like face. 'I think we can do anything we like to you. In fact it might be quite pleasantly interesting *having* you here.'

Putting everything she had into it, Holly suddenly looked past them at the door and shrieked, 'Nick, help!'

In the instant that they both automatically turned towards the door, she threw the cassette recorder across the cabin at the far light fitting and at the same time reached up to the wall light above her head, catching at the ornate brass arm and pulling it with all her strength. There was the rending sound of metal tearing away from the wood panelling as the screws holding the fitting came away from their sockets, and then the electrical wires started to appear and got stuck. The far light bulb had exploded into tiny particles of flying glass when the cassette player hit it and the men had instinctively ducked, but now they saw what was happening and came charging towards her. Holly gave one last, desperate pull and the wires came free again. Then, mercifully, there was a loud bang as the system fused and the cabin was once again plunged into darkness.

Holly took a wide leap to the side just in time, and behind her heard the two men curse as they collided into one another.

'The door! Quickly, cover the door!' one of them shouted.

But she had already thought of that and had decided to try to get out by one of the windows instead while the men knocked into each other in the darkness as they searched for her. Pushing aside the curtains, she spent several agonising seconds feeling for a catch, then held her breath as she fumbled it open and quietly, hardly breathing, started to slide the window open.

'Quiet! What was that?' Stavros called out as the window squeaked a little.

'I heard nothing. Where the hell is she?' the other man returned furiously.

Holly picked up a low table near her and flung it across the cabin in the direction of where she thought the door was. The men gave a shout and started for the noise, and in those few precious seconds of confusion Holly was up and had scrambled unceremoniously through the window and had started to run along the deck away from the cabin. There was no moon now and it was too early for dawn, even the anchor-light was out—she must have fused every light on the boat. Twice she stumbled into things in the darkness, banging her hip quite painfully so that she almost cried out, but she hobbled on looking for somewhere to hide where the men wouldn't find her, somewhere small where she could curl up and be safe. Of how she was to get off the boat she didn't even think; impossible to try to steal the dinghy and row away, that was the first place they would expect her to go to. No, better to hide and wait for daylight. The boat couldn't sail on indefinitely, it would have to refuel some time.

Then she felt something hard and uneven underfoot and stooping down found that it was a ring let into the deck, which meant that there must be a hatch underneath. If she could hide in there . . .

She bent to pull it, but just then a torch shone into her face and Stavros shouted, 'Got you!'

He made a grab for her which she evaded and then she started to run, but her foot caught in the deck ring she had pulled up, she was thrown off balance against the rail and then fell headlong over it, plunging down the length of the boat's side into the blackness of the sea.

She seemed to go down for ever before at last she managed to turn and strike out for the surface, her clothes weighing her down and her lungs full of the water she had swallowed when her scream had suddenly been cut off as she had hit the sea. Treading water, she coughed and spluttered, despair in her heart because now the men would come for her and take her back to the boat. Looking up, she saw Stavros shining the torch over the side and lifted a hand to him. The beam of light caught her and she heard the man laugh. He shouted something to the other man, but he made no move to come for her and then, unbelievably, she heard the boat's high-powered engines throb into life. God, were they going to run her down?

Swiftly she turned and began to swim as fast as she could out of range of the torch, then veered off at a tangent in the hope that they would go the other way. She thought that if they did catch her up she might be able to dive deep enough for the boat not to hit her, but it was the screws she was afraid of; on such a big boat they might be powerful enough to suck her into them and cut her to pieces.

Kicking off her shoes, she swam as she had never swum before, but her jeans were dragging her down with every stroke and she had to waste a few vital minutes while she pulled them off and

also her shirt, letting them sink to the bottom. She
made much better progress then, and when she at
last stopped to rest she saw that the boat was a
good distance away, seemingly going round in
ever-widening circles, the torch playing on the
water as it searched for her in vain.

Pretty confident now that she had outdistanced
them, Holly began to worry that the sea might do
the men's job for them. All she knew was that she
was somewhere in the Mediterranean and had no
idea which way to turn to reach the nearest land—
if there was any within swimming distance, that
was. Then she took herself in hand to balk the
rising panic; the boat had been anchored only a
quarter of a mile or so from Kinos, if she kept
going she must reach it soon. If she was heading in
the right direction *and* if the current didn't carry
her right past it, of course. But she couldn't just
tread water and wait for daylight as she would
very much liked to have done; the men might come
upon her, and the current would carry her along
anyway, so she might just as well swim.

It was nearly three hours later before the grey
cold light of dawn revealed the low dark mass of
land only a few hundred yards away to her right.
If the sun hadn't come up she would have gone on
swimming right by it. Trembling with exhaustion
and cold, Holly from somewhere found hidden
reserves of strength and swam doggedly towards it.
Her legs gave way as she reached the beach and
she had to crawl out of the water on her hands and
knees, collapsing, her last dregs of energy gone, as
she reached the soft cool sand.

The sun had dried her and was burning hot on

Holly's back before she opened her eyes again. Someone was stooping over her and she looked up to see a familiar face examining her.

'Well, well! A mermaid, no less. Welcome to my island, Miranda,' the real Felix Riddell said with a smile on his still extremely handsome face.

CHAPTER FOUR

HOLLY stared at Felix Riddell bemusedly, her mind refusing to believe what her eyes told her. He reached down and helped her to her feet, but she was still so weak that she had to cling to his arm for support.

'Where—where did you say this was?' she asked unsteadily.

'Fallipos. Didn't you know?'

'No. No, I thought I was swimming the other way, to Kinos.'

'And you missed your way—how unfortunate!'

There was irony in Felix Riddell's voice, but it was lost on Holly. She remembered the way the yacht had come after her and her long, despairing swim, and she began to shake uncontrollably, her teeth chattering despite the heat of the day.

'Here, you'd better have this.' He let go of her for a moment while he slipped off his open-fronted shirt and then helped her to put it on. It was only then that Holly realised that her bra must have come off when she was swimming and she hastily raised her hands to cover herself.

'Oh, it's much too late for that. I've already seen *all* your charms.' His eyes wandered down her body and settled.

Holly glanced down too and saw that where her nylon panties were still wet at the front they were quite transparent. She flushed and hurriedly turned away from him.

'If—if you'll be kind enough to lend me a towel and some dry clothes I'd be very grateful, Mr Riddell,' she said stiffly, his tone getting through to her.

'You know who I am, then?'

'Yes,' she admitted.

'And I suppose that after I've given you some clothes you'd like to stay and talk to me for a while, is that it?'

Holly would have liked just that very much, but she could tell from his manner that it was the last thing that was likely to happen. She turned her head to look at him.

'I—I don't know what you mean?'

'Don't you? Oh, I think you do. You're not the first reporter who's tried this means of getting an interview with me, you know. But I must admit that you're the most attractive yet. Although the last woman was Italian and was completely naked,' he added, grinning.

Holly pulled the shirt tighter around her and began to walk back along the beach. Felix Riddell followed her a few paces behind.

'Is there somewhere I can hire a boat to take me back to Kinos?' she asked.

'It can be arranged. And you won't have to pay, it will be my pleasure to provide it. Besides, I hardly think you were able to carry any money about your—er—person.' Holly's back stiffened, but she kept on walking silently. After a few moments he said sarcastically, 'You're not trying to tell me by this air of injured dignity that you're not a reporter, are you?'

Holly stopped and turned to face him. 'No, I'm not a reporter. I'm a photo-journalist.'

For a moment amusement shone in his eyes as he came up to her. 'Oh, that's quite another thing, of course.' Then the eyes grew steely. 'But leading to the same thing. You used this trick to come here and interview me, didn't you? Tried to use my well known susceptibility to female charms to reach me? And how far were you prepared to go, I wonder? The Italian woman assured me that I could do anything I wanted.'

Holly had been through a lot since last night and this sort of sexual crudity was the last straw. Close to tears, she yelled at him angrily, 'Damn you, Felix Riddell! Yes, I did come to Greece to interview you. But only because it had already been fixed up between my paper and one of your employees. And then last night, when I got on your yacht, I found they'd cheated me. It was only a man pretending to be you, after all.' Her voice broke on something dangerously close to a sob. 'And when I found out they tried to keep me on the boat, but I ran away and fell overboard. And then they tried to run me down and I've been swimming and swimming for hours. And now you start being damn rude, and it's just about the last straw! So if you'll tell me where I can get a boat I'll leave you and your rotten island just as soon as I can!' Then, like a fool, she burst into tears and had to turn and run away from him up the beach to hide her face.

He let her go and waited for a good five minutes before coming up to where she was sitting on a stone seat at the beginning of a flight of broad,

shallow steps leading up from the beach. Holly
wiped the back of her hand across her eyes and
blinked up at him. His body in just a pair of blue
Bermuda shorts was still fit and athletic even
though he must be nearing fifty. Whatever he did
on his island, he hadn't let himself go to seed.

Sitting down beside her, he said, 'It seems
there's more to this than I thought. What's your
name?'

'Holly Weston.'

He glanced down at her ringless fingers. 'Well,
Miss Holly Weston, you'd better tell me exactly
how you get here.'

Holly would very much have liked to have
showered the sea-salt from her body and hair and
to have borrowed some fresh clothes before she
did so, but she realised that she probably wouldn't
even get these out of Felix Riddell unless she told
her story first. He seemed quite ruthless enough to
just put her in a boat and send her back to Kinos
as she was. So, haltingly at first, she told him the
whole story, everything.

'I realise I was an utter fool to believe Stavros,'
she admitted finally, 'but it seemed so plausible—
you being struck down by some illness and losing
your looks. Why else would you imprison yourself here?'

He looked at her enigmatically. 'Why, indeed?'
Standing up, he pulled her to her feet. 'You'd
better come up to the house and I'll find you some
clothes.'

She looked at him uncertainly. 'You do believe
me, don't you?'

'These men—what did they look like?'

'The one who pretended to be you was dark and swarthy, and the other one, Stavros . . .' she shuddered, 'he was awful, terribly thin with a face like a skull, as if it had no flesh on it.'

Riddell had stopped and was staring at her intently. A look of fierce anger grew in his eyes as he said, '*Now* I believe you. The swarthy one—he was my valet for several years until I had to dismiss him recently. And the other is the chief mechanic on my yacht. At the moment he's supposed to have it out for sea trials after some repairs. They must have plotted this together and waited until they had an excuse to take the yacht before they sent word to you. Yes, yes, they could have done it. I gave the captain and the rest of the crew leave this week. What exactly did they tell you?' he demanded abruptly.

As Holly told him they walked together up the steps and emerged into a garden, a green paradise where no such trees or flowers should ever have grown. It could only have been created by transporting tons of earth to cover the barren rocks. The plants, from exotic flamboyant trees of the West Indies to English roses, tenderly grown and constantly watered, making a haven of shade, with here and there a lawn and sheltered bowers heavily fragrant with hanging honeysuckle or bougainvillaea. They came to a little white stone circular temple, its domed roof supported by statues of ancient Greek goddesses that looked as old as those she had seen in one of the temples at Ephesus and just as beautifully sculptured. But she was given no time to stand and stare; Felix Riddell strode briskly along another, wider path set between a bank of hibiscus bushes, their large scarlet flowers glowing in the sun, and then up another flight of steps that wound up a quite steep hillside and out on to the terrace of his villa. And now Holly just had to stop and stare. The villa was built into the hillside; its rooms with their stone balconies and the outside twisting staircases, half hidden by exotic trailing plants, all seemed to be a part of the rock slope. There was even a waterfall which cascaded down to a swimming pool set into a paved patio.

'But—but it's beautiful,' Holly breathed. 'Is the waterfall for real?'

The millionaire shook his head. 'No, it's pumped down from a tank on top of the hill.' He went to hurry on but turned back when Holly laughed.

She looked at him in amusement. 'How un-romantic! You really should at least have said that it came from a stream that has magic powers; and that the ancient gods and goddesses drank from it would have been even better, of course.' Then she shrugged. 'But I don't suppose you'd bother with all that for someone who's just an unwanted in-truder.'

Felix Riddell studied her face, almost as if he was seeing it for the first time, his eyes going over her fair hair, still speckled with sand, the grey eyes beneath fine level brows, her straight nose and the clean lines of her mouth and chin. Holly tilted her head rather defiantly under his regard, and he asked abruptly, 'How old are you?'

She frowned, but saw no reason for not telling him. 'I'm twenty-four.'

He shook his head almost in disbelief. 'And I suppose you're hopelessly romantic?'

Holly looked away and reached out to touch a trailing stem of purple bougainvillaea, concentrating on it. 'I was once.'

'But you're not any more?'

'No.'

'I see.'

She turned her face to look at him. 'Do you?'

'Oh, yes.' He smiled wryly.

Remembering his past history, she said, 'Yes, I suppose you do.'

She let go of the spray of flowers and by tacit consent they both turned and walked silently towards the villa.

He led the way through wide patio doors standing open to the sun and into a large room that was a surprise; Holly had expected to see sumptuous decor and priceless ornate, antique furniture, but the room was really very plain, with a polished wooden floor with just two or three brightly-coloured locally woven rugs, and roughcast walls painted white to give a stark background to several French Impressionist paintings that even to Holly's untrained eyes spelt Van Gogh and Utrillo. The furniture, too, was plain; a couple of settees with deep, squashy cushions, a baby grand piano in one corner, and the only concession to conventional ideas of luxury—a really good set of hi-fi equipment and a whole wall of shelves filled with records and tapes.

'You'd better come through to my communications centre first and then I'll find you some clothes.'

Riddell led the way up a spiral staircase and into a corridor with several rooms opening off it, the doors all tantalisingly shut. The communications centre made Holly's eyes pop. It was almost like walking into an aeroplane cockpit, with a huge and complicated-looking radio transmitter, telex machines that clattered continuously, racks of telephones in different colours, as well as several computer systems. There were two men manning the room and Felix Riddell crossed to speak to one of them, who immediately picked up a phone and began to talk into it urgently.

'We should have a trace of the yacht within an hour,' the millionaire said as he rejoined her. 'Although if they think that you were drowned they might even bring it back of their own accord, thinking themselves safe.' He smiled grimly. 'It will be interesting to see their faces when they find you here, waiting for them.'

Holly, too, found that thought very satisfying after the way they had tried to run her down. Then she realised that the first thing they would do, whether the men returned to Fallipos or not, would be to cash the cheque she had paid them. Catching his arm as he was turning to go out of the room, she said quickly, 'Mr Riddell, may I ask you a favour? The cheque I gave to Stavros— could you please telex my newspaper and ask them to stop payment on it immediately?'

His eyebrows rose and he said rather scathingly, 'They got the money out of you, did they?'

Her voice hardening, Holly retorted, 'I thought they'd delivered the goods!'

He laughed, suddenly seeming ten years

younger. 'A drugged and masked caricature of me being the goods?'

Holly decided to get her own back a little. 'Well, he did seem to know an awful lot about your past life. Especially about your women—he knew a great deal of detail about those.'

His eyes narrowed. 'Did he, by God?' Then, blandly, 'I hope you didn't believe it. Anyone who could make up such a plausible reason for my being here would obviously make up those sort of sordid details as well—just to titillate you and make you forget the more important things he'd glossed over, of course.'

Holly's mouth opened as she realised that he was mocking her, but before she could make a retort he turned and said, 'Come along, I'll show you where you can change.'

He went down another corridor which opened into a gallery overlooking a huge dining-room which had a great fireplace stacked with logs in one corner, a luxurious extravagance on an island where every log would have to be shipped in from the mainland. He halted by a door further along the gallery and said, 'You'll find everything you want in here. When you've finished go down the outside stairs to the patio.' Then he pushed open the door, gave her a brief nod and walked briskly back towards the communications centre.

This room had yielded to modern comforts more than the others Holly had seen, with a wooden four-poster bed hung with flowered chintz, a dressing table, and soft carpet underfoot. It was one of the rooms with a balcony overlooking the garden, and Holly immediately went to stand on it and look out at this green paradise set in the clearest of seas and under the bluest of skies. For a few minutes she just drank in the beauty of the place: the richness of the flower-filled garden, the warmth of the sun, the heavy scent of the oleander that draped its red flowers like colourful curtains on either side of the balcony, and the silence broken only by the soft murmur of the sea and the gentle buzz of a honey bee that drank its fill from the silken flower heads. Perhaps for the first time in her life she began to realise just what money could do and how it could enhance the lives of those who possessed it in unlimited quantities, but that it could create something as perfectly beautiful as this she had never imagined in her wildest dreams.

Turning back into the room, she discovered a bathroom opening off it and also a dressing-room lined with wardrobes which, when she opened the doors, she found to be full of women's clothes, all new from the looks of them and bearing labels that made her stare reverently. And there weren't only clothes, but also dozens of pairs of shoes in several sizes and drawers full of delicate lace underwear, all still in their pack-aging. Holly gazed in awe, wondering just who all the things were intended for; hardly for chance visitors like herself, so presumably Felix Riddell still had female guests on the island from time to time, and far more than just one, if the variety of sizes and colours was anything to go by.

Holly took her time over her shower, using the shower lotion she found in the bathroom together with an expensive shampoo for her hair. Then she wrapped herself in a thick bath towel not much smaller than a bed sheet and padded back into the bedroom where she explored the dressing-table drawers until she found a hairdryer; by now she was quite sure that Felix Riddell had overlooked nothing that would add to the comfort of his female guests. She spent a blissful half hour looking through the clothes and would dearly have loved to try most of them on, but in the end she chose the simplest sundress and sandals that she could find, feeling that as she was only an uninvited and unwelcome intruder she had no right to anything at all, let alone something expensive. But she did go a little overboard with the 'Joy' perfume she discovered, together with a large make-up kit in one of the drawers, but then what woman could possibly resist the scent advertised as the most expensive perfume in the world?

Almost reluctantly, she left the lovely room and walked along the balcony to where the outside staircase was cut into the rockface, twisting down to be for a while in deep shadow and then in bright sunlight where jasmine flowers cascaded over the balustrade and shafts of the sun's rays turned the stone to gold, a metamorphic change surpassing that of any ancient alchemist.

Felix Riddell was waiting for her on the patio, seated at a round garden table and with another casual shirt over his shorts. He looked up as she approached and quite openly studied her as she walked towards him, his eyes running over her appraisingly. But he made no comment on her appearance, merely motioning her to a chair.

'I expect you're hungry?'

'Mm, starving!'

'Then I'll order breakfast for you. You'll have to excuse me not joining you, but I had mine some time ago.'

'Of course. What is the time?' Holly asked. 'Unfortunately my watch wasn't waterproof and it's stopped. And I didn't see a clock anywhere.'

'You won't,' Riddell answered with a short laugh. 'That was one of the first things I did away with when I came here. No more living by the clock and chasing time, cramming as much into the day as I possibly could. The only place where there's a clock now is in the communications centre where I have a digital international time clock so that I don't get people out of bed when I telephone them. No, here on Fallipos I let time take its course, with the result that it almost seems to stand still. But if you really want to know what the time is,' he glanced up at the angle of the sun, 'then I'd say it was between ten-thirty to eleven o'clock.'

Holly had been smiling to herself while he had been speaking, and now he turned his head and caught her. 'I suppose you think that's a very Bohemian attitude to life?' he demanded rather sneeringly.

Holly laughed. 'No, I think it's a wonderful attitude if one is rich enough in money—or time—to do it. No, I was just wondering what all the sales staff of the quartz watch manufacturing company you own would say if they could hear you.'

He grinned. 'I guess it wouldn't be very good for business, would it?'

An elderly manservant came then with a

heavily-laden breakfast tray, and Holly bit hungrily into the hot rolls spread with home-made butter and honey, washed down with several cups of American coffee. While she ate her host asked her questions about her career and these she answered readily enough, telling him about some of her previous assignments and her early years in journalism.

'You're rather young to be sent on a job like this, aren't you?'

'I suppose so,' Holly confessed, 'but there aren't that many female photo-journalists around, especially those who can take off at a moment's notice to more or less anywhere in the world.'

'You intended to take photographs of me?'

'I hoped to.' She smiled ruefully. 'But I had to abandon all my gear on board your yacht and I expect Stavros will have thrown it overboard by now so there won't be any evidence that I was ever aboard. Lord, my editor will go mad when he hears he has to replace that little lot!' A thoughtful smile curved her mouth. 'I wonder how Stavros will explain the light fitting I broke. Perhaps he's pulled into some port now and is desperately trying to get it fixed before he brings the yacht back.' Then she looked at him rather guiltily. 'I'm sorry about the lights, but it was rather an emergency, you understand?'

'Oh, quite,' he answered gravely. 'Please feel free to pull my boat to pieces any time you like.'

Holly looked at him quickly, saw the amusement in his eyes and laughed. Sitting back in her chair, she said with a sigh, 'Oh, it is good to be alive!'

His eyes became grave again. 'It was very foolish of you to go off with them without some sort
of safeguard. Didn't you tell them at the hotel
where you were going?'

Holly shook her head. 'I wasn't sure exactly
where I was going myself. And you have to be prepared to take risks if you want to get good stories.'

'Where are you staying? I'll get someone to ring
and let them know you're safe.'

'Oh, that won't be necessary, thanks. I'm only
staying at a taverna in Melmia and I'm sure no
one there will worry about me if . . .' she stopped,
suddenly remembering Nick, and went on slowly,
'if I stay out all night.'

But Felix Riddell had seen her hesitation and
picked it up quickly. 'There is someone?'

She shook her head. 'I remembered that I did
tell someone that I was going to interview you, but
I'm sure he won't have given it another thought.'

'He?'

'An Englishman I know who happens to be on
holiday here.'

Thankfully a buzzer sounded discreetly then,
preventing him from questioning her further as he
picked up the receiver of a telephone and listened
for several minutes. Then he replaced it and smiled
with some satisfaction. 'My yacht has been traced
to Piraeus, the seaport that serves Athens, and I've
arranged for the two men to be brought back
here.'

'The police will bring them?'

'No, not the police. I have my own means of
dealing with those who are disloyal to me.'

Holly looked at him and shivered suddenly,

glimpsing for a moment the cold ruthlessness that had carried him to the heights of power and fortune. Not for anything would she want to be in the shoes of Stavros and the other man when they faced Felix Riddell.

He gave her his attention again, saying, 'You say that you can take off at a moment's notice; does that mean that you have no family commitments?'

'Yes,' Holly answered carefully, 'but I have them organised so that I'm able to do my job.'

'I see. And just what are your commitments? Parents, boy-friends? A lover, perhaps?'

Holly's features tightened at the bluntness of the question, but she replied evenly, 'None of those. But I'm sure you're not really interested in my private life, Mr Riddell.'

He sat forward and looked at her intently. 'Oh, but perhaps I am. Perhaps I'm very interested. Tell me about your private life, Miss Holly Weston, tell me all about it. I want to hear every detail: who was your first lover; how many men you've been to bed with; who cured you of being a romantic. Come, tell me all about yourself,' he commanded with a definitely nasty edge to his voice.

Holly frowned, not pretending that she hadn't understood where he was heading. 'I haven't asked you any questions about your personal life, Mr Riddell.'

'No, but that's why you came here, isn't it? To probe and pry into my past, to hold an autopsy on my marriages, find out about my business interests. And most of all, of course, to find out why I shut myself away on this island. That's the truth now, isn't it?' he demanded forcefully, his fist hitting the table.

For a long moment Holly looked back at him without speaking, then she said slowly, 'That was the story I came to Greece to get, yes. But only if you'd chosen to give it to me of your own free will. Since it turns out that it wasn't you who had agreed to an interview, then I have no right to ask you any question, and I won't do so.'

He stared at her for long seconds, complete surprise on his face. 'A reporter with moral scruples—I don't believe it!'

'I work for a very reputable journal, Mr Riddell, not one of the sensationalist newspapers. We would have checked every fact that I'd been given before we published the story.' She smiled thinly. 'Somehow I doubt if either my paper or you would have been very pleased if we'd had banner headlines branding you as a deformed idiot.'

A look of horror came over his face. 'Good God, no!'

'Although,' Holly added thoughtfully, 'it would have forced you to repudiate it. You'd have had to come out into the open then.'

'So I would. Perhaps we've both had a lucky escape.' He looked at her keenly. 'So you're really not going to ask me any questions?'

She shook her head, smiling, but adding provocatively, 'Not unless you want to tell me, of course. But you know, you're going to have to tell your story some time. Those men could easily have duped a reporter who hadn't done his homework thoroughly. And—I don't know how much you keep in touch with gossip columns and the like—

but there have been a great many rumours going around about you lately: that you're a drug addict, recovering from a nervous breakdown, that you're imp . . .' She stopped herself hurriedly and tried to cover the hesitation by adding quickly, 'Some even say that you've died and that a consortium is running your business. Which could be very bad for your stock market shareholdings if it gained any ground.'

. Felix Riddell shrugged dismissively. 'Those kind of rumours have been circulating almost since the day I moved here. I'll know how to deal with them if they start to get out of proportion.' His eyes fixed on her steadily. 'But there was one rumour that you changed your mind about telling me; what was it?'

To her annoyance Holly found herself starting to blush. 'Oh, it was nothing, really.'

'Then tell me,' he commanded in a tone that brooked no denial.

'Well——' she looked down at the table, tracing along the edge of it with her finger. 'Well, they—er—they did sort of mention that you might be impotent.'

She had expected him to be angry, but to her surprise he laughed heartily. Leaning forward, he reached out to cover her hand with his. His eyebrows rose and there was a look in his eyes that Holly couldn't fail to understand. 'I can assure you that that's one rumour that is definitely untrue. In fact I'll be pleased to prove it to you personally if you'll give me the chance?'

Before Holly could even begin to form an answer they were interrupted by the sound of foot-

A special offer for readers of Mills & Boon

Four Mills & Boon Romances-FREE

We have chosen four Romances for you to enjoy FREE
and without obligation as your special introduction to
the Mills & Boon Reader Service.

Mills & Boon Romance

SEEN BY CANDLELIGHT
Anne Mather

Mills & Boon Romance

THE IVORY CANE
Janet Dailey

Mills & Boon Rom

THE MA OF CAR LINDS
Margaret

steps and Felix Riddell turned round, a frown on his face, but his hand still holding hers. There were three men crossing the patio towards them, two of them were holding guns which were steadily trained on the third man, who was obviously their prisoner. Holly took one look at the third man and froze into a stunned silence.

Felix Riddell demanded angrily, 'Who the hell is this? How did he get here?'

One of the men with the guns answered tersely, 'He sailed his boat into the bay. We warned him off, but he kept right on coming, even though we fired at him. He says he's come for the girl,' he added, nodding towards Holly.

'But I see that I needn't have worried.' Nick spoke for the first time, his tone heavy with sarcasm as he looked pointedly at their joined hands.

Holly hastily drew hers away and put it under the table.

Felix Riddell looked from Nick's face to hers. He stood up. 'Do you know him?' he asked her.

Nodding reluctantly, she replied, 'Yes, he's the Englishman I told you about.'

'Ah, yes.' He addressed the two men. 'It's all right, you can go. But later I shall want an explanation from you two on how he managed to land here.' This was said with a frown that boded them no good, and the men's shoulders sagged as they took themselves off. Turning back to Nick, he said, 'So you thought she needed rescuing, did you?' He moved round to stand in front of Nick, drawing himself up to his full height. Both of them were tall men and well built, but the years of dissipation had begun to show on Felix Riddell, in the slight thickening of his waistline and the lines round his eyes, whereas Nick had still the suppleness and vigour of youth. An instantaneous antagonism seemed to have sprung up between the two and it seemed to Holly that they faced each other like boxers squaring up for a fight, or a king stag preparing to defend his ground and his harem of does from a challenging newcomer.

Sarcastically Riddell added, 'And so you decided to do your Sir Galahad act to impress the lady.' He glanced at Holly. 'Are you impressed?'

Nick, too, turned to look at her and Holly found that she couldn't have answered for the life of her.

His lips twisting into a cynical smile, Nick said, 'It seems that I wasted my time. The lady only needs saving from herself.'

'So why don't you take yourself and your boat back where you came from?' Riddell said harshly. 'I'll bring Miss Weston back when she's ready to go. And in future when you're warned off, stay off.'

Nick put his hands in the pockets of his jeans and leant nonchalantly against the table. 'Either she comes with me or we both stay.'

Riddell's brows drew into an angry frown. 'Do you want me to have you thrown out?'

His voice silky but holding a definite challenge, Nick said, 'Go ahead and send for your henchmen and let them try—if you can't do it yourself, that is.'

Projecting herself into the sudden tension, Holly said hastily, 'I'm quite ready to go now. I'm sorry that I intruded on you, Mr Riddell, but thank you for lending me the clothes: I'll send them back to you just as soon as I get to Kinos.'

He drew his eyes away from Nick's to look at her. 'Keep them,' he said briefly. Then, persuasively, 'There's no need for you to go yet, Holly. I told you I'd put a motor-boat at your disposal. Why don't you stay and have lunch with me? Maybe we can talk some more about why you came here.'

Holly looked at him quickly, hopefully, wondering if he was considering letting her do an interview after all.

Seeing the gleam of interest in her grey eyes, Felix smiled down at her, the lazily seductive smile that had won him countless conquests in the past. 'Why don't you tell our well-meaning but extremely interfering friend here to take himself off?'

Before she could answer Nick stepped forward and put a hand on her shoulder in the age-old possessive gesture of a male for his mate. 'Perhaps the situation hasn't been made quite clear to you,' he said, addressing the older man and looking him straight in the eyes. 'The lady happens to be my wife.'

There was a short, rather shattering silence, and then Riddell looked at her and said coldly, 'Is this true? Are you married to him?'

Her face pale except for two bright spots of colour high on her cheekbones, Holly answered steadily, 'In theory.'

Felix Riddell's eyes sharpened. 'But not in practice?'

Even with Nick's fingers biting deeply into her shoulder, she replied with a firm, 'No.'

CHAPTER FIVE

HOLLY carefully refrained from saying a word until she and Nick had been escorted down to the small harbour by the two guards and had boarded his boat and were sailing back towards Kinos, but all the time her anger and resentment at his high-handed action was steadily growing. Nick, too, had kept a tight-lipped silence as he went about the business of raising the sails and steering them away from Fallipos. He had removed his hand from her shoulder the moment she had denied him, but he had still refused to go without her, so there had been nothing for it but to leave at once; no way could the two men have spent any more time together without there being a nasty confrontation of some sort or another.

The wind filled the dull red of the sails as they passed out of the protecting arms of the harbour bay, setting the rigging creaking and the waves lapping merrily against the sleek hull, but Holly was oblivious to the music of the sea and the wind, she was entirely caught up in her own emotions and turned on Nick furiously.

'How *dare* you come for me? Just what right do you think you have after all these years to just walk in and start interfering in my life? I could have *killed* you!'

Nick laughed unpleasantly. 'Spoiled your pitch, did I, Holly? And just as you were getting really friendly with the great man too. From the look of it he was just on the point of propositioning you when I turned up.'

This was so near the truth, even though she was sure that Felix Riddell had only been funning, that Holly felt herself start to colour guiltily. Which, of course, only served to make her angrier than ever. 'Whether he was or not is none of your damned business. How I lead my life is my own affair. You gave up any right you might have had to question it the day you walked out on me.'

Nick's dark brows drew into a frown. 'You're quite right; what you do doesn't concern me. I came to find you only because your paper has been calling you since dawn this morning. The hotel-keeper had seen us together and when he found that you hadn't slept in your room last night he came over to my boat to see if you were with me.' He smiled thinly. 'After I explained that I was the last person you would have spent the night with, he told me that your paper wanted to get in touch with you urgently and he asked me to take the call because his English isn't that fluent. It seems they were afraid you might have been duped by the person you were supposed to meet. Your editor had found out that a trick had been tried before or something, and he wanted to catch you before you fell for it.' His eyes ran over her, noting that her clothes were different from the ones she had worn the day before. 'I take it that your being out all night means that you did fall for it?'

Holly glared at him. 'Well, that's just where you're wrong. They were very clever, but I saw through them.'

'So how come you end up by being with Felix Riddell?'

For a moment she opened her mouth to tell him the whole story, but then hesitated; even though she had seen through the imposture she had a pretty good idea that Nick would still condemn her as a fool for putting herself in such a dangerous position, especially when he heard that she had fallen overboard and had to swim for it. No, the less he or anyone else knew about it the better. So she merely replied shortly, 'I've already told you that it's none of your business,' and turned to see how far they were from Kinos.

But the mocking tone in which he said, 'Afraid to tell me?' brought her sharply round to face him again.

'No, I'm *not* afraid to tell you, I just don't choose to, that's all,' she snapped, furious again. 'If you hadn't barged in when you did I might even have persuaded Felix Riddell to give me his story.'

'Yes, I noticed how persuasive you were being,' Nick agreed dryly. 'Who was doing the propositioning, him or you?' His tone grew insulting. 'Or was he just thanking you for spending last night with him?'

'Why, you . . .' Overcome with rage, Holly sprang to her feet, took two furious steps across the deck, and, before Nick could stop her, hit him hard across the face. Her anger at the present situation had triggered it off, but behind the slap was the pent-up hurt and resentment of the last seven years. Bitterness welled up like a flood and once started she couldn't stop. 'You louse! You swine!' With every epithet she hit out at him blindly, wanting to hurt, to give as much pain as she had suffered.

Her first blow had taken him by surprise, but then Nick raised his right arm to defend himself, his left hand still holding the wheel as he tried to steer the boat and capture her flailing hands. Then he gave a curse and let go of the wheel completely so that the boat yawed and came round, the sail flapping emptily against the mast.

'You little spitfire!'

He reached out to grab her, but she was in such a blind fury, beating against his chest with her fists, trying to claw at his face, that it took a few minutes for him to catch her wrists and twist them behind her back. Even then Holly still struggled and fought; twisting in his arms and arching her body as she sought vainly to get free. She began to butt him in the face, and Nick swore savagely and wound a hand in her hair, jerking her head away so sharply that she winced with sudden pain.

'Damn you, you little wildcat! Stop it!' He shook her then, shook her till her teeth rattled, his voice as angry as her own. And when he let her go she stood before him, no longer fighting but trembling with spent rage and emotion, tears running unhindered down her cheeks. As Nick looked at her he gave a strange, strangled sort of groan. 'Oh, God, Holly!' And then he pulled her roughly, almost violently to him and kissed her devouringly, his fingers digging into her arms, his lips bruising hers as he took her mouth with a savage intensity, not caring whether he hurt her or not.

'No!' She tried to pull away, horrified at what

was happening, but he dragged her back hard against him and put his arm down to hold her body close while the other hand he put at the back of her neck so that she couldn't turn her head away from the cruel ravishment of her mouth. Impossible to break free, so Holly tried to hold herself rigid, to dissociate herself from his embrace, but then the harder fight began as memories started to flood back; the strong hardness of his lips that had caressed her body so many times, the sharp tang of the aftershave he had always worn, the sheer animal masculinity of him; all the evocative sensations that had lain dormant in her subconscious, deliberately pushed out of mind for so long, came back now to fill her with all the sensual desire that his kisses had always aroused in her. It had always been like this, right from the very first; she had never been able to resist him when he set out to arouse her, soon capitulating and moaning with desire as his hands and lips explored her, caressed her.

With a choking cry Holly tore herself from Nick's arms, her hands going up across her chest as if to protect herself from him. 'You rotten swine! Take your filthy hands off me!'

Nick gazed at her, his breath ragged and uneven, his face for a moment naked and vulnerable, then he seemed to make a conscious effort to pull himself together. 'You had that coming,' he said harshly. 'You've been asking for it since the moment we met.'

'That's where you're wrong,' Holly managed. 'It's the last thing I want from you!'

Nick's jaw tightened. 'You wanted it once. You

used to almost beg me to make love to you.' His voice became grim. 'But then that was *all* I could give you, wasn't it? Your parents made sure of that.'

Unevenly, Holly said, 'Leave my parents out of this. What they did . . .' She shrugged tiredly. 'It's over and best forgotten.'

Nick looked at her sharply. 'You know, then, that it was their interference that split us up?'

She nodded. 'Yes, I realised soon after you'd gone.'

'We might never have parted if it hadn't been for them.'

Holly smiled bitterly. 'Oh, I'm quite sure we would. If you cared for me so little that you could just walk away and never even try to write or contact me in any way, then I'm quite sure that our marriage wouldn't have lasted much longer than it did, in any circumstances.'

While she spoke Nick had been looking at her searchingly, but now he took a hasty step towards her. 'Holly, I . . .'

But she moved away and said quickly, 'Nick, let's leave it, *please*. It all happened so long ago. It's over and done with now. What's the use of tearing each other apart, raking it all up again?'

He stared down at her for a long moment, then said slowly, 'Does it—tear you apart?'

Holly tried to turn her head away from his searching gaze, not answering, but he put his hand up to her chin and forced her to face him. 'Does it, Holly?' he asked again, a note almost of urgency in his voice.

She tried to read his face, to find out what he

wanted her to say. Did he want her to say yes because it would give him sadistic delight to know that he still had the power to rouse her emotions, or did he genuinely want to know? Holly found that she wasn't prepared to give so much of herself away, and countered with, 'Does it you?'

The urgent light died out of his eyes and he let her go and stepped back. He smiled without humour. 'As I said, women are always afraid to answer a direct question.' Then he turned abruptly away and went back to the wheel of the boat, ignoring her.

Holly turned with a sigh of relief to lean over the rail and watch the outline of Kinos gradually come nearer. It was true that she had realised that her parents had been responsible for the break-up of their marriage soon after Nick had left, but that hadn't been the direct reason. At first, in the first week or so after Nick had gone, she had been positive that he would either come back, or else that he would have found them somewhere else to live and insist that she join him, but as the days had gone by and there had been no word from him, her parents had started to talk of divorce, taking it for granted that she would agree. The bitter realisation that he had indeed left her made her so stunned that Holly hardly realised what they were saying, and it was only when they went over her head and made her an appointment with the family solicitor that Holly came to her senses. By then she knew that she was pregnant and told them, expecting them to drop all talk of a divorce and do their best to help her find Nick so that they could try and patch things up. But to her horror, her parents' reaction was that it made no difference; she must go ahead with the divorce and have an abortion. As her mother said, 'You surely don't want that ungrateful upstart's child? Not after what he's done to you—and to us?'

Bitter scenes had followed then, with her parents trying to persuade, and when that didn't work, to bully her into having an abortion. But Holly had been adamant in her stand, hoping, but with ever-increasing despair, that Nick would contact her. After several weeks, when hope had at last died and her parents' continual nagging became intolerable, she had packed her clothes, drawn what little money she had out of the bank, and grimly left their house to live in a tatty, one-roomed bedsitter in London. At first it hadn't been too bad, she had found a job as a waitress in a hamburger bar quite easily, but as her pregnancy increased and became obvious, her movements slower, she had been dismissed and had to rely on National Assistance handouts to live. She had let her father know her address, as much in the forlorn hope that Nick would get in touch with her, as anything, but they had made no attempt to contact her or come to see her, and when she wrote again to let them know that they had become grandparents, the letter was returned marked 'NO LONGER AT THIS ADDRESS'. There had been times then, when she was cold and hungry, afraid to let the baby cry in case she got thrown out by her landlady, that she had hated her parents for not standing by her, but with the new maturity thrust upon her she had come to realise that it was her own stubbornness that had brought her down. If she wanted to keep her baby, then she would have to rely on her own resources.

Of Nick she tried not to think at all, knowing now of her parents' deliberate campaign against him, she could understand why he had left and forgive him for it, but nothing could make her forgive him for not caring what happened to her after he had gone, for not trying to make a go of their marriage outside her parents' home.

She turned now to look at him, standing tall at the wheel, his hair ruffled by the breeze. It had been a hard and bitter struggle to keep and rear his child. She wondered suddenly what he would say, what he would do if he knew, if she came right out now and told him. Holly smiled grimly to herself; he would probably take her back to Kinos as fast as he could and then turn round and get the hell back to Australia or wherever he was going without a moment's pause, rather than have even the possibility of being saddled with a wife and child he didn't want. The smile became even more bitter; maybe he might even ask the classic question: 'Who's the lucky father?' But as she watched him he lifted his head to look up at the pennant flying at the top of the mast and her heart gave a dizzying lurch; there was no need to ask who Jamie's father was, he tilted his head in exactly the same way as Nick when he looked up at her, with the same long-lashed blue eyes and the firm, determined chin. No one, seeing them together, would ever question his parentage.

Nick turned his head and caught her watching him. His eyes met hers and held them steadily until the memory of that bruising kiss came vividly back and Holly dropped her own, a slight flush of colour in her cheeks. He said, 'Will you be going back to England now that your assignment is over?'

'Yes, there's nothing here to stay for now,' she agreed stiltedly. 'I'll leave tomorrow morning.'

He shook his head. 'There isn't another ferry until Wednesday. You'll have a couple of days to wait.' He hesitated, then said, 'I was thinking of making a trip some time to Samos, that's an island about half a day's sailing from here. Pythagoras, the mathematician, was born there, and you can see the remains of the temple of Hera. If you like we could go tomorrow, spend the night there, and sail back the day after so that you can catch the ferry on Wednesday.'

Thrown by his sudden invitation, Holly said bluntly, 'Why on earth do you want to take me?'

Nick shrugged. 'You're at a loose end and I thought it might amuse you.'

Holly sniffed disparagingly. 'I should hardly think it would be amusing to spend so much time in each other's close company when we can't even exchange two sentences without ripping into one another.'

Keeping his voice level, Nick said, 'Maybe we ought to give it a try for that very reason. To see why we have this effect on each other.'

'But that's obvious,' Holly returned with a frown. 'It's because of what happened between us in the past, of course.'

'Is it? Seven years is a hell of a long time, Holly. I was just a student then and you little more than a schoolgirl. We've both changed, become adults.

The bad times we went through then shouldn't have lasted to colour our emotions now. Not,' he added slowly, 'unless they went very deep. And if they did that, then they must have mattered a lot—to both of us.'

He had been looking at her steadily as he spoke, and it was this, as much as his words, that silenced the harsh retort Holly had been going to make. Instead she turned away and looked blindly out to sea. 'I—I don't know,' she stammered.

'Think about it. Maybe if we talked the thing through . . .'

But Holly broke in sharply. 'No! What's the point in holding an inquest now? The corpse is already rotten in its grave!'

Nick was silent for a moment. Then he said rather flatly, 'All right. If that's the way you want it. So just come along for the ride.'

'I don't know,' she said again. 'I'll have to think about it.'

They were silent then until they sailed into Melmia harbour and Nick had moored the boat. He vaulted lightly over the rail on to the wall and then reached down to give her a hand, but she stumbled as the boat moved under her and he had to catch hold of her to prevent her falling, lifting her bodily on to the harbour.

'Oh!' She gave a gasp as she found herself held close against him, his arm firmly round her waist.

For a moment he continued to hold her, his eyes on her face so close to his own. Holly thought for a few crazy seconds that he was going to kiss her again and stiffened, but he merely said brusquely, 'I'll be at the taverna at eight tonight. You can tell me then whether or not you want to go to Samos tomorrow.'

He released her then, so suddenly that she was taken by surprise. Giving her a curt nod of farewell, Nick jumped back on board and began to busy himself reefing the sails.

Holly began to walk slowly back to the taverna, her heart still racing in her chest. Her thoughts went back to the fight on the boat; Nick had said then that she had asked for it, implying that she'd deliberately started the fight to provoke him into finishing it the way he had. But that wasn't true at all, at least not consciously; all she had wanted then was to hurt him. And when he had started to kiss her she had resisted by every means in her power. It was only as it went on that it had evoked memories of the good times, the wonderful, halcyon times when he had made such ardent love to her. Then, too, he had been uncontrolled, his desire for her overriding everything else as he had taken her in a frenzy of wild passion that had raised them both to the heights of physical ecstasy. Even now, just thinking about it still had the power to make her skin prickle with heat, to send waves of sensuality and longing coursing through her body.

Holly came to a sudden stop, cursing herself for a fool. She was behaving like a bitter, frustrated spinster, relying on fantasies for her kicks. And that was all it was, really, a fantasy; something that happened so long ago and for such a short time that it had taken on a dreamlike quality. Or had, until Nick had brought it all so rudely back to reality, to the present instead of the dim and

distant past. Brought it back so vividly that when
he had helped her off the boat and held her in his
arms she had wanted him to kiss her, wanted urgently to feel his mouth on hers, to have his hands
touch her until he had roused her to the peak of
desire, to . . . Holly shuddered, forcing her mind
away. Such thoughts were the height of madness.
This was the man who had walked out on her and
that was all that mattered. That fact, and only
that, was what she must remember, hold in her
mind. Everything else must be firmly shut out.
Both for her own sake and that of her little son,
she must not let ancient memories of shared joy
intrude into her life now. The path she had chosen
was a lone one and didn't include any permanent
male companion—and not for a moment would it
include Nick Falconer! She had given herself to
him in love and trust once, but she would never do
so again.

But there was still the problem of the expedition
to Samos to be worked out. Had his motives been
purely altruistic? Somehow Holly couldn't see it,
any more than she could understand why Nick
sought her out or had come after her to Felix Riddell's island. It couldn't be possessiveness or jealousy; if he'd felt those emotions he would never
have left her in the first place. Although the way
he had squared up to the millionaire had definitely
had a 'hands off, this is mine' belligerence about it.
Holly sighed. Drat Nick Falconer! Why the hell
did he have to come back into her life? she thought
grimly. In fact, why had he ever come into it at all?
But that thought brought her up short; if there
had been no Nick there would be no Jamie. But

apart from that ... Holly paused outside the taverna and turned to look back at the boat where Nick was stowing the last sail. No, she knew now, in a sudden blinding revelation, that despite all the grief and pain that had come after, not for anything would she have missed those few ecstatic months when they had been lovers.

Going into the taverna, Holly told the relieved Alexis Lambis that she was quite safe and then went up to her room to change out of the clothes Felix Riddell had lent her. He had said she could keep them, of course, but she was determined to return them. Even if he only had the things thrown in the dustbin at least her conscience would be clear. Her mouth puckered into a moue of chagrin at the failure of her assignment. And worse than that, she had lost all her precious camera equipment. She could just imagine the Editor's face when she told him, and her spirits sank dejectedly. The paper would provide her with new equipment, of course, but the Editor wouldn't be pleased, especially as she didn't even have a story to justify the loss. And when he heard that she had actually met Riddell and not got an interview out of him, he'd probably hit the roof!

She slept through most of the afternoon, then went down to the beach to swim and sunbathe for an hour or so before getting changed for dinner. During that time she had thought of little else but Nick's invitation, but even when she went down at eight to meet him, she still hadn't made up her mind. One minute she thought that she would accept, to prove to herself that she was immune to him as much as anything, the next she decided that

she couldn't, that she was still far too vulnerable
to him and being alone with him for two days
would be bound to lead to disaster one way or
another. Quite which way her mind shrank from
pursuing. If he hadn't kissed her on the boat
everything would have been clear-cut; she definitely wouldn't have gone with him because they
rowed all the time, but now ... now there was a
fatal fascination about the idea. Holly knew there
ought not to be, knew that the only sane thing to
do was to stop short right now and have nothing
more to do with Nick, to just keep out of his way
until she could leave the island. But that kiss had
left her weak and confused, incapable of making a
decision, her body filled with a yearning that she
thought had died long ago.

Nick was waiting for her at one of the tables on
the terrace, wearing a lightweight tan safari suit
this time. He stood up as she walked towards him,
looking at her appraisingly. Holly found that she
couldn't meet his eyes and sat down hurriedly,
making a business of arranging the stole she had
brought with her round her shoulders until she
had had time to collect herself a little and could
face him with a degree of composure.

She was afraid that he would come straight out
and ask her for her decision, but fortunately he
just asked her what she wanted to eat and then
told her something of his job, explaining what he
did and where it had taken him during the last
seven years. Then it was her turn to talk about her
work, her face becoming animated as she did so,
her hands expressively emphasising her point.

They continued to talk on safe, uncontroversial

subjects while they ate, but afterwards Nick subtly brought it back to a more personal level.

'You've obviously been quite a success in your career. What made you take it up in the first place? I don't remember you ever wanting to when we were together.'

'No.' Holly picked up her glass of wine and ran her finger idly round the edge. 'I decided to take it up soon after—you went away.'

They were both silent for a moment until Nick said, 'But why photo-journalism?'

'It was just journalism at first, the photography came later, when I had more time.' She hesitated, then said, 'I needed something that I could do mostly at home, that gave me some free time to attend to—other things.'

'Like the full social life you've always been used to,' Nick interrupted sardonically. 'All the cocktail parties, dances, and coffee mornings you couldn't live without.'

Holly's chin came up. 'Of course. What else?' she retorted in cold sarcasm.

A puzzled look came into his blue eyes. 'What did your parents think of your work? It wasn't exactly what they had in mind for you, was it? They approved wholeheartedly of the social butterfly existence you were living.'

Holly became interested in her glass again. 'They had nothing to do with it. In fact, they knew nothing about it.' She shrugged. 'They probably still don't. You see, I—I left home shortly after you did. I haven't seen my parents since.'

Nick stared at her incredulously. 'You left home? But didn't they try to stop you? You were only seventeen, still under age, surely they . . .'

'You forget,' Holly interrupted tightly, 'they were no longer my legal guardians—you were. And as you weren't around to express your wishes on the subject . . .' She let the sentence tail off, the words she hadn't said as expressive as those she had.

Nick was still staring at her, his mouth drawn into a thin line. Heavily he said, 'Why, Holly? Why did you leave home? Was it because of what had happened to us, because you realised that it was your parents who had . . .' he paused, 'who had come between us?'

'Who had made life intolerable for you, you mean, don't you?' She sat back in her chair and looked out to sea, at the water lapping gently on the shore, curling in soft waves of phosphorescence in the moonlight, as she wondered how much to tell him. Slowly she answered, 'It was partly that, but there were—other things.'

'What other things, Holly?' he demanded insistently when she didn't go on.

Speaking with difficulty, she replied, 'They—they wanted me to get a divorce straightaway—but I refused. There were rows—so I left.'

Nick tensed and sat forward, his eyes on her face intently. 'Why didn't you want a divorce?'

'Because I . . .' Her hand began to shake and she hastily set down the glass. She would have put her hand in her lap, under the table out of sight, but before she could do so Nick reached quickly out and covered it with his, holding it firmly so that she couldn't escape. She raised eyes that were suddenly afraid. 'Please, Nick. I don't want to talk about it any more.' She tried to pull her hand away, but he wouldn't let go.

'No, Holly, you can't stop now. *You have to go on.* Why didn't you want a divorce?'

Holly stared at him, unable to hide her vulnerability. 'Because I ... At first, you see, I—I thought you would come back.' His hand tightened on hers, tightened till it hurt. Biting her lip, she looked away and was silent for a long moment. Then, her voice changing completely, becoming harsh and bitter, she went on, 'And then, when I was sure that you weren't, that you'd gone for good, there was no point in getting a divorce,' adding venomously, 'What would be the use of being free when I had no intention of ever marrying again? I may have been fool enough to marry you, but not such a fool that I didn't learn by my mistake. If nothing else those few months with you taught me never to put my trust in a man again!'

Shaking with emotion, she glared across at Nick, but he was staring at her with a strange, almost bemused expression in his eyes. Leaning forward across the table, he said urgently, 'Holly, *you* never got a divorce; has it ever occurred to you to wonder why *I* didn't?'

She smiled crookedly. 'Only once. And when I realised what the answer must be I certainly didn't want to think about it any more.'

His eyebrows rose. 'Just what answer did you come up with?'

'The right one. That it was convenient for you to remain married because it was a way out of any entanglements with women who wanted to tie you down, who weren't satisfied with just an affair and wanted to make it permanent,' she answered curtly.

An angry glint came into his eyes for a moment and she felt his fingers tighten on her hand again, but then he relaxed and said, 'And did it never occur to you that you might be wrong? That my reasons for not getting a divorce could be identical to your own?' He hesitated, then said slowly, 'That they might even go farther than that?'

Holly stared at him, her throat feeling suddenly tight. 'What—what do you mean?' she stammered.

Earnestly he said, 'Holly, I didn't just walk out on you. I did . . .'

'Excuse me. Miss Weston?'

Holly looked up rather dazedly to see a man in a dark, Naval-looking uniform standing by the table. Vaguely she was aware of Nick's furious 'Hell and damnation!' as he let go of her hand.

'Y-yes, I'm Holly Weston.'

The man gave a courteous little bow. 'I am in the employ of Mr Riddell, madam. He asked me to bring this to you.' And he held out her bag of photographic gear and her cassette recorder, luckily still intact.

'Oh, you found it! Oh, how wonderful!' Holly's face lit with pleasure and relief. Without thinking, she added, 'I was sure those men would have thrown it overboard after me.'

'No, madam, it was found safely aboard the yacht.' He took a white envelope from his pocket and held it out to her. 'Mr Riddell also asked me to give you this letter and to wait for your answer.'

Holly took it from him and slid open the envelope, aware, without actually looking directly at him, that Nick was frowning in disapproval. The letter was brief and to the point.

'You may well be right about me having ·to come clean with my story. Why not come over to Fallipos tomorrow so that we can discuss it further? Yours, Felix Riddell.'

Hardly able to believe her good fortune, Holly didn't hesitate before turning to the messenger. 'Please tell Mr Riddell that the answer is yes, I'd be pleased to visit him tomorrow.'

'Very well, madam. The yacht will call for you at ten tomorrow morning, if that is convenient for you?'

'That will be fine. Thank you.'

The man gave another small bow and left them alone again.

His voice tight, Nick said, 'I take it that means you won't be coming with me to Samos tomorrow after all?'

'No. I'm sorry, Nick, but as you've probably guessed, there's a possibility that Felix Riddell may give me an interview—and I can't afford to pass up a chance like that.'

'Not even for a prior engagement?'

She looked at him steadily. 'I hadn't said that I'd definitely go with you, Nick.'

'No more you had.' He sat back, anger in his eyes, his tone heavy with contempt. 'So instead you're going over to Fallipos. Running to do Felix Riddell's bidding when he crooks his little finger at you. And will you be just as willing to meet his terms for an interview?'

Holly's face paled. 'And just exactly what do

you mean by that?'

'You know darn well what I mean! Just what lengths are you willing to go to to get this story?'

Angrily Holly got to her feet, but Nick reached out and caught her arm. 'Oh, no, you're not running away from this one.' Exerting his strength, he forced her down into her chair again. Holly glared at him in impotent fury, angry as much with her own weakness as with him. 'Let go of me, you swine!'

Nick grinned maliciously. 'Not until I'm good and ready. I'm beginning to realise just how much you've changed. Tell me, where did they teach you to prostitute yourself for a story—at the School of Journalism?'

'How *dare* you!' Holly's eyes blazed. 'For your information, I've never, *never* had to use sex to get a story—and I don't intend to start now!'

'No?' he asked jeeringly. 'When I found you with Felix Riddell you were holding hands and definitely *not* behaving like strangers who'd just met.'

Shrugging rather helplessly, Holly said, 'That was just—just a joke. A reaction to something I'd asked him.' Nick's eyebrows rose in disbelief, and she added fiercely, 'Believe it or not; I couldn't care less. I don't have to defend myself to you. And just because we happened to live under the same roof for a few months it certainly doesn't give you the right to question me now.'

'And shared the same bed. Don't forget that!' Nick interrupted grimly.

That silenced Holly as nothing else would have done. She stared at him for a long moment, her eyes large in her pale face, then she blinked and looked down, putting up her free hand to lean her head on it.

He released the grip on her arm, moving his hand down to cover hers as he said urgently, 'Holly, please don't go to see Felix Riddell tomorrow. Come with me to Samos instead.'

She started to shake her head. 'There wouldn't be any point. We have nothing to say to each other and . . .'

But he broke in quickly. 'Yes, there is, Holly. I've a great deal to tell you that you don't know. Things that could make all the difference to us.'

'No,' she answered firmly. 'I came here to do a job and that must come first. I'm not here on holiday like you. I have responsibilities even if you haven't.'

His eyebrows rose in surprise. 'What responsibilities?'

Biting her lip, Holly hastily covered her slip by saying, 'To my paper, of course. They pay me to go after stories, not to pass them up because I've received an invitation to go sailing. And if they heard that I'd let slip an opportunity like this they'd probably fire me.'

Nick took his hand from hers and sat back in his chair. 'Would you like another drink?'

'No. No, thanks.' Holly shook her head, glad that he seemed to have taken no for an answer at last. For a few minutes they sat in a rather strained silence, Nick looking broodingly out to sea, while Holly wondered just what it was that he had wanted to tell her, things he'd said she hadn't known, that could make all the difference to them.

Briefly she wondered if he had just made it up as a lure to persuade her to go with him, but then she dismissed the idea from her mind; whatever else he had been, Nick had never been devious. Always, in the past, he had been completely open and above board, had never tried to deceive her in any way. So if he said he had something to tell her . . . She opened her mouth to ask him what it was, but he forestalled her.

'What did you mean when that man of Riddell's gave you your gear back and you said you were afraid it had followed you overboard?'

Holly looked discomfited. 'Oh, that. It was nothing.' She glanced at his watch and gave a pretended gasp of surprise. 'Good heavens—eleven-thirty already!' Standing up, she picked up her case and nodded to him. 'Thanks for the meal, Nick. Sorry I can't make it tomorrow. I expect you'll be moving on soon, so I'll say goodbye as well as goodnight in case I don't see you again.' Then she gave him a bright, false smile before walking quickly away.

He hadn't said anything, just watched her go, although Holly half expected him to try and stop her, but he merely sat there silently drawing on his cigarette, his expression completely unreadable.

It was almost with a sense of release that Holly shut the door of her room and dropped her case on the table. She supposed she ought to check its contents, but it would have to wait until the morning; right now she was too tired to bother, her complete lack of sleep the previous night hitting her now. And the last few hours with Nick hadn't helped; she had been as tense as a coiled spring, unable to relax, her emotions like trip-wires ready to be set off by the slightest jar. Only now that she was away from his menacing presence could she start to unwind, to sit on her bed and lean back against the wall, eyes closed, hands shaking a little from the release of tension.

The rap on her door broke sharply into her almost trancelike state. More asleep than awake, Holly automatically got up to answer it, only briefly wondering who it could be. But when she opened the door and saw Nick leaning his long length against the door jamb, she came fully awake in an instant. Immediately she moved to slam the door in his face, but he put his foot out to stop her and then calmly pushed his way in and closed the door behind him.

Eyes blazing, she said furiously, 'If you don't get out of here this minute I'll start screaming for help!'

Nick's left eyebrow rose sardonically. 'Go ahead—but don't forget that we're in a still rather primitive area of Greece. The people here have very basic ideas about what rights a man has over his wife—and one of them is definitely visiting her bedroom whenever he feels like it.'

'They don't know I'm your wife. I don't use your name any more,' Holly broke in heatedly.

'But they will when I show them the photograph I have in my wallet; you in your virginal white and me in the morning suit your parents insisted on,' he explained tauntingly.

Holly's face paled. 'You—you still carry that around with you?'

'You never know when it might come in handy.'

'I can imagine!' she retorted sarcastically, but then looked away, feeling totally confused. Haltingly, she said, 'Why have you come here, Nick?'

He didn't answer immediately, but waited for her to look at him again, to see the lazy, mocking smile on his lips before he lifted his arm from where it had been partly hidden at his side and held her stole out to her. 'You left this behind. It fell off the back of your chair.'

'Oh! I—I see.' She moved forward slowly and reached out to take it from him, then stopped suddenly.

Nick's eyes gazed down into hers, the mockery gone from them now and in its place an entirely different light. Softly he said, 'Come here.'

Holly began to tremble and she said in a stammering entreaty, 'No, Nick. Please—no!'

But he let the stole fall to the floor and put his hands on her shoulders to gently draw her towards him. He kissed her slowly, deliberately, exploring her mouth with his lips in tiny little kisses that made her insides seem to take fire. She gave a little moan under her breath and stirred sensuously, moving closer to him, but he held her off, not letting her get too near. Then his right hand left her shoulder and began to move downwards, caressing her neck, her breast and on down to her hips. Desire grew, filling her body with intense yearning, and she began to writhe under his hand. His kiss became more passionate then, his tongue touching her lips as she opened her mouth under his. Suddenly he put both his hands low on her hips and pulled her hard against him, letting her know how much he wanted her. Holly gasped as she felt his hard body against hers, heard him groan deep in his throat as she put her arms round his neck and pressed herself against him, returning his kisses with a fierce hunger.

His hand moved up to twine itself in her hair, his lips bruising, but then he pulled her head away so that he could see her face.

His voice thick and unsteady, he said softly, 'It was always good between us, Holly. Whatever else was wrong, this was always perfect. Even the very first time, when you were still a virgin; it was one of the most wonderful experiences of my life. And it was for you too, wasn't it? Wasn't it?' he repeated, his head coming down to kiss her neck, her throat, his breath burning her skin.

'Yes,' she moaned softly. 'You know it was.'

He sought her lips again, compulsively, his dominant sexuality demanding submission. 'I want to make love to you, my darling one,' he murmured against her mouth. 'Just the way it used to be.'

It may have been that last phrase, or perhaps the endearment, one that he had never used when they were together, that brought Holly back to reality, that made her suddenly shiver as if she was very cold and deliberately move out of his arms. He looked down at her in surprise, his eyes dark with desire, his pulse unsteady.

Tightly she said, 'I think you got it wrong, didn't you? You don't mean make love at all; you mean that you just want to have sex with me. Because that's all it would be.'

'No, Holly, that isn't so.' Nick took a hasty step towards her, his hands reaching out for her, but she backed away.

'No?' Her voice became jeering, bitter. 'What are you trying to tell me, then? That you never stopped loving me, or that now you've seen me you've fallen in love with me all over again?'

Nick's hands dropped to his sides. Slowly he said, 'Something like that, yes.'

Holly laughed jarringly. 'You must be crazy if you expect me to believe that! The way I read it, if you'd loved me you'd never have left me. People don't just walk out on those they love—not if they really care about them. But perhaps you didn't know that. Perhaps you thought I'd just fall into your arms the way I did before. Well, all right, I admit that you can still turn me on. And that's all you want really, isn't it?' Her voice unsteady, she faced up to him. 'For some crazy reason you just want to prove to yourself that you can still make me, that after all these years you still have the power to dominate me sexually.' She looked up into his eyes, gone glacier-cold now, and shivered convulsively again. 'Okay, so I admit it,' she repeated, her voice rising, 'so why don't you . . .'

But Nick stepped forward and caught her by the elbows jerking her towards him. 'But I haven't, have I? Not yet.'

She stared up at him, suddenly frightened. 'What—what do you mean?'

'You know exactly what I mean. Even though I excite you, you're letting your head rule you so that you back off at the last minute. You're a coward, Holly. You're willing to make verbal submission in the hope that I'll be satisfied and leave you alone, but you're afraid to give yourself to me in case you find out that what you feel for me is more than just physical need.'

'That's all it could possibly be,' Holly broke in defiantly. 'That's all it ever was!'

'Was it?' Nick's brows rose as he let her go. 'I never took anything from you that you weren't prepared to give.'

'No? How about that last time?' she demanded, the hurt raw in her voice. 'I certainly wasn't willing then.'

His jaw tightened. 'That was—different.'

'Yes,' she agreed harshly. 'Unforgettably different!'

There was a short tense silence which Nick broke by saying heavily, 'It isn't over between us, Holly. Not yet. Too much has been left unsaid, too many old wounds opened up for us just to walk away from one another.' He paused, then added deliberately, 'And you know as well as I do that before we're through we're going to make love again—*and it's going to be soon*. That, too, is still between us.' He bent to pick up her stole and tossed it on the bed. For a moment he looked at her, but when she didn't speak, said mockingly, 'Sweet dreams, Holly,' and left the room, shutting the door softly behind him.

CHAPTER SIX

FELIX Riddell's yacht, the *Apollo*, captained by the same man who had brought her the message the previous evening, picked Holly up punctually at ten the next morning, and took her over a sea as calm as glass across to Fallipos. At the jetty she was met by an austere English butler who conducted her—led was hardly the appropriate word—to where Felix Riddell waited for her in the large room that overlooked the garden.

He moved forward to greet her as soon as she came in, a lazy smile on his handsome face. 'Good morning, Holly. I trust you've now fully recovered from your unfortunate dip in the sea?'

She smiled. 'Yes, thank you. I'm fine.' She held out the parcel of clothes she had borrowed. 'And thank you for lending me these clothes, Mr Riddell.'

He waved the parcel aside. 'I believe I told you to keep them. And the name's Felix.' Putting a hand under her elbow, he led her to the long settee and poured her out a Martini without bothering to ask her what she'd like, then he sat down beside her, one arm along the back of the seat. His eyes ran over her critically, as if he was summing her up all over again, but Holly returned his regard steadily, in no way intimidated. He smiled, his eyes crinkling up at the corners. 'Tell me,' he said lightly, 'are we likely to have that husband of yours charging in on us again today?'

She shook her head, aware of the warning behind the question. 'I hardly think so,' she answered coolly.

'Good.' He stood up. 'How would you like to see my picture gallery?'

Holly's eyes widened a little in surprise; Felix Riddell was rumoured to have an art collection that rivalled that of the late Paul Getty, including the most comprehensive set of French Impressionist paintings in the world. But he was like a miser with his hoard, never lending any of his paintings to exhibitions or allowing connoisseurs or other collectors to study or photograph them; many of his friends hadn't even been invited to look at them. So Holly felt more than a little overwhelmed by the unexpected privilege, then thought sardonically that perhaps he had a secondary collection that he allowed his visitors to see.

But in this she was mistaken; his picture gallery was like a massive walk-in safety vault with huge steel doors at the entrance, the paintings hung on bare white walls and lit by electric light. The rich colours of Cézannes, Van Goghs, Gauguins and many others leapt at her in the long, stark room, overwhelming her at first by their sheer number and magnificence, but gradually, as she looked back down the gallery, she felt an infinite sadness that the power and beauty of the paintings should be shut away like this, hoarded for one man's pleasure.

Felix had led her slowly along, speaking knowledgeably of the paintings and their artists, and at first she had asked excited, eager questions, but as she grew silent he glanced at her with a puzzled frown.

'Doesn't art interest you?' he asked her abruptly.

'Yes, very much. I used to spend hours in art galleries in London when I was living in digs; they were the only places where you could go and get warm for nothing,' she added with a reminiscent smile.

'But you don't like these pictures?'

Holly gave a slight frown and answered slowly, 'Of course I like them, they're wonderful paintings, but ... I'm sorry, I don't mean to offend you, but I can't help thinking that so much beauty ought not to be shut away, they ought to be shared so that everyone can see them. I'm sure the artists never intended them to be locked away like this.'

'Do you have any idea of the value of this collection?' he demanded.

She shook her head. 'I'd hate to even make a guess. But surely,' she paused and looked at him uncertainly, 'if a picture is taken out of circulation, then its value can only be judged by the amount of time you spend looking at it? Today you've spent about two minutes or so in front of each painting, but you probably spent ten minutes reading a newspaper, so the newspaper is worth five times as much to you as a painting.'

Felix Riddell stared at her for a moment and then burst out laughing. 'That is the most upside-down philosophy I've ever heard! But I must say it's original, I'll give you that.' He glanced back down the gallery. 'I suppose you're one of those people who think that all great paintings should be in public galleries; but has it never occurred to you that a painting won't last indefinitely, that it has to be kept in ideal conditions to preserve it as long as possible? And what better way to spend one's money than in trying to save as many of these great works as one can? Only the other day the Italian police recovered some paintings that had been stolen from a small gallery some months before, but the thieves had stored them in an old shed where they'd been pecked at by chickens and soaked by rain and snow, so that they were all ruined beyond repair. At least I know that something similar will never happen to these while they're in my keeping.'

Holly laughed lightly and held up her hands in surrender. 'Okay, okay, I admit that there are two sides to every coin, but I still can't agree that they should be shut away like this.'

Felix, too, laughed, an appreciative twinkle in his eyes, but continued to argue with her over the subject in a friendly way as he showed her out of the gallery and clanged the great steel doors shut behind them, sealing them by setting the buttons of an electronic gadget set in the wall.

'The locks are linked to a programmer in the computer room upstairs,' he explained. 'No one can open them without my orders.'

He then took her over the rest of the house, acting rather like a guide in a showplace as he pointed out the pieces of sculpture and other objets d'art in the various rooms. For a few fleeting moments it seemed to Holly as if he was setting out to impress her with his wealth, although why he should want to she couldn't think. But he certainly seemed to be going out of his way to entertain a relatively unknown journalist who had intruded into his privacy. Holly looked at him with a puzzled frown between her brows; wondering if he just enjoyed showing off his possessions or whether he had some other motive in pointing them out to her. But then she shrugged the thought away; what other reason *could* there possibly be?

They had lunch out on the patio in the shade of a jasmine hedge, a wonderful meal that was a mixture of the most delicious Greek and French food. During it Felix put himself out to amuse her, making her laugh with anecdotes from his past about the rich and the famous people he had met. He was a witty and clever raconteur, knowing exactly how much detail to put into his stories and the precise moment for the punchline, so that Holly enjoyed herself immensely, tears of laughter in her eyes.

'Oh, no!' she gasped at one of his more way-out anecdotes. 'He didn't do *that*? Not the *President*?'

But Felix assured her that it was true. 'But don't spread it around or I might never get invited on his yacht again,' he added with a grin.

Holly sat back and gently swirled the glass of Napoleon brandy he had poured for her. 'Would that disappoint you very much?'

It was the first time she had asked him a personal question, but so far he had made no mention of giving her an interview for her paper and she was eager now to know where she stood, so she tried this as a tentative lead-in.

But Felix merely smiled and answered, 'Not too much, no.' He poured brandy from the crystal decanter into his own balloon and raised it to her in a silent toast. 'But I've been talking too much.

How about telling me something about yourself?'

'But I told you all about my career at breakfast yesterday.'

'You also told me that you hadn't any commitments,' he pointed out wryly, 'and ten minutes later your husband showed up.' He waited for her to speak, but when she didn't, he said softly, 'Was he the one, Holly? The one who took the romance out of your life?'

She looked down at the table. 'Something like that,' she agreed, trying to keep her voice as even as she could.

Felix watched her keenly. 'So what is it between you two? Are you separated, divorced, or what?'

'I suppose you'd call it separated, although we've never consulted solicitors to make it legal or anything,' she told him reluctantly.

He frowned. 'So why is he with you now?'

Holly raised her head. 'Look, do we have to go into this? I'm sure that my marriage can be of no earthly interest to you, so I'd rather just drop the whole subject, if you don't mind,' she said shortly.

'But I *do* mind.' His tone was so forceful that Holly's eyes widened in surprise. Setting down his glass, he leant forward, his eyes regarding her steadily. 'I want to know what your position is in regard to your husband, Holly,' he paused, then added deliberately, 'and I want to know exactly what your feelings are about him.'

Holly blinked, taken aback by his sudden vehemence. Slowly she said, 'He isn't with me. He was already here when I arrived, on a sailing holiday round the Greek islands. It was pure coincidence that he happened to be at Kinos when I came here to interview you.'

'He didn't know you were coming?'

Shaking her head, she said decisively, 'No, he couldn't have done.'

'When did you last see him, write to him? You may have mentioned it and forgotten about it.'

She smiled wryly. 'Oh, no, that's quite impossible. We haven't seen each other or communicated in any way for the last seven years.'

'Seven years!' Felix stared at her in amazement. 'But you must have been just a kid then?'

'I was seventeen. As you say, just a kid,' she agreed bitterly.

Felix's hand came out to cover hers. 'What happened?' he asked gently.

She glanced quickly at him, a refusal to speak about her personal life again hovering on her lips, but there was such a kind, concerned look in his eyes that the words died unspoken.

His hand tightened on hers. 'Tell me,' he commanded.

'There's nothing to tell, really. We were both just too young—me especially. We lived with my parents and they didn't get on with Nick. So he left—and forgot to take me with him. Absent-minded of him, wasn't it?' she added with heavy irony.

Felix was watching her frowningly. 'How long did it last?'

'About six months—give or take a few fights.'

'I see.' He sat back. 'And I suppose seeing him here so unexpectedly has brought it all back, made the hurt raw again?'

Her hand trembled under his. 'It has a bit, yes.'

He grinned. 'The British skill at understatement!' Then, 'When is he moving on?'

Holly shrugged her shoulders and retrieved her hand. 'I don't know. He seems to be sticking around.' She didn't think that she had given anything away in her voice, but Felix looked at her shrewdly.

'Maybe he wants you back?'

'No, I'm sure that isn't his reason for . . .' she broke off, a faint flush in her cheeks.

'So what is his reason?' Felix pursued. He looked at her face, then said thoughtfully, 'Or maybe I can guess. He wants to go to bed with you again, is that it? Wants to satisfy his curiosity about what he saw in you in the past, about what kind of woman you are now.'

'I should hardly think he'll find that out just by sleeping with me again,' Holly retorted acidly.

'That's where you're wrong.' Felix leant forward and picked up her hand again, easily overcoming her resistance, and holding it in both of his. 'A man can find out everything he wants to know about a woman when he makes love to her. A woman has no secrets in bed.' He paused, looking down at her hand and playing with her fingers, before saying almost casually, 'Are you going to let him?'

Despite herself, her hand jerked in his. 'That's none of your business,' she returned coldly.

He lifted his head and looked at her steadily. 'Maybe it's not—but I'd very much like it to be,' he added deliberately, his eyes holding hers.

Holly stared at him for a long moment. Impossible to have misunderstood, impossible not to read the message in his eyes. In some confusion, she pulled her hand away and stood up. 'If—if you'll excuse me, I'll just go and freshen up.'

'Of course.'

He, too, stood up and Holly could feel him watching her as she walked across the patio and entered the villa. Once in the cloakroom, she thankfully locked the door behind her, grateful for a little privacy in which to collect her thoughts. Slowly she crossed to the mirror over the marble sink and stared at her reflection in the glass. Her skin was quite tanned now, but even this healthy glow couldn't hide the dark smudges under her eyes, or the frown of worry in them. She hadn't slept much last night, even though she was tired, after that row with Nick. She had lain awake, thinking about him, her body still hot and frustrated from the way he had kissed her, caressed her. The thought of his fingers touching her making her toss and turn on the bed, longing for fulfilment. She wanted him to take her, she knew that, wanted it desperately, after all these long empty years. For a while she had even been on the point of getting up and going to his boat, to wake him and tell him that she'd changed her mind, that she wanted to go to bed with him. But pride held her back. To go to him now would be utter weakness, almost as if she was saying that all the hurt and unhappiness he had caused her didn't matter. It would be a betrayal by her own body. So she had deliberately made herself remember the bad times in a feeble attempt to strengthen her resolve, a resolve she knew would be sorely tried the next time Nick tried to take her. And that there would be a next time, she had no doubt at all. He had said he wanted her, and she knew him well enough to know that he would ruthlessly pursue that aim—and what the end would be she was afraid to even begin to imagine.

She bent to wash her hands and sighed exhaustedly; this assignment was going completely wrong. First Nick had exploded on to the scene, and now Felix Riddell was causing complications. His last remark had made it perfectly clear that he was interested in her, which raised added problems, the most important being had he just invited her here for his own ends or did he really intend to give her an interview for her paper? Holly swore under her breath. Damn all men! She had managed to keep free of them for so long, and now they were threatening to disrupt her life again. Almost viciously she re-applied her lipstick and then strode back out on the terrace, in no mood for even the mildest flirtation, ready to snap Felix's head off if he tried it. In fact, she would almost have welcomed the chance, so that she could lose her temper, tell him just what she thought of old men chasing young girls, so that he would have nothing more to do with her and she could pack up and go home, never to see either of them again!

But Felix was more than her match when it came to experience of women; he took one look at the belligerent light in her eyes and kept the topics of conversation completely impersonal for the rest of the afternoon, so that gradually she relaxed and began to enjoy his company again. So much so that once or twice she tried to steer him back to the question of an interview, but he refused to commit himself one way or the other, merely grinning and changing the subject.

They went for a swim from the beach where she had been washed up, then had a game of tennis before changing for dinner, Holly again borrowing a dress from the extensive wardrobe he kept for female guests. She had been in two minds about staying, uneasy about his intentions, but apart from that one remark after lunch, Felix had made no attempt to make a pass at her, and when he saw her hesitate, had smiled and said, 'And of course my yacht will be waiting to take you home whenever you're ready.' So they had dined by candlelight, on the richest, most wonderful food she had ever tasted, served on dishes of the finest porcelain once owned by the Tsars of Russia, and drank wine from crystal glasses that reflected the light in a rainbow of colours. Then they sat in the big lounge and listened to music from equipment so sophisticated that the orchestra seemed to be all around them. A log fire took the chill off the evening, and Holly grew sleepy and comfortable.

Felix came over to take her empty glass from her. 'Another drink?'

She shook her head and straightened up from where she had been half-lying on a settee. 'No, I must go, it must be getting late.' She glanced around and then remembered that he didn't have any clock in the room. 'How do you tell the time when it's dark?'

He laughed. 'Oh, I just go to bed when I feel tired and get up when I wake. But there's no reason why you shouldn't know the time.' He crossed to his desk and took out a slim black box from the top drawer. He held it out to her. 'Here.'

Slowly she took the box from him and opened it. Inside was a watch on a slim gold band—real gold! After only a moment Holly shut the box again and handed it back to him. 'I'm sorry, Felix, but I can't accept this.'

He frowned. 'Why not?'

'You know perfectly well why not.' She stood up agitatedly. 'I'll go and change.'

'Holly.' Felix reached out and caught her arm. 'Don't read something into this gift that isn't there. It isn't even a gift really—just a replacement for the watch you ruined when you went into the sea off my boat.'

'It isn't necessary; I can get my own watch mended when I get home.'

Rather exasperatedly, he said, 'That watch is made in one of my own factories; I keep a dozen of them here to give to friends.'

'Maybe you do,' Holly answered unsteadily. 'Maybe an expensive gift like that is nothing to them, or to you. But it is to me—*and you know it*.'

'All right.' He looked at the heightened colour in her cheeks for a long moment, then let her go. 'All right,' he repeated. 'I'll tell them to have the boat ready to take you back to Melmia in twenty minutes.'

He was waiting for her when she came down in her own clothes and took her elbow to guide her through the moonlit garden to the jetty. But just before they emerged from the trees he stopped and turned her to face him.

'Will you come again tomorrow?'

Holly hesitated, wondering if there was any point.

Guessing the reason, Felix said earnestly, 'Look, I know you still want the interview, but I haven't yet made up my mind. I'd like us to get to know each other better first. I need to be sure that you'd give me a sympathetic hearing before I commit myself.'

There was a note of sincerity in his voice that enabled Holly to make up her mind. 'All right, I'll come tomorrow.' She held out her hand and smiled at him. 'Thank you for a wonderful day.'

He took her hand, but instead of shaking it carried it to his lips. 'Goodnight, Holly.'

It was late when the yacht pulled into the harbour at Melmia, but there were still a few men sitting on the terrace of the taverna, involved in one of the constant, unending arguments that were their greatest pleasure. As she hurried by, Holly glanced quickly up, half expecting to see Nick at one of the tables, but the men were all native Greeks. Then, as she climbed the outer stair, she saw him on the deck of his boat, leaning nonchalantly against the mast, smoking a cigarette. Quickly she turned and ran up the rest of the steps and dived into the corridor, hoping against hope that he hadn't seen her, but knowing full well that he had. In her room she hurriedly locked the door, then ran to the window. He was no longer on the deck and she couldn't see him on the street. Hardly able to breathe, she waited, expecting any second to hear his rap on the door, hear him demand that she let him in. But all was quiet and still, even the Greek men soon taking themselves off. Slowly she relaxed and undressed, then went to close the shutters. Nick's boat was in darkness, like all the others in the harbour, swaying gently to the soft roll of the sea. She pulled the shutters to, closing Nick out, closing her mind to whether or not she would have opened the door to him if he had come to her room.

The yacht came for her at the same time and she again spent the day very pleasantly with Felix, learning to play squash in one of his two squash courts and after dinner watching a newly-released American film in his private cinema. Again he had said no word about the interview and again he hadn't made a pass, although when he said good-night to her before putting her on the boat, he this time kissed her lightly on the lips. 'Until tomorrow,' he said softly.

Nick's boat was still tied up at the jetty and he was again on deck smoking a last cigarette, but as he saw her disembark from the yacht, he threw the stub into the sea and went below. Almost as if he had been waiting up to see her safely home, Holly thought, feeling half resentful, half ... but what her other feelings were, she wasn't quite sure herself.

The next two days followed the same pattern with only a couple of phone calls from the Features Editor to disturb it. Holly had already told him that she was working on Felix Riddell, but he was becoming impatient with her lack of progress.

'You don't understand the situation,' she explained. 'He's a tough nut to crack. If I try and push him he'll just tell me to go to hell. But I'm sure he will make up his mind before too long.'

'Okay, stay with it. You've done fine to have got so far,' the Editor assured her. 'But try to clinch it as soon as you can, will you? If any other papers get wind of the likelihood of him telling his story, they'll all be there like a pack of wolves.'

But it was the next day before Felix finally made up his mind. After dinner he led her to a room she hadn't been in before and which he described as his den. The walls were lined with shelves of books, many of them extremely early and valuable ones from their titles and cover bindings, although Holly was far from being an expert. He poured out a couple of drinks from a decanter on an antique sideboard and gave one to her.

'Let's drink a toast, shall we?'

Holly smiled. 'By all means—but what to?'

He looked at her quizzically. 'To you. To my new biographer.'

She stared and then gulped. 'I—I don't understand. You mean you want me to write your biography?'

He nodded, amused at her stunned expression. 'That's right. I've been thinking about it for the last few days, and I sent to London for examples of some of the work you've done in the past. Now that I've seen them I've decided to give you the job.'

'So *that* was why you wouldn't make up your mind?' Her face glowed with excitement. 'Oh, Felix, I'd love to do it. And I'll really do my best for you. You won't be sorry, I promise.'

He laughed and put his arm round her waist. 'I know I won't. I'm sure you'll do a great job.'

She turned to him impulsively. 'When can we

start—tomorrow? I'll bring my cassette recorder and we can do enough for my newspaper article, and then I'll fly back to England and get leave of absence for a few weeks so that I can . . .'

'Hey, hold your horses!' Felix interrupted her. 'I said a biography; I didn't mention the newspaper feature.'

Holly stared at him blankly, the excitement gradually leaving her face. 'But I have to do that. I can't just forget about it and do your biography; it wouldn't be right.'

'Well, right or not, that's the way it has to be,' he said brusquely. 'And besides, printing an article beforehand would steal a great deal of thunder from the biography, wouldn't it?'

'It might, yes, but . . .' Holly thought quickly. 'Look, if you don't want the article written, would you agree to let my paper serialise your biography just prior to publication? That's been done many times before without harming the sales—in fact it quite often boosts them.'

Felix rubbed his chin thoughtfully. 'Okay, I'll buy that. Yes, we'll negotiate a deal with them straightaway.'

Holly laughed happily. 'That's wonderful! Oh, Felix, I'm eternally grateful. I'll fly over tomorrow and arrange it.'

Felix put his other hand on her waist. 'That won't be necessary; we can get in touch with them through my telex system. And besides,' he smiled down at her, 'I don't want to lose you, even for a day.' And drawing her to him, he bent his head to kiss her. He must have felt Holly stiffen, but he went on kissing her, not letting her go for some time. Then she stepped back and looked at him bleakly.

'Just what are you trying to say?'

'You know perfectly well,' he answered thickly. 'I want you to stay here and live with me, Holly.'

'Be your mistress, you mean?' she said coldly.

He reached out and again pulled her close. 'We'd be *lovers*, Holly. You must know how I feel about you. I never thought I'd fall for anyone again, but I've fallen for you more heavily than any woman before. I want to . . .'

'Stop it!' Holly jerked away from him, her face white. 'You're wasting your time.' Agitatedly she took a few paces away from him as she tried to find the right words. 'Felix, I'm sorry, but I don't feel the same way. So let's just drop the subject, shall we?'

Felix stared at her, a look almost of disbelief on his face. Then he said, 'But we get on well together, don't we? You've enjoyed the days you've spent here with me?'

'Yes. Yes, of course I have, but . . .'

Stepping quickly across to her, he said, 'Do you realise the kind of life I can give you, Holly? Anything and everything you want. Clothes, jewels—you'd have nothing but the best. We'd live here on the island together, just the two of us, but if you wanted to we could travel, go wherever you like. And I'd be generous, Holly. You wouldn't have to work ever again. No more running round the world chasing stories or living in cheap hotel rooms.'

Holly had been vainly trying to interrupt and at last she managed to stop him. 'But I *like* the life I live, can't you see that? I've worked hard to get where I am and I enjoy my job. And to live off your wealth, to have everything handed to me on a golden plate—where's the challenge in that? Okay, so maybe you've lived your life, answered all the challenges and can sit back and take things easy, but I still have mine to live.'

She paused and looked at him unhappily. 'And there's nothing you can give me that I want. All right, so it was exciting for a while to live like a millionaire; to wear beautiful clothes and have a mink coat put round me against the chill on an evening stroll, to be waited on and spend all the day in idle pleasure. But it was only exciting because I knew it would soon end, because I'd soon be back in my own world. If I lived like that all the time, never working, I'd be bored to death in weeks, the island would become a prison.'

She moved to leave the room, but Felix caught her arm and turned her to face him. His voice was sharper now, with an edge of anger to it. 'No. You wouldn't be bored, Holly. Do you think me so inexperienced a lover that I wouldn't make you happy and contented? Once we'd slept together you'd want to stay with me for always.'

He tried to take her in his arms again, but she pushed him away, her face set. 'I'm sorry, Felix, but the answer's still no. There's nothing you can give me that I don't already have.'

His mouth setting into a thin line, Felix said harshly, 'You don't have a man.'

Holly's face paled. 'I don't need a man. Not you, or anyone,' she retorted. Quickly she crossed to the door. 'Don't bother to see me out. I'll make my own way to the boat.'

His voice stopped her as she was about to leave. 'Do you know what you're giving up?'

She glanced back, a bitter smile on her lips. 'Oh, yes, I know that very well. I'm giving up every chance of writing not only your biography but the article as well.'

'That isn't so.' Holly had turned away, but his words made her look back over her shoulder in surprise. 'Your acceptance or refusal of my—offer had nothing to do with that. I'll give you the interview if you still want it. But the biography . . .' he shrugged, 'perhaps it would be better if we forgot about that, in the circumstances. Being alone with you for weeks on end, on a purely business basis, might be more than I could stand.'

Slowly Holly turned back into the room. 'You— you mean it? You'll give me the interview—and with no strings?'

He smiled crookedly. 'No strings. Come as usual tomorrow, and bring your cassette recorder.' Then, brusquely, 'You'd better go now. I'll tell them to have the yacht ready for you.'

It was almost midnight when the boat dropped her at Melmia harbour and turned to go back to Fallipos. Holly watched it for a few minutes before letting her eyes look in the direction of Nick's boat, drawn there as if from the pull of a powerful magnet. He wasn't on deck, but there was the glow of light behind the curtains screening the cabin windows. And really there was no need for him to look out for her, he must have realised by now that he had only to hear the noise of the yacht's powerful engines entering the harbour to know that she was safely back.

Slowly Holly climbed the stairs to her room, her thoughts in some confusion. Her rejection of Felix's proposition had been purely instinctive, she had even found it a little repulsive, although why she did so she wasn't quite sure. It certainly wasn't because she found him physically repellent; even though he was almost old enough to be her father he was still a very handsome man and he had a youthful outlook that easily bridged the age gap between them. He had touched her often and when he had kissed her it hadn't been unpleasant. In fact, Felix was a very experienced man who knew how to handle women and how to make himself attractive to them. So why, then, had she found the thought of becoming his mistress so repugnant? Crossing to the window, Holly leaned on the ledge and looked out, turning the problem over in her mind until she came to the conclusion that it was *because* Felix found it necessary to set out to make himself attractive that she had been put off. It suggested a degree of falseness in his character, and how could you ever rely on or trust someone who didn't act completely naturally with you?

She smiled slightly to herself, remembering the inducements he had offered her. How little he knew her character if he thought that clothes and jewels could influence her decision! How much more satisfaction seeing in print an article that you'd gone to endless lengths to obtain, had sweated and slaved over to get the wording exactly right. Okay, she had enjoyed their conversations together, had been stimulated and amused by him. He was the sort of person she would like to have as a friend, to meet, have dinner and laugh with occasionally. But he wasn't the sort of person she felt she could go to in trouble, or to confide in. Why, she hadn't even told him about Jamie.

But then she hadn't told Nick about Jamie either. She came out of her reverie a little and realised that she had been gazing down at Nick's boat the whole time. It was getting quite late and yet the light still burned in his cabin; perhaps he was reading before he settled down to sleep. That was one of the things they had shared—a love of books. Almost every night they had been together they had read in bed for a while, until Nick had reached over and taken the book from her hands and pulled her down beside him. Holly's eyes filled with sudden tears and she blinked them angrily away. Nick had never had to put on an act to make himself attractive, he possessed an arrant masculinity that made women physically aware and drew them to him like a magnet. And she had been so proud, so over the moon with joy when, of all the girls who had wanted him, he had chosen her. And Nick wasn't the promiscuous type; even after their marriage other women had made advances to him, had made it plain that they were available, but Nick hadn't even given them a glance, had only laughed at her fears and petty jealousies and told her that he was a one-woman man, and then had taken her in his arms and convinced her in no uncertain terms that she was definitely that one woman.

But now? She had sensed right from the start that he was different, far more widely experienced with her sex. There was a hardness about him that had never been there before, as if he really didn't give a damn. And the way he had kissed her, that, too, had shown her that there had been other women in his life, loving him, sharing his bed!

Holly straightened up suddenly, and without giving herself time to think about what she was doing, picked up her stole and ran out of the room and down the outside stairs. The moon was high in the night sky, casting a silver glow over the sleeping town, the walls of the cube-like houses creating sharp triangles of deep shadow at every corner. The terrace of the taverna was empty, although there was still a glow of light from the doorway leading to the kitchen where Alexis Lambis and his family would be having their own belated supper now that all the customers had gone home. Holly hurried on down the harbour, not really knowing why she was going to Nick, or what she would say when she got there, just knowing that she *had* to see him.

Her heart beating painfully in her chest, she paused for a moment on the quay just above Nick's boat to recover her breath and try to compose herself a little. But as she stood there one half of the double doors leading to the cabin opened and the light spilled out on to the deck. She drew back, startled, then thought that Nick must have seen her and be coming to help her aboard. But the voice that came from the cabin definitely wasn't Nick's, it had a French accent and was feminine and husky.

'Oh, Nicholas, *mon chéri*, that was wonderful, *ravissant*!'

Holly hastily stepped back into a block of

shadow and drew her dark stole over her light-coloured dress as the doors opened fully and Chantal d'Arneau stood in the doorway and turned to put her arms round Nick's neck and kiss him on the mouth, her body pressed against his. '*A demain, chéri*,' she murmured throatily, and went on to say something else, but Holly didn't stay around to hear. She stopped further into the shadow and slipped down the alleyway between two houses, running quietly along an inner path that she knew would take her back to the taverna and the sanctuary of her room.

CHAPTER SEVEN

HOLLY lay awake for most of that night, alternately cursing herself for being a stupid fool or thanking her stars that she hadn't gone to Nick's boat earlier and walked in on him with the Frenchwoman. She shuddered at the thought, imagining the scene. She had acted purely on impulse, for once letting her heart rule her head, and look where it had got her! By running to him like that she had lowered herself to Chantal d'Arneau's level. She wondered whether the Frenchwoman's husband knew that she was visiting Nick on his boat at night, and if not, how on earth the woman managed to sneak away and back again without being seen or missed. But perhaps the poor man was used to his wife's promiscuous behaviour, Holly thought cynically, and either turned a blind eye or complacently accepted it. For all she knew it might be the accepted thing among the rich set they obviously belonged to, to have casual holiday affairs. And had Nick really sunk that low, that he'd let himself be used like that?

Holly turned to bury her head in her pillow, trying to shut out the pictures that filled her mind, but for the first time in years she cried herself to sleep.

Felix sent his yacht for her as usual the next morning, but Holly was late and kept it waiting at anchor for several minutes, and when she did go aboard went straight inside to the cabin, her eyes hidden by dark glasses. There was a constraint between them today which Holly didn't even try to dispel. She got down to business right away, asking him questions from the long list she had prepared when she first came out to Kinos, which seemed eons ago now. Felix answered readily enough, often making lengthy answers when she asked him to fill out his replies, but there was a frown between his brows as he watched her and noted her tenseness. At lunchtime he called a halt and insisted they talk of other topics over their meal, whereas Holly would rather have gone on with the interview. All she wanted now was to get enough information for her article and to go home to her son. She ate very little and answered him only in monosyllables, impatient to get on. But Felix seemed in no hurry now, although at first he, too, appeared to want to get the interview over. Holly had expected that, had been sure that her rejection of him would have made him at least brusque with her, if not downright nasty. To most men, especially of Felix's age, the physical refusal of their advances by a young girl must come as a double blow, not only to their pride but to their vanity, highlighting the fact that they are no longer an attractive proposition. But for some reason she couldn't fathom, Felix seemed to want to get back on their old footing. Ordinarily Holly would have been pleased and happy to do so, glad to have him just as a friend, but she began to suspect that Felix might have thought she was just playing hard to get and be working up to asking her again, so she decided to keep it cool and by her manner let him know in no uncertain terms that she wasn't interested.

After lunch they started again, sitting outside on the patio, but Holly developed a blinding headache and found it almost impossible to concentrate. She asked the same question twice, apologised stumblingly, and put her hand up yet again to her aching head.

Felix stood up abruptly and crossing to her chair, firmly took her notebook from her hand and switched off the tape recorder. Holly opened her mouth to protest, but stopped as he took off her dark glasses and looked down grimly at her eyes, dark shadowed and still slightly puffy from the previous night. His mouth tightened.

'You've been crying.'

Holly started to shake her head in denial, then realised the futility of it. 'It's nothing to do with what happened between us last night, if that's what you're thinking. Let's get on, shall we? I'm not even halfway through yet.'

She held out her hand for her glasses and after a moment he gave them to her, but said, 'No, we've done enough for today. You don't look at all well.'

'I have a headache, that's all,' Holly admitted defensively. 'If you could just ask someone to find me a couple of aspirins, I'll be fine shortly.'

'No, we'll leave it now and carry on tomorrow, if you feel up to it. Let's go inside, out of the sun.' He led her indoors and poured her out an iced drink. Then he left her a few minutes to come back with a bottle of painkillers. 'Here, take a couple of these.' He poured two out into her hand and watched her as she swallowed them. 'You young idiot, why didn't you tell me earlier that you weren't feeling well?'

'I—I wanted to get the interview over.' She turned and went to sit on a settee, leaning her head back against the seat and shutting her eyes for a few blissful moments. When she opened them she saw Felix looking down at her, concern in his face.

'Why don't you go upstairs and lie down for a while?'

She managed a weak smile. 'I'm sure it will go away soon. I'm sorry to be such a nuisance.'

'My dear child!' Felix ejaculated, then bit off what he had been going to add and crossed to pour himself a drink, turning afterwards to study her again. 'You say it wasn't our,' he sought for a safe description, 'our . . . disagreement last night that upset you? Is that the truth?'

Holly gave a rueful smile. 'It didn't help any, but it wasn't the main cause, no.'

'What was it, then?'

She looked away before saying shortly, 'It really isn't any concern of yours, Felix.'

'Which means that it was that husband of yours who made you cry,' he guessed, a wry twist to his lips. 'What did he do—try to force himself on you again?'

Holly stood up and faced him coldly. 'No. *Yours* was the only proposition I received yesterday. As a matter of fact I haven't even spoken to him for several days. And now, if you don't mind, I think I'd like to be taken back to my hotel. I'm sorry about having to cut short the interview—I'm sure you're as keen as I am to get it over with as soon as possible.'

'Holly, look, about last night . . .' Felix came over to her and reached out as if to take hold of her arms, but she moved away.

'It's all right, you don't have to say anything.' She lifted an unsteady hand to her head. 'I'm afraid I was rather rude to you, I'm sorry.'

'Hell, no. I should be the one to apologise.' Felix appeared as if he was going to say something else, but looked at her white face and changed his mind. 'We'll talk when you're feeling better. Phone me from the hotel tomorrow if you feel up to it and I'll send the boat for you.'

'Yes, all right,' Holly agreed tonelessly, and allowed him to escort her down to the quay and help her on to the yacht.

By the time they got back to Melmia the pain-killers had helped a lot, but she still felt very tired, so she decided to go for a quick swim and then relax on the beach for a while. There were diffe-rent people on the sands today, the ferry having brought a new set of holidaymakers. A couple of young men looked her over appreciatively as she passed, but she ignored their attempts to talk to her and walked further up the shore, looking for a quiet spot away from everyone else. She found it where two largish rocks jutted out from the beach forming a roofless cave with a stretch of pure, clean sand a few yards wide between them.

Holly didn't swim for very long, just enough to cool herself off, then she retreated to her patch of beach and lay down on her towel, her head in the shadow cast by one of the rocks, the rest of her body in the sun. She tried to go to sleep, but it eluded her, her mind was still too full of Nick and the Frenchwoman. There had been no sign of her or any of her friends on the beach today, and their boat hadn't been in the harbour, so presumably they had gone sailing for the day—unless they had left Kinos altogether. Was that what it had been last night, Holly wondered; a farewell fling before Chantal d'Arneau and her party moved on? Or had she been heard going back to her boat so that her husband found her out and decided to remove her from Nick's dangerous proximity? It would be interesting to see whether or not their boat came back that evening.

Turning on to her stomach, Holly let the soft sand drift through her fingers. Perhaps Nick was so smitten with the Frenchwoman that he might also sail away, follow them to wherever they were headed. But this new, harder Nick didn't seem as if he would ever let a woman get close enough to him to upset his plans in any way. If they couldn't fit in with him it was just too bad. A 'so long, it was fun while it lasted' attitude. Not that Holly cared either way, of course; it was nothing to her how many women Nick had, now or in the past. She stared at the fine sand flowing gently from her hand; so why, then, had she cried last night? For the old Nick, for the one who had never looked at another woman when he was with her? Or was it guilt, because it was her fault that he had become the man he now was? She had been so blind then, so terribly blind.

Abruptly she got up. This kind of self-recrimination just wouldn't do. She knew from past experience that it only made things worse, eating away her shaky confidence and making her more open than ever to hurt and unhappiness. She had found then, when Nick went away, that action was the only answer, so now she ran down the beach and plunged into the sea again, swimming out strongly against the swell.

The two youths must have seen her, for they, too, swam out and caught her up as she turned back. They spoke to her first in a language she didn't understand, and she shook her head as she tried to swim away from them. But they came after her and one said in bad English, 'You in trouble. We help, yes?' and caught hold of her arm.

'No, I'm all right.' Holly tried to protest, but the second youth grabbed her other arm.

They were in shallower water now and the two men could stand up, although Holly was still floating. They were laughing at her, leering grins on their faces, as their free hands began to explore her body. Holly opened her mouth to scream, but they pulled her under so that she choked and gasped on swallowed water.

'You like this game, yes?' One of the youths, his dark hair plastered to his head, laughed in her face as his hand started to pull off the bottom half of her bikini.

The next moment he disappeared beneath the surface, his hand torn from its grasp on her arm. There was a froth of struggling arms and legs and Holly's eyes opened in amazement as Nick's head broke the surface, her assailant hanging limply from the arm lock in which Nick held him. The other youth, too, was gaping in astonishment, and then he hastily let go of her and plunged away, heading for the other end of the beach as fast as he could swim.

'Are you all right?' Nick seemed hardly even out of breath.

'Y-yes, thanks.' Holly reached down and wriggled back into her bikini. 'What are you going to do with him?' She nodded towards the half-dazed youth.

'I know what I'd like to do with him,' Nick said grimly, 'but I suppose we'll have to let him go.'

He half carried, half dragged him nearer the beach and then loosened his hold so that the youth fell to his knees in the water, then he got up and staggered away in terror, his head constantly looking back in case Nick was coming after him.

When he had gone, Nick turned to look at Holly, putting out a gentle finger to touch the red marks on her arm where they had held her. 'Did they hurt you very much?'

'No.' Holly shook her head, but then trembled. 'But it wasn't—very pleasant.' She walked out of the water and back up the beach and bent to pick up her towel. 'I felt so *helpless*.'

Nick took the towel from her and wrapped it round her shoulders, then began to rub her back. 'You need some lessons in self-defence.'

'Yes,' Holly agreed with a certain amount of irony in her voice, 'I suppose I do.'

Nick caught the implication and his hands stilled as he looked down into her face for a long moment. Then he said abruptly, 'You're back early today. What happened—did you have a row with your millionaire?'

'No, I didn't—and he isn't *my* millionaire,' Holly pointed out, her tone hardening.

'No?' Nick's left eyebrow rose in disbelief. 'You surely aren't going to tell me that it takes as long as this to get the facts for one article?'

'Of course it doesn't.'

'So just what have you two been doing for the last week—playing chess?' he asked, his lips twisting into a sarcastic sneer.

'Yes—among other things, if you must know,' Holly returned, angry now. 'Not that's it's any of your damn business what I do with my time.'

Nick's eyes blazed. 'And I suppose it's none of my damn business who my wife gives her body to either?'

'No, it isn't,' Holly began furiously, 'because I don't consider myself to be your wife. In fact I . . .'

Even through the thickness of the towel, she could feel his grip tighten on her shoulders. 'Have you been to bed with him yet? Have you?' he demanded savagely.

'What's the matter?' Holly jeered. 'Are you jealous because I prefer him to you? Well, you're right to be, because he's a far better lover than you ever were! He's twice the man you . . .' She stopped abruptly, the words choked off as Nick put his hand to her throat, his eyes murderous in his set face.

'Is he, by God?' His expression changed. 'Or is the attraction just the obvious one that he's rolling in money? Is that why you let him proposition you—for what you could get out of him?' he sneered.

Holly knocked his hand away and stepped back.

'Well, whatever I see in Felix, it's perfectly obvious what you see in Chantal d'Arneau!' she retorted fiercely.

Nick's eyes fastened on her face. 'Just what is that supposed to mean?'

'It means what the hell right have you to question me when you're in the middle of a sordid affair with another woman yourself?'

A guarded look came into his face. 'What gives you that impression?'

'Oh, it isn't an impression,' Holly shot back caustically, 'it's a fact. I saw her leaving your boat last night.'

His eyebrows flew up in astonishment. 'You *saw* her?'

'Yes, kissing you goodnight and thanking you for the wonderful time you'd given her,' she answered, her voice as cutting as a razor's edge.

Something flickered in his face and there was amusement in his voice as he said, 'Well, at least I have one satisfied customer who's willing to give me a reference.'

'Why, you——!' Holly's voice shook with rage. She raised her arm to hit him, but Nick caught her wrist and held it.

'Holly, listen, there's nothing between . . .'

'No, you listen,' Holly put in, her voice vitriolic. 'When I met you again I was filled with all sorts of doubts and uncertainties, but this past week has taught me a lot. And I'm perfectly certain of one thing more than anything else; that I want to be free of you. Free for ever. As soon as I get back to London I'm going to sue for a divorce!'

Nick's grip tightened on her wrist for a moment,

but then it eased and he let go, his expression un-readable. 'I see. And just when do you intend going back to London?'

Holly took a couple of deep breaths, trying to calm herself. Her nerves were in a sudden vacuum now that the decision had been taken, the words said. Her voice surprisingly steady, she answered, 'I'm not sure. Probably the day after tomorrow.'

'There isn't a ferry that day.'

'It doesn't matter. I'll hire a boat to take me to Piraeus, and then I can get a plane from Athens.'

'Perhaps you'll look me up before you go,' Nick said flatly, 'so that I can give you the address of my solicitor. You'll need it for the divorce,' he added pointedly when he saw the wary look in her eyes. 'And maybe you're right, maybe it would be best this way. After all, we don't have anything to hold us together.'

'No.' Holly turned away, unwilling to meet his eyes and unable to find anything else to say.

After a moment, Nick said heavily, 'If you're ready to go I'll walk you back to the taverna. Those two chaps seem to have taken themselves off, but I'd rather you didn't go back alone.'

Holly slipped her sundress over her head and bent to put on her flip-flops. 'I haven't thanked you for coming to my rescue,' she said stiffly.

'Think nothing of it, it's all part of the service,' he answered with flippant irony.

But there was no sign of the youths and Nick left her at the edge of the town, with a mere curt nod of farewell, and strode off down one of the side streets, leaving her to make her own way to the taverna. Now that the die was cast, Holly felt a curious sense of unreality and relief from tension. It was as if the bond holding them together had suddenly snapped and she was left dangling in mid-air, at the end of one part of her life but not yet having started on the next. For the first time she was glad that she had seen him again, that things had come to a head, and the decision she had been putting off for years finally made. But there was sadness there too, and a sense of desolation and failure. Because that was all divorce could ever be, an admittance of failure to make good from a bright and wonderful beginning.

The next morning she phoned Felix and asked him to send the yacht for her, determined to get the interview finished that day. With this in view, she kept strictly to business, refusing to let Felix sidetrack her and being very businesslike. Over lunch he tried to lead her into more personal conversation, but Holly was politely distant, ready to talk on general topics but steering well clear of anything that might edge on to her private life. Felix looked at her in some bafflement, unable to get by the defensive wall Holly had thrown up between them.

In the afternoon they finished the interview and then he agreed to let her take photographs, and she used up several rolls of film on both him and the house. When she had done she was about to pack her camera back in the case, but Felix stopped her.

'Lend me your camera; I want to take one of you.'

Reluctantly she handed it over and Felix made her stand against a background of flowers in the garden, the purple bougainvillaea and red hibiscus filling her nostrils with their heady scents. Without thinking she reached up to a branch above her head and pulled it down, the better to smell the heavenly perfume. She felt a sudden sadness, knowing that she would never see this lovely place again, and closed her eyes for a moment, trying to imprison its beauty in her memory.

'Holly.'

She opened her eyes to find Felix staring at her. There was an almost desperate appeal in his eyes as he quickly crossed to her, the camera forgotten, and gripped her arms. 'Holly, don't go. I need you so much. Can't you see what you mean to me? Please say you'll stay.'

'Felix, no, please!' Holly tried to disengage herself, but he was holding her too tightly. 'We've already been into all this. I don't want to be just your mistress . . .'

'And this time I'm not asking you to be.' A rueful smile came to his lips. 'After the last time I swore I'd never do this again, but if it's the only way to keep you with me . . . I want you to marry me, Holly, to be my wife. I'm not going to lose you now, not after having found you. I never thought I'd fall in love again, but I have, harder than ever before. And you'll be my last love, Holly, I swear it.'

He bent to kiss her, taking her acceptance for granted, his lips already possessive. When at last he let her go, Holly moved away, unhappiness in her eyes. During the course of that long interview she had learnt the real reason for Felix's settling in Fallipos and cutting himself off completely from his former life. He had said, 'I simply woke up one morning with the most colossal hangover, my whole body feeling foul from too much food and drink and too many cigarettes. And I didn't know where I was—or a thing about the woman I was in bed with. It was then I realised that I was rapidly killing myself, and that the only way to stop was to get myself as far away from temptation as possible. At first I thought of shutting myself away in one of those monasteries where you can go as a guest to rest and think, but you can imagine the sort of field day the press would have made out of that if they'd got wind of it, so I decided to play the eccentric millionaire and create this hideaway for myself. And I've grown to love it here, so much that I never want to leave it.'

His confession had given her a much better understanding of him, and for a moment she almost wavered; it would be so easy to just opt out, to let Felix take over her life and Jamie's and never have any worries ever again, to live here in this peace and tranquillity. And Felix had said that he needed her. She felt an overwhelming surge of compassion for him and gratitude that he should want her so much. No one had ever told her they needed her before, not even Nick when they were together, but then she thought of Jamie, of his constant but unspoken need of her which was far greater than Felix's could ever be, and common sense reasserted itself; Felix had lived and played to excess before he came here, whereas she had only just begun to live and Jamie not at all.

Her voice firm, she said, 'I'm sorry, Felix, but I can't marry you.'

'Because of your husband?' He dismissed her marriage with a wave of his hand. 'You can file for a divorce immediately. You won't even have to leave here to do it, it can all be done for you by lawyers in London.'

'No, it isn't that.' As gently as she could, she said, 'I don't love you, Felix. I like you, yes, very much, and I'd be proud to have you as a friend. But I don't love you, and I can't live with someone I don't love.'

A bleak, defeated look came into his eyes. 'And what if I told you I couldn't live without you?'

Slowly she answered, 'I'd say that you were too big a man to resort to that kind of blackmail. You lived without me before, Felix, you'll soon forget that I ever existed.'

He shook his head. 'No, that I'll never do.'

Holly picked up her camera and Felix escorted her down to the quay, silently accepting his defeat, but before helping her on to the yacht he kissed her again, with a fierce, yearning hunger as if he couldn't bear to let her go. Then he said unevenly, 'Maybe I've been here too long. Perhaps I'm ready to face the world again and strong enough to withstand all the excesses that brought me down before.'

Reaching out to gently touch his cheek, Holly said with sincerity, 'Oh, I hope so, Felix, I really do.'

He let her go then and she stood in the stern of the boat as it pulled away, watching Felix and his island recede into the horizon and out of her life.

Back at Melmia, Holly hired a boat through Alexis Lambis, the fisherman owner agreeing to leave early the next morning, then she phoned her office to tell them of her plans before going up to her room to pack her things. As she wanted to make an early start the next day, she changed into a black silk blouse and matching skirt and went down to the terrace to eat a couple of hours earlier than she would normally have done, intending to have an early night before the long journey ahead of her.

Then there was only one thing left to do. Holly walked slowly along the quay towards Nick's boat, the blood-red of the setting sun setting the sky on fire and turning the whitewashed houses to soft pink in its reflected glow. She walked past the spot where the French yacht had been moored, its place taken now by a converted fishing smack, and paused on the harbour wall by Nick's *Argosy*.

She supposed she ought to shout 'Ahoy there!' or something to announce herself, but knew that she would feel ridiculous, so instead she clambered down on to the boat and rapped on the cabin roof.

Almost immediately Nick pushed open the doors and stood on the steps, looking at her.

'You—you asked me to look you up before I left,' Holly said, when he didn't speak.

'Yes, of course. Come in.'

He went back down the steps and put up a hand to help her down, but she pretended not to see it and managed alone. The cabin was compactly fitted out with a galley on the right, opposite a dining section with a table now folded away and a row of seats down one side. Beyond, towards the bow, she could see into another cabin fitted with a wide bunk, neatly made up with pillows and a blanket. Holly took one glance, remembered

Chantal d'Arneau and quickly looked away, her face set.

'Won't you sit down and have a drink?' invited Nick.

'Thanks, but I won't be staying. I only came because you said you'd give me the name of your solicitor,' she answered stiffly.

'Of course. I'll write it down for you. And perhaps you'd better give me the address of yours.'

Hastily Holly fished in her bag for paper and pen, and wrote it down for him. Then she turned to find that he was watching her. He glanced at the paper when she handed it to him, then slipped it into the pocket of the pale blue denims he was wearing.

'Afraid I'll have to search round a bit for mine. It's a firm that was recommended to me by someone in Australia. The card should be about somewhere, but it's easy to lose things in a small boat like this. In the meantime, we might as well have a drink. Yours was a vodka and tonic, wasn't it?' He opened a well-stocked drinks cupboard and poured out a vodka for her and Scotch for himself.

'Now, what shall we drink to?' he asked as he handed her a glass. 'I suppose the obvious thing would be to our future happiness.'

'Apart,' Holly added caustically before he lifted the glass to his lips.

He smiled crookedly. 'As you say—apart.'

Holly sat down on one of the seats because the cabin was so small that standing made her too close to Nick for comfort, while he leant against the edge of the galley, making no move to search for the address.

After a couple of swallows, she reminded him tartly, 'You said you were going to look for that card.'

'There's plenty of time,' he returned easily. 'I take it your prolonged interview with Felix Riddell is now finished?'

'Yes,' she agreed shortly, refusing to be drawn.

'So you'll be going back to London to write up your story. Any idea where they'll send you next?'

She shook her head. 'It could be anywhere. But I hope to have some time at home first.'

He raised his brows. 'Home?'

'I have a cottage in . . .' she paused, 'in the country.'

A quizzical look came into his eyes. 'I hardly picture you in a country cottage with roses round the door. I should have thought a flat in the West End of London was more in your line.'

Holly set down her glass and stood up. 'Well, you never did know me very well, did you? When you get round to finding that card, perhaps you'll send the address to my solicitors?'

Nick made no move to stop her as she left the cabin, merely following her up the steps to the cockpit. But then he said, 'Before you go perhaps you wouldn't mind giving me a hand for a minute? I've been having some trouble with my engine and I'd like to try it out, make sure it's running properly.'

Holly turned back reluctantly. 'What do you want me to do?'

'Just steer the boat for a bit while I check that the engine is pumping the water through.'

'You mean take it out to sea?' Holly asked uneasily. 'Why can't you run it here?'

'I'd have to have the throttle wide open and it makes too much noise,' Nick explained casually. 'The sound of the engine reverberates on the harbour wall, and also it creates too much wash; it would make all the boats move about when the owners are trying to cook their dinners, which wouldn't make me very popular. It won't take very long,' he added, 'and I'd prefer to get it right before it gets too dark.'

'Oh, all right,' Holly agreed reluctantly, long experience of old and reluctant car engines making her sympathetic to his difficulties. 'What do you want me to do?'

'I'll take her out of the harbour and then perhaps you could take over while I get down into the bilges.'

He cast off the mooring lines and started the engine, to chug quietly out of the harbour heading towards the sunset, the sea flecked with purple and gold in their wake. Once clear of the bay, Nick turned the boat to starboard and Holly took over the wheel, sailing parallel with the shore. Automatically she obeyed Nick's instructions to accelerate or slow down, and then they sat idly on the water while he made some adjustments.

Holly had never been out to sea at sunset before, especially a Mediterranean sunset, and gradually she became lost in its magnificence, watching it slowly sink, glowing purple at the base of the orb and lightening to molten crimson above, shafts of blazing orange and gold reaching up into the deep blue of the sky. It was very quiet, the sea very still, as if the whole world had stopped and was breathlessly watching the miracle of transition from day into night. The sun sank lower, was suddenly blinding in its last brilliant intensity, and then it was gone, the heat and light and spirit lost from the day.

With a deep sigh, Holly slowly came back to reality to find Nick standing silently behind her, he, too, caught up in the beauty of the sunset. Its glow was still on his face, reflected in his eyes as he gazed down at her.

'I'll take over now.'

Holly moved aside as he took the wheel and turned to watch the last dying rays as the boat came round. This, too, was a memory she wanted to hold on to and treasure, but she was filled with an inexpressible sadness, knowing that memory could never bring back the brilliance and beauty that she had just seen.

Concentrating as she was on the last dying rays of the sunset, Holly didn't realise where they were until she heard the rattle of the anchor chain and looked round to see that Nick had sailed into a small deserted cove surrounded by steep cliffs that made it inaccessible except by sea. The anchor splashed down and the boat came broadside on to the shore, about thirty yards from the beach.

As Nick cut the engine, Holly turned to him questioningly. 'What's the matter? Isn't the engine working properly.'

'Yes, it's fine.' Deliberately he added, 'It always was. I just wanted to get you alone.'

Holly stared at him. 'You tricked me into coming with you? Well, just what was the point?' she demanded angrily. 'We've said everything there was to say and come to the only conclusion possible; that we never want to see each other again and intend to keep it that way—permanently.'

'You're right,' Nick agreed sardonically, 'we *have* said everything we're going to say to one another for the time being. In fact we've already said too much—and all of it the wrong things.'

'Then why on earth...?' Holly began hotly, then came to an abrupt stop as she saw the look on his face.

'Because we've some unfinished business, you and I.'

'No!' The word came out in a gasp of fear, then hurriedly, 'Look, if it's because of what I said about you and Felix...'

Nick laughed harshly. 'Oh, no. This is nothing to do with Riddell or any other man there's been in your life. This is just between you and me.'

'No!' Holly gasped again, and made an involuntary movement to escape, but Nick reached out and caught her, pulling her to him, imprisoning her hands against his chest.

Roughly he said, 'I've been trying to make you come to your senses since the moment we met, but it seems there's only one way to get through to you.'

Terror in her voice, she stammered, 'No, Nick, please. Please don't!'

'It has to be this way.' Picking her up, Nick kicked open the cabin door and carried her inside, then set her down on her feet. He took her arms and put them down at her side, then Holly stood as if turned to stone as he undid the fastening of her skirt and she felt it slip off her hips and fall to the ground. His fingers sought the buttons of her blouse, became impatient so that a button tore and clicked to the floor. He pulled off her blouse and let that, too, fall to the ground, then his hand moved to the fastening of her bra. She shuddered as his hands found the soft swell of her breasts, cool against his fingers. His lips touched her throat, murmuring her name, then went on down, caressing, urgent.

The memory of that last time, when he had taken her against her will and then left her, when he had given her a child, came forcibly back, filling her with fear, and she suddenly put her hands against his shoulders and pushed him violently away. Nick lost his balance and fell back, giving her time to turn and run for the door. She stumbled up the steps, sobbing with panic, running across to the rail and throwing herself into the sea as he burst out of the cabin after her.

The water was still warm from the sun, enfolding her like a blanket, but Holly paused only to kick off her sandals before striking out desperately for the shore, no clear idea of what she was going to do, intent only on getting away.

Behind her, Nick tore off his clothes and then dived cleanly from the deck, coming to the surface and breaking into a powerful crawl in one smooth, graceful movement. He caught her as she felt the bottom beneath her feet and began to run through the shallows, catching her arm and spinning her round. Holly fought him silently, kicking and clawing, tears running down her face because she knew it was a fight she couldn't win. She slipped on the wet sand and fell to the ground, Nick falling with her, their legs still in the lapping waves as they rolled over and over.

Suddenly Holly collapsed, letting him pinion her arms against the sand, his body heavy on top of her. They were both panting, breathless, and for a few moments lay inertly, then Nick's mouth sought hers, pushing her head back against the sand, forcing her mouth to open. Holly gave a little moan, trying to jerk her head away, but his lips continued to ravage hers, demanding submission. For a moment she continued to resist, but she could feel his body hard against her own, his thighs imprisoning hers. She moaned as her lips parted in the final surrender, her insides taking fire as Nick let go of her wrists to fondle and caress her. Then all other sensations deserted her as she lost herself in his embrace.

The water swirled and eddied around them as Nick reached down to pull off the rest of her clothes, then he made love to her in a frenzy of triumph and longing, their mutual ecstasy wild and prolonged. There was no night or day, no land or sea, only the two of them lost in a vortex of sensuality as old as time itself.

CHAPTER EIGHT

THE stars were out and the first shafts of moonlight lighting the sky when Nick at last stood up and looked down at Holly lying at his feet. He stood tall and strong as a tree, the drops of water running down his thighs and legs. Holly looked up at him sensuously, mouth parted, lids half closed, her face softened by satiated rapture.

Nick smiled down at her, his eyes caressing her nakedness. He bent to pick her up and Holly put her arms round his neck, clinging to him and burying her head against his shoulder. Wading out into the sea, he laid her on her back and swam with her the last few yards, then hoisted her on to the boat, before carrying her down to the cabin. He found a big, soft towel, and put it round her, intending to dry her, but Holly reached up to twine her hands in his hair, pulling his head down so that she could kiss his throat, bite his ear.

'Behave yourself, woman!' He tried to towel her back, but Holly moved closer to him, rubbing herself sensuously against him until he groaned deep in his throat. 'You minx! Later. I have to talk to you.'

'No, I don't want to talk.' Holly ran her fingers over his chest, touching, exploring, rediscovering her power over him.

He stood it for a little while, then let the towel drop so that he could hold her, kiss her with

174

hungry passion. Then he led her into the forward cabin and gently laid her on the made-up berth, her fair hair falling across the pillows. For a moment he sat on the edge of the bunk, his eyes dark with desire as he fondled her.

Holly opened her arms to him. 'I want you, Nick. I want you now.'

He smiled, and as he came down on her he said forcefully, triumphantly, 'You're my woman, Holly. You belong in my bed.'

When Holly awoke she found the little cabin in darkness except for the glow of a cigarette end as Nick lay smoking quietly beside her. He put it out when she stirred and put his arm round her, pillowing her head on his shoulder. Holly sighed contentedly and snuggled up to him. It had been so long, so very long since they had lain together like this.

Tenderly Nick pushed the hair off her face and stroked it gently as he said, 'Holly, there's something I've got to tell you. I . . .'

She stiffened and interrupted fiercely, 'If it's about that French tart . . .'

Nick laughed. 'No, it isn't.' He balled his hand into a fist and hit her playfully on the chin. 'And I *wasn't* having an affair with her. If you'd hung around a minute longer you'd have seen her husband and another couple leave with her. I'd invited them over to the boat for supper and a drink in return for an invitation they'd given me. It was the food she'd enjoyed—not *me*, you jealous little cat.'

Holly smiled in the darkness and nuzzled his neck, exploring it with little kisses. 'I was, wasn't

I? But she wanted you, though.'

'Just like Felix Riddell wanted you,' Nick reminded her gently.

She grew still and said with difficulty, 'Nick, what I said about him—it wasn't true. I didn't go to bed with him.'

'I know.'

'You do?' Holly's eyes opened wide in surprise. 'But how could you possibly know?'

He ran his fingers slowly down her arm so that she shivered deliciously. 'A man can often tell when a woman hasn't been made love to for a long time—her body tightens up, makes her almost like a virgin again. And you haven't, have you?'

'No,' she whispered. 'There hasn't been anyone since you.'

'Oh, Holly! My darling girl.' His hand tightened convulsively on her arm. 'And Riddell? He didn't mean anything to you?'

'No.' Holly shook her head.

Nick gave a sigh of relief. 'If you knew the agonies of jealousy I went through seeing you go off in his boat every day. I wanted to tell you then how much I wanted you back, but everything seemed to be going wrong between us, and you'd built up such a wall around yourself, that I was afraid I'd only make things worse. If it hadn't been for the fact that you came home every night, I think I would have kidnapped you long since. And when I thought of you, possibly in his arms and making love to you, I wanted to go over there and tear him apart.' He paused to explore her bare shoulder with his lips. 'So I was wrong about him all the time,' he murmured indistinctly. 'It was just business?'

'Oh, I wouldn't say that,' Holly answered casually, and smiled to herself when his head jerked up. 'He *did* ask me to be his mistress.'

'Oh, he did, did he? I hope you told him to go to hell?'

'No,' Holly replied equably, 'I said no, thank you, as a nicely brought up girl should.'

He laughed softly. 'Minx! And I suppose that brought the interview to an abrupt end?'

'On the contrary, the interview didn't start until I'd turned him down.'

His brows drawing into a frown, Nick said, 'You mean that he used it as an inducement for you to accept?'

'No, there were no strings to either of his offers.'

'Either . . .? He asked you again?'

'No. The second time he asked me to marry him,' Holly replied calmly, mischievously enjoying his discomfiture.

'Did he, by God?' Nick sat up and stared down at her. 'I trust you told him you were already married?' he said harshly.

'He didn't seem to think that was of much importance.' A thunderous look came into Nick's eyes and he opened his mouth to make a biting retort, but Holly went on, 'But I told him that I didn't love him and that I could never give myself to a man I didn't love. Now or ever,' she added softly.

Nick's expression changed immediately and he lay down again to gently trace the outline of her face with his fingers. 'Oh, my lovely girl, if I could only tell you how much you mean to me!' But he must have felt her stiffen, the hurt not yet completely gone, and he said urgently, 'Listen to me, sweetheart. I didn't just walk out on you. I wrote to you at once telling you that I was going to look for a new job and somewhere for us to live. That I'd come for you as soon as I found somewhere. But when I telephoned a few days later your mother said that you wanted nothing more to do with me, that everything was over between us. I came round to the house, but your father said you'd gone to stay with friends and ordered me out. So then I spent ages travelling all over the country calling on all the friends and relations I thought you might have gone to. During that time I'd applied for the job with the construction company again, and when I was sure I'd got it and knew where I was going, I went to your parents' house again and pushed my way in when they tried to keep me out. I ran up to our room, but it was empty, all your clothes gone. I went through the other rooms and then I tried to make them tell me where you were. I was angry—God, how I was angry! I said some pretty foul things to them and they called the police and had me slung out.' His voice filled with remembered bitterness. 'It was then I came to the conclusion that what they had said was true—that you really didn't want to see me again.'

Holly lay motionless beside him, realising with growing horror how her parents had interfered to wreck her life even more than she had known. When he had finished she put her head in her hands and moaned. 'Oh, no! No! Oh, Nick, I missed you so much and I was so alone. I wanted to die.'

She began to cry, in sorrow for the years they had lost, for the terrible waste, as well as for the hurt that Nick must have suffered.

He let her cry for a little while, then gently lifted her head and kissed the tears away. 'Hey, don't you want to hear the rest?'

Trying to control herself, Holly took a long, shuddering breath. 'Yes. Yes, of course.'

'Well, when I went away that first time I was pretty mad, but somehow I could never push you out of my mind or hate you, as I tried to do. I loved you very much, you see,' he said simply. 'So every time I came on leave to England I looked for you, but without any success. And then when I did find you, it was in Australia of all places.'

'In Australia? But I don't understand; I've never been there.'

Her eyes had grown accustomed to the darkness now and she saw him smile. 'No, but a magazine with one of your articles in it, together with a small picture of you on the editorial page, found its way to the site where I was working. I immediately phoned your office, but they wouldn't give me your address, so I pretended that I might have a story for you and they told me you were shortly coming here on another assignment.'

Holly sat up and put on the light so that she could see him properly. She stared down at him. 'You knew I was coming to Kinos? It wasn't a coincidence?'

He grinned smugly. 'Hardly. I caught the next plane and broke a couple of world records to get

to Greece, and hire a boat, and sail out here before
you arrived. I just made it; the ferry you were on
sailed in a few hours after I did.'

She was silent for a moment, going through the
implications. 'And did you come here hoping that
we—that this might happen?' she asked slowly.

A serious look came into Nick's eyes. He
reached up and gently began to massage her shoulders. 'I'd like to say yes, but to be honest, I just
didn't know. I only knew that I had to see you
again, to hear from your own lips that we were
finally through. We're two grown-up people now,
not kids any more, and maybe I thought we could
meet and find out where and why we went wrong.
Help us build for the future.' He smiled wryly and
his fingers tightened on her shoulders. 'At least
that's what I told myself, but I'm afraid that when
I met you everything suddenly became far more
basic than that.'

'So I noticed.' Holly lowered her head so that
her hair fell forward and hid her face. She said, as
lightly as she could, 'Well, now you know that you
can still make me. You've laid your ghosts and can
start again as soon as you're free. We'll both be
able to now that we don't have any feelings of
guilt or bitterness about each other.'

His hand lifted the curtain of her hair. 'Is that
what you want—to go ahead with the divorce?'

'Yes, of course. We've both built up different
lives for ourselves,' Holly answered, trying to keep
a light tone, but unable to meet his eyes.

Nick laughed softly and pulled her down to him.
'Oh, Prickles, what a terrible liar you are!' His lips
found hers. 'I love you,' he murmured against her

mouth. 'I've never stopped loving you, and I'm never going to let you go again.'

He made love to her again then, rediscovering a long-forgotten fire that had blazed and burned so long ago. It was different—and yet the same as she remembered. Love and gentleness were there now, as well as heat and passion. Bitterness disappeared as they gloried in each other's sensuality, lifted to dizzying heights of ecstasy that washed away all hurts and fears. And at last they lay in exhausted, contented sleep in each other's arms.

Holly woke first and sat up, careful not to disturb Nick who, even in his sleep, had placed a possessive arm across her waist. The light was still on and she reached up to turn it off, letting the first rays of morning sun filter into the cabin. It was chilly, so she pulled a blanket up from the foot of the bed and drew it over them. Nick stirred and smiled in his sleep. She looked down at him tenderly, wanting to touch him, but afraid that he might wake. For a long time she sat gazing down at him, thinking about him, about her son and of the future.

At last she gave a little sigh, her decision made, and slipped from the bed to shower in the tiny bathroom and to dress, or at least to put on as many garments as she could find; one or two rather vital ones seemed to be unaccountably missing. Then she made a couple of mugs of coffee and carried one in to Nick, bending to kiss him awake.

He stirred and opened his eyes, putting a hand behind her head to pull her down and kiss her properly. 'Why are you dressed? Come back to bed,' he demanded imperiously.

She smiled. 'I'm a working girl, remember? I have to get back to Melmia to work on my story and phone my paper.'

'Do that tomorrow.'

He reached for her again, but Holly moved out of the way. 'First things first, okay? Here, I've brought you some coffee.'

With a reluctant groan, Nick sat up and looked at his watch. 'It's barely seven o'clock.'

'I know, but I want to tell them that I've got the story and to hold a space for it in next week's edition.'

'All right, I'll drink this and take you straight back.' He smiled and pulled her down on to his lap. 'And while you're on to them, tell them that you won't be back for a few weeks, that you'll be taking a second honeymoon sailing round the Greek Islands.'

He kissed her again, the coffee forgotten, until Holly laughingly reminded him.

She watched him as he dressed and shaved—remembering—so that it almost seemed as if time had stood still, that they had always been together like this. On the way back to Melmia he talked about which islands they would visit, steering the boat with one hand, the other round her waist, holding her close to him, enjoying the feel of her body against the length of his.

When they got to the harbour, he said, 'Do what you have to do quickly, darling, I'll be waiting here for you.'

'What are you going to do?'

'I'll go and buy some stores in the town. Enough that we can sail for a few days without having to put into port unless we want to.' He grinned happily. 'I've an idea we might just be too busy for any sightseeing for quite a while!'

He turned her round to kiss her goodbye and was surprised by the intensity with which she returned it and the way she clung to him. 'Hey, what's this?' Nick put up a finger to her eyes as she blinked back sudden tears.

'I know—silly, isn't it?' Holly gazed at him for a long moment, as if she couldn't get her fill of looking at him, then she said quickly, urgently, 'I love you, Nick,' and clung to him again.

Putting his arms round her, he held her close. 'I know, sweetheart. But we've got all the time in the world now.'

Before he let her go he kissed her again and said, 'Hurry back. I can't wait to get you to myself.'

Holly smiled and walked quickly along to the taverna, turning at the top of the steps to look back and wave to him.

In her room, she quickly changed her clothes and then watched from the window and saw the fisherman from the boat she had hired come to the taverna for her. A few minutes later Nick left the *Argosy* and walked into the town. As soon as he was out of sight Holly picked up her cases and hurried down the stairs. The fisherman took her luggage while she paid her bill and then she was running across the harbour to the boat, praying that Nick wouldn't come back unexpectedly and see her. She stood in the stern, watching anxiously, as the boat got under way, but there was no sign of him and she slowly relaxed, gazing back at the island until it had become nothing more than a jagged outline against the horizon.

The greenness of the English countryside after the stark beauty of Greece was both welcome and overwhelming. The richness of trees and bushes, the deep green of lawns and undergrowth seemed to crowd in on the narrow lanes, trying to win them back. But it was good to be there, to smell the honeysuckle that grew against the cottage wall and to hold her son in her arms again. But there was time only for a few hours with him before she had to go to London, where Holly filed her story, receiving hearty congratulations from both the Features Editor and the Editor himself. The photographs, too, were of a high standard and they planned to make it the main feature for the following edition. Holly took advantage of the general air of approval and asked for a couple of weeks' holiday, which was given readily enough. But before going home to her cottage, Holly turned to her boss and said casually, 'Oh, by the way, if a man called Falconer, Nick Falconer, should happen to ask for me, would you give him my home address, please.'

'Okay, will do.' He made a note on a pad. 'What is he—a lead for another story?'

'Something like that,' Holly agreed, turning to go home at last, and wondering bleakly whether he would ever be asked for the information.

It was three days before Nick came. Holly was up in the front bedroom of the cottage when she heard a car in the lane and looked out. It was a Saturday and Jamie was at home, playing in the garden in the sun, almost lost among the tall fox-gloves and lupins as he looked for his new rabbit that he had let out of its cage yet again. The car pulled up outside and Nick got out and walked up to the gate, checking the name on it to make sure he was at the right place. Holly drew back, suddenly breathless, her pulse racing.

As Nick lifted the latch Jamie heard it and emerged from the flowers, leaves in his hair and a smudge of dirt on his face. 'Hallo. I've lost my rabbit.'

Nick grinned. 'I'd better shut the gate, then.' He crouched down to Jamie's level. 'What colour is it?'

'It's white and he hasn't got a name yet. Just Mr Rabbit.'

'Well, perhaps it's still in your own garden. Did you come through the hedge?'

Jamie frowned. 'This *is* my garden. Mr Rabbit lives in that cage over there that Mummy made for me.'

A puzzled look came into Nick's eyes as he sought to work out the situation. 'Why didn't your daddy make it for you?'

Jamie's eyes, blue and innocent, looked up into Nick's face as he said simply, 'I never had a daddy. He went away before I was borned. But Mummy says I can look after her when I'm big enough instead,' he added importantly.

Nick stood up suddenly and stared down at the boy. In the window Holly raised her hand to her mouth, biting her knuckles hard, in an agony about what he would do next.

His face white, Nick said harshly, 'What's your name?'

Jamie looked up at him uneasily, scared by his tone, and realising that this tall man was a stranger, and he'd been told never to talk to strangers. But despite his fear he faced up to him. 'James Nicholas Falconer Weston,' he answered in a breathless rush because he'd only just learnt it all and it was hard to remember.

Holly's heart lurched as she saw the look on Nick's face, saw him stare at his son and see his own features mirrored there. Slowly he went down on to his knees and put out a tentative hand to touch the child's hair, his mouth twisted almost in pain. Then he said hoarsely, 'Hallo, son,' and pulled the boy to him to hold him very, very close.

Some instinct must have told Jamie that he was safe, because he didn't cry or call out, but after a while he began to wriggle and Nick loosened his hold. He picked him up and stood up. 'Let's go and find your mother, shall we?'

And suddenly life came back into her limbs and Holly was flying down the stairs and through the hall. They were halfway up the path when she tumbled through the door and then stopped precipitately, her hair flying about her head.

Nick saw her and for a moment his eyes blazed with anger. 'You idiot! You crazy, crazy idiot!' But then he held out his free arm to her and she ran to him, tears of happiness running down her cheeks. Nick's eyes, too, were wet as he buried his head in her neck and said roughly, 'Why the hell didn't you tell me?'

But it was some time later, when they had both recovered a little and Jamie had gone off to look for his rabbit again, that Holly answered that question. She led him to the wooden seat under the old apple tree and said rather incoherently, 'I didn't want you to come back to me because you *had* to. I wanted you to want to. I had to be sure, you see. Sure that it wasn't just a—a sexual hang-up. I thought that, perhaps, once we'd made love again you might realise that it *was* only sex you wanted after all, and you'd be glad I'd gone away. And I couldn't risk telling you about Jamie in case it made you think it was your duty to come back— or something stupid like that. You do see, don't you? I had to be sure that you loved me enough to come after me again.'

'Oh, Holly!' He put a hand on either side of her head and looked at her face for a long moment before he bent to kiss her hard on the mouth, his lips bruising in their need and intensity.

Too choked by emotion to speak, Holly buried her head in his shoulder when at last he let her go, and felt him stroke her hair.

'God, if I'd only known,' Nick muttered thickly. 'What you must have gone through to keep him and bring him up on your own! Didn't your parents help you at all?'

Holly straightened up and pushed the hair off her face with a trembling hand. 'No, they wanted me to have an abortion and to divorce you. And— and I couldn't do that, so I left. They . . .' She bit her lip hard. 'I suppose they must have destroyed your letter, and I must have left just before you came to look for me. I didn't think you wanted me any more, you see.' Her eyes looked up at him, dark and haunted. 'Oh, Nick, if only I'd waited!'

He swore savagely under his breath, then said urgently, 'I'll make it up to you, my darling, I swear it.' His hands gripped hers tightly, warm and strong. 'I've been offered a directorship of my company, based here in London. We can be together always, the three of us.'

'Oh, Nick!' Holly moved into the safe haven of his arms, her happiness complete and overflowing as Nick kissed her again and again, as if he still couldn't believe that she was really his at last.

'Mummy, I found my rabbit!' Jamie's piping voice interrupted them as he ran round the corner of the house, clutching the poor animal to him. 'Why are you kissing that man?' he demanded suspiciously.

Nick laughed. 'There was definitely a possessive note in that question. When are you going to tell him who I am, and that he'd better get used to seeing me kiss you?'

Holly stood up and held out her hand to him, her face radiant with love and happiness. 'What's wrong with right now—and let's tell him together, shall we? Oh, Nick, we've both been waiting so long for you to come home!'

The Mills & Boon Rose is the Rose of Romance

Every month there are ten new titles to choose from — ten new stories about people falling in love, people you want to read about, people in exciting, far-away places. Choose Mills & Boon. It's your way of relaxing:

March's titles are:

GREGG BARRATT'S WOMAN by *Lilian Peake*
Why was that disagreeable Gregg Barratt so sure that what had happened to Cassandra was her sister Tanis's fault?

FLOODTIDE by *Kay Thorpe*
A stormy relationship rapidly grew between Dale Ryland and Jos Blakeman. What had Jos to give anyone but bitterness and distrust?

SAY HELLO TO YESTERDAY by *Sally Wentworth*
It had to be coincidence that Holly's husband Nick — whom she had not seen for seven years — was on this remote Greek island? Or was it?

BEYOND CONTROL by *Flora Kidd*
Kate was in love with her husband Sean Kierly, but what was the point of clinging to a man who so obviously didn't love her?

RETRIBUTION by *Charlotte Lamb*
Why had the sophisticated Simon Hilliard transferred his attentions from Laura's sister to Laura herself, who wasn't as capable as her sister of looking after herself?

A SECRET SORROW by *Karen van der Zee*
Could Faye Sherwood be sure that Kai Ellington's love would stand the test if and when she told him her tragic secret?

MASTER OF MAHIA by *Gloria Bevan*
Lee's problem was to get away from New Zealand and the dour Drew Hamilton. Or *was* that her real problem?

TUG OF WAR by *Sue Peters*
To Dee Lawrence's dismay and fury every time she met Nat Archer, he always got the better of her. Why didn't he just go away?

CAPTIVITY by *Margaret Pargeter*
Chase Marshall had offered marriage to Alex, simply because he thought she was suitable. Well, he could keep his offer!

TORMENTED LOVE by *Margaret Mayo*
Amie's uncle had hoped she would marry his heir Oliver Maxwell. But how could she marry a maddening man like that?

Masquerade
Historical Romances

*Intrigue
excitement
romance*

CHANGE OF HEART
by Margaret Eastvale

Edmund, Lord Ashorne, returned from the Peninsular
Wars to find that his fiancée had married his cousin.
It was her sister Anne who had remained single for
his sake!

LION OF LANGUEDOC
by Margaret Pemberton

Accused of witchcraft by Louis XIV's fanatical
Inquisitor, Marietta was rescued by Léon de Villeneuve
– the Lion of Languedoc. How could she *not* fall in
love with him, even knowing that he loved another
woman?

Look out for these titles in your local paperback shop from
13th March 1981

The Mills & Boon Rose is the Rose of Romance

THE STORM EAGLE by *Lucy Gillen*
In other circumstances Chiara would have married Campbell
Roberts. But he had not consulted her. And now wild horses
wouldn't make her accept him!

SECOND-BEST BRIDE by *Margaret Rome*
Angie would never have guessed how the tragedy that had
befallen Terzan Helios would affect her own life . . .

WOLF AT THE DOOR by *Victoria Gordon*
Someone had to win the battle of wills between Kelly Barnes
and her boss Grey Scofield, in their Rocky Mountains camp . . .

THE LIGHT WITHIN by *Yvonne Whittal*
Now that Roxy might recover her sight, the misunderstanding
between her and Marcus Fleming seemed too great for anything
to bridge it . . .

SHADOW DANCE by *Margaret Way*
If only her new job assignment had helped Alix to sort out the
troubled situation between herself and her boss Carl Danning!

SO LONG A WINTER by *Jane Donnelly*
'You'll always be too young and I'll always be too old,' Matt
Hanlon had told Angela five years ago. Was the situation any
different now?

NOT ONCE BUT TWICE by *Betty Neels*
Christina had fallen in love at first sight with Professor Adam ter
Brandt. But hadn't she overestimated his interest in her?

MASTER OF SHADOWS by *Susanna Firth*
The drama critic Max Anderson had wrecked Vanessa's acting
career with one vicious notice, and then Vanessa became his
secretary . . .

THE TRAVELLING KIND by *Janet Dailey*
Charley Collins knew that she must not get emotionally involved
with Shad Russell. But that was easier said than done . . .

ZULU MOON by *Gwen Westwood*
In order to recover from a traumatic experience Julie went to
Zululand, and once again fell in love with a man who was
committed elsewhere . . .

If you have difficulty in obtaining any of these books from your
local paperback retailer, write to:
Mills & Boon Reader Service
P.O. Box 236, Thornton Road, Croydon, Surrey, CR9 3RU.
Available April 1981